D1449666

THINGS PAST TELLING

THINGS PAST TELLING

A Novel

SHEILA WILLIAMS

THORNDIKE PRESS
A part of Gale, a Cengage Company

LIBRARY OF CONGRESS CIP DATA ON FILE.
CATALOGUING IN PUBLICATION FOR THIS BOOK
IS AVAILABLE FROM THE LIBRARY OF CONGRESS.

ISBN-13: 978-1-4328-9830-4 (hardcover alk. paper)

Published in 2022 by arrangement with Amistad, an imprint of HarperCollins Publishers

Printed in Mexico
Print Number: 01   Print Year: 2022

This book is dedicated to the
Grandmothers —
Blessed are they who remember.

THEY WAS THINGS PAST TELLIN', BUT I GOT THE SCARS ON MY OLD BODY TO SHOW TO THIS DAY. I SEED WORSE THAN WHAT HAPPENED TO ME.

— Mary Reynolds, *formerly enslaved, Black River, Louisiana (WPA narrative — interviewed in Dallas, Texas, 1937. Mrs. Reynolds's age, approximately 100 years.)*

■ ■ ■ ■

PART I
IN THE BEFORE TIME

■ ■ ■ ■

1

Liberty Township, Highland County, Ohio
May 1870

I sit in the sun. Old bones like the sun. Nicholas say, "Momma Grace, you're going to fry up to a crisp, you keep on settin' there!"

I tell him, "Let me fry!"

The sun feel good, only thing takes the ache in my joints away is its warmth. It spread across the backs of my hands like butter.

Frances whips out of the door, marching over to where I set. Oh, Lordy, that woman. Moves so fast, like she a soldier on a march.

"Momma Grace! You didn't eat your breakfast. You going to waste away, you don't eat." She frowns.

I can't see her too good but I know Fanny, and I know she frowning. Shame to mess up a pretty face like that. But her worry is out of love.

"Not much hungry, Fanny," I tell her. "Old as I am, I wastin' 'way anyhow."

I chuckle — I like that little joke.

Nicholas grumbles. No sense of humor in that boy.

"Momma Grace, you need to eat."

I shake my head, rub my knees. Oh, that sun do feel good on my bones.

Put me in the mind of a story I heard . . . long time gone now. Whose story that? 'Bout Zekiel out in the desert, think that where he was, with bones. Dry. He connect them . . . dry bones. Zekiel he . . . I did wonder what that boy doin' out the middle a nowhere with . . .

"Momma Grace?"

"I do eat, Nicky. Just enough."

He and Fanny eye each other, I feel it. I know what they thinkin'. *What can you do with this woman? Set in her mind. And her mind wanderin'.* I smile to myself, lean back on the little pillow Calico made up for my chair. Feel like I'm on a feather bed sittin' up. That gal of mine is a wonder. She can make anything, do anything. How I get such a child?

The sun warm. I think I'll just take me a —

Admiral bark like his head gonna come off. Somebody comin'. That fool dog. Noth-

12

ing that hound like more than work his mouth. Then he growl. Oh. Somebody white comin'. I do not know why Nicky trained that animal to growl only at white folks . . . Well, yes, I do. Nicky use the same name for all his dogs. This only the fourth . . . fifth? Anyway, that hound comes from a long line of dogs named "Admiral" and they all was taught to bark at white folks. Can't see this man well, better wait till he get closer up. I can hear his voice. Oh, now he comin' closer. Nicky must have grabbed Admiral's collar. My one eye good but the other one, I see only shadows. There's voices, words going back and forth, but not conversation. This is business, I tell by the tone. What's he saying?

What's the family name?

How many are you?

And who are you?

A census-taker man, I 'member the one came through afore the war, years, decades ago. This Ohio good about counting up its people. That man could not get his head wrapped around me and the children. Seemed to him I had one colored child and one white one and he was trying to figure how that happened. I told him to look in any field at the cow and bull. Better n' that, ask your momma.

This man's voice is high and thin, reedy-like. 'Minds me of the Kaintuckian. His voice used to hit my ear all wrong, too, sent a chill down my back. Well, he gone now. Nicky speaks, his voice deep and booming, the voice he uses for white folk, polite but not deferential. He wasn't raised to be deferential. I chuckle again. At least Nicky is trying to be polite. Fanny? I feel her simmerin'. Just imagine her face, skin pulled close to her cheekbones, her dark eyes 'bout to skewer that man. That gal has a short fuse, she's done with this nonsense already, I can hear it. I see the 'numerator now, he nothing out the ordinary. Just another white man dressed in brown and gray clothes.

The man licks his finger and turns to the next page. There's a breeze and it catches the paper and plays with it. As head of household, Nicholas answers the man just like his mother taught him. "Always answer polite, like you were raised. But that's all. You're a free man just like him." Calico has told him this since he could talk. Good thing he listened to her. I've answered many white men in years and years, too, some polite-like and some not.

"There's me, Nicholas. I am forty-five —"

"Where are you from?" the white man interrupts. I hear Fanny take a breath. She's

14

standing just behind me so I can't see her face but I know it looks like thunder 'bout to roar.

"Ohio."

The man writes deliberately, forming each letter as if he were just learning it.

"Color?"

What kind of question is that?

"Mulatto," my grandson answers. What kind of answer is that? He's not . . . just light that's all. He marks off the other family one by one. The man is writing furiously, trying to keep up. "My wife, Frances, about forty-two years old, from Virginia. She's mulatto. Our oldest, Samuel, is out on his own, then there's Shelton, he's out at work. Apprentice to . . ." I hear the pride in his voice. The world turn 'round on those boys. Shelton's training to be a blacksmith. But Nicky will have to be careful. Pride is something white folks don't like to hear from us.

"Your wife from Old Virginia?" the man asks.

Is there a new one?

"Yes. But all of our children were born here in Ohio."

In my head, I hear my grandson say, *And all of us are mulatto except . . .*

Zekiel he connected them dry bones.

I close my eyes and let the sun warm my eyelids. Sun. Warmth. I remember . . . there was a place where I was warm every day and liked to feel the sun on my skin. Now I feel the 'numerator's stare. He has to count me, too, but I know what he thinking. He thinking I'm no count. And I don't talk much anymore, already said most of what I came to this earth to say to the people I wanted to say it to.

My grandson answers for me.

"She's my grandma. Maryam Priscilla Grace. P-r —"

"I know how to spell it," the man barks.

I feel Fanny's fingers dig into my shoulder. Hold your temper, gal.

"How old is she? She looks old."

"A hundred and twelve. Born in 1758. Or '68. I'm not certain, neither is she. She is pretty old. At least ninety."

"Can't you ask her?"

Nicky tells the man that I don't talk much. A few moments pass and I know that he's making a gesture that means I'm a little squirrely in the head now. Not that he believes it, he just does that so that folks leave me alone. I decide to snore a little bit. Behind me, Fanny snorts.

"Momma Grace . . . she's . . . blind," Nicky continues.

Maybe. But I do see.

"And where's she from?"

"Virginia."

My backbone twitch.

No, I'm not! But I am speaking only to myself. But yes I am from Virginia, lived there many years. But no I'm not. Not from there. That Virginia is like Ohio, home but not home. Only my lives there . . . and the lives I lost, made it familiar, the crops I planted, the babies I helped into the world, the earth where . . . seeds and sins . . .

Virginia is familiar and I know it. But it's not . . . where I'm from.

Fanny interrupts.

"Excuse me, sir, but do you want to know where Momma Grace is *from*? Or where she was *born*?"

I hear that pride again. Fanny can read and write and figure. She teaches school. She a force, Fanny is.

"Does it matter?" the man asks. He sounds annoyed and I know . . . I can feel what he thinks of me. I know what he sees: an older-than-time colored woman of unreliable sight and no value, probably invalid and not worth two cents much less $1,500, what Nash got when he sold me to McCulloch. He clears his throat. "Officially," he tells Fanny, "it says 'birthplace.' "

17

"All right then," she says, minding not to unsettle the man by sounding too grand. "Momma Grace was born in Africa."

The word strikes me in the face, as if Fanny had slapped me. I near stood up.

Africa.

I never heard that word until I came . . . here. And since then, I've been from so many other places, names strange to me, living lives that I've near forgotten. But won't. Can't.

Tennessee. A stop.

Old Virginia, they say there's another one now.

Jamaica, I remember the smell of it. I remember the first place I stood on hard earth after days at sea . . . that wide beautiful dark horrible deadly sea where bones float along the waves and the finned fish follow. The key. Looks so much like . . .

South Carolina and that island, where the Igbos walked into the sea.

Norfolk.

And now this here, this Ohio and a swollen fast running dirt-brown river. I've been so many places to be from and then, there the place that Frances said. *Africa.*

Not what I remembered it called. A peculiar word, hard to form the sound with my mouth. Not what I called it by when I . . .

was . . . there in the before time.

"What'd you say, Momma Grace?" Nicky asks. "Sometimes, she mumbles a bit," he says to the census-taker man.

I opened my mouth but nothing come out, open my eyes, and blink. The sun strong fore it move on to light the other side of the world. The world where I am from. I see it, the place I left and have a name for. The thought of it closes my throat. The smells . . . sounds of birds calling, birds that don't fly here. It's been years, decades, several lifetimes, I wonder if it's there anymore. In the time after I stumbled off that big boat, I knew many from . . . there. Some like me with words I knew as close as my mother's heart. And there were others. I had learned some of their words from the markets, their faces brown but different from my own. Many had strange ways, some bowed to bad-tempered gods. They sang different story songs of places and doings from across an ocean of water and sand. Then I knew many, people like me, brought away from . . . there.

What happened after all the people were carried away? Did the land sink beneath the waves of the dark brown blue waters? Or was it deserted now? A wasteland like the blue people spoke of in their tales, sand like

19

waves, no trees, no water? No people?

Had they all . . . had *we* all been brought here?

It was called many names by us, each saying something different yet meaning the same place. But no one from there ever used that word. *Africa.*

No one.

And now, I had lived so long that I wondered if I was the only one left in this place, this America, who remembered it.

Was I the last one?

"Where you from, Grandma?" the man yelled.

And I don't like anyone to call me "grandma." That not my name.

Through her teeth, Fanny said, "Momma Grace can hear just fine."

"Edo," I said to the man. "I am from Edo."

I close my eyes and let the hot sun kiss my eyelids.

2
MAN KILLER

About 1758

I walked through a door of no return with two things, my life and my name. Since that time, I have lived many lives, slipping them on and off like shawls, some made of rough wool, others of cloth light as Chinese silk. I been called many names, and answered to them though none was mine. They were shawls of a kind, given to me by others who thought they should belong to me.

My true name, I keep close to my heart.

I never speak it.

It is the name my parents give me in the before time. Few people in this place ever heard it and they are dead now, gone to the land of shadows and whispers. In that time, when I was a child, my parents called me by many endearments but not by my birth name. My sisters and brothers called me by other names, too, some kind and teasing, some not. I did not like it then. Now? I think they did me a blessing. My true name did not fall lightly from others' lips and so it has remained mine. No one here can spell it. I cannot spell it myself. It has been many years since I heard it spoken. Its obscurity has become my strength.

My girlhood is like a story one hears at night when the work is done, while the children sleep, with embers glowing on the hearth the only source of light. It don't sound exactly real and if I heard the story told, I would think it belong to someone else. A story about a girl from some far'way place, not me. A girl whose name means "little bird."

My father had three families over his lifetime, including the time that I know about, three wives, ten daughters, and six sons. But unlike many men in our village, he kept one woman at a time.

"What would I do with two wives?" I'd heard him ask, a wry smile on his face and subtle laughter emerging from his throat. "What man can make two women happy at the same time? What man can make *one* woman happy at any time?" Those listening joined him in levity.

His first wife was a girl not much older than I was when I left or so went the story that my sisters told. Then, Father was barely a man. They were happy together until her lungs weakened and she died. Father's second wife, my mother's sister, bore daughters and sons one year after the other until her womb gave out and she, too, died. Women do not live long in our country.

Father's second wife died so long ago that few in our village could remember what she looked like. But my father said that she had been beautiful, graceful, and compliant and that her daughters, my sisters Ayana, Te'zirah, and Jerie, were much like her — or so they reminded me near every day.

When my mother came to our father's bed, she brought wit, a resilient spirit, and a strong back to the marriage along with a sizable dowry. Tradition bound my father to her legally but it was her beauty and intelligence that bound her to his heart. She was a wise woman called, and trained since childhood in the ways of healing, midwifery, and divination. Some of our people said that she was a sorceress, others called her worse names. My mother never gave a thought to sour words. "You can get much done, my little bird," she reminded me often, "if you care little for what others say about you."

My mother was delivered of twins from her first childbed, a boy and a girl. This double birth was a powerful omen. The girl was born first, big and feisty; she screamed at the top of her lungs the moment she emerged, kicked and squirmed in the midwife's arms, impatient to eat. My mother, exhausted from pushing out the child, could not nurse her until the second baby was born. Smoke and incense filled the birthing house with an intoxicating haze. The swirling fumes were no accident — they had been chosen and blended beforehand by my mother. She used the tools of her craft on herself. The smoke sharpened a laboring woman's focus while the dense spicy incense calmed anxiety and helped breathing.

Mother sat upright on a mountain of blankets, her legs thrown open, head back, eyes closed. Her body dripped with sweat and her reddish mahogany skin stretched across her huge belly as she grunted to push the child out. She clenched a smooth wooden handle between her teeth and held onto thick hemp ropes to steady her body. While the maid bathed her forehead, the chief midwife checked the opening flower of the birth portal as it expanded and contracted.

"Slowly, slowly, listen to the sound of my voice."

"Maysha, slow, slow . . ." The women's voices melted into one chorus of encouragement and comfort. My great-auntie, one of the women in attendance on that day, said that my mother let out a scream that sounded like a warrior's battle cry just before she pushed her babies into the world.

My mother said that she remembered nothing about the ordeal except the murmurs of the midwife's voice using the words chanted by midwives since time began, and this was how it should be. These were the same words that my mother used when she attended at births, and the thick dense haze created by the incense, ground from a spice that came from an island in the east, was a tool of her art. The smoke swirled around, hissing and slithering like snakes moving through the sands at night.

When the second baby finally slid out, the women went silent. No one moved. All held their breath. The head midwife grabbed up the boy and manipulated his body firmly with her hands. The cord of life was wrapped around his neck, and his little face was flattened and wrinkled and had a bluish cast to it. One of the women shouted, "He has a footprint on his face! The other child has stomped him to death in the womb!"

The little boy was put to Mother's breast but would not or could not suck. The girl baby, bad tempered and loud, her fists clenched tightly, her legs tucked up into her body, latched onto the nipple with such ferocity that the new mother gasped. Her breasts, grown huge and tight with pregnancy, gushed, and the baby girl gulped greedily.

The boy died. The spirit that he did not use returned to the land of shadows. Our father was sad but rejoiced in the birth of his fourth healthy daughter. My mother rocked and cuddled the surviving child and sang to her. The women carried back to their homes dark words about the fat female baby who nursed well and belched loudly and the puny little boy who had been too weak to nurse at all.

I was eight years old before I heard the story of my birth, before I learned why some of the people shifted their eyes away from me, fingering their amulets whenever they saw me pass. They called me "Man Killer."

3
LITTLE BIRD

All these daughters! My father could not credit it. Three came before me, the children of my aunt, Father's second bride, tall, slender, beautiful girls with faces that even the royal sculptors coveted as models for their work, especially my sister Jerie, who was so beautiful that the queen mother was said to be jealous. Or so I heard once eavesdropping on her women as they relieved themselves near the mangroves near the river. That wife was said to have been the perfect woman, sweet in spirit, obedient in demeanor, and lovely in face and body. Her name . . . if I ever knew it, I have forgotten. She died in childbed before I was born and took her child with her. But she left behind Ewua, my oldest brother, and a trio of daughters, whose laughter, gossiping, and words filled my childhood with wonder and dread. My beautiful and terrifying sisters. From them I learned to dress myself, eat properly, make offerings, do chores, and braid hair. From them, too, I think, I learned to be resilient. It was Jerie taught me that, Jerie who tormented and teased me past the point of tears. Jerie who taught me how to survive.

The sixth child of my father, the fourth daughter and buried in the middle of such a group, I grew up loved but overlooked. One of many, never a special one. I was not seated on an Iyoba's throne (so my sisters reminded me over and over), nor was I at the center of any world, Benin City, Edo, or anywhere. I was barely walking good when I learned this.

I remember, dimly, a day when I had burrowed myself onto my mother's lap, reached for her breast, and began to suck. She thumped me on the cheek and pushed me away. They say I screamed as if my arm had been cut off.

"No!" Mother said sternly. "No more. You are too big now. Go with Te'zirah, she will give you a drink. Go!"

I fled, screaming, tears spilling out of my eyes. After that my mother's belly grew large and round and not too much after that, a baby, another boy, sucked greedily at her breasts. I was no longer the treasured, spoiled baby girl. Yet another boy followed and another. I was shooed away to the back wall of Mother's house, ignored, teased, and forgotten. Even my name, unusual that it was (or so Father told me) became like an unneeded robe left behind. Mother called out the names of each one of my sisters, even my younger brother, before calling for me by name.

The middle child gets lost, never the treasured eldest, especially if a son, or the baby, who can be cuddled and indulged because he or she may be the last. At six or seven, I decided that I did not want to be called by my little brother's name. That I no longer wanted to be the "forgotten one," that I would figure out a way to make my mother, to make everyone, remember my name. That I would discover how to make them see me. And so I became a master of mimicry, repeating what others said, using exactly their words, language, inflections, and gestures. I told their stories.

It was the best life I could have chosen for myself. It was a game where I was the player who always won. Small enough to fold myself almost in half, I listened, watched with purpose, and, without realizing it, sharpened the tools that would support my craft. The cacophony of voices, animal sounds, and commerce on market day were nothing to me, my ears were sharp and sliced through the din to pick out every word uttered by the complaining Yoruba woman who kept the large chickens. The laughter that wrapped itself around the washing songs of the Igbo women did not keep me from catching the musicality of their speech. I repeated them to myself until I could say or sing them without thinking. The turbaned ones' speech worried my tongue. I knew a few words but could not say them.

Eavesdropping is as natural as breathing for a neglected little girl. She is small enough to hide behind this or under that, slim enough to flatten her body against a wall to become a breathing shadow, and — which may be the most important — a little girl who is the fourth or fifth daughter (who can remember which?), the sixth or seventh child (out of ten) born to a man who has had three wives, is of no interest, of no count at all. She can go anywhere. She is a nonperson; even her dowry is insignificant. She passes in and out of a circle or a house and is invisible. She is both present and not present.

And so she hears and she listens. She figures out the words of the Mende woman whom Idie owns as a slave. She has learned

30

the proper greeting of the strange pink-faced men her father calls "the Portugee" who make trade with the king. She has learned the words of insult of the Akan, a greeting from the Ife women who trade pleasant words with her mother, a word or two of the guttural Arabic overheard from a man squatting with discomfort in the tall grasses. My mother says he is of the blue people, returning from pilgrimage at Timbuktu.

And this made my sisters laugh and my mother smile. My brothers, who would not admit that they were in awe, still teased me, acting as if they were the oba or warriors and held authority over me. But even they began to take me aside, talk to me, ask me questions and listen to my advice. "How do you say this?" "What does that word mean?" They listened to my stories, the ones I told from eavesdropping on the Dahomian women in the markets, the brass people, the Fon craftsmen.

Mother giggles and covers her mouth with her hand. My brother Ogu in her arms suckles contentedly. Too much, I think. Mother looks thin.

"Little Bird, you are a naughty girl," Mother teases me, still giggling from the story I have just told. "The turbaned one is a priest, it is not good to make such a joke. His god will be angry."

But she is still smiling.

Jerie smacks me on the top of my head.

"Ow!" I yell, pushing her away.

"You are such a baby," she scolds, "it was just a tap."

I glare at her. It was harder than a tap I think.

"It will be your fault if he sends a curse on us," Jerie says, her voice dripping as always with self-importance and sarcasm. "The turbaned one's god is more ill-tempered than all our gods together!"

Mother makes a sound of warning and Jerie sighs but says nothing more. The baby fusses and Mother is distracted. Jerie pinches me — hard — on the arm and leans in so close that her nose almost touches mine.

"Your fault," she hisses.

It was about this time that Father began to notice me, the time that I became to him more than just a fourth daughter, a dowry. This was unusual — women and men kept to separate places, by work and by custom; girls with women, boys with men. But Father was one who walked a path that he alone had blazed, and, like my mother, he did not worry much about the opinions of others. Already considered peculiar because he had one wife when he clearly could afford two, Father took me with him from time to time, on his errands of business. If I ever knew what his business was I have forgotten. I think that he took me as company, because he did not have a son who could serve as companion: Ewua, my oldest brother, had married and was living in Benin City, serving the oba, and Ogu was three years old and still a baby and of no use to anyone. I was eight and old enough to keep up with him on his journeys, to help carry and run errands but not old enough yet to be taken over by the women. I had no breasts and would not start bleeding for many years so they had no interest in me. And so, Father wrapped my head as the Malian did ("You make an ugly boy!" Jerie commented, wrinkling her nose at my altered appearance) and took me with him, to Benin City, to Calabar, a strange and lively town on the water, a place populated by strange people, where the tall ships with white wings rested between sailings.

In a way, I became my father's surrogate son.

"My little eagle," he would tell me sometimes, a rueful smile on his face. "This is not right that I should teach you to hunt, to move about the country like a boy. You should be learning how to be a good wife. Yet without the wrap around your head who would think you are a girl?" He'd laugh. "What kind of man wants an eagle for a wife?"

I did not understand. In our journeys, especially those through the forests, Father had taught me about the creatures who lived in the cliffs, in the forests and grasslands among the trees and on the plains. I loved the stories he told about the serpent eagle that soared above my head then swooped down gracefully to catch a snake for her supper. They were the best of mothers, strong, devoted, and watchful. They were fearless. And they hunted relentlessly to feed their young ones.

"They fly so high, Father," I answered. "They see far away, they catch the snakes for their hatchlings. They fight to keep their nests safe." *Why wouldn't they make perfect wives?*

"What you say is true, Little Bird. As hunters, they are unmatched." He steadied my hand. "Aim high, take a breath to steady your hand, and fix your eye on your prey."

My stone found its mark and the plump bird fell out of the tree. It was my first kill and I was delighted.

"I am like the mother eagle!" I exclaimed, doing a dance of celebration.

My father put the animal into his sack. To me he said, "You will make a fine mother, Daughter." He smiled at me, patted my head, then looked back toward the horizon. To himself he said in a voice so low that I nearly didn't hear, "But few men want an eagle in their bed no matter how skilled she is with a spear."

When we returned home, my father returned to his storehouses and his councils. I followed the winding trail through the forest back to the village. Chimaobi, his brothers and friends, all of them cousins of mine in one way or another, caught me just as I reached the outer boundary.

"Bird Woman!"

Chimaobi. I hated him even though Mother said that it wasn't useful to hate. But then, I told myself, Mother didn't have to spar with him almost every day.

I ran; I was fast but Chima was older than I and larger and I knew that he would catch me. Behind my back, I heard his friends laughing and decided to stop. I turned around to face him.

"That is not my name," I said, looking him in the eye. Chima had a round face and small eyes, beady like the serpent eagle. He

35

was stupid. He reminded me of a toad. "And when I finish training with my mother, you can call me 'Lady Eagle.' " This last bit I added to annoy him. I was too young to train with my mother but he didn't know that. Mother had a certain reputation. Chima hated me not only because my father was a respected elder but also because I was not the daughter of a minor wife. My mother was a lady of status whose dowry had been substantial. His mother was a third wife who barely had a hut to call her own.

"You are a little demon, that's what you are!" Chimaobi began, his litany unchanged from our almost daily encounters. "My mother told me. You're a man killer. Stomped your brother to death before he was born."

There were those words again. *Man killer.* How long would I carry them around on my back like a sack of stones?

"You're a scrawny bird, too!" he continued, laughing. "With skinny arms and chicken legs and a beak for a nose! Ha, ha!"

The laughter of his friends emboldened him and he lunged toward me.

"Bird woman, chicken woman . . ." He had a stone in his hand and just as he threw it, I turned to run. But I slipped and fell. If

I hadn't fallen, Chima, whose aim was terrible, would only have grazed my foot. But fate was not on my side. The stone found its mark on the side of my forehead. He grabbed me up and shook me.

"Chicken woman, chicken woman . . ."

With my free hand, I smacked him, hard, against his ear and he screamed in pain.

Good.

I wrestled free and scampered down the hill, the sound of Chima's voice yelling after me, the words of the other boys' taunts and their laughter ringing in my ears.

"I've been looking for you."

The sound of Jerie's voice fell on my ears like a boulder. It was hard to know whose voice I dreaded hearing the most, Chima's or hers.

"Your mother . . ." My sister was always careful when talking to me about distinguishing between my mother and hers. "My honored aunt sent me to find you . . . what have you done to your head?" I growled at her. As if I would smash a rock against my own head. She reached out to touch me with her delicately shaped palm, then thought better of it. "You're filthy. As usual." Her light brown eyes danced with hostile amusement and undisguised satisfaction. "Your mother won't be happy."

She grabbed me by the arm and pulled me along toward Mother's house, the largest in my father's compound, being careful to keep my dusty, grass- and mud-stained blouse away from the immaculate robe that she wore. Bullying me was this sister's favorite occupation besides gazing at herself in a mirror, having her hair dressed, or applying cosmetics to her eyes, cheeks, and lips. She dragged me along, moving quickly, and I stumbled as I tried to keep up. Jerie was four years older than I and many hands taller. My legs could not move as quickly as hers.

Jerie. I smile now when I think about her. But then? "Jerie the Beautiful" as she was called, was our father's most desirable daughter; her bride price was enormous and our family had many offers for her. I don't think she would have minded so much, my being dirty most of the time and tramping along behind our father, except that I was *her* sister and, therefore, an embarrassment.

"I have found her!" she announced, pulling me into Mother's house by my ear. With a triumphant flourish, she pushed me forward.

"Ow!" I yelped, nearly falling at my mother's feet.

Mother sighed loudly. She reached out to

me with her free hand, the other arm wrapped around her newest baby, another boy, who was asleep.

"Little Bird, where have you been and why are you so dirty?"

"She's been rolling around in the mud with those boys again." With Jerie in the room, there was no need for me to speak. Her voice dripped with disgust. She waved her hand toward the servant, who cowered in the corner of the hut. "Do something with this robe! She has gotten dust all over it!"

Mother cut her eyes at Jerie, then turned her attention back to me. She was used to my sister's bursts of temper.

"What will I do with you, my little bird?" she asked sympathetically. She patted the cushion next to her and I sat down. Mother stroked my cheek with the back of her hand. A long stripe of black dirt crossed the barely visible veins like a dark tattoo. I was mortified. Mother frowned, then reached for a damp cloth, one that she probably intended to use on the baby.

"Mother, I want to change my name," I blurted out. "I don't like it. People make fun of it. They call me 'Bird Woman' and 'Chicken Woman.' I want another name. Mother, can you and Father please give me another name?"

My mother smiled, her dark eyes scanning my face. She brushed away the escaping tears and cupped my chin in her hand.

"When you are a woman and married, you may call yourself whatever you wish. For now, you are my little bird, my red eagle. And, I think, that someday, you may be glad that I gave you that name. The red eagle is strong, brave, and resourceful. She soars high and sees much."

"Hardly." This comment came from Jerie. "Dirty, dusty, and rough is more like it."

"Jerie." Mother's voice was stern even though she was smiling. "The goddess has given us many roles." She paused, watching as my sister shrugged off her robe and began to admire her image in the mirror that the servant held for her, a treasure that Father had bought in Benin City.

Jerie's skin was smooth and dark like the reddish-brown clay vases that we'd seen in the markets. Her shoulders were well shaped and her waist was small. Her breasts, large and full for one so young, hung like pears on her chest. Jerie really was beautiful. She turned her body this way and that as she tried to get a better view. Mother shook her head.

"You my niece are given the body and face

for a man to lust after and admire. You were given a body for love and for babies." Jerie smiled with pleasure at Mother's words. "Your sister's gifts are for a different purpose." Mother looked at me again, then turned her attention back to the baby. "To protect, to fight, and . . . to survive." My mother's voice sounded as if it were coming from far away, from a place that only she could see.

Mitti, the servant, made a quick sign for protection when she thought Mother wasn't looking. Jerie and I set aside our mutual animosity and exchanged glances. My mother had that effect on people.

It was usual for men in our village to choose wives who were of our people but from another village. But my father had done more than that. He had chosen his wives, both Jerie's mother and mine, from among the "old people" of our tribe, connected by blood but who had come from lands south and west of the stone gates built by the ancient ones, ancestors of the blue people. In these places, the goddesses were as powerful as the gods, and, it was said, their kings were guarded by women who carried bows, spears, and shields and rode camels into battle. Mother didn't hunt or fight but she could see far beyond the mists and shadows, and the herbs and potions she mixed healed many ills, both of the body and of the spirit.

"Does that mean that I can ride with Father? When he journeys to Benin City?" I asked eagerly. There was nothing I would have liked better than to be far away from Chimaobi and his taunts and my sisters, especially Jerie.

"No, you silly girl," my nemesis answered in place of my mother. "You'll have your bleeding time soon. And then you'll be married." She smirked. "If Father can find someone who'd want to marry such a scrawny little rodent."

"Jerie!" This time Mother's voice was not indulgent. It sliced through the air with the snap of a whip. My sister closed her mouth quickly and lowered her head. "You have teased your sister enough. Cover yourself! It's time for you to draw water." I scampered up and moved toward the entrance. "Little Bird, don't dawdle and *don't* get dirty! Jerie! Are you listening?"

"Yes, Aunt."

It was a daily ritual and, next to traveling with my father, it was one of my favorite diversions even though I had to tolerate the company of my sisters. We didn't go alone. There was a caravan of unmarried daughters carrying the tall jugs on their shoulders and heads, winding their way through the brush and the boulders and the coarse sand toward the well. It was a procession of earthbound goddesses, and even though they tormented me, I was proud of my pretty sisters.

Ayana, seventeen, led the way, followed by Te'zirah, thirteen, and Jerie, who was sixteen. They were my cousins as well as my sisters but we looked nothing alike. Jerie and her sisters were golden-brown skinned with black hair and light brown eyes. Tall for their ages and well formed, both Ayana and Te'zirah displayed the lushness of body that made Jerie so distinctive. And they had been taught well by my mother and carried themselves with grace, smooth and sleek like big cats. I sighed as I stumbled along behind them. Mother was teaching me those things as well but I wasn't as good at these lessons. And it didn't help that I had not inherited any of my sisters' looks or grace.

"She was my sister but we, like you and Jerie, had different mothers," Mother had answered when I complained. Her eyes danced with laughter. "Sometimes, that makes all the difference."

I didn't think it was funny. As I marched along tripping over stones that I was too preoccupied to see or getting poked in the face by branches left to swing by my sisters, I wondered how much easier my life would be if I were tall and shapely like Ayana or beautiful and graceful like Jerie. Then I wouldn't fall over these stupid boulders.

"Don't worry, Bird Girl," Jerie teased me, taking one of the water jugs from my hands and passing it over to Te'zirah. "Next year this time, you'll have to carry all these jugs by yourself. You and Te'." Te'zirah's eyes widened. "Ayana's wedding is in two moons. And Father is arranging a marriage for me, too." My heart skipped a beat at the thought of life without my tormentor. The water jugs were heavy but I thought Te'zirah and I could manage. It was nice to think of. "Besides," she added — Jerie always gave you one more thing to think on — "Your mother, my honored aunt, has decided that, of all her daughters, *you* are the one to be taught her art and skill."

"Me? Why me?" I whined in despair. The pleasant daydream of Te'zirah and me walking congenially along the path to the well without the constant teasing of our older sisters shattered. Jerie shoved me forward. I almost dropped the water jug. "Why not you?"

"I will be married and have a handsome

husband."

I could feel my shoulders slumping in despair. I couldn't wait to get back and ask Mother if Jerie spoke the truth.

"Why me?" I croaked. As if by asking the question again I would get a different answer.

Jerie's answer was silence paired with a smug and devious grin. She couldn't know that only one of us would fulfill her prophecy.

4
OUIDAH

I will never forget the sound of my sisters' laughter. It was like music, the sweetest song of the most gifted bird, a trill of lightness, of spirit, it was laughter for its own sake. Jerie, Te'zirah, and Ayana entertained themselves, and me, with jokes and stories. They did not include me in their banter, they were older, after all. I was of no worth at all. "You're a baby, you cannot understand," I was told, usually by Jerie. It didn't matter. It wasn't the joke that made me smile with pleasure, giggle from my belly. I did not have to hear or understand the story about this person's mishap or misfortune. The end of the story, the point of the joke, none of this mattered.

Only the sound of my sisters' laughter mattered. Their voices were lyrical, brilliant like the rising sun over the treetops in the forest, shiny like the reflection of torchlight on the warriors' shields when in formation;

they twinkled like the songs of the stars. Their laughter was a chorus, the same melody, the voices complimentary, fitting together like the bright threads woven to make a blanket.

My sisters walked ahead of me, in order, by age. And I was the youngest and the slowest and followed behind, still the child. It was a day like any day, the time for the chore of fetching water and carrying back to our home. One of many chores that we completed in a day, a chore delegated to the daughters of the family.

The forest was thick that year, the rains had been good, the sun had shone when it was supposed to, warmed the earth, tickled the roots and seeds and made them grow. Our father said that the gods were content and had blessed us with the fruits of their contentment. But the lushness that gave my father satisfaction made it difficult for me to see my sisters, and, it seemed, they moved farther and farther away even though I could hear them as clearly as if they were standing at my elbow. From moment to moment, I caught sight of Ayana's yellow robe, a bright biting shade that had been dyed to mimic the orioles that visited our land every summer. Te's voice cut in from time to time: "Little Bird! Keep up!" I made a face at her attempt to add authority to her words. She was only two years older than me but was spending more time with the others than with me. Her moon time had come. I was now the only child in the group. A low murmur that was Jerie's voice, telling one of the funny stories (gossip) that she was known for. I did not hear the name of the hapless victim, her words floated past me too quickly. But it wasn't long before gales of laughter filled my ears, the signal that the story had ended, that someone had most certainly ended up in an unfortunate situation, and I laughed, too, even though I couldn't hear exactly what happened. Ayana's deep, rumbling belly laughs caressed my ears as did Te's higher-pitched giggles that melted into a long series of "ha-ha-ha's" and Jerie's bark of delight that quickly became the richest and yet silliest sound that ever emerged from between the lips of my most formidable sister.

Laughter.

The laughter of my sisters. For several precious never-to-return moments. And then, an interruption. Another sound inserted itself. Not laughter.

Something else.

It happened fast. Everything at once. Flashes of darkness blocking out the rich

green of the trees. Movements. Something . . . some things . . . moving like
lightning here. There. All around us. Every
sense was ignited. The carefree trills from
my sisters descended first into shrieks then
into full-throated screams of surprise and
then terror. An emotion I had never felt
before. It stopped the breath in my lungs,
the beat of my heart. The blood in my veins.
The sounds of guns — a roar unforgettable
once you've heard it, and I had on my visit
to Calabar with Father — yelling, the voices
of men but not our men, not my father or
my uncles or other kinsmen, the tones were
deep and menacing, words I did not know.
The scents of the forest had changed, too,
from green, rich, and damp to dry, dusty,
choking, and thick. Smoke. Something was
burning and the ash filled my throat though
it felt like dirt in my mouth. I coughed then
choked. My head jerked around, looking
back toward home then up. A huge spiral of
black smoke clawed its way toward the
clouds. Home was burning.

My skin itched. My feet . . . I had stopped
walking. My feet felt as if they were sinking
into the spongy dirt. I was like stone. Cold.
A sensation that I would not feel for years
to come in a place I did not yet know
existed. And yet it was there, it was real and

it had rooted me in place, locked up my muscles so that I could not move.

Screams. Smoke. The trees were alive with the sound of birds screeching as they escaped, feet pounding the ground, running. Predators. Hunting. Me.

My eyes flooded, my sight was blurred. I was surrounded by the forest and by a fog, by the smoke. I couldn't see; I didn't know what to do, even where I was. I remember . . . that I started to cry, opened my mouth to call for Mother. But from nowhere, a vise encircled my upper arm, jerked me out of the cold, shook me to silence. Jerie's face close to mine, her nose was inches away from my face. The look in her eyes . . . She spoke in a voice I did not recognize, sharp and low, more like a growl. No laughter, no joking. The order given by an older sister who expects to be obeyed without question, without pause.

"Run."

Their war cry was like thunder and the ground shook under their weight. Footsteps like giants. Or so it seemed to me. I saw this through a child's eye. I was ten years old.

They came out of nowhere like an unexpected rain shower. But the raindrops were cudgels, spears, and fists. They were giants who moved like panthers. They were wizards whose speed was no match for the small steps of a frightened little girl — Jerie and I had become separated, I didn't know where Ayana and Te'zirah had gone — they were demons who had woven a smoke-filled fog to blind us, beings from a place so terrifying that it had no name that you could speak aloud.

We scattered, screaming, running in all directions, zigzagging our way through the trees, hoping to elude them, knowing that they couldn't follow each one of us. And that was true in a way. Who they were, I didn't know then. Mende, Igbo, Dahomian, Yoruba. Their language, shouted and clipped, was familiar and yet not. As for their purposes, I knew what they were. They needed only to catch enough of us to satisfy their mission. They were slave traders.

The water jar fell to the ground and broke, drenching my feet.

I ran until I couldn't feel my legs, until I couldn't breathe. Ran in the only direction that made sense to me, away from my home, away from the river. My breath came heavy but quick as I gulped in the smoke-filled breeze that made me cough and burned my eyes. My ears rang from the cracks of thunder from the guns. I didn't know where

I was going, didn't know where my sisters were although I thought that I could hear their voices and . . . screams all around me, or so it seemed then. Te's screams turned my blood cold, my cousin Sharisha calling for me, Jerie cursing, using words I had no idea she knew. Me, I said nothing, called for no one, and didn't scream.

"Make yourself small," Jerie had whispered before she pushed me away, the feel of her hand like stone against my arm, before she ran herself.

I did what she told me. They caught me anyway.

I had tripped over a fallen sapling, scratched my legs and tore the flesh from my palms when I fell. I scooted myself into a hollowed-out tree, then folded up into a ball, trying to ignore the ants whose nest I had invaded.

The giants were everywhere, their huge feet stampeding through the trees, parting them as if they were just tall grass. They yelled at each other, commands or directions, their voices were deep and sharp. I had caught some of their words as one of them passed. The elaborate pronunciation that I had heard at the markets once, that I mimicked when Mother wasn't paying attention. Dahomian.

Feet the length of a small dog stopped in front of the hollowed-out tree. Then two large arms, the width and length of tree trunks, reached into the opening and pulled me out. His dark eyes were slits in his reddish-black face; his nostrils widened then blew out puffs of air with the sound of a bull. A growl that passed for laughter rumbled up from his chest.

"Ah!" Meaning, *Look at what I have! A little bird!*

I struggled, tried to wiggle out of his grasp as he tucked me under his arm as if I were a large sack of grain. He smacked me across the side of my head and it made me dizzy. Before I passed out I heard him say, "Be still."

I woke up with iron bands around my ankles. Lying next to me — we were connected by a thick, heavy chain — was a boy about my size. He was sleeping. I shook the chain to rouse him but he didn't move.

A shadow passed over me. It was one of the giants. I sat very still as if that would make me invisible. He snorted, nudged the sleeping boy roughly with his huge foot, then nudged him again, rolled him over, dragging me with him.

"This one's dead," he said in his language, gruff and loud, the sounds rough against my ears. His gaze slid over me as if I wasn't there, seeing but not seeing, as if I were a blade of grass or a stick. A stone. He exchanged abrasive words with one of the other men, who spat an expression of disgust, then he gestured broadly with his long arms. Another giant unchained the boy from me then attached me to another person, a woman. The bracelet was heavy around my ankle.

I don't know how many of us there were. I saw face after face after face behind me until they became a blur. None of them were people I knew, not my sisters, no one from our village. A lump formed in my throat. It stopped me crying, stopped me speaking, stopped me breathing. Near stopped me thinking.

The sound of the whip rippled through my ears. Startled, a man in front of me lurched to his feet and took a couple of steps, the movement taking me by surprise, and I fell. The giant cracked the whip again, barked out a command.

Walk.

We walked for days, for weeks, forever. The slave traders — they weren't just Dahomians, I heard Mende and Fon, too — led us through the forests, zigzagged, threaded us through the brush and the river waters like the gold thread I'd seen once woven into the Iyoba's robe. They stopped from time to time, to give us a hint of water, something undigestible to eat. They unshackled the sick, dying, and dead from among us. And there were many. A man in front of me, leg out to take a step one moment, flat on his face the next. A girl farther back, dropped to her knees, and never got up. There were whispers that she had delivered a child, too soon, and that she and the child, both ailing, were left behind. And there were others, an older woman here, a boy my age there. It happened every day, maybe every hour, I don't know. I lost the way of keeping time. Terror and loneliness had silenced my tongue and dried my tears. The stench of death curbed any appetite I might have had. I heard the moans and cries with every step. I saw the horrors in my sleep. I still do.

One word only from the leader.

Walk.

We did. And walked so far and for so long that I was sure that the land would run out. That we would find ourselves on a high cliff and fall off into a pit of darkness because there were no more steps we could take, no more steps in existence. I have met others from that time who took this journey, there are not so many now. Who walked forever to the dark waters and then floated to this place where we have been. An Igbo woman who called it the "long walk." An Angolan priest who said it was the time of many steps. And others who have called the walk by many names, some lovely and poetic, some not. We have argued about the number of days it took, the heat, the rains, the corrals in which we were kept. One thing we have never argued about is the memory. Not one of us can forget.

For me, it was not so much of a long walk as a long drag. There were many whose hands were bound. All of us were shackled. We dragged ourselves across the land of our mothers and fathers, digging up mud, roots and grasses, rocks and blood. Scraping the skin from our legs, the skin peeling away from the soles of our feet, dripping water and piss and blood into the earth. Leaving these drops and pieces of ourselves behind. As we did everything else.

They sold four men and four boys to a group of pink-faced men during a stop in a clearing. On another stop, when they had unchained some of us to relieve ourselves, two men broke away and ran into the forest. But they were captured, one of them brought back and shackled at his wrists and his ankles. The other was brought back beaten and bleeding, his body in pieces.

Under the cover of night, we were led into Ouidah and put into a pen like the one my father used for his goats — one of the men behind me whispered that it was called a "barracoon," a funny-sounding word. It was open to the stars at night, the sun in day, and the rains when they came. I remembered poking at one of Father's goats with a stick. Now the thought of it made me sad and ashamed and I asked the goddess for forgiveness. Now I was the one to be poked at with a stick and teased.

I had been to Ouidah before. The first time I was with Father, his companion for a business mission. I was eight or nine but tall for that age and able to walk the streets by my father's side, which was why I had been chosen. I still looked more like a boy than a girl. I remember feeling proud. Te'zirah had pleaded for the honor but Father said that she was too pretty and would be a distraction. She wasn't (and neither was I) but she had started breasts and perhaps that's what Father meant. It doesn't matter now.

The city was a sprawling, dirty, noisy mess, its streets teeming with carts, animals, and people. I loved it then. The oxen, cattle, goats, and chickens I had seen and heard before in our village, in other villages where my mother went to market. But not the people. I walked with Father, staying close as he had instructed but tripped over my feet (and Father's), bumped into passersby, and nearly walked into the path of a caravan of camels except that my father grabbed my arm.

The English and some of the Portugee had pink-colored faces with strands of straw-colored hair escaping from beneath their headwraps — Father said they were called "helmets." Other white-faced men had dark hair, near dark as mine, and eyes to match. And swirling around us were women in various colors, intricately wrapped headdresses, their baskets over their arms or carried by their servants. They were a marvel, laughing and chattering away to each other in a slippery sliding kind of language that I did not know. Some of them looked like women from my home, others had come from somewhere else with their sand- and cinnamon-colored skin, thin noses, and eyes colored gold like sand or gray and blue like the sky.

I had never seen anything like this. It was a place to stop my heart beating with its sounds, its smells, and the humming energy of its citizens. I remember . . . On that visit, I felt only excitement. And pride that Father had chosen me to see this, to have this memory. I did not see the barracoons on that visit. But I was not a visitor now.

One night a blanket of silence settled on the city reaching from the vast estates at the forest's edge to the barracoons near the coast. The markets were closed, the cries, laughter, and music bubbling up from the festivals and streets diminished into a series of mournful melodies and then nothing. The citizens of Ouidah had celebrated themselves into a stupor. The animals awaiting transport, including us, settled into ourselves. Those who could sleep did. Those who could not — and I was one of those — made ourselves small and waited. Waited for the nightmare of night to end so that the nightmare of day could begin.

The rains had come and gone, the few clouds left behind floated away quickly on the wind as if trying to catch up with the storm. The moon was a sliver and sent no light but the black sky was dotted with sparkling lights that seemed to flicker, first bright then dim, bright then dim. I thought it was the gods talking and wondered if they were talking about me and the others there, caught in the country, now held in this pen like goats. What had we done to deserve this? What had I done?

The stars did not share their conversation with me. I watched for a sign but there wasn't one. I drifted off into a sleep of no dreams and no rest.

What was time? Days and nights? Some-place along the walk, I lost the how of it. Forgot what it meant when the sun rose and set, it all became one time to me, one long never-ending day-night. I forgot who I was and became no one, a nothing, of no worth to anyone except the slave traders. I was a girl child, surrounded by strangers, people from other villages; no one knew my place, my parents, my face. They couldn't speak my words. I was like a pebble on the ground, one of many. Unnoticed. Unremarkable. Small.

I woke up one morning from a sleep that was no sleep. Women were keening, men were yelling, and children were crying. A group of men — including the Dahomian — were moving quickly through the barra-coon, grabbing this person and that person, dragging them outside and chaining them together. Several women, some men, a few children, a little boy who reminded me of my little brother. And me. They dragged us through the streets toward the coast and, once there, lined us up then pushed us down onto the sand, the loud roar of the waters booming behind us. Another, a yellow man with eyes like a cat's, shouted at us as he walked past, stopping to examine our hair, our teeth, as if we were the goats that my family treasured. He pointed as if counting. The water was coming in and I felt the thick wet sand forming a circle around my bottom.

"What does he say?" one of the women whispered to anyone and no one in particular. She spoke the words of Edo.

The yellow man spoke the language of the Igbo but he was not Igbo.

"He say stay here," I whispered.

The other women, hearing my words, nodded, glancing at me with large eyes. They arranged what was left of their robes around their legs and thighs for modesty before sitting down.

The men, including the yellow man, who seemed to be the headman, stood apart from us, their heads down, their gestures agitated, their voices muted. Their words floated past me on the sea air but I did not understand them. I yawned. My stomach cramped. I was hungry and thirsty and felt sick. I closed my eyes and let the sun warm my face and the breezes brush across my eyelids. It was quiet. Strange after the constant murmurs in the barracoon, the cries, moans, shouting within it and the combustion of the city streets around it. But now, the only sounds were the low murmurs of the men in their circle and the water lapping against the shore. I opened my eyes and looked toward the sea.

The tall ships. I had seen them before. On a visit to Calabar with father. Then, I had thought them regal, mysterious, magical. Their white sails lovely and graceful in the billowing breeze.

I had asked Father about these ships, the first time I glimpsed them from a ridge above the city. And he, like any good father, had told me that they were trading ships, carrying bounty and treasure to the great Kongo kings of the southeast, to the Malian chieftains of the north, and to the Temne. Father had woven a tale of adventure and treasure, a bedtime story crafted to lull an excited child to dreams of glory. He did not tell me the truth — how could he? I was too young. But maybe he did without realizing. He was not gifted with the sight as Mother was, to see across the landscape through the mists of time to the future. He could not have known that the treasure he spoke of, which would one day be loaded onto the tall ships with their brilliant white sails, was me.

One of the Dahomians picked me up and dropped me into a small boat, where I joined ten others, men and women, and several children. He and another yellow-faced man rowed us to a white-sailed ship docked in the harbor. The first person I saw once I climbed over the railing was a pink-faced man holding a whip. The second was Jerie.

5
HOME

I screamed.

"Ah! Jerie!"

"My Little Bird, Little Bird, oh . . . little one," she crooned, wrapping her arms around me, her skin soft and strangely cool. I buried my face into her chest and cried, hugged her tight, my hands curling into fists as if to hold us in a clasp forever. I felt Jerie's bones against my arms. It was like clutching air. The lush body once admired by all in our village and beyond was gone. My sister was as thin as a twig.

The whisper of a sob escaped from her lips, from the mouth of the regal girl who was not given to sighs, who rarely cried. She kissed the top of my head, murmuring words of affection. The pink-faced man barked at us, his words hitting my ears like sharp stones. He shoved us aside as he pulled the others over the side of the tall ship. Caught off guard, Jerie stumbled then righted herself, never letting go of me. Like a strange four-legged creature from our father's stories, we hobbled out of the way and took refuge in a small, dark alcove.

"Let me look at you." Jerie held my face between her palms. Our foreheads touched. She took a deep breath, a long, ragged gasp that rattled in her chest as if she were inhaling sand. Then she coughed. It was a horrible sound. I looked at her. She smiled.

"You are sick."

She shook her head.

"No, I am well, only a little hungry."

I knew that it was more than that.

Her skin, once a rich mahogany brown, was brownish gray and dry; the sculptured bones that had given her face its beauty and strength now protruded; her eyes rested deep in dark-ringed sockets. She had long ago lost her headwrap. Strands of white hair curled around her temples. Jerie was sixteen.

I would not have known my sister if not for the look in her eyes. It grabbed me by the heart and pulled. Her eyes, dark brown and still luminous, held me before her arms did. In them, I saw our parents, our brothers and sisters, our homeland. I heard the music played at our oldest brother's wedding, the drums; I saw the long line of women and girls, including my sisters, wind-

65

ing our way through the forest to the wells. I saw Father. I even saw Chima. I saw what was behind us and in the same moment, I saw signs of what was to come, though I lacked the maturity to understand. And there was more. In Jerie's eyes, I saw what had come.

I closed my eyes, pressed my lips together, and said nothing. Tears. I felt Jerie's touch on my chin.

"No, little sister," she said in a loud, insistent whisper. "You will open your eyes and watch. And you will open your mouth and speak." She glanced over my shoulder at the activity at the railings. One by one the people grabbed up from the barracoon where I had been kept were being helped over the side. "You will listen and learn. Now is not the time to sleep or cry; it is the time to stay awake.

"How you have grown, Little Bird," Jerie murmured. "Almost as tall as me." Her fingers poked into my arms. She gently pushed me away as if to get a better look, then frowned. "And filling out." She did not sound pleased. Warily, she looked around as if we were being watched. Then she hugged me quickly and wrapped her arm around mine. "Stay close." The tone of her voice was sharp.

I remember wondering why Jerie was so watchful, worried that someone would hear us. There was much shouting, men running, carrying crates, leading goats and people. It was impossible to hear anything. The tall ship was in the throes of being loaded, its hold readied for the journey. No one noticed us at all.

There is much to do before a tall ship sets off. The unloading of cargo, the loading of cargo — for the *Martinet,* that was people — the inspections of the sails, the supplies. The pulling up of the anchor. The sailors were everywhere, in the hold, on the masts and on the decks, not one of them stayed still or in one place for long. And once the white wings caught the wind, the ship creaked and groaned, like an old man stretching his bones in the sun. And then it moved. This was a sensation that I had not had before. Every muscle, nerve, and organ in my body was swaying, undulating from side to side and back to front, each at a different pace. I felt sick but I couldn't be sick. I wanted to scream but my throat was closed. I wanted to run to the railings, climb over, and jump into the waters. But my feet were rooted into the rough wooden deck. I wanted to grab up the sandy shore of Ouidah, hold it in my hand, and never let go.

And while the others cried and vomited around me, I stood as still as I could next to my sister, who did not cry or vomit, and felt the swaying motion of the ship beneath my feet get stronger as the boat moved out into the dark swirling waters. My sister and I watched as the brown green earth and white sand–colored buildings of Ouidah grew smaller and smaller and then disappeared into the horizon. The ten-year-old who I was and would never be again wondered where my world was going and if it were coming back. Jerie's fingers dug into the flesh of my shoulder and it hurt.

"Are they going to take us home?" the ten-year-old me asked.

Jerie took a deep breath, then let it out slowly. By some magic, despite the noise and the splashing of the waves against the side of the ship, the whooshing sound of the sails as they pushed against the winds, I heard the raspy rattling sound of air escaping from her chest.

That moment comes back to me in dreams, always part of another memory, never by itself. It needs the support of other more pleasant thoughts to soften its blow. As if anything could make it kinder. It slithers in, quiet and unnoticed, like a garter snake sneaking into your cabin before dawn to get warm. It is a memory that changed me, that built a wall around the before and me. I cannot forget the look on my sister's face, of pain that is beyond pain, of loss that slices the heart and leaves you bleeding inside until the blood fills your throat and chokes you.

I knew then and I know now that she wanted to lie, to color my hopes, to quell my worst fears, to soften the blow of the hammer on my soul.

"No," she said.

6
THE TENTH DAY

Stay close.

I had so many questions. What had happened to us? Where were the pink faces taking us? What . . . My sister's breath was gentle against my ear: *Say nothing. Listen.*

I did everything she told me. Jerie was my sister, mother, teacher, and protector. She was all the family I had. In those early shape-shifting days of the journey across the dark water, I stayed as close to her as a third arm. We slept on a platform next to the stairs leading to the hold of the ship. Turn your face one way, the stench of the hold made your eyes water. The other way? I caught whispers of the sea, the air cool against my skin. I felt the rain against my skin at night, washing the heat and filth away. We were shackled together but I did not mind. As long as Jerie was with me. The rest of the hold held horrors, sights, sounds, and smells I cannot give words to. Even though I was no longer alone, as I'd been in the barracoon, on the long walk, and in the bowels of the tree outside our village, I was terrified beyond speech. The warmth of my sister's hand against mine was the only comfort I had until the night came. And another horror seized me.

A pink-faced man unshackled my sister's ankle from mine and grabbed her arm. I pushed at him, yelled "No!" His dirty white hand closed and became a fist to slam into my face but was diverted by my sister's slender arm. He spat out a few words. Jerie shook her head and held up her open palm toward his face. For a moment, he said nothing, then he grabbed her arm again, roughly let it go, and climbed up the stairs. Each step sounded hollow and full at the same time, a moan of dread that filled my ears.

Jerie turned to me.

"Stay here. Do not move. Say nothing." She slid off the platform, the heavy chain following her like an anchor, weighing more than she did.

"Where are you going?" I shrieked, holding on to her with both arms.

Gently, she untangled my grasp and leaned her face close to mine.

"I will return. Stay. Do as I tell you. Stay."

With that, she pressed her forehead against mine and left, her footsteps having no sound at all, as if she were a ghost.

I did not move. I barely took a breath. Wet myself and cried silently in shame. All around me were frightening sounds, voices, crying in a swirl of octaves. The creaking wooden hull of the ship moaned as if it, too, were grieving. Whispers. Murmurs. Words that I knew and words I did not know. It rained early, just after Jerie was taken away. The air was heavy with moisture mixed with odors of despair and terror.

My mind swirled, all of the words binding together into one thread, the remnants of sobbing into an ominous pattern. The understanding I had of others' words, for fun, for stories, that had made me smile . . . now this knowing terrified me.

Where are they taking us? Mende.

Are they cannibals? Are they going to eat us? Edo.

I'm sick. Bassari.

They will feed us to their gods as a sacrifice. Dahomian.

Can't breathe . . . can't . . . Igbo.

Don't be a fool! They are not going to eat us! Fula.

They mean to sell us to work in the Portugee chief's mines! Akan.

We must fight! Yoruba.

I can't . . . breathe. Igbo.

I knew nothing, had only more questions. I gathered up all of the words and tried to remember each one, turning them over and over in my head. So that I could ask Jerie when she came back. If she ever did.

I did not sleep.

She stumbled down the stairs at dawn followed by the pink man, who roughly re-attached the chain. I remember asking her what had happened. I remember, will always remember, that she said nothing. In the daylight, when we were dragged up the stairs on deck, I saw the bruises on her slim, delicate neck and on her arms. I did not ask her again.

The mind of a ten-year-old child is more like a water jug than a basket. The basket can be filled with grain or with leaves or fish. And because it has spaces between the woven reeds, even if it is woven tight, something, some small thing, sneaks through, escapes. A blade of grass, small leaves, or a tiny fish. If filled with thoughts and knowing, some worthy slice of knowledge will escape. But not in a jug. You fill it until it can hold no more.

And my mind was like that, spinning around and around in the hold of the slaver ship. I watched and saw things no child should ever see and, at some point, my mind overflowed. I saw more than I could speak of. After a few weeks, my nostrils went numb and I no longer gagged on the stench. I turned my ears against the cries for help, the moans of pain and the shrieks of assault and brutality. And turned them toward the lessons that my indomitable sister was imparting. They kept my mind busy and distracted. Away from the nightmares. Away from the nights that one or another of the pink faces unshackled Jerie's ankle from mine and dragged her up the rickety wooden stairs.

The *Martinet* pitched back and forth, near tipping over once in a wild rain that blew up sudden. The dark waters taught me that you can die and then die again. And after each dying, you are different, not who you were, not what you were. Some days after the *Martinet* sailed, the dark waters swirled and rose to meet the night sky, though it was day. It rained but not the rain that Jerie and I knew, not the gentle rains on the plains near the big city or the heavy nourishing rains that flooded our rivers yet gave richness to the soil. These waters met the black clouds and drowned us all, dropped the ship again and again into a never-ending sea until I was not sure where the sky ended and the water began. Thunder pounded our ears, booming drums that knew only one song, lightning in a circle. Jerie and I clutched each other as tightly as we could — we would drown together or survive together in our terror, we did not care which.

The ship rose up on the waves then fell with such a force and so sudden that I was sure it would plunge beneath the waters and hit the bottom of the sea. If there was one. A time passed, the sky cleared, the ship righted itself, and the white wings filled with gentle winds as if no storm had ever blown. A thin sweating man with light greenish skin and black clothes gave us a speaking when we were on deck, moving his hand this way and that in the air. He gestured to us one by one. Later I learned that the black-coated man was a priest and had given us a kind of blessing. He had also gifted each one a name in keeping with his god. Mine was "Mary Priscilla Grace."

My stomach soon emptied and in a few weeks did not bother much with the motions of the ship. One of the pink faces, a young one, spoke to me in a stew of many tongues including mine, trying to make me understand that I was now like him, a sailor, a man of the water. He said that I had the "sea legs."

I had lost count of the sun's risings and settings, had not thought much about the moon's growing from a sliver to an orb shining like the ivory white of a cowrie shell in the pitch-black sky. Jerie scolded me for forgetting to say my prayers of thanks to the sky goddess. My lack of piety and ignorance worried her and she scolded me. But why should I pray? If the goddess was truly powerful then she would know that we needed deliverance. None had come. I owed her nothing. My sister coughed and coughed. In the gloom of the tiny alcove on the deck that we'd claimed as ours, I saw that her face was twisted in pain.

"Little Bird, don't mock the gods, give thanks for the gifts they have given . . ." She finished her lesson in a fit of coughing and then she groaned. My stomach tightened in fear. Jerie's voice, once smooth, its warm tones lilting with wit, was now coarse and raspy from the constant coughing and vomiting. We had both been ill from a lung contagion and from what the sailors called "bloody flux," but where I seemed to be healing, Jerie was not. If she was talking, she coughed every few words. Her bowels had moved so often that there was nothing left in them but black water, and her stomach, distended as if she were to give birth, was empty. For days, she had given me her ration to eat along with my own because she couldn't keep food down. Jerie was five years older than me but I was now stronger than she was.

"Don't talk, sister," I said, patting her arm and wiping her face with a tiny corner of my shift, the cleanest part that I could find. I wrapped myself around her because she could not sit up without support. "Just rest." I felt her head drop against my shoulder. The white-sailed boat rocked this way and that, a motion that I was now accustomed to but still did not like. Jerie murmured something.

"What did you say?"

"Don't think . . . ." She coughed as if her heart were coming out, then cleared her throat and said, "Don't think because I am . . . You must still do your studies. What is that word?" I made a face in the darkness and felt my sister's chuckle. Her bones quivered against my side. She was so thin that every breath she took felt as if it were my own.

"Word?"

"Listen."

I knew what she was talking about. Word

by word, she was making me learn the speaking of the people around us, not as a game as we used to do at the markets, but as a kind of training, a teaching. Jerie instructed me to listen carefully to the chatter bubbling out of the huddle of Yoruba men in the opposite corner, the Igbo woman and her child sitting next to us, the Fula woman whom the others whispered was a witch, and the Portugee sailors who went up and down the creaking wooden ladders to throw food and water at us or drag us up to the deck.

"What did he say?" Jerie asked again, referring to the Akan man who yelled and cursed at everything and everyone but especially at the Yoruba brigands who had captured him and the Portugee who had purchased him and were piloting the ship.

This time, it was my turn to chuckle.

"He say . . ." The man's voice was at its highest volume now and the Yoruba were screaming back insults. "He say their mothers are like dogs and their fathers crawled out of a river."

Jerie tried to laugh but coughed instead.

"So now you tell me, sister. How many tongues do you know?"

I sighed. My belly growled with hunger but I had learned to ignore it.

"Ewe, Yoruba, Fon, some of the Fulani, some of the Arab . . . a few words of the Anglais and Portugee. Some Asante. Eight."

"Bassari."

"Yes, Sister. Nine."

"Good. You will know enough words to speak, to trade, to make your way . . ."

I had decided that, due to the fevers, my sister's mind was going. I knew it. She repeated things over and over, admonitions, the words of the others, slave and sailor alike. She made me repeat rules of behavior; she reminded me of herbs and roots that could be useful in case of illness. She spoke of the "new place" — it had no name, this place that we were all going, where I would have to make my way and trade. Trade what? With whom? Yes, I had learned words from the others, had listened to their whispers with an understanding that gave me the meaning of barely two words out of five. But it was only enough to assure me that the "new place" was full of misery. The Hausa said that we were to be eaten. The Mende wailed and tore at their skins. They said that we had been captured by sorcerers and would be changed into rats. The Fulani said that we were to be made soldiers for a war. The Akan said that we were slaves to work the fields and mines and waters of the white people. And no matter who we were or what gods we revered, we all mourned the distance from our families, our villages, knowing that when we died, our souls would wander the world, tormented, ghosts searching for the gods who had abandoned us and the ancestors who were far away across the waters. What ghost could cross the waters?

Every few days, how many I could not say, they — the sailors — dragged us up the ladders to the decks and drenched us with water. It was a "bath," they said. Their words, even the ones I could understand, dripped with disgust. They sneered at us. They made us stand even though so many of us were weak from the sicknesses, and some of the women — the young Igbo mother — were taken away crying and returned to the hold later, wearing expressions of stone and saying nothing. Like my sister.

This day, I held on to Jerie as best I could until I found a place for her to sit. I made her as comfortable as I could. She was so weak that she needed my arms to steady her and my legs to move us both. In the daylight, her appearance was shocking. She was as thin as a person could be who still breathed, her flesh barely covered her bones. The complexion that I had coveted was now gray. Her eyes, once luminous with laughter and intelligence, were large, sunken, and old-looking, and my heart sank in despair and fear. She was the only family I had. I was desperate for her to get well but I did not know what to do. Jerie was no more than sixteen years old. She looked as if she were one hundred. She inhaled deeply, coughed, then leaned back against the post and closed her eyes.

"Your lessons . . . are not over, Little Bird," she said softly. As if to answer her, a seabird cawed and Jerie smiled. "What is that?" she asked me. "What is the word?"

I gave her the word for "bird" in four languages.

"Good." She patted my hand. "You are ready."

I left her there, sleeping, with the sun on her face, and stood up to stretch my back and legs. I had been hunched over for so long that near every part of my body ached and groaned. Like everyone else, I shuffled across the deck, my movements slow and labored. My legs felt as if they could barely hold me. We wouldn't be on deck long, we never were. Once the water dried up and we each managed a few gulps of clean air, the sailors came and readied us for our return to the hold. I looked out across the waters, in every direction, and saw nothing but sea and sky. The sun was hot, orange, and round. It looked like the same sun we had in our village but I wasn't sure. Nothing else was the same. I looked toward the east and thought about the days that had passed separating us from our parents and our brothers and sisters . . . all of us. Too many to count.

We would not go home again.

I was so lost in my thoughts that, at first, I didn't hear the ruckus behind me. A voice caught my attention, one of the Akan men, and I turned around to see the sailors poking at my sister. I ran toward them, waving my arms and yelling as if they were wild dogs that I needed to disperse.

"Stop that! Leave her alone!"

"This one's dead," they shouted.

"No, she isn't! Don't touch her!"

I pushed my way through them and slid down to my knees. Jerie had fallen over, her eyes half-closed, her mouth open. I gathered her into my arms and whispered in her ear. "Jerie, wake up. Wake up please. *Please,* Jerie."

I shook her. Her head flopped over as if it were barely attached to her body. Her eyes were slightly open but they did not see me.

I felt a sob rise up in my chest like an invader.

"Jerieeeee . . . No, no, no, no . . ."

The sailors, some of them as young as me, stood around us in a semicircle, making a sign with their hands, some moving from foot to foot, looking at each other and over their shoulders at the people. They had no idea what to do.

"Jerie . . . please wake up, please!" I kissed her forehead, her cheeks, her slender hands. She said nothing. She saw nothing. She was gone to the place of shadows. And I was going to the new place, the land of the pink faces, without her.

A low deep murmur began to rise from the bowels of the *Martinet,* a humming sound that matched the roar of the waves, that made the sides of the boat vibrate. The humming soon flowed into the high-pitched keening led by the women, supported by the baritone voices of the men. The sound had risen from the hold, a chorus of Hausa, Fula, Yoruba, Akan, Arabic, and Bassari. Different words, same purpose. It was the sound of mourning. And I was the chief mourner. Days later, after I had recovered myself, the Igbo woman said that I shrieked so loudly that the timbers of the big boat had trembled and the white sails deflated in terror. She said it turned her blood to stone. The captain, unnerved by the cries, commanded a quartet of Akan men to carry me back to the hold. I was still screaming.

Before they took me, they had to pull my arms away and pry my fingers off of my sister's body. I would not let her go. I grabbed the sailor whose job it was to throw her over the side. And when he finally did, I tried to jump in the waters, too. I would not eat. I would not drink. I tried to starve myself to death and they forced food and water down my throat, holding my mouth open with a hard cold silver devil until I choked. I wanted to die. In some ways, I think I did. I became what the Yoruba call the dead but not dead.

My grief sent me to a place of unknowing, of not being. A world of darkness and whispers. Even now, I see those days as having no color, filled with shapes but no faces. I remember in slivers and shards. When I was younger, I had this nightmare each time I slept. But I've lived a long time now and other nightmares have come along to supplant it. It comes to me now and then, when I am tired or if it's late and I've stared too long into the fire. The memories are fragmented now, pieces, bits. I don't know what is true and what is not. Except one thing.

After all these years, I know that Jerie, my sister, is still dead.

I spent my days and nights chained in the little alcove that I had once shared with my sister. The pink faces were afraid that I would jump over the side. I did not eat or drink. I did not sleep. The Fulani woman came . . . or was it a woman of the Yoruba? She cleaned me and tried to make me drink water. One of the men, he was a war chief in his own land, stood before me, feet planted wide, nostrils flared, his voice booming with authority. He lectured me on my duty as an obedient daughter, that I owed my ancestors my life, that it was my responsibility, as a daughter of the Edo, to survive and be strong. Because of Jerie, because she had made me learn his tongue, I understood his words. But I did not answer and finally he walked away.

The world of shadows — the world of the spirits — kept me close for many days. I felt the ship's rocking and swaying. I heard the chatter of the people, the words of the sailors above me, the screeches of the birds, the splashing of the dark water against the side of the hull. I heard and did not hear. I saw faces and did not see them. Except for one. I saw Jerie. As she was before, her beautiful round face, her smile like sunshine and the dimples in her cheeks, her body strong and healthy, before.

She was always with me. Scolding me, teasing me. Her voice flooded my ears. Her face . . . beautiful, reddish brown in color, and sculptured like the carved statutes of the Iyoba, the way it was before we came to the big waters . . . Jerie consumed my vision.

Little Bird, you are lazy and badly behaved as always! Disrespectful! What would your mother, my honored aunt, say? How like you! And all the time I spent teaching you, and guiding you so that you will be a useful woman!

I do not feel useful.

What does anyone care about your feelings! It is about duty. It is about respect to our parents and to our ancestors! You must pay your debts to them.

I am respectful.

You are foolish. You must wake up. You must be ready to use the lessons that I have taught you. Use them to make your way. Use them to live.

No.

You must live.

No.

For our ancestors. For our parents. For me. You must . . .

No.

You must live.

Then she went away. And there was quiet.

This time when the Fulani woman came to me with the small cup of water, I took it with both hands and nodded to her, and thanked her using the few words of Fula that I knew. She was surprised. Then she smiled at me and nodded, her large eyes luminous like a pool of water in moonlight.

"We thought you were gone away," she said.

7

Carolina Cove, Queen's Bay, Jamaica
About 1769

There was a storm and then another and another. The dark waters were nothing but rising curls of black waves, screaming winds, and thunder. The sky god threw fire down on us. The sun disappeared and the skies stayed dark, so dark that I couldn't tell where the sky ended and the waters began. I could not tell how many hours or days or weeks passed. Daylight, the sun, and time had run away together. The *Martinet* passed through a caravan of storms, each one longer, louder, and more terrifying than the next. I was not afraid.

The winds roared, splitting then shredding the white sails as if they were paper, setting the ship rocking from side to side, taking on water that left ponds on the deck. At times, the side rails disappeared in the swirling brown blue water and it did not look as if they would appear again. The faces of the pink-faced men shifted white with fear. Even the fat one they called "Captain" was pale. The men yelled at each other as they scurried across the decks tying down everything that could be tied down, wrestling with the massive sails, bailing water. They made signs with their hands, a gesture I took to be a prayer to their gods for deliverance. Others fingered strands of beads they pulled from their pockets, their lips moving without sound, praying to their god who had deserted them as my gods had deserted me. A low vibrating song of woe rose from the bowels of the ship. No shrieks of terror or pleas for salvation. Despair had penetrated the hold. The *Martinet* had sailed beyond the place where prayers could be heard.

I was shackled to the same little alcove that I had once shared with Jerie. The roaring winds slammed against me as if I were made of leaves, pressed me against the wall then lifted me up as if it had fingers, and it was only the heavy iron bracelet around my ankle that prevented me from being blown across the slippery deck and thrown into the sea. The salt water pelleted my face, found its way into my eyes and burned them blind with refreshing intensity. It filled my nose and mouth until I choked. I leaned against the wall and, even though I knew it was useless, said my own prayer to the queen of all our gods, Ayiba. But mine was not a prayer for deliverance; it was a prayer for death.

But I didn't die. The *Martinet* did not sink. She sailed through the last of the storms like a dancer from festival, her head, the masts, held high, her body, the stem forward and intact. The dark waters turned blue-green, the skies cleared, and the sun, once absent from the world, sent heat to dry up the water-soaked ship. And, as if shrugging her shoulder at the retreating winds that had once blown rain sideways, the *Martinet* glided into the quiet cove on the island of English Jamaica on a warm blue-skied day, her hull riding the waves as if she were floating on clouds.

I smelled the island before I saw it. In some ways it was familiar. The pungent odor of wet earth mixed with sand and shit and the bones of dead things from the before time tickled my nostrils and I sneezed. An odor that bit my nose then, as quickly as it had come, drifted by on a light breeze; the sea spray, once gritty and sharp, was soft and warm against my cheek, scented with what I would soon learn to call "vanilla." I heard the calls of the island's far-flying birds before I ever saw the flapping of their wings. Watched the rabid activity of the pink faces as they climbed up and down the ropes like monkeys and ran across the deck carrying this or that, yelling at each other over their shoulders, their boxy faces marked by relief and open-mouth smiles that revealed yellow teeth. The first I saw of the island was a lonely tree broken away from its roots and its land long ago, bleached white and stripped black in places, its jagged bow rising and falling with the waves. It was too large to have drifted away from . . . home, my home, the place I lived before. It had to have come from this new place, the place that Jerie had groomed me for, that had no name for me yet, where, according to my sister's plan, I would use my facility for languages and make my way.

I was alert now, sat up and became watchful of the hive of movement around me. I waved at a young pink face who had tried to teach me some of his words in exchange for mine and beckoned him to me. He wasn't much older than me, his pink face spotted, his straw-colored hair matted and wet. He smelled worse than I did. But he was friendly and curious. And he had been useful. Over the past few weeks, I had gathered up his words greedily (along with the extra rations that he sometimes brought), committing them to mind and waiting until the best time to use them. I saw him moving toward me, awkwardly juggling two square woven baskets, swaying back and forth with the odd crab-like gait of his bowed legs.

He called my name, mispronouncing it the way he always did.

"What is? Where we are?" The order of his words was still beyond me but when he nodded and smiled, I could tell that he knew my meaning.

The baskets, damp with sea spray, began to slide out of his grasp. I lunged toward him as far as the leg iron would allow and we struggled to get control of them. Together we maneuvered the baskets over to a small tower of similar containers.

"Thank you," he barked. He, too, was trying to make sense of my speech. He was English but had spoken in Yoruba, the language I used with him. As Jerie had instructed, I kept my own language to myself. *Better if they don't know.*

"What is?" I asked again, gesturing toward the horizon where green and brown earth was coming into view.

"Coming into port," he said, "Carolina

Cove. Jamaica."

The *Martinet* did not dock in Carolina Cove but dropped anchor in the small bay. The young Englishman and his mates lowered longboats into the waters and filled them with baskets and other cargo, bolts of cloth, bottles of port, and a good number of the Dahomian, Asante, and Igbo men and boys. As they were rowed away toward the docks, the Akan chief, the man who had scolded me for grieving for Jerie, raised a war cry among his countrymen that was taken up by the Dahomians, too. The pink faces did not like it, their complexions grew red. And one of them silenced the man with a sharp crack of his stick across his back. After that, the only sounds I heard were the call of the seabirds, the whipping sound of the white sails in the breeze, and the waves beating up against the hulls of the ships docked in the harbor. I did not step one foot on Jamaica. The *Martinet* sailed away just before dawn the next morning, its belly refilled with human and nonhuman cargo.

The tall ship made its way north or so the spotted pink face told me, bound for a place called "Savannah," proud that he was using what he thought were my words. The *Martinet* seemed to float from island to island without stopping, following the dark green

93

patches like stepping-stones in a shallow river. The swirling, angry dark waters were left behind. The air was warm and moist, the storms that had plagued the *Martinet* were gone. Rains came and went but the winds were light and the lightning kept its distance. I was shackled into the alcove once again and day and night blended together. Days, maybe months passed. I didn't care. Time had no meaning for me. The dark heavy mantle of loss covered me once again. And even the Fulani woman's gentle touch and soft words of persuasion could not move me.

The air was warm and smelled of earth and grasses and spices. The sun was hot and familiar, like the sun I knew. It had been away. Hiding? From the storms and the turbulent dark water? But now it had returned, taking the place of the weak cold sun that had followed the *Martinet* like an evil hex across the dark water. The ship now rocked on gentle waves, their whitecaps catching the light, sparkling like silver in the sun, the splashes soft and playful. I was sleepy. It was easy to be sleepy when the boat rocked like it did and the air was soft. Some days I could not keep my eyes open. I slept through the nights and much during the days, and even when I woke, I felt sleepy and sluggish, confused. In no time at all, I fell asleep again. I could tell by the Fulani woman's expression that she worried about me.

"Wake up, little sister. No one should sleep so much." She brought her face close to mine, looked deep into my eyes, studied my face with hers, the irises near black in color. She told me to stick out my tongue. "You have the sleeping sickness," she said in a tone of sad authority. But there was nothing wrong with me. I slept. I dreamed, living in a world that was beyond my reach when I was awake. A world of wishes, a world that, for me, would never be again.

Jerie's face floated in and out of my dreams. As always, she admonished me.

Wake up sister! Save your own life!

And I cried. She teased and comforted me.

You are a silly little bird! What on earth will I do with you?

And I laughed. I called to her. She wore her favorite dress, deep blue with black designs, her slender arms wrapped in gold bracelets. Sometimes she turned around and smiled at me, held out her hand, the bracelets jingling against each other, beckoned me to come with her. And I laughed again and ran. Or I tried to. My feet were made of stone. I could not move. Jerie beckoned to me again. Called my name. Still, my stone-bound feet were too heavy to lift. But it was too late. The dark waters had returned, flooding my sight, and the smooth tones of her voice were fading away as the water's roar got louder and louder. With each dream, Jerie's voice grew soft, faint, sounded as if it was far away, like an echo, then . . . like the breath of a breeze, blowing softly at the top of the trees. Cool, soothing, and light. Then gone.

Something loud and large tore a hole through the side of the *Martinet* and split the timbers of the deck, the side walls of the hull, and the floor of the alcove where I had been dreaming. It uprooted crates, baskets, and people, sending them everywhere, some overboard. It jerked me out of the region of the near dead, grabbed me by the arm, and sent me sprawling across the deck with the chains attached to the shackles around my ankle following me like lost children in search of their mother. The sound set the ship pitching back and forth violently, the storm of sound roaring in my ears. But this storm brought no rain or winds. There was no lightning: the skies were sunny and blue, cloudless. This storm of sound came from big guns — "Cannon," they were called — the scorching-hot missiles shrieked through the air, landing not on but through the floorboards of the ship, crushing anything and anyone in their path, until there was not much left to mark its presence. Except fire.

The hold filled with smoke. Voices raised in desperation and there was a sickening chorus of pleas for help from those chained below. Panic. The smoke was like a snake, slithering through every crevice, opening, or crack, moving as if it had a map to direct it to its prey, trapping our legs and arms with invisible ropes, drowning us in dry unbreathable oceans of white and gray and deep stormy blue. We were choking to death. It burned my eyes and filled my chest so quickly that I couldn't breathe and thought for a moment that Jerie was right and that I had been too stupid to know it. My life had worth to me and now a huge white snake of smoke was trying to take it away.

And I, who had wanted to die and thought with childlike arrogance that I could die just by willing it, was overcome by something I did not recognize, rising from my feet through my legs and torso into my arms to the top of my head. It wasn't fear. It was fury. I battled this . . . thing, swinging my arms and coughing between screams as I struggled to breathe, kicking as far as the shackle would allow, crawling along the deck to find a breath of fresh air. Fighting to live then choking on the white death and losing my way. I couldn't see, couldn't . . . see . . . could not.

Water splashed against my face. It was cold, dirty, and salty. I gagged on the taste of it, felt the grittiness against my skin, burning the cuts and scratches on my legs and arms. The salt stung my eyes. I spat out a piece of seaweed but I felt it and tasted it and smelled it. I pulled myself to my knees and looked around. I was topside, on the deck.

I held up my arm against the blinding sun. My ears filled with the sound of the waves rumbling around me. It was still a sunny, mild day with soft warm breezes smelling faintly of vanilla and cinnamon. The swirling blue-and-green water looked cool and unthreatening. A bulky ominous shadow loomed over us. The *Martinet* had somehow been righted and was now attached to a huge ugly black-hulled ship by a family of ropes as thick as my waist.

Only thirty of us remained after the dock-ing in Carolina Cove, and now we huddled together facing a group of men who didn't look at all like the crew of the slaver *Martinet*. I wondered where they had gone, including the young pink face who had tried to be my friend. One of the men barked at us; none of us understood his words but we caught his tone. I tried to stand up but my legs were wobbly. Behind me and on either side, the people murmured among themselves, their expressions somber and watchful.

The men who surrounded us now were a collection of miscreants. They were young and old and ages in between; they wore no uniforms, meaning they weren't king's men, not Anglais or Spanish. No one man resembled another. Some wore black hats, some no hats at all, others bandannas. Some were men who reminded me of the Portugee and Creoles who lived at Ouidah and in the French port of Saint-Louis farther up the coast. Others were pink faces, English or Spanish or maybe Dutch. I had heard of but hadn't met any Dutch. There were some French, I recognized the words. And then there were many who were in-betweens, shades of brown and tan and gold with black hair and red hair and brown hair. And in the center of this group was a tall black man who wore the clothes of the English, but had the face of the Akan and the scars to mark it. He studied us with an intensity that left me trembling. No white man had ever looked so terrifying. He would have been considered handsome in my country. I allowed myself to think about what my elder sisters would say about him: their remarks on what a fine man he was and how he carried himself like a war chief or prince. A noble forehead and sculptured nose like a king of Edo whose image the craftsman created out of prayer and wood for the devotions of the Iyoba or that the goldsmiths and brass people would model out of boiling metal. He was as dark as the night but his eyes seemed light, as if they had fire within them. I shuddered. If he was the leader, I could only feel that this was not a good thing. Some of the most ruthless warriors were of the Akan. And they had a reputation for trading people.

He spoke over his shoulder to his men and in his speech I caught a word familiar, here and there, the singsong mishmash of creole tongues I'd heard. And Akan. Behind me, the whispering swirled anew, now soft and anxious, a low buzzing of questions. And there were curses on this Akan, if that was what he was, whose people were enemies for some in our group.

I lowered my head and pretended to pick at my feet as I listened through the comments of the others behind me so that I could more easily hear the words of this man who now had the power of life or death over me, over all of us.

Amina, a woman of the Hausa, whispered close to my ear, "Little Bird, do you know his words? What does he say?"

Without raising my head, I turned toward her and murmured, "He is of the Akan, I think, and he take us to a place . . . called Key. He is . . . not a slave trader." The tall man's commands were spoken in pieces, fragments constructed well enough for me to gather his meaning.

And in obedience to my sister Jerie's lessons, I learned a new word that day.

Pirate.

8
CAESAR

"You. Girl."

I froze, pressed my lips together so that nothing escaped from my mouth. Next to me, I felt a muscle in Amina's shoulder harden as she, too, became a piece of stone. I lowered my head. I decided that the tall man was not talking to me. There were other girls in our group. If I was still and did not breathe, he would not see me. I would be invisible.

"You girl! Come!"

I was too frightened to look up. I heard a sound as if he had snapped his fingers. Then he barked out a word: *"Vite!"*

The French-speaking man grabbed me by the upper arm and dragged me to a place in front of the tall man, then dropped me on the deck, hard. I screamed. The tall man bark once more. The Frenchman shrug and murmur what sounded like an apology as he backed away.

"You talk when I talk," the tall man say. His words were those of the Asante. I said nothing. His men look one at the other. It came to me that they did not know what he was saying.

He walked toward me and the planks beneath me quivered under his weight. I was scared, so scared that I could not breathe. My throat had closed. I could only look down. He stopped. His huge feet were directly beneath my gaze.

"You answer me, girl. Do you know my words?"

"Yes," I croaked in answer.

He reached down and pulled me to my feet with a gentleness that surprised me. I raised my eyes to meet his. It was like meeting the sky god. He was a giant and he wore a sash of bullets across his body. But his eyes were kind.

"You are of the Asante?"

I shook my head.

"What is your name?"

"Maree Pres-cilla. Pres-cilla Grace." I still could not pronounce the name that the *Martinet* captain had gifted me, the name that I did not want. He had said it was a Christian name.

"No. Your true name."

I told him.

"Ah, the little bird," he said, sounding satisfied. "Who are your people? What is your country?"

"Edo," I said. It was the one place word that I knew was near my village.

"Hmmm," he commented then, "but you know the Asante. You know my words. And you know other words I think. Asante. Yoruba."

I bobbed my head.

"Yes."

"Speak out, Little Bird!" His voice was like thunder. "Mende?"

"A little."

"Igbo."

"Yes."

"Hausa."

I, the itinerant child, who had caused my mother concern because I was not the right kind of girl to develop into the right kind of wife, "the parrot" as Jerie called me, had picked up enough pieces of the languages of our trades to satisfy this giant.

"You know the words of the white men?"

"Some."

"How you learn this?"

"I — I listen. At the market with my . . . m-mother and sisters."

"Ah. A little spy."

He used a word of the Anglais and I did

not yet know the meaning of "spy."

He reached down and lifted my chin. I was trembling so hard that my teeth were chattering. He was smiling. This time, he spoke in my language, but simply, using words in the way of a small child.

"Who your father?"

I told him of my father and of my mother of the village near Edo town just a mile from the Iyoba queen mother's birth home. I told him about my older sisters and brother, the baby whom my mother had just birthed. My father's craft. He nodded, satisfied with my answers. I had replied to him in his own tongue and he seemed to relax. As we spoke, his crew began to talk among themselves, casting curious glances at me.

"Silence!" the tall man bellowed. The cries of the gulls were the only sounds remaining. He had used the Anglais but everyone understood what he meant.

"You tell them," he said to me, gesturing toward the people like me who been brought up from the slaver's hold. "What I say. In their words, so all can understand." I nodded. He studied me for a moment then seemed to come to a decision and stepped back. I was surprised to see that the Frenchman who had handled me roughly walked over and stood by his side as if he, too, was to make a pronouncement.

"I am Caesar, once known as Akande. This ship . . . this slaver" — he pointed toward the *Martinet,* spat out the word as if it were filth — "Is now mine. You, people of the Yoruba, Fulani, Igbo, and Mende . . . Akan" — at this a cry went up behind me, as those who were now known as his countrymen proudly saluted with their voices. "You are all free men and woman, slaves to no one." He looked down at me and nodded slightly. "Tell them" — he meant the others who had come from the hold. "Tell them what I say."

I took a deep breath to steady my wobbly legs and my voice and repeated his words, using the tongues that I knew from the many days in the hold, repeating the message until they all stood, smiling with relief, nodding in affirmation. The men and boys would be allowed to serve Caesar either on one of his ships, and he had many, or at his base on an island, a place called "Caesar's Key." As for the women and girls, and there were not many of us, he could not take us back to our homelands, but if we wished, he could take us to the island of Jamaica, where we could live in one of the large towns of Maroons; "Moor Town" he named it. It was a city controlled by an Obeah woman named Nanny and populated by people from our homes, people who had rebelled and escaped the slaveholders, setting up villages of their own in the mountains. The people murmured as they digested Caesar's words and a few of the women wailed. I understood and would most likely have cried with them but I could not.

"This girl child is of Edo. She is my sister." He turned and spoke to his men in a combination of broken Portuguese, French, and Anglais. "She will be called Maryam and she will be under my protection." He held up one finger. "No man is to talk to her without my permission. Woe to any man who touches her. I will castrate him and throw him over." His men exchanged uneasy glances. "No man."

When Caesar finish his speaking, he sent the people to a place where they could wash and get food. Me, he told to follow him. He led me to a place, a "cabin" he called it, just off the deck of the ship, said the Frenchman would bring water and clean garments for me to wear; that I was to stay there until he called for me.

It was a small place, the room, with a table, a chair, and a pallet for use as a bed. So many ways I could describe it now, with the hindsight of maturity and the knowing I have of the English words. But then, it was as strange to me as everything else that surrounded me: the kidnapping, the tall boats with their billowing sails, the shackles and the loud clanging chains . . . and the vast never-ending waters that had brought me . . . here. Wherever "here" was. A porcelain bowl with flowers painted on it set in the corner; it was pretty and I picked it up to examine it closely only to almost drop it when the faint stench of human waste touched my nose. The little place was dark and stuffy, there was only one window and it wasn't large enough to admit much air or light. I peered outside and saw the waves rolling in the distance.

"My sister," Caesar say to me just before he left the cabin. "Mind what I do." He took my hand in his giant one and placed it on the latch. "Turn this, like this, and the door will not open. You will be safe. Turn the other way." He show me. "And it open for you. Try."

With trembling fingers, I turn the knob the one way and then the other. Caesar nodded his satisfaction. Because he was tall and I was not, he crouched down and looked me full in the face.

"You know my words." He had said this

to me many times, as if he were amazed that it was true. How long since he had heard the words of his fathers?

"Yes."

"From this day, you will be my translator. Do you understand?"

I shook my head. Caesar smiled.

"You listen to my words. And to the words of those who talk with me. Here on this ship and in my business. You tell me what is said so that I will know that the words of my business are true, that those who I trade with are honest."

"And . . . if the words are . . . wrong? Not true?" I tried to follow the cadence of his Akan speech.

His lips formed a straight line and the look in his dark eyes hardened.

"They will be dealt with."

I felt cold despite the damp warm air.

"They will be killed?"

Caesar's eyes softened and he smiled. But his smile did not comfort me.

"They will be dealt with."

It wasn't long before I felt a vibration beneath my feet. My stomach lurched. The *Martinet* was moving again. I wondered where it was going. One of Caesar's men mentioned a town named "Havana" and then a "key," but those words meant nothing to me. Someone pound on the door, calling out my new name in French, *"Marie! Marie! Ouvrez la porte! Vite!"* I jumped, startled at the noise and afraid that the man would burst in and hurt me. But I remembered that the door was locked and I was the only one to unlock it.

"Enfin!" It was the Frenchman. I would have to pay attention to his words now, too. He shoved a bundle of clothing into my arms with such force that I took a step backward. "Himself say *s'habiller, vite.* Here is some food and water. He will need you when we dock in Sainte-Cecile. Before we sail home."

He marched toward the door, a sour look on his face.

"Wait . . . ah . . . monsieur."

He glared at me, a snarl curling his lips upward. *"Eh bien?"*

I bit my lip. I had only a few words of the language of the Frenchman. *"Ou est . . ."*

He waved his arm from one side to the other. "Out there."

I unfolded the bundle of what looked like dull rags. The hard funny things the Europeans called "shoes" and two garments, one a white . . . "shirt," I think it was called, and the other was a pair of leggings like the ones the white men wore. I looked up at the

110

Frenchman.

He shrugged his shoulders.

"It is the bad luck to have a woman on ship. So it is that Caesar sends these clothes for you. So that the men do not become . . . anxious." He used two fingers to make a sign, tapping his forehead and chest. "They take the other women to the *Calabar.* You are the only" — his eyes flickered — "woman on the *Black Mary.*"

Again, I must have looked confused. The Frenchman snarled his impatience.

"He renamed this cursed slaver." He smiled as far as his rotten teeth would let him. "*Après toi. Le* Marie Noire."

I had other names that I had not chosen. I was to be called "Maryam." The Frenchman called me "Marie," the sailors from Hispaniola called me "Maria," and I was to dress like a boy. I wondered if the Igbo was right. The tall ship had sailed off the end of the earth and I was in a strange world.

I was eleven years old.

9
THE *BLACK MARY*

From that day I was Caesar's beloved sister. He was the captain of the *Black Mary* and on her consort, the *Calabar,* the man-of-war. He was the head man. He was royalty and I was also. And as royalty, I did not work. I was dressed like a boy yet I did not swab the decks, fetch, or carry like the other boys on board. The idleness allowed me to heal, the food added flesh to my bones, and the little cabinet that Caesar gave to me was a quiet place to sleep, but I was bored. I pestered Caesar to give me a chore, an errand. He laughed, his large white teeth gleaming in the sun.

"You want to empty slop jars?" His laughter bubbled up from his massive chest. My cheeks warmed and I felt foolish.

"No . . . Honored Brother."

"It is not the use of your skinny arms that I need. For now I have more than enough men to keep us afloat. I will have need of you soon enough, Little Bird. You will have words aplenty to cipher. Rest. Eat. Tonight we dock at Sainte-Cecile. I will need your talents then."

"Where are we going?" I asked my honored brother, who indulged me and allowed me — but only me — to pester him with questions. In the before time, I would not dare to address a man directly, a man like Caesar. A girl, especially a girl who had not yet been through the passage, would have little of use to say to such a man. But I was seeing the world through different eyes. More than that, I knew that this was a different world.

The man-of-war and my namesake dropped anchors in an isolated cove, tucked away where there were no camp lights or people. Or so I thought. The *Black Mary* was empty of the rest of her human cargo and her hold filled with boxes, baskets, and crates of various sizes. But no people. I had asked if Caesar plan to sell me. He laughed.

"No trade in people," he told me. "Only cloth, rum, other treasures."

Then, with the Frenchman at the helm, the slaver that was left the little cove and its mothership behind and sailed away, silent as a shadow, hugging the coastline until the lights of a small harbor came into view.

"Listen to me, Beloved Sister," he said, not taking his eyes from the harbor as the ship moved closer to the dock. "I tell you what to do and you must do it without mistake." He glanced down at me. "Without mistake."

Being a child of a warm country, I did not know then the word to call it, this feeling. The breezes that filled the sails of the *Black Mary* were warm, the air heavy with moisture. But I was cold. The sharpness of his words left gooseflesh on my arms. There was a threat behind the endearment that he used only for me.

"Y-you will kill me if I . . . make a mistake?"

Caesar did not look away from the Frenchman's back.

"Yes."

It was a festival and a market all together. The noise of the people going here, going there, on foot, in canoes, in wagons and on horses, music of a kind I had never heard, after the murmurs of the waters, the whispering Caribbean breezes, the noise of Sainte-Cecile town was deafening. It 'minded me of Ouidah, the confusion, heat, and wildness. There were undercurrents, too, of danger that 'minded me of Ouidah.

I didn't need Caesar to tell me that I was to stay close to him and to the Frenchman. It would be too easy to get lost, by misstep or misadventure. I saw many people from the before time woven here and there within the throngs of people in the main street. Slaves or no, I was not sure. But I was very sure that I did not want to be captured again.

We were to meet Big Jacques, a trading partner of Caesar's. A pirate, too, cast as a "merchant" as they all were. He had a reputation for larceny, as they all did. Beyond that, not much was known about him. Caesar was bringing him rum, cloth, and a commodity that Jacques coveted; its name I did not learn. In return, my honored brother was to receive a treasure of silver and gold. My purpose was simple.

"Big Jacques will speak *en français* but I am told those are not his words. He is of the Anglais. His . . . first mate will speak for him. You will listen. To Jacques's words and to his mate's words. You will listen to the words of those around him. Every word, every joke, may have worth. You will say nothing. You will look as if you know nothing. You will stand or sit as I tell you. I will not decide his offer until I consult with my adviser."

Adviser? A word I did not know.

Caesar looked down at me and gently touched my shoulder. It was near dusk but I could still see his expression.

"*You* are my adviser. I will do my business with him once you will tell me what I need to know."

"How am to do that?" I still did not understand what I was to do.

"I said this to you." Caesar's response was sharp. "You will listen."

What I had taken for a festival was in truth a market. There was a price for everything and everyone. The laughter, the dancing and drinking, were the masks of the god whose glory was celebrated, a god named gold or silver. A god of coin. And, in this place, his chief priest was Big Jacques.

He was a fat man, dark as far as pink faces go, with black hair and a beard of hair braided as tightly as my own would have been if Jerie was . . . He sat on a throne of mats like the oba as he was carried through our village. He was surrounded by men and women in a place that looked as if it had once been a fortress. It was open to the breezes but still hot and suffocating in the heat and I wondered why he did not ask the servants — were they servants? — to fan him. He stood when Caesar entered the place, with me and the others following behind him, and he laughed, showing a mouth of gold- and silver-capped teeth, emitting a loud sound of pleasure as he grabbed my honored brother and hugged him, then patted him hard on the back. The sound was as loud as a slap.

He had the blue eyes of the English but when he spoke to Caesar, he spoke only in French, which was translated by the Frenchman, not by me.

Jacques clapped his hands and food and drink were brought. Rum. And food! So much food! I did not see all what filled the bowls but the smells made my mouth water and my belly growl. Later I saw what was left of a stew made with fish. I was a child and always hungry! But I knew that it was not my time to eat but to listen. Caesar sat down. The bearded man laughed again and swept his arm toward the rest of us, gesturing for us to sit, eat, and drink. But my honored brother shook his head slightly then scowled and barked a command, that we were to stay where we were, that we were not to eat or drink. In obedience, we squatted on the floor opposite Caesar and Jacques. As was planned. But for me. Caesar made a show of snapping his fingers. He gestured to a sliver of straw mat next to his feet. I was to squat there.

The potentate was impressed.

"You are better with your slaves than I!" he said, his plated teeth sparkling in the torchlight as he chewed his food with vigor, his mouth open. "Obedience! *Comme ça!*" he added in French. Caesar's eyes flickered. The fat man's words were various. French here, a word or two of the Portugee, he threw words around like treats for his dogs. Some I knew, some I did not. But as I sat there, perched on my haunches, scratching the floor with the nail of one finger, I listened as I had been ordered. Remembering what Caesar had asked of me. Willing my ears to catch every phrase, every whisper.

"He is not of the *français,* that is for certain," Caesar had said earlier as we walked through the streets, "though I am told his speech is correct."

"No one knows of his real name or where he is from," the Frenchman added. "And he uses that mulatto *l'enfant de chien* for his interpretor."

I had seen the "mulatto" when we entered, noting that he whispered in Jacques's ear, that he smiled a lot and nodded his head. He reminded me of the yellow man in Ouidah, the one with the freckled face and Igbo nose who had cracked his whip at me and ordered the men to load us onto the boats that took us out to the slaver waiting in the bay. The Creole who was as bad as any Dahomain slave trader. His light eyes, the color of watered-down rum, gleamed with deceit when he spoke. I lowered my head and listened.

Caesar ate little and drank less, although you had to be watching carefully to notice. It seemed that when his cup was filled, he drained it. He laughed at the fat man's jokes and berated the Frenchman loudly and more than once for not correctly passing along his words. And all during the dinner, I listened, to the yellow man's words, to the throwaway words of the Big Jacques, and to the murmurs of those around me — Jacques's other men and hangers-on, the women — their tongues loosened by rum and something called the poppy.

It was agreed that my honored brother would retire to his ship to prepare for the exchange of cargo and coin to take place after dawn. It was late when we left the pirate's lair with Caesar shouting his good-byes, laughing at his own jokes and singing, weaving from one side to the other, the walk of one who had taken too much spirits. I walked alongside with his hand on my shoulder as if I were a walking stick.

"He is not of the Anglais or the French, he is . . . from another place, the English colony, Virginia. He and the yellow man are brothers."

Caesar's deliberately uneven gait came to an abrupt halt. The Frenchman's eyebrows rose. The two exchanged glances.

"Brothers?"

I nodded.

"Same father . . . a laborer from the Anglais, in-den-ture." I repeated the word I had heard although I did not know then what it meant. "Different mother. Jacques mother die. The yellow man's mother was wet nurse. It is her language that he speaks."

"Ah," Caesar started walking again, his steps zigzagging across the dirt road.

"He speak the English only, *le français* a few words, and the Fon he learn at the breast."

The Frenchman frowned at me.

"He sound . . . like he know it," he said, meaning the words that the fat man spoke in *le français.*

I shook my head slightly then yelped in pain. Caesar had stepped on my foot.

"He do not," I said. "He . . ." What was the bird my sister had called me? "He . . .

parrot. He repeat only."

We were at the shore, clambering into the longboat that would take us back to the *Black Mary.* Caesar got in, then turned and lifted me into the boat as if I were no heavier than a bird's feather.

"So. What does the parrot want?"

"Smith," I said. "His name is Jack Smith." I couldn't help myself. I grinned.

Caesar grinned back.

"So. What does the Jack Smith want?"

They were waiting for him. It was the darkest part of the night and quiet. Even the stars were silent. Long before the red sun rose, we heard them coming, their oars slipping in and out of the water with as much sound as a minnow's sigh. They must have thought themselves lucky. The *Black Mary* was dark and still, like a ghost ship. The crow's nest was deserted. To even a trained eye, it must have seemed that Caesar and the crew of the *Black Mary* were deep into the sleep of rum.

Caesar's men shot the longboats out of the water, then sent a cannonball into the camp. The men who weren't shot and didn't drown, including the yellow man, were captured. Caesar demanded a ransom, which, at first, Jack Smith refused to pay.

He said that the raiders were filthy turn-coats. Caesar agreed and offered to return their heads to him as a warning to others. Smith paid the ransom. He also purchased the cargo that had been the purpose for the *Black Mary*'s visit in the first place at a higher price.

As we sailed out of the saint's cove, Caesar placed five gold coins in my palm.

"This is your share, my sister," he told me. "Collect enough of these, you may buy anything you wish. Even a worthy husband when you are old enough!"

I mark this moment as the first time in my life that I held coin of my own earning in my hand.

10
CAESAR'S KEY

Today, if I had the gold and silver coins that Caesar gave me over the time that I spent with him, I would be a wealthy woman. I would have been able to buy a fine house, land, cattle, horses, and chickens and still have coin to spend. I would have been able to buy people, too, if that had been my wish. I would have fine soft clothes and an elegant cheroot pipe. Over the next few weeks, as the *Black Mary* and her companion sailed north, Caesar used the same method at each stop and became richer for it.

I learned much about Caesar and about his world, now my world. Not by his words. By listening, watching. Turning over the scenes and words in my head until they made sense to me. Until they became real.

There were many like him, like Caesar, the pirates. Their white-sailed ships of every type — stolen from the pink faces of every port — patrolled the warm Caribbean seas, engaging the English or Spanish only when they had to, evading them otherwise. Alliances within their society were various and did not last. Caesar said that few love affairs lasted from sunup to sundown. The *Black Mary* and her consort never stayed anchored in any port or bay for more than two sunsets. Caesar was known for leaving at the hour of darkest night, three o'clock in the morning, before birds stirred, before dawn broke.

There was a price on all our heads. My honored brother was mindful of this. And so he was unpredictable. He appeared in ports, coves, and cays, unexpected and uninvited. He left without notice. His destinations, mysterious. It was said of Caesar that his footprints did not appear in wet sand until two days after he raised anchor.

The redcoats — the name used for the Anglais king's men — had a navy that covered the dark waters as far as the horizon; the Spanish had the same. Other pirates controlled an armada of ships. Caesar did not. But he was not bragging when he said that he did more with longboats and two sailing ships than all of them. He slipped in and out of ports, traded his cargo, and left, rich and undetected. He was away before his enemies and those who sought to capture him knew that he had arrived.

He knew all of the pirate kings, their women and their weaknesses. And so he used a kind of magic to gain advantage. He created a kind of entertainment for them unique to their desires or vices, and in the doing, diverted their eyes from his real activity, seeing only what he wanted them to see. The Frenchman functioned as his emissary and his translator; he was the voice of Caesar, stood at his side, spoke and gestured with authority. I was at Caesar's side, too, but no one noticed me. I was a simpleminded boy (I did not yet look like anything other) whom he patted on the head as like a dog. I kept my head down and my ears open and was invisible though I was in sight. The eyes and attention of Caesar's prey rolled over me as they would a blade of grass in a field. They didn't see me at all.

We meandered northward through warm calm seas, weaving in and out of the shallow straits, stopping here and there at islands of various and colorful names: Mayaguana, Cay Lobos, Rum Island, and Cat Island, meeting and trading with others of similar occupation and indifferent allegiances, sometimes trading, sometimes not. But whatever the purpose of Caesar's detours, the outcome was never in doubt: he filled the hold of the *Black Mary* with coin and jewels to please himself and necessaries to satisfy a village of people, from sugar to the finest sewing needles. And once he had done this, his ships floated north and then east toward a small mountain of an island that had no name on a map but many birds and a sheltered cove where anchored ships of various loyalties docked, whose crews had taken refuge there.

It was one of many slivers of land that made of themselves barriers to the Spanish colony. Small, sandy, lush, some of them so flat as to be washed away at high tide, others larger with dark mounds rising above the dark green-blue valleys toward the clouds. Malaga Key, mapped and named by a shipwrecked Spaniard in an earlier time, was not a "cay" at all but a mixture of sand and mountain, valley and marsh. The lost Spaniard named it after the place that he came from. Caesar named it after himself.

Sailors call them the "sea legs," when your insides and your outsides come together to hold you on the deck of a ship, when you can take the swaying and the rolls and valleys of the water without feeling as if your insides will come out of every opening on your body. I had crossed the dark waters in a misery of terror, loneliness, and sickness. By the time I walked the plank to the *Martinet*-that-was and it slid across the light blue waters of the Caribbean, I felt only the movements of my feet. My innards didn't roil or quiver as they used to. I walked with the rocking instead of against it and felt my toes clutching at the wooden planks on the deck as if they were claws. O'Brien, one of the oldest men in Caesar's crew, cackled at me, grinning with a mouth more full of gums than teeth.

"Ye got yer sea legs, Black Mary, ye do. Yew'll be climbin' yon mast afore ye know!" He raised one skinny finger toward the crow's nest. It looked like a white twig twisted with knots.

"Non! Elle n'est pas de sailor," the Frenchman bellowed back at him but in good humor. "She's a translator, not a salty!"

The raucous laughter and conversation that followed his retort kept the men occupied while I walked along the deck toward the railings. But I wasn't there to throw up.

We'd been at sea for two days with no sign of land, no sightings of other ships. I did not know where we were going, Caesar did not share his bearings with me. But that day, as I held my hand across my brow to block the glare of the sun, I saw flocks of seabirds circling in the distance and a dark mound emerging on the horizon. Land. But what land? As we got closer, other mounds of dark green, black, and tan appeared, I felt a tremor growing in the pit of my stomach. These were not illusions. The last time I saw land like this, the collection of colors, deep rich evergreen, palm trees, tall and willowy with light green tops and the soft tan of the sand . . . I was near the lands of the Fon, I was near home. The breath caught in my throat. It could not be. Was I dreaming? Worse, was I seeing things that were not there?

I sniffed the air and was rewarded with the smells of damp soil and a sweet perfume. The birds screeched and chirped as the ship turned slowly then moved parallel to the shore. The waters calmed and I couldn't help myself, I started jumping up and down, the joy filling me up to my throat. Figures moved along the shoreline. I could see the colors of their clothing: bright colors, scarlet, yellow, white, deep blue. And I could see the colors of their faces. Tan, brown, black, yellow.

Home. I am home.

I heard my mother's voice, my father's

laughter. The giggles of my younger brother, the teasing of my older sisters . . . Jerie. I wondered how I was going to tell our mother that Jerie slept now beneath the dark waters. I saw the shrine that would be built in her memory, heard the chanting of my great-aunts, the deep-voiced murmurs of the elders, and I tasted the sweetness of ripe fruits. But it was just a wish.

"Land ho!" A voice from the crow's nest. Caesar's hand on my shoulder.

"What is this place?" I spoke in Edo, forgetting.

He looked down at me, a slight frown on his face.

"What did you say?"

I repeated my question in his words, my hopes choking me now instead of my wish.

Understanding filled his dark eyes, he nodded slowly.

" 'Tis home," he answered. "Your new home. This island is called a 'key'; they call it *cayo* in Spanish." A wide grin stretched across his face. "It is my island. I call it 'Caesar's Key.' "

"It looks like . . ." I caught myself before I said the word, either in Edo or Akan. Water filled my eyes and I wiped them with the back of my arm. I looked up at him but his eyes were closed.

"It does," he said. "And if I close my eyes and only let the sun warm my face . . . and if I take a long breath . . . then I catch the fertile perfume of the earth of my fathers, the dark scents of the riverbank after flooding. I hear what they call the 'larks' calling and the sharp sweetness . . . too sweet . . . of the nandi flower blooming as it releases its perfume."

I let the tears roll down my cheeks. Caesar's fingers pressed into my shoulders, then he released his grip.

"It was cruel I think . . . ," he said, "to choose this place as mine. It fools me every time I sail into the cove. Everything about it reminds me . . . of Entume, my village, my warriors, of my wives and children. But now it is my new home, the home of my wives and my children, and my men and their wives and children." He looked at me. "I chose it because of its isolation. Because I can defend it, I am safe, away from the English king's men and the Spanish and it is of no interest to the colonials. And yet . . ."

I heard him take a long breath.

I am not a seer, the gods did not honor me with those gifts as they did my mother and her mother. I do not read the mind as people say, and the mists of time do not lift

130

high enough for me to see very far beyond. But at that moment, I knew what Caesar was thinking. I knew what his greatest wish was because it was my wish, too.

"I will not return, will I?" I coughed out the words. "Home."

"No, you will not," he said, still staring out to sea. "Nor will I."

Caesar's Key was a sliver of land, a wisp of a place in the blue-green sea, a slice of what would be Floride that had broken off and floated away. It had sand and palm trees, a small and dense forest, and even a mountain of black rock, formed, so Caesar said, when the earth goddess belched a long time ago. The settlement, populated only by the families of the crew, was built up by small low buildings of many designs, some that reminded me of my home, others like the cabins of the pink faces that I had seen along the coast of Jamaica, and still others that took the form of the longhouses of the first people of the place, gone now. It was all new and strange and fascinating and familiar. The people gathered at the dock, children dancing with joy, smiles on every face. The crew, men I had spent several months with, some taciturn and often ill tempered, beamed with joy, and I was

surprised to see them embrace some of the
women and pick up the children whom they
claimed as theirs. It was a place like Ouidah
but it held no fear for me. There were pink
faces here and there but mostly tan ones
and brown ones and black ones and in-
between ones. And Caesar — who claimed
two wives in this place — fell into a crowd
of children, all colors and sizes, all clamor-
ing for his attention, while his women —
wives — stood aside, smiling with pride,
one of them a woman of the Igbo, the other
a woman with light yellow skin and curling
dark hair who wore the sharp features of
the Malians from the north. It was like a
festival and I was pulled along by one of
Caesar's young ones, a boy of six or seven,
who said that I was to live in his mother's
house.

"Father says that you are his honored
sister! My aunt!" The little boy spoke so
quickly I barely caught the words. He'd
grabbed my hand and now pulled me into
the center of the crowd that thronged the
dirt road. "You will live with us, my aunt!"
He giggled and flashed a set of white teeth
at me, one of which was missing in the
front. "That's funny! You're small to be an
aunt!" His words, a mishmash of Anglais,
Igbo and Hausa and the *français* and other

tongues, poured out of his mouth. He danced along the street, and to keep up, I had to dance with him. "Oh! Here's my mother!"

The Igbo woman studied me with large dark eyes and a serious expression. I knew that she took measure of me, to decide if I was a threat to her, a rival. But she, like her son, saw a child, a girl not yet bleeding. Her position was secure. And I, I remembered my mother's teaching. I stopped before the older woman and lowered my head in respect.

"My husband say you are his sister," she said slowly. "That you are . . . ," she paused, "his speaker."

I nodded. For once, the "speaker" was mute.

"I am Nneka. You are welcome in my house." The antics of her dancing son caught her eye and she frowned. "Kwe! You stop that! You are worrying your honored aunt!"

"Thank you . . . Sister," I said, speaking slowly so that the words would be correct. "My name is . . ."

What was my name? Little Bird? Priscilla Grace?

"I am Maryam," I said, remembering the way that Caesar had pronounced the new name he'd given me. "Maryam."

Nneka nodded, as if she was accustomed to such names.

"Come with me." She ran her hand lovingly across the top of her son's little egg-shaped head. "Kwe and I will show you where you may sleep."

Later, Caesar's son took me along the beach to show me his favorite shells and to bother crabs. There were a few dwellings here and there but mostly the surrounding forest was deserted until we came to a fence that was made entirely of shells. I had never seen a thing like it. I followed the length of the shell fence with my eyes as it wound its way into the forest. In the gloom, I could just make out a small cabin, like a long-house, that stood in a small clearing, blue smoke curling out of its chimney. I thought that was strange since it was hot there just like in my own country.

Kwe shrugged his shoulders and grabbed my arm.

"That's Aunt Cat's house," he said, dragging me away back toward the docks. "We don't come here unless she call us. And she did not call us. Don't want her to see us . . ." The look in his dark eyes was somber.

"What's wrong?" I asked. "What are you

afraid of?"

The boy didn't answer at first, just pulled me harder as if he wanted me to move faster.

"Not . . . afraid. But Aunt Cat, she is powerful. And my mother would not be pleased if I made her angry." He shook his head and marched on without looking back. But I did look back and saw a woman standing in the shadows at the edge of the forest near the opening of the shell gate.

"Who is she?" I asked Kwe, feeling a chill around my shoulders despite the heat and the heavy moist breeze.

"She the medicine woman," he whispered loud enough for the fish to hear.

The first night I spent on Caesar's Cay was magical; if I closed my eyes, I would have thought that I was home, across the dark waters, looking toward the rising sun. The evening meal was a fest, to celebrate the Asante homecoming, to give thanks to the gods, all of them, Yoruba, Igbo, Christian, Muslim, for bringing Caesar, his men, and me safely home.

There was food, the women had been cooking all day, and the pots gave off aromas that made my mouth water, aromas that were familiar, although some were not. Fish stews, chicken and rice, beans, a pig roasted over a pit, a delicacy that those who followed the turbaned ones did not eat, settling themselves some distance away and upwind.

I ate until I was almost sick.

The dancing made me laugh — those who spoke the Gaelic hopped and tapped to the quick shreiking sounds of the stringed wood, an instrument that looked like the kora that I had once seen a Mandinka man play; the Spanish among Caesar's men swayed to the tunes that sounded like a woman crying; and under it all, at the start of every song and at the end, long after the last tone faded, there were the drums. Hours after the last beat was struck, I heard them. Even in my dreams, the beats firm and steady, speaking. The hands that beat them belonged to men of the Hausa, and of Benin and also of the Taino and the Muskogee, who lived in places I had not yet visited. The drums played by hands from the east and west shores of the dark waters told the stories that the Gaelic drinking songs could not, that the Spanish ballads would not. The drums told the story of children stolen, misery and loss when the ancestors on the western shores watched their children felled by musket balls, pestilence, their ankles decorated with iron chains.

I swayed, too, but not to the music, I was

sleepy. I had eaten, laughed, talked, and done something that I had not done since the day the Dahomians swept me and my sister away many days, weeks, months ago. I played. The children had several balls and we kicked them and threw them. We played a game of catch-me and used an old length of rope to play what the Anglais called "tug-of-war." I let the younger boys chase me and then I chased them back. I ran and ran until I thought my legs would fall off.

I forgot. From that moment I stepped onto the sand beach of Caesar's Cay, I forgot all that had gone before and became a child again. We pretended we were warriors and did battle on the beach, falling dead and getting sand in our hair, our ears, everywhere! I closed my eyes, inhaled the soft cinnamon scent of the air, and remembered . . . My feet slapped the wet sand and the warm water splashed against my legs. I ran and muscles that I hadn't used for a long time ached for days afterward. I remember it with pleasure.

And the sound of laughter so long away from my ears. The men, the women, the giggles of children, shouts and yelling my name as we ran. The gurgling of the fat babies that we teased with little toys made by a salty, whom I would never had thought a craftsman. He straightened the little head of the cloth doll he had fashioned and passed it over to the little girl, barely a year old, who smiled and drooled, one tiny tooth prominent in her open mouth. He was so gentle, this man who had wielded the cannon near by himself. I grinned at him and in the shade of the palm leaf canopy, I saw the blush cross his cheeks. "My daughter Ana," he said with pride. "Marie says she is strong and has a bear's spirit."

"Marie?"

"The medicine woman. The children called her 'Aunt Cat.' She is the midwife also."

I cast my mind back to the strange shell enclosure that I had seen from the shore on my walk with Kwe.

I was in a new world among new people, different from me yet . . . I knew them. The talk around me, the laughter, babies crying, music . . . I was not afraid. Or worried. I was home now, a new home, I had a new family, I had been accepted and had status. And I was safe. No one would hurt me or trap me. Or kill me. I was content.

I was ready for sleep. I must have drifted off, because the only thing I remember is being lifted up, my body rocking back and forth, a deep voice murmuring in my ear.

Caesar. I was settled into a soft nest that smelled faintly of sweet grasses and freshly washed linen.

"Sleep, Little Sister. Sleep."

I got to be a child again on that day, the day we landed at Caesar's Key. I got to be a child one last time.

11
Little One

The *Black Mary* and the *Calabar* cruised the eastern Atlantic and the Caribbean near constantly, stopping in so many ports that I could not count and did not get all of the names, strange as they were to me: Cay Lobos, Abaco Cove, Little Inagua, Cove de Sainte-Marie, Isla de Navassa.

Caesar was eager to gather all the bounty that he could before retreating to the cay before the onset of what he called the "storm season."

I shuddered, remembering the rains that drenched our land in the before time, the rivers swollen with water, the year that a village where my father's cousins lived was swept away. Young as I was, even I could recall a time when the water fell for days and my parents despaired. Crops, people, and even whole villages were washed away, snakes walked the land, and nothing grew, because the earth, saturated and tired, rejected seeds and simply turned to mush. In this place where water was, where the dark waters were a two days' sail toward the rising sun, I could not imagine what a rainy season would be like.

"It is more than the rain," Caesar explained. "There is a wind that comes, out of the eastern sea. It form a storm, the sky is black, fire come from the clouds. The waters can swallow a ship, even a man-of-war, quick than the time you blink. The waves are taller than the trees." He gestured toward the palms swaying in the gentle breeze. "We must be safe in the arms of the key by storm time." He stared past me, frowned. "I think the storms come early this year. The waters are too warm."

And so, to outwit the black-cloud storm, Caesar hopped like a frog around the blue-green seas. He baited the English, parlayed with the Spanish, and negotiated with *les français.*

I did as I was told.

I spoke only to Caesar. My head swirled with unfamiliar faces and clothes, new words, strange accents. I lost many of the words of the Portugee. They were many as sailors but their ports and towns were farther south in the seas where Caesar did not go. More and more, I heard the words

141

of the Anglais and *les français.* And when we were out of port, Javier taught me the words of the Spanish. Our final port of call was Magdalena, a pirate's haven on the northern edge of the island of Cuba. The *Black Mary* opened her sails and turned northward toward Caesar's Key and Angel's Cove, where she would dock and rest, tucked away from the worst of the storms. The *Calabar* left a week before, groaning under the weight of supplies and treasure.

On a morning just past dawn, I took up my place on deck near my honored brother. I felt strange, tired and giddy at the same time, feverish but not. My legs were wooden yet barely held me up. Caesar looked me over, a frown forming on his face.

"Beloved Sister, you don't look well."

I swallowed hard, felt as if my insides were coming out. My stomach had tightened into a knot as if a melon were pushing through my skin, tearing me apart from the inside. Swallowing again, a wave of panic swept over me. I didn't want to shame myself by puking or, worse, shitting in front of him. But I couldn't move. My head throbbed, and my vision shifted. Black spots everywhere, a whoosh of warmth flooded out of my body and I felt my head fall to the side.

So this is death, I remember thinking

before the black sky covered my eyes.

I know now but did not know then that, sometimes, when a mind is lost, it recover itself one sense at a time. It is the hearing that comes first. As I came to myself — I had not died — I felt nothing, no pain, no sickness, and my bones had no weight. I heard myself breathing, my chest fill then empty, the soft whoosh of air leaving my nostrils. My legs sank into a mattress and my head sagged against a pillow. The sound of voices floated by, one familiar, the other, not.

"Elle n'est sais pas." She didn't know. Caesar.

"No. I don't think so."

A woman's voice.

". . . did this . . ."

"Qui est . . ."

". . . *rien*. She is young, very young, such a little thing. *La pauvre jeune fille.*"

"I will find who did this and . . ."

"*Enfin!* She will hear you! *Calmez.*"

"Will she live?"

"Oui."

"And the child?"

Their voices were clear to me if their words were not, a stew of sounds, languages, my dreams mixed them up. Portuguese with Fon, Edo with Fula, Arabic and French and the Anglais wrapped around each other. My mind struggled to untangle the words and phrases. She . . . Me? I was ill but would live. The woman said so. Caesar would find . . . would kill . . . someone. Who? Why? And there was a baby somewhere but it was not crying. The woman said that it could not live or did not live. Ah! The medicine woman, Marie Catherine was her name. I had not met her face-to-face. But she was the healer and a midwife. That is why Caesar asked about a baby. She spoke a kind of French mixed with words of a tongue that I had not heard before.

"Get out. This is women's business," she said with authority. "I will send word if I need you."

Pain cut through my abdomen. I woke up, gasping. Tried to sit up but could not. Someone . . . the woman? Yes, the brush of soft fabric against my arm and a faint scent of spice and flowers caressed my nose. I opened my eyes but her face was a blur of tan and white. She placed her palm on my forehead then touched my cheek with one fingertip, murmuring endearments in a language that I did not understand, not French or Edo or Portuguese or even the patois that I had heard from some who were born in the Jamaica. Her voice was low and

144

calm, melodious like my mother's. I was drifting off to sleep when I felt a pressure within my belly and another stab of pain. I yelped and opened my eyes.

"Ah, you are awake. Good."

For a moment, I saw my mother's face, dark eyes sharp with wisdom but soft with love. Then the face of another woman took its place, one of my great-aunts or godmothers, a medicine woman of her village. Slowly, my eyes focused.

I had not seen anyone who looked like her. She was mestizo or, maybe, a Creole woman, with dark tan skin and black almond-shaped eyes like my mother's, a white cloth wrapped around her hair. She smiled, then placed the back of her hand against my head.

"You are mending. No fever. I am sorry to have caused you pain." She glanced down at where my hand rested on my stomach. "I had to make sure that your womb clears itself. *Savez*?" She frowned as if gauging my awareness. Repeated her question in Portuguese, then in *le anglais.* "Do you understand?"

I nodded but I did not understand.

"I will give you water but you must drink slowly. Your stomach is not yet strong. Some broth later, maybe bread. But not yet." She stood up and turned to leave, her skirts swirling around her. Then she stopped and looked back at me, smiled. "I am Marie Catherine."

"I — My name is . . ."

Marie Catherine smiled and touched my cheek with her palm as my mother had done.

"I know your name, Little Bird."

Marie Catherine gave me water. It was cool and refreshing and tasted of mint. Something to make me sleep. The next time I woke, the sun's rays were lower on Marie's rough-hewn log walls, casting shadow and heat.

It was afternoon.

I was in pain.

Marie Catherine touched my forehead, then pressed her palms gently but firmly on my stomach. I groaned; she sighed.

"I am sorry but I must do this." She pulled back the sheet and lifted my legs gently, then cleaned me with a damp cloth and water. One of the cloths was stained with bright red blood — I caught a glimpse before she put it out of sight. I must have soiled myself. I remember being ashamed, so ashamed that I couldn't look at her.

"Do not worry, child, it must be done. Part of being a woman." Marie Catherine caught my gaze again and leaned close. "You do understand? What I am saying?"

I shook my head.

"I — I understand the meaning of your words, Aunt," I told her. "But I do not understand . . ." The throbbing in my stomach had returned and was making me miserable.

"Ah." She leaned back, squeezed my shoulder gently, then stood up. "I will get you something to calm your stomach."

She helped me sit up on the pallet, placing pillows behind my back before handing me another cup of the spiced water.

"What is this?" I asked her.

She smiled slightly. "It will help the pain."

Later she brought a bowl and soup and, swatting my hand away, fed me herself.

"It's a broth, chicken with vegetables and herbs," she explained. "To build your strength and heal your womb."

"Womb?"

Marie Catherine's dark eyes narrowed as she searched my face.

"*Dite-moi.* Do you understand what happened to you?"

Tears spilled from my eyes. I was ashamed of my body's weakness.

"I — I wet and . . . s-soiled myself," I managed to spit out, choking back a sob.

"In front of . . . Caesar and . . . Luc a-and . . . all of them." I couldn't look at her. All I could think about was how humiliated my mother would be if she knew of my behavior, of how I could not control my body functions. What would Jerie have said?

Marie Catherine lifted my chin with her finger.

"No, Little Bird, you were delivered of a baby."

A baby. She said the word as naturally as if she'd said good morning. A baby? How had I . . . without my realizing, my hands sought out the small mound that was my stomach. It was sore but no longer hard. The little lump that had been there . . . No.

Questions froze on my chapped lips. *How . . . why. No. Not possible.* I had not had the rites yet, the ceremony . . . Marie Catherine shook her head slowly.

"You . . . You did not know this? That you were with child? But how can that . . ." She sat back in the chair that she had set next to the bed. "You are very young. Fourteen? Fifteen?"

"Twelve. I think."

She inhaled deeply and closed her eyes. When she opened them, her features had hardened into a mask of calm, a calm that looked so dangerous that I shivered. There was a passing breeze in the little room, cold, sharp, a burst of air that had lost its way.

"I see. Who is the father?"

Father. Baby. These words meant nothing to me. I knew what a man and woman did together, or thought I did. I still had much to learn. I was taken before I had been through the rites. I had not yet had my first bleeding when I stepped on to the tall ship.

I stared at Marie Catherine. I could not go beyond what she had told me. I had been delivered of a baby. A child. And yet, if that was true — and I had no reason to disbelieve her — then how had I . . . My thoughts flew from here to there, swirling like the water in tide pools, around and around and . . . No. And then I knew. And so did Marie.

She was a sorceress, of that I was sure. Because her eyes grabbed mine the moment I remembered, pulling out the truth that I had tried to forget. At dusk some moons ago, seven? Eight? Green Turtle Island, Hope Town, it was. A busy but not so busy street, an alcove between hovels, a strong arm around my shoulders, wrenching my neck, an unseen man's breath in my ear.

An errand for Caesar, taking papers to another comrade, a man who spoke Portuguese and had only a few words of Anglais.

I was to give him the papers, give him a message for his ears only, and return with his response. I was the one whom Caesar trusted for the errand. And I had done what he asked, exactly as he asked it of me. My mistake was returning to the *Black Mary* by taking a shorter way.

Hope Town is a small but busy place; its main streets are lively and broad for such a small town, crowded with people and market stalls, commerce everywhere. There are few trees left and no shadows. But the side ways are not sunny or crowded or wide and the one I chose had only two people on it — him and me. I heard his steps and turned to see who was behind me, but I was too slow. He grabbed me around the shoulders and dragged me into an alcove that was set back from the alleyway, a niche that was too isolated and hidden for even the midday sun's rays to reach. A few words only, guttural, hard, and slurred. Anglais. His body smelled of rum, sweat, and filth. He held me with one hand, tore my britches down with the other and with one thrust plunged himself into my body, breaking what little understanding I had of the world, of good and evil. I remember that he stopped, once, uttered a French expletive, and thrust his hand up my shirt, grabbing my breast as if he wanted to tear it off. Then he plunged into me again, this time with a ferocity that left me shrieking until he smacked me across the back of my head. And then he shoved me down on the cobblestones and I knew that he was going to stab me or slice my head off.

But he didn't. He cursed at me again in a language I soon learned to recognize and then he was gone, leaving me shaking, pissing myself and broken, my insides feeling as if a monster had reached in and torn them out. I do not remember how I managed to get back to the ship, to clean myself up enough to pass any scrutiny from Caesar or the others. But I did. And then I tried to forget. Which I did. But at that moment, sitting in the soft heat of late day, looking over my cup of water at Marie Catherine, I said nothing, because I did not know what to say.

I couldn't tell her *that.* I could not see that day again, feel the . . . against my back and the breaking of my . . . I could not. I would not. And, somehow, Marie knew that, knew exactly my thoughts, could see exactly what I saw as if she were behind me, looking over my shoulder at the horror that I had tried to forget. But she said nothing.

"The . . . child." Two little words. I felt as

if I were walking across a dry riverbed covered with sharp jagged stones that sliced into the bottoms of my feet. Blood seeping into the water, swirling away from my sight.

"She was . . . It was too early. And you" — she stroked away my tears with the back of her warm hand — "You were too young."

"Can I . . ." I did not even know what to ask her. But Marie knew and shook her head slowly.

"*Non.* I have given her the prayers and buried her where the breezes will cool her face and the rising sun will take her blessings. Her spirit will float away in warmth and safety." I did not ask her anything else, because I could not bear to hear the answers.

I have thought about this moment many times over my life. This little girl was my first child and, for many years, my only child. I have wondered what my life would have been like had I not been so young, had she not been born too soon. I have thought about what she might have looked like but the face I see in my head is always a blur. I did not see the face of the man who overpowered me. Marie Catherine had not seen him either. But she had seen my child. And later that evening after Caesar came to look in on me and consult with Marie, I remembered more of the conversation they had with each other earlier, on the day before I completely woke up, in the moments when I floated between the real world and the world of dreams.

Caesar growled and bellowed like an angry god.

"I tear him apart! Rip his cock off, his legs, his —"

"How you find him, heh? How you know what man to slice up? Will you burn Hope Town to the ground? Hang every man over twelve years from the masts of your *Black Mary*?"

"I will know."

"Just like a man. *Fermez*!"

Her voice cut through his like a dagger.

"You do not know him. Even she does not know him. Put your fury away and pray for her to be well, body and spirit."

Caesar grumbled again, his angry words rumbled in his chest like swallowed thunder.

"What was the child?"

"*Une petite fille,* pale, fragile." *A little girl, pale, fragile.*

"White." Caesar spat.

"*Oui.*"

12
MEDICINE WOMAN, TOO

Over the next few days, I slept. I drank what seemed like buckets of the spiced water that dulled the ache in my stomach. I slurped at bottomless bowls of soup. Soon I was able to eat more, pieces of bland whitefish with rice, then, later, a stew of vegetables and shrimp. Marie Catherine fussed over me like a hen would a chick, bathing me as if I were a baby and dressing me herself. She would not let me exert myself. And when I woke in the middle of the night, shrieking or sobbing, because the stench of the no-faced man filled my dreams, or moaning because my stomach and sides throbbed with pain, Marie pulled me into her arms and comforted me like the child I still was, calming me with the light melodies she sang in her own language, one that I did not understand. The dreams have stayed with me but now are infrequent visitors. I healed, in time, due to my youth and Marie's care.

And when storm time retreated and the blue-green seas of the Caribbean were calm again, it was time for Caesar and the Frenchman to depart again on their business. But this time, he was not taking me with him.

I argued with him in every language I knew. But all he did was throw back his majestic head and laugh, his large white teeth gleaming in the brilliant sunlight. Marie Catherine and the Frenchman laughed, too.

I was not amused.

"Who will prevent the Anglais captain from cheating you?" I demanded, spitting out the rough Asante words as I had heard him do, my hands on my hips, thrusting out my chin in defiance. "And Wellington is a fiend and a liar, you have to watch him every moment, count each of his eight fingers, twice, to make sure that he hasn't swindled you!" I added, referring to Caesar's nemesis, a light-fingered scoundrel whose penchant for thievery had cost him one finger and one thumb.

Caesar roared with laughter again and placed his massive hands on my shoulders.

"You are more my sister than if you were of my own blood," he said, proudly. "But I think only of you." He leaned down and I

155

felt the soft brush of his lips across my forehead. "I would not risk you for all the gold that Alonzo Rijas has in his coffers nor of the emeralds that I plan to relieve Wellington of. You must rest —"

"I have rested!" I told him.

Caesar would not be moved.

"Maryam, listen to me. This will be a short trip, the waters are tranquil, the winds soft. We slip down to Cay Lobos, we relieve the old Anglais rascal of some of his emeralds —"

"Or all of them," Marie Catherine added in a low voice. Caesar glanced at her. She was smiling mischievously.

"And we slip back. Before *les jour des morts.*" He held my chin in his fingers. "You will not know I have gone. Now rest. Eat. Do what Marie tells you, my sister."

Caesar and the *Black Mary* sailed away. And this black Mary stayed behind. I needed more rest, and my honored brother agreed. But it was more than that.

I could not go back to what I was. I could not play ball with Kwe and the other boys, even if they would allow it. I could not splash in the surf with the other children and play chase. Because I was no longer a child.

In the before time, accompanied by my

mother, my sisters, and my aunts, I would have been escorted into the realm of women, been changed somehow, from a girl child to a desirable woman, with a bride price set by my father. My hair, now braided, dressed, and wrapped, would be different; Jerie would have taught me the proper way to wrap my gele. And I would never walk like a child again; never talk the same, using the words of a child. No magic could be more powerful. I don't know how many days the change took, but I do know that once I left the women's house, I would not have been the same Little Bird that I was when I entered.

The Dahomians, the pink faces, the tall boats. The dark waters, this place, they changed all of that and me. The women's house that I entered, that remade me forever, was not the one of my sisters, my mother, my aunts. I had a child, who was born, took a breath, and then died, all in the time it took for a spirit to sigh. And in giving birth, I became a woman, entering and leaving the women's house with one step. And what Jerie had foretold would become stone: that my mother's craft would be mine. From the moment that my child took her first and last breath, Marie Catherine began preparing me, training me to be a midwife.

The women of Caesar's Cay were not easily persuaded. They cut their eyes at me, said that I was too young to treat their ailments, which I was. They said that I would use the wrong potion and make them sick instead of heal them, that I had not experience to watch over them in labor, which I did not. Their murmurs became complaints became a chorus of dissatisfaction. Marie Catherine silenced them with sharp words.

"Our beloved sister was taken from the lands of her ancestors, our mothers, she has crossed the dark water. She is the daughter of a wise woman, a foreknower. Healing is in her blood, passed to her by the wish of her grandmothers. She knows without being told. And she was born one of two." That Marie knew this of me without being told was proof of her power.

There were gasps and some of the women fingered the sacred objects they wore on fine leather rope around their necks; some were amulets, others, partial to the rituals of the black-robed ones, wore small wooden crosses. Now they glanced warily in my direction, an experience familiar but now unsettling. The birth of twins was, then and now, a singular occurrence, to be remarked upon and pondered, steeped in mystery and power.

"She will know the herbs, the roots, and the grasses by smell and by touch. And she has known the circle of life even though she is young."

The murmuring had stopped by this time, replaced by the focused silence of listening. The birth and death of my child was no secret on the cay. The hillock where she was buried had become a shrine where the women left flowers and other offerings.

"I will teach her all that I know. And in my teaching, she will remember. But hear this: Maryam's gift was passed to her through the blood of our grandmothers."

The complaining murmurs of the women had become a chorus of chants, the sacred "yes" of the goddess.

I looked over at Marie Catherine and she nodded. *It is done.* I had not been asked if I wanted this destiny.

And yet it was mine.

Jerie's prophecy had come true.

I pouted. I was still very much a child. I took out my displeasure on Marie Catherine, the one person who did not deserve it. My mother would have been ashamed of me, would have thought she'd brought me up badly. Jerie would have scolded me

harshly and pulled my ears. I was uncooper-
ative. I did not want to drink the spiced
water that cut the pains in my middle. I
tried to pick at my food but Marie's stews
and soups were mouthwatering. And many
a night when she told me to sleep, I stayed
awake and tried to pick a conversation with
her, to test her resolve and authority. I chat-
tered like a parrot but it was no good. Marie had slipped her sleeping herbs into my
tea. I was no match for a vodou queen.

Not that I am certain that's what she was,
even now. I will never know. I knew her only
as "Marie Catherine," as a revered aunt, a
skillful teacher. And for the next five years,
when I wasn't traveling with Caesar, I spent
my time on the cay and I lived with Marie
Catherine, who taught me the arts of healing and the craft of midwifery and of what
it was to be a woman.

I was an eager student. The herbs, roots,
and medicines were in my blood. Mother
had been a wise woman among our people.
It took me no time to master the look and
names of the herbs, roots, plants, and other
compounds to stop bleeding, to heal cuts
and sooth a troubled head, a quivering
stomach, or an upheaval of the bowels. We
went foraging nearly every day both on the
cay and off, combing through the dense

brush, a terrain similar to the coastal areas of my country, the places where the brass people lived. Marie taught me the purpose of every living thing and reminded me that life could be long and that I might not spend all of my years in the safety and relative isolation of Caesar's Cay.

On one of our outings, she leaned over and pulled up a handful of greens, roots, and mud. The earth was damp from recent rain and moisture dripped from the ends, the brown water leaving a trail across the lower half of her white apron.

"Et voilà," Marie said with satisfaction, passing a handful over to me. "These will cook nicely in the pot. The broth they make will feed your heart, keep you strong, and protect you from the lung contagion." She placed the green tops in the palm of her hand and gestured for me to lean in close. *"Regardez* . . . there is a brother to this weed that lives on Jamaica and a sister who lives along the coasts . . . in the colonies *les anglais* call Georgia and Carolina. They are easy to find if you know where to look."

She fixed me with a penetrating gaze. Her eyes were dark brown, so dark that they might have been black. "And I have taught you that. Yes?"

I nodded, studying the green mess in her

hands, attaching the image to my brain.

"And I think you will find these have cousins farther in the Americas. I know that I have seen them in *les Virginias* as well."

"You have been . . . there?"

Her smile was slight.

Her eyes were guarded. "I have been many places."

She made me watch when she set bones (a process that made my stomach flip) and taught me how they fit together. Soon I was helping her treat Caesar, his men, and the myriad of ailments that overcame them, and their women and children, too, who had settled on the cay because it was quiet and secure and because it was the one place to which they knew their men would return.

I learned the healing easily enough, the bad stomachs, joint aches, setting right the arms out of place, but the idea of being a midwife filled me with dread. The first time I watched a baby born, I vomited even though I'd seen my mother give birth years earlier, in the before time.

I ran from the cabin.

Marie settled Amie's son and then came after me, finding me hunched over, still heaving. She was furious.

"What is wrong with you? Never! *Never* do you leave the side of the mother! Never!"

"I — I can't do it . . . I can't . . ."

Marie Catherine handed me a cloth to wipe my face and made me take a few sips of water to rinse out my mouth before reprimanding me again, just as harshly as before.

"You can. You will," she barked at me. "I will not be here for all time. *You* will not be here for all time." At this, I stopped coughing and stared at her. How could she know this? "And you . . . you must know the art. From this, you will make your way." She snapped her fingers. "*Comme ça.* It is struck on your path."

"How do you . . ." I shook my head.

Marie Catherine inhaled sharply and opened her mouth to speak, but a voice from the cabin silenced her.

"Marie!"

Marie looked at me. This time, her expression was stern, but her eyes were filled with concern. She placed her palm on my cheek and pushed the cup of water back into my hands.

"Wipe your mouth. I must go to Amie. We will talk of this later. You have much to learn."

And I did.

Amie's child was a boy, healthy and fat. We left late that afternoon, the mother and child being made a fuss over by the other women and by his amazed father. But it had been a long labor, almost an entire day, and now it was evening and Marie was resting, her feet spread across an ornate tapestry-covered ottoman that Caesar had brought back for her from Santiago. Now it was my turn to care for her. I set a cup of tea on the small table beside her chair. She waved her hand at the steam that rose from the hot liquid.

"Ahhhh, *bon.* No one brews the tea like you, my Mary." She smiled slightly, the weariness spreading across her face, then she picked up the cup and took a small, tentative sip.

"Attends!" I warned her, using the more refined French that she was teaching me. *"Il fait . . ."* The word eluded me.

Marie laughed, a lovely sound like the tinkling of small bells.

"Il fait chaud," she said. "*Oui.* But . . . ah, so good!" This time, she slurped the liquid.

I removed her shoes. She winced but waved off the pain. Her feet had swollen. I massaged her feet and calves. She had stood nearly all eighteen hours of Amie's labor. It was a wonder to me that she could move at all.

"You have magic in your touch," Marie

cooed, closing her eyes after setting the cup back on the table.

"*Eh bien,*" I mimicked her accent. "It is time for you to . . . *dormirez* . . ."

Eyes still closed, Marie smiled.

"*Dormir.* And sleep, it will come soon enough. For now, we return to your lessons."

I looked up from my labors.

"What lessons?" For me, attending my first laboring mother was lesson enough.

"I am teaching you about being a woman."

A cool breeze fluttered across my shoulders.

I was not ready. I did not think I would ever be ready.

"*Écoute,* my little Mary and do not turn away." In the darkness, I heard the strike of a match. The flame lit up Marie's face in a strange but beautiful golden frame. "You have had an encounter with a man but you have not made love with one. What happened to you was not of your choosing. You have had a child but this, too, was not of your choosing. You were . . . taken. But it will be different, Little Maryam, with a man you love."

I had taken a breath when Marie started talking. I was still holding it.

"You barely had your first bleeding, it is

no wonder that you are discomposed, that seeing a child born makes you sick. You have only your experience to account for it." She stopped, sighed, and took another pull of her pipe. "You were too young."

"T-the . . . child . . ." Even though some time had passed, I could not make my mouth form the words "my baby."

I felt the warmth of Marie's palm as she laid it across my hand. "She is with the gods."

Again, I felt the odd fleeting brush of a cool breeze. This was not the first time or the last that Marie would refer to "gods" instead of "God." In a way that I cannot put words to, I knew that Marie, while appearing at times to accept the teachings of the pink faces' Christian god, did not give him all of her allegiance. For reasons I could not describe, I was comforted by knowing this.

"We begin at the beginning, with a woman and a man and what they do with and for each other. Then we move to the child they create, si tu desire. And then we talk about the mother and the child." She exhaled a small cloud of smoke that curled itself into a tiny snake that climbed its way toward the open window. Her eyes gleamed in the waning light.

"I will know a man? I will have a husband?" I was afraid to ask and afraid to hear Marie Catherine's answer.

"Yes," she said.

"Will . . . Will I have children?" I asked.

She sees beyond the curtains, Caesar had said of Marie Catherine. Like my mother, she was a gifted one who saw through the mists of time and place. She stared at the smoke until it was gone, then she turned her dark-eyed gaze on me.

"Yes," she said quietly. "But they will not all be yours."

13

1 FEMALE ABT 16 YRS DARK
WELL FORMED

The ground shifted. One moment, I slept, alone, in a cabin on the *Black Mary,* safe and cool, rocked gently by the waves, or on a pallet in Marie Catherine's cottage with the sound of the surf caressing my ears. And in the next, I was away, my ankles in irons, the skin bleeding raw, barefooted, damp and miserable on a decrepit listing piece of a ship, its planks wet and rotting, its hold half full of men and boys from Angola and the kingdom of Congo. A British man-of-war had caught Caesar unawares, set the *Black Mary* on fire, and now towed the *Calabar* alongside, restoring it to its English name, the HMS *Bristol.* They had killed or captured all on board, taken the booty Caesar had collected from Saint Thomas and from the Spanish pirate One-Eyed Cisco. The crew separated. The white men not killed in battle were executed for treason. Those who were left, the black men, the brown and yellow men — and me — were captured and sold.

Caesar was not with us.

Some way, amid the yelling, the explosion of cannon and muskets, the fires and the thick smoke, he escaped. Only the gods knew how — Caesar's gods and mine. Many stories about that. He was dead. Shot then drowned, some said. No. Hacked to bits, others claimed. Silence when the issue was pressed. No one would admit he had seen a body, whole or not. Not even the king's men.

The *Black Mary* burned, its pieces and parts hissing like snakes as they fell, smoldering, into the sea, the tall masts swaying like palm trees in a gentle breeze then plunging with violence, spears aimed by the sky god's hand. The ship that had been my sometime home rolled to her side then sank without a sound. One blink, she was floating, black smoke pouring from a door-size gash, red flames dancing wild. The next time I looked, the *Black Mary* had vanished, not a curl of smoke to mark the spot. Gone. And all the men who sailed with her, gone. But not Caesar.

"Pas de mort, il est disapparu," the Frenchman told me in the hours before he was hanged. *"N'est pas ici."*

169

Escaped. Disappeared. Dead. What was true? I have no answer. All I know that is true is that I never saw him again, living or dead.

In a moment, in the time it takes for a breeze to pass, a bush to sway, the waves to roll in from the sea then back again, the sands had shifted. The soles of my feet standing in one place, now another. And everything different. Place, people, weather.

I learned some time later that Caesar's Key was raided, too. But when the Anglais king's men stepped onshore, there was no one there, no women, no children, no one. Anything and everything and everyone of value that Caesar had stashed away over the ten years that he had roamed the Caribbean was gone. Or looted. Never found. Some said hidden in caves or buried in the sand. Protected by a vodou woman's spell. The Anglais burned the huts, the cottages, any dwelling that they could find, destroyed the docks and left, frustrated. Caesar, Marie Catherine, the women and children of the men of the *Black Mary,* disappeared. I never saw any of them again, and I would know their faces no matter how much time has gone. It is whispered that the king's men only thought they had destroyed every dwelling on Caesar's Key, that, in the early morning, especially when the cool fog rises from the dense forests along the northern coast, Marie Catherine's cottage is seen in the distance by lookouts in the crow's nests of passing ships, with pale blue smoke rising from its chimney and a white-turbaned woman standing by the gate.

I have gotten used to the angles of my life, standing on one type of ground, then learning to stand on another. I had been my own woman on Caesar's Key and on his ships. I had been the much-beloved sister. I had spoken in knowledge, had my words weighted as much as Caesar's, was respected just like the men even though I was barely a woman. On the key, I had practiced my craft, as Marie Catherine had taught me, healing, soothing, guiding children into the world. Now that ground had shifted and I was orphaned once more. No family. No country. No status. The skin around my ankles bled, tormented by sores, was unaccustomed to the rough, poorly made iron of the shackles. And I was taken before I could gather my caches of herbs, salves, and medicines or my medicine basket. I was no longer Caesar's beloved sister, Maryam. I was no longer Maryam the wise woman, apprentice to Marie Catherine. With one fire of a cannon, one swipe of a sword, I was no one again. A black from somewhere. A woman. Of no status. Of no count. Property. Worth whatever coin they said or valued by my weight in pounds of tobacco.

The ship docked in the port of Savannah. Maybe the trickster god was having his joke on me. Savannah had been the final destination of the *Martinet* all those years ago before Caesar intercepted it and took it over. My arrival in this place had only been delayed.

They dragged me from the ship onto a platform set up dockside, the iron chains pulling at my skin; their weight made walking impossible. I hated the indignity but I could only shuffle, trying not to stumble. The auctioneer, a fat, pink-faced man with the accent that I would soon learn to recognize as Irish mixed with the slow, rounded tones that marked the drawl of this new place, this Savannah, had a ham-sized hand, his fingers so swollen that his rings made grooves in his skin. He gripped my shoulder then shoved me toward the front of the platform and with one sweep of his hand tore the shirt from my body.

"Look at those teats!" He guffawed. "She's a breeder no doubt about it. Match her up with one of yor niggers or bed her yerself!" The laughter was like thunder in my ears. My cheeks burned with humiliation. The open mouths and pink cheeks became a blur of faces with no eyes, no features, as the tears flooded my vision. I tried to snatch the shirt from his fat hand. He slapped me and growled in my ear, "I'll feckin' knock yer eyes out yew dew that again." He turned back to his audience with a face-splitting smile. "She got spirit too. Just what yew want!" A wink. The audience erupted with laughter. "Now. Who'll start the bidding? How about eight hundred pounds? She's a breeder, a strong field hand, and . . . so the nigger gossip goes, a midwife. Yew can hire her out or . . . let her deliver the babies you get on her!"

The sound of their laughter made me sick. A few of the pink faces yelled out numbers but their words were lost because of a fracas taking place at the back of the crowd, a small circle of people talking loudly, waving their arms about. The ruckus drowned out the auctioneer and he held his arms open as if to concede defeat.

"Gentlemen! I'm trying to do business here!" he yelled out, pretending to be good-natured. "Now, last bid was from Master Singleton. Do I have nine fifty —"

"Midwife! We need a midwife at Petal's!" The plea came from a tall gangly man wearing a dark hat, weaving through the crowd, stopping each woman he met. "Are you a midwife, madam? No? Do you know of one? You, madam?"

The auctioneer decided that it was time to take back control of his potential buyers before they lost interest altogether. He stepped forward on the platform and grinned, dropping my shirt in the process. Seeing my moment, I scrambled forward and grabbed it, slipping it quickly over my head.

"Is it a midwife yer lookin' fer? I got a midwife here!" he yelled, gesturing toward me, his tone ugly with laughter and sarcasm. "What you think? Are ye interested? Nine hundred and fifty pounds!"

The man had reached the front of the platform and looked up. His face was long, his cheeks hollow, as if his meals were irregular. His dark hat was near as dark as his hair that hung to his shoulders. He didn't say anything, just looked at me. Then he looked back at the auctioneer.

"She'll do. Will ye hire her out?" he asked, and reached into his pocket. "I'll pay ye two pounds for a day's worth of 'er time. There's a laboring gal over at Petal's."

"Yew can have 'er all to yerself for nine hundred and fifty pound! Or five hundred pounds of tobacco!" the fat man said, pocketing the silver as quickly as he could in case the tall man changed his mind. There was more laughter.

The man shook his head and did not smile.

"Petal don't trade in slaves. Just need 'er to help the gal is all. Bring 'er back when she's done." He nodded toward me, his gaze on the chain. "Take off the irons."

The fat pink face paused, looked at me, his smile gone.

"Best leave 'em on. She is one of them Guinea niggers, they can't be trusted not to cut your throat, not seasoned. Might try to run on yew." He held out the length of chain in his hand.

The tall man in the dark hat looked at me, full in the eye, the way Caesar had, to send a message without speaking.

"She won't run," the tall man said. "Take 'em off."

He was the tallest man I ever see, tall even without his hat, taller than Caesar. But skinny. Legs long, thin like sticks. He move fast through the crowded streets, weave in and out like a water snake. I ran to keep up. Good luck for me that he *was* tall. I could see him over the crowd. Once, he stop, look down at me. I look up at him.

Like a conjurer, he pull a bundle of blue cloth from no pocket I could see and push it into my arms.

"Put it on."

It's a coat. I do as he says.

"Keep up and be quick about it."

I am quick.

The streets of this Savannah are crowded, hot, and made of stone. I stumble, trip, and bang my toe against their up and down. That tall man don't miss one step. It's a crooked street, slopes toward the water. People everywhere, all kinds. I listen. Some words I know. He take me along the waterfront, smelly, loud, dirty, like every port town I ever saw on this or any side of the dark waters. Coin going from one hand to one hand. Coming and going. On the dockside, ships taking goods in and sending them out. Cargo, all kinds. Rum. Spices. Cloth. Steel. People. All brown.

A river on one side, tall lopsided buildings on the other. Tall man turns, grabs me by the sleeve of the blue coat, and guides me to one of them, tall, grimy, but with a black painted door, shiny-like and brass door knocker and knobs. The two steps from the street to that door swept clean and scrubbed. He knocks.

A few knocks, then a short, scrawny woman opened the door. She was not smiling. Dressed like a housemaid who had forgotten her apron, she had a pointed beak for a nose, thin lips, and dark eyes. Wisps of reddish-gold hair escaped from the white cap she wore on her head. Anglais or Irish from the look of her. There were many of them in this part of the world.

"Took ye long enough," she said. By her words and her tone, I knew that she was not an Anglais and not the housemaid despite her dress. She looked as if she was about to say something else when she saw me. She looked long and she looked hard. Then she said to the tall man, "Tell me she's not the midwife."

He grinned.

"She's not the midwife. Now let us in."

A bloodcurdling scream pierced the air.

"Jesus, Mary, and Joseph!" the woman said, slamming the heavy door behind us. "She keep that up, I'll whelp the bairn meself." Again she gave me a look. To the tall man, she said, "She's just a girl."

He bowed his head in agreement.

"She's a midwife. Least the slave trader says . . ."

"I don't —"

"I know, Petal. She's hired out is all, I'll

have to take her back. Ain't perfect but she's the only help I could find."

"What's your name, girl?"

I told her.

The woman sighed and looked at me again. Another earsplitting scream broke through the quiet. From the end of the hall, a door opened and a woman with bright yellow hair stuck her head out. She was naked from the waist up.

"Goddammit! Tell that bitch to shut up!" she barked. "It's disturbin' me clientele!"

"Don't make such a fuss, Li'l!"

Despite her lack of clothing, the woman named Li'l looked as if a fuss was what she was going to make. But she thought better of it, set her jaw and turned around. "Now, me darlin', where were we?" she cooed to an unseen listener. The door slammed shut.

"You'll have to do," Petal said at last. She grabbed me by the arm and pulled me across the threshold. "No time to waste, girl. The child's comin' fast. Now, I've done what I do in these times, from what I know, which ain't much, and from what Mrs. Tootle tell me, when she's here."

"When she's sober," the tall man said in a low voice.

Petal threw him a glance.

"Hot water, clean cloths, an extra sheet,

coverin's for the baby, and . . ."

I nodded.

"Thank you . . . mistress." I had to remember how to address white women. "And if you have these . . ." I rattled off a few names, herbs, bark. Without my basket, I had little to offer except the knowing between my ears and the hope that some of the sundries I needed could be found. Petal frowned but told me that she would check her stores and do what she could. The laboring woman screamed again.

"Yew best get up there. Do what ye can, I'll gather up the bits you asked for."

I nodded and walked quickly toward the stairs in the direction that she pointed.

"Go with Jones. Third landin', second door on the right, not that the screamin' moanin' and groanin' wouldna direct ye. She's a right devil so mind yerself," Petal said, her voice carrying despite that she was near halfway down the long hall.

"Yes, mistress."

"And don't call me 'mistress.' I'm nobody's mistress." She laughed and looked back at me. "I 'spect you the same."

Following Mr. Jones, I climbed the stairs for what seemed like half my life before I reached the third landing. Petal was right about not bothering with directions to the laboring woman, who was called "Tulip," her screams and curses led me right to her door. On the way up the stairs, the tall man, Jones ("Don't need t'call me mister, Richard is my name") explained that I was in a boardinghouse and sometime brothel (in case I hadn't figured that out) and all of "Petal's girls" were named after flowers. She had a passion for flowers and gardens. The naked woman downstairs, Li'l, was known as "Lily," while "Petal" had been born Margaret.

"Tulip, here's the midwife . . ."

The dark-haired woman who lay in the bed, propped up on pillows, her legs thrown open, stopped midscream and stared.

"And Petal be up with —"

"Get that niggah outa here! Now! Get her out! Get. Her. Out!"

And she opened her mouth wide enough for a cow to step into and screamed again. I think the floorboards rattled.

I went to her, tried to check her belly and her heart, but she swatted then spit at me, calling me names that even I — who had spent the last five years living with pirates who had some of the foulest language — had rarely heard.

"No niggah bitch will ever touch me nor my baby! Get her oooouuuuut!"

Disgusted, I stepped away from the bed and grabbed the damp cloth that Jones passed over to me; I wiped my face. Behind me, from the open door, I heard Petal's voice.

"Now, what's this then?"

"Get me a real midwife!" yelled the woman in the bed. "Aieeeeee . . . . !" She did not look or speak like a tulip. "Not this filthy girl . . ."

Petal marched into the room at the front of a regiment, her arms full with linens, followed by two women carrying buckets of water, a kettle, and a basket of what I took to be the herbs and plants that I had asked for. She passed over the items to me and continued her arrangements without breaking a step.

"Stanzie. She is the midwife. Her name is Maryam and you b'have yerself."

"No niggah's going to —"

I opened my mouth to tell this frothing demon from the dark regions what I thought of her but Petal spoke first.

"Stop acting like a silly cow and shut yer trap!" Petal pointed at me. Her tone was sharp as razors. "She's all we got. It's her or noffing. Now ye settle yerself and let her do her work. Richard, out! This is woman's werk."

Tulip's mouth was open but no sound came out. Jones smirked and stepped out of the room. The other women who helped Petal carry the water and cloths smirked also, biting their lips when Petal glared at them.

"Now then." She looked at me and nodded. "Get to werk, you."

Tulip flinched when I touched her but least she didn't spit. I took no notice, just went about my business. With Petal's help, I arranged the pillows and cleaned her, and arranged the bedclothes to catch the worst of it when the baby arrived. A murmur from the corner of the room caught my attention. One of the women held a cup in her hands, the steam floating up toward her pox-marked face.

"Here's the . . . tea that you wanted," she said, shades of the Français that she had spoken as a child softening her words.

"Merci," I said, taking the cup in my hands. The woman with the pox face stared at me. I turned to Tulip.

"Drink."

Her dark eyes blazed with anger but her lips were pressed together. She wasn't about to say anything, not with Petal in the room. But she raised her hand as if to bat the cup and its boiling contents onto the floor.

"Não," I growled at Tulip in her own language.

She stared at me as if seeing me for the first time, and her eyes widened.

"You know my words," she said in Portuguese.

The same thing that Caesar had said to me. Long time gone now.

Use your words, Little Bird.

"Some, yes."

She inhaled slowly then grimaced as her body twisted to push her child out.

From then on, she talked, then screamed, then talked some more. So many words poured out of her that it was if she had saved them up for me. Her birth name was Constanza and she was from a fishing village with a name that I could not pronounce. She had run away from a dead mother and a drunk of a father when she was thirteen and in love. She had been married to a mariner or so she'd thought; once they landed in Savannah, he'd tried to sell her labor and she'd run away. Petal took her in and put her to work. The oldest work a woman can do besides cook. But Petal was kind, kept a clean house, and did not put up with brutes among her clientele. Or babies. Constanza's would be sent away once it was weaned.

I crooned to her using some of her Portuguese words and to her daughter once she arrived, a pink-faced squirmy thing with hardly any hair, very different looking from most of the children I had delivered on Caesar's Key and the other islands. Strong and, it seemed, good-natured, the little girl nursed right away and Constanza, with tears in her eyes, thanked me over and over and told me that her daughter's christening name would be "Bonita Maria" after me.

14
NORTH FROM SAVANNAH

I would have stayed with Petal if I could. She wanted me, her man Richard wanted me, said there was always work for a midwife and what the Anglais called a "physic."

"Bones don't set themselves and there's always aching guts t' soothe not to mention that someone's got to deliver the babies." Petal's jaw tightened. "Even a few in me line o'werk." She sent Richard to bargain with the Irishman. Her plan was to buy me from the auctioneer then strike papers for my freedom. I would owe her but I would be free. "I don't hold with slavery," she said.

I tended to Constanza and little Bonita while Petal tidied the room.

"No much better than a slave meself," she said, gathering the soiled linens into a bundle that was larger than she was. "Came here in fifty-eight, fifty-nine with me ma'am from the parish workhouse. Tobacco merchant Maryland way bought her contract."

The bundle of sheets and clothes had grown so much that I could barely see the top of her head. "But then she died." No words for a moment as she worked the linens into a ball. "And I was by meself. The merchant sold my labor to a farmer. Ten years. Whew!" She set the linen in the hall by the open door and wiped her forehead with the back of her arm. "I was barely ten meself. Had my first baby near two years later. My next a year after that." Picking up the chamber pot, she raised the window and pitched it out. "The old bastard that owned me . . . owned me labor took me afore the church wardens and *those* bastards bound me up for another fifteen years. Here. Give me that baby."

The baby was nodding off and Constanza was snoozing. I picked up the child and covered the mother. Petal rinsed her hands and reached out.

"Ahhh . . . the wee pretty thing. Hair like silk . . ." She nuzzled the sleeping child's neck and sighed. "Oh, the lovely smell of a new one. How I miss that."

"Where are your children?" I asked.

Petal's expression didn't change.

"Ah, the first one, he died, too small to live. The second . . ." She bit her lip and looked down at Bonita. "Well . . . they took her from me once she was weaned. And sent me off to Prince George County to work on another o' the fat bastard's farms. She was colored you see. And so she was taken . . . probably sold somewhere. And I was bound for another twenty-five years."

My shoulders tightened. I had learned much in my time with Caesar, much from Marie Catherine. But I had spent no time in the English colonies. I knew nothing of their ways. It was a surprise to me that a white woman of the English could be like a slave, too. I said so to Petal.

Petal was singing to the baby, prancing around the small room like a butterfly, her tiny feet flitting across the floor.

"Ah, 'tis. My indenture labor was extended because of the colored child that I bore. Twenty-five years!" She kissed the baby on her nose. "I was sixteen then. Twenty-five years for a woman in this place?"

I couldn't figure as good as Caesar but even I knew that twenty-five years was a lifetime and for women, could be death time. If contagions and brutality didn't carry off a woman, childbed did. Besides Marie Catherine and now Petal, I'd met few women who had more than thirty-five years.

Her eyes locked with mine and she nod-ded.

"Aye. And was I plannin' to wait around for the fat fool to beat me, work me into the ground, or fill me belly with so many babies that me insides turned to porridge?"

I had tended to such as those.

"So the answer is no."

"Aye. I ran. Nothin' t'keep me there. He . . . He'd taken the child, bound her out to some family after she was weaned. Sold her, more like. So what was there to stay for? I stole some coin from his strongbox, bribed a stevedore . . . with whom I was acquainted . . ." Her eyes twinkled with mischief. "And made me way here. Never looked back." She held the baby close to her chest and stroked its tiny head with the tip of her nose. "Hope to find that daughter someday. Even if only in me dreams." Her voice softened. "I named her Rose."

I cast away the dreams I had about the daughter I had borne but never seen; the child whom I could not think about without crying. That had been years ago, in another time, another place, when I was another person, a girl child barely past her first bleeding. My throat closed and I pressed my lips together.

"You have . . . another child?"

Petal grinned.

"Aye. He. Richard and I have a son. Big, hearty boy. I sent him west, to the Creek lands to be raised by Richard's sister and her husband. He's near twelve now." By the sound of her voice, I knew that she was full to bursting with pride. "Taking up the cooper trade just like his uncle."

Waiting for Richard to come back from the docks was like waiting for the grasses to grow even though I was not idle, not for one breath. Petal set me to treating the little aches and irritations of her ladies and neighbors, and she fed me, too. A stew of chicken, rice, and okra, the meal so familiar but not what I'd expected from an English-woman until I visited the kitchen and paid my respects to Tamar, a woman of the Wolof. And so the time did pass pleasant-like. I began to hope that Richard's skill of haggling could get me a place in another new world but one that I could see myself in.

It was not to be. The Irishman had struck a deal that made him a profit and kept me a slave. And sent a sheriff's man with a pistol to Petal's door to collect me.

"Did all I could, Maryam," Richard told me with a look of disappointment. Petal frowned. "The Irishman sold you to a planter from up Virginia way, man called Nash." His shoulders drooped. "Your physic skill intrigued him so he bought your contract. A thousand pounds."

Both Petal and I gasped. My time with Caesar had taught me the value of money, gold, silver, tobacco, whatever currency you could name. A thousand British pounds was a lot of money for a girl from Edo place.

Richard shook his head slowly.

"Unfortunate for you to be young and skilled. You will heal up him and his people. Says he has a farm with fifty or a hundred slave workers depending on which way you ask him. He figures you heal them up too and serve as midwife. And then . . ." Richard stopped and raised his eyes up to meet mine. "You are young enough to have children."

I'd heard the word "breeder" and knew what it meant. The Anglais liked things orderly. They kept figures and charts in thick leather-bound books full of bloodlines and descriptions, of cattle, of horses. Of people. They would put me with a man of their choosing or they would try. A cold pit formed in the bottom of my stomach.

"Can't you . . . . could you buy me? Offer him to hire me out?"

Richard looked tormented. Petal looked worse.

"I tried. He wouldn't do it, wouldn't consider hiring you out. This Nash is pleased with his . . . purchase."

The sheriff's man collected the fee that Petal had agreed to pay the Irishman. I felt as if I'd been kicked in the stomach. Had been in Petal's barely a day's hours and felt as if I would be safe there, could live a life there. And now the winds were shifting again, taking me off on another unwanted journey, just like the waves of the dark waters. As I stood in the doorway and bid them goodbye, Petal grabbed my hand and squeezed it. I felt the cold weight of coin in my palm. She pulled me close and hugged me as she whispered in my ear so that the sheriff and Nash's man could not hear her words.

"This is for all ye did for Constanza and her child. Remember this, Little Maryam, never take less for your labors, my girl. A good midwife be worth her weight." She stepped back and studied me from top to toe, then murmured with a small smile on her lips, "If ye may want to up yer fee a bit ye may want to fatten up!" Both she, Richard, and I laughed. The sheriff's man, uninvited to share our joke, frowned and bellowed at me to get stepping.

As the wagon and flatboats took me northward through the Carolina into Virginia, along the coasts and rivers, I thought about the coins. I'd stitched them into a seam on the inside of my calico dress, hidden well. It was not the first time that I had been paid for my craft; Caesar had given me coins every time I listened and spoke for him. But those coins had been lost in the sea. Now, in this new life, in this new place that Jerie had told me about, this was the first time I had been paid money for practicing my craft. I made a vow then — on my sister's life — that it would not be the last.

■ ■ ■ ■

PART II
THE DAUGHTER OF
A STRANGE GOD

■ ■ ■ ■

15

White Maple Grove, Chesapeake County, Virginia

I was bought by a man named Robert Nash. It took six weeks to travel from Savannah to Nash's farm, a journey near as long as the one I took across the dark waters. May because Mister Nash trade, buy, and sell along the way, make so many stops, at farms, at villages. Mister Nash know every person there is on this road and he call them by name. The ones he don't, he make it his business to find out. He calls that "commerce." Nash was a pink-faced man with reddish hair and the thinnest lips I ever seen on a person. His blue eyes were watery-like and he blinked a lot as if the sun and the air worried him. He spoke the slurring mixture of English common in this part, accented with bits of words that I recognized from the Irish. He look like a walking slug with his stick legs and round belly but he think and move quick like a bird. He cleared away space in the back of the wagon for me to sit, pointed and scurried away as if he was afraid he would catch something. His man Durfee, who also spoke the Irish, snorted and held out his hand to help me up. When I took it, he clamped down so hard on my fingers that I near shouted in pain. Durfee pulled me toward him and spoke close in my ear.

"Won't chain yew down 'cause he say so. But I know you people better'n he think he dew." His hot breath came in puffs against my cheek. "I don care if ye are a gold-weight nigger worth five hundred pound tobaccy, try to run I'll shoot ye."

He half-lifted, half-shoved me into the wagon.

The wagon was driven by Jupiter, Nash's colored man. Nash and Durfee rode horseback alongside. Jupiter nodded in my direction but did not speak. What he knew or thought he kept. The wagon was packed full of supplies, sacks of grain, crates of port and other spirits, protected from the bumps and rocks in the road by straw and old cloth, boxes of crockery what called "china," bolts of fabric and other treasures, as Nash called his purchases — and me — 'long with a large leather satchel that looked fit for the midden heap.

"This is an old physick's bag, I bought it off a tinker," Nash had told me, thrusting the sack into my arms. "You can make use of it on your visits."

The dark-blood-color skin was not long wet in some places, dry near to dust in others. The satchel was past saving but the sundry inside was worth a look. Most what I could use was gone but there was bottles, vials, small cloth packets, and a couple slim blades that was sharp still. I pulled a throw-'way end piece of cloth from a crate and wrapped them up, careful not to get cut, put the rest in a tight-woven coil basket that a Wolof woman had give me. Everything I had was lost when the king's men took Caesar's ships. Now I had to make me a new kit.

I was one of Nash's purchases, a "treasure" like his bottles of wine and heavy books. Unlike the port, I was to earn him what he call a "return on his investment." To my surprise and his, I did just that, before we traveled even ten miles.

From the first turn of that cursed wagon's wheels, I bounced and rolled with every jolt as it moved, marked by so many bruises and aches that I was physick to myself. The roads were near gone in most places, not more than cattle trails, rough and marked with holes everyplace else. I rode in the back with the sacks, boxes, and crates and felt confused in my mind and angry. Back and forth like the waves of the dark waters, seemed I never stood on the same ground for long before it shifted and changed. I had come to accept my life as a midwife and free woman of value during my years on Caesar's Key. A person who had respect not only as Caesar's "honored sister" but as myself. Now I was no one again, of value only to this man who had paid English pounds and tobacco for me. Mister Nash's "thousand-pound nigger woman" Durfee called me as if I had no name, as if I was a stick from a tree. I was so wound up in my head that I thought to escape, though I did not know where I should go. I studied the landscape as we rode along, the trees and shrubs and grasses, watched the waterways, how high or low they were. The land was familiar, yet not. The people . . . well, it seemed I was in the land of white people. I tried to make a plot. But my plotting didn't last. Before the midday, we came 'cross a wagon turned over in the road, wheel split. The driver had fallen off and hit his head and it was bleeding. His woman was wailing and held her arm. Her face was red with cuts. The contents of the wagon were scattered across the ground like fallen leaves. The horses had run off. My new life as Master Robert Nash's colored medicine woman began and didn't let up until the buckboard rolled into the yard of the quarters at White Maple Grove some weeks later.

Stopped in Charleston and treated four men with the flux (including Master Nash), two with disruption of the bowels, and five whose stomachs gave out from too much rum. Set one broken arm and two shoulders dislodged from a fight, ease the monthlies of the innkeeper's daughter and the troubles of the innkeeper, whose foot was near unrecognizable due to gout. Eased a poor girl's breathing, she had the consumption. Helped a Welsh barber (he *said* he was a physic, too) amputate a rotting leg and was near sick myself from it; made a poultice for a woman whose man had punched her in the eye. In the Carolina, in a cluster of homesteads we visited, I tended to a baby, treated stomach ailments, and soothed the misery of a washerwoman.

Her mistress, several months gone with a baby, waddled up to me after having a few words with Master Nash.

"Robert . . . your master, Mister Nash, says that you can treat ailments and such.

My Nansy, she's poorly, has been for a month. Says her head won't stop aching." Aside from her huge belly, the woman was thin as a stick and rabbit-looking, two yellow teeth protruding from between her lips. "I think she's malingering but my husband . . ." She looked over her shoulder at the tall man standing near the wagon in heavy conversation with Durfee. The man look more like her grandfather than husband. "My husband, Mr. Robinson, gives his permission for you to tend to her."

"Yes, mistress," I murmured.

I followed Mistress Robinson 'long an alleyway of cabins and she stopped and gestured toward a smallish one that looked near to coming down on top of whoever was inside. "In there," she said. She looked me up and down as if trying to commit my image to memory. Her spooky-looking gray eyes stopped on my face. She made a small sound in her throat. "Nansy was born in-country like you." Her words dripped with vinegar.

"In-country" mean this Nansy came from across the dark waters. I went to the open door and stopped, tapped on the frame. Was gloomy inside, I could just make out a figure in the corner, what I first mistook for a heap of blankets.

"What you want?" The woman's voice was low and raspy as if she'd been coughing hard. Or crying.

Igbo.

"I am . . ." I gave my true name. "Maryam, they call me here. I am sent by your mistress to tend you."

I spoke in her words.

Nansy was standing in front of me before I finished speaking. Her face was streaked with tears and her eyes were rimmed in red. Her mouth was open in astonishment.

"You are . . ."

She was a woman of my mother's age, her hair covered by a white kerchief. She looked as if she had been crying for weeks.

"Yes, Aunt," I answered, touching her gently on the arm. "I am a daughter of the Edo and a midwife. But I am come to tend your head." She closed her eyes and more tears streamed down her face. My throat closed up.

I put my arm around her shoulder. Wiping her face with the back of her arm, she gestured toward the steps, swept as clean as glass. Nansy's cabin was near a ruin outside but it was tidy inside.

"It is cool here, sit. Please."

So we sat, spreading our skirts across the rough wood plank step. A cool blow of air, like the flutter of a bird's wing, brushed our cheeks, rustled the leaves, then worried a group of noisy black birds, who cackled displeasure. Sitting shoulder to shoulder there, we did not speak. We did not need to. After a while Nansy sighed. She knew what I was 'bout to tell her. That Irishman wouldn't linger long.

"I am sorry, Aunt, but I cannot tarry. I travel with Master Nash and his man will come soon to fetch me. What has made your head ache so?" I asked to be polite, to be respectful of her. I knew grief when I saw it.

She turned her face toward mine and made a fist of her hand and pressed it against her chest.

"Little Sister," she said in Igbo, her voice thick. "It is not a sickness of the head but of . . ." She pounded her chest lightly. Her voice descended into a sob. "Master Wesley sold my man away . . . to . . ."

Nansy spoke the name of the place where her man had been sold. But I didn't know it, didn't know the English colonies. Would it have mattered if I did? Her man was gone. If I had learned anything in my time around the English, he would not return. And she was in grief. I thought of the little Fulani woman who had tended to me on the slaver, who watched over me after Jerie . . . The woman who helped me back to the land of life. Who would watch over Nansy? Who would bring her back?

There was little I could do. Her wound would not heal. It would seep until the day she die. She knew it. I knew it.

I bathed her head and eyes with rosewater, left her a packet of chamomile to make a tea that would help her sleep. I massaged her shoulders, rubbing in the soft-scented oils of a salve of lemongrass that Marie Catherine had taught me to make. I did what I could in the short time I had to soothe her body, knowing that there was nothing I could do for what truly ailed her, nothing I could say to take the pain away or fill the emptiness it would leave.

We thought you were gone away.

Durfee came to fetch me. He watched as I took leave of Nansy using what words of respect I could remember in her tongue, giving her what blessings I knew in mine. I stood before her and we clasped hands. Our foreheads touched.

He scowled at me.

"She's one of those Africky neggars like you."

I said nothing. I never heard of "Africky" until I came here.

"What's wrong with her? Mistress Robinson said she is lazy."

I wanted to whirl 'round, grab the cutlass that I knew he kept at his side, and slit his throat, as Caesar and the Frenchman had taught me — in case I had to protect myself, they said.

"Master Robinson sold her man away to a place called Al'bama."

Now it was the Irishman's turn to say nothing until we reached the wagon, but he was burning to know. As he handed me up into the buckboard, he asked, "Yew took long enough to bid her farewell. What did yew say to her? In your Africky tongue?"

I studied his pale face, looked into his dark storm-sky-blue eyes and square jaw. Durfee wasn't bad-looking as far as the pink faces go. But he had a mean way about him. There was a river of bitterness flowing just beneath his skin.

"I say goodbye."

By the time we reached Robert Nash's farm, I had delivered three babies, set four broken arms or legs, soothed uncountable stomachs and bowels and monthlies, and eased the suffering of an old mulatto Creole woman's passing to the land of spirits although her family said she was going to the Christian god's heaven. By my reckoning, I had paid Nash back his thousand pounds and earned some for myself. My payment from him was a run-down cabin at the edge of the camp on his northeast farm, the one nearest to his brother's, along with a chair, a pitcher, a bowl, a pot and a broom. I stood in the doorway and stared into the dim interior that had space only enough for me to turn around. There was a small hearth at the back but it wasn't lit. There was one window. The whitewash was near gone, soaked into the rough brittle surface of the walls; the ceiling looked 'bout to cave in; sunlight flowed through a gap between the planks where the roof had given way, pieces of blue paper flakes peeling off, scattered 'round the floor like leaves.

My chest was heavy as if I had a cold coming on. Make a home out of this? It didn't have so much as a pallet in it. What would I sleep on? My thoughts swirled around my head and the only way I could think to calm myself was to move. I picked up the broom and swept, back and forth, twigs, dirt, dried leaves, spiderwebs, as if the back and forth would sweep the confusion from my brain and bring order to my thoughts.

"We help you do that."

I near dropped the broom. Three women stood in the doorway. Two of them were so familiar-looking that I thought I was seeing my sisters Ayana and Te'zirah. The third was shorter and rounder and bore the soft round nose and plump cheeks of the Mende women who had bartered with my mother at the markets. They smiled.

"Welcome, Sister," one of them said, the one who looked an older version of Te. "I'm Elinor, this here Keysa, and my girl, Sara." She stopped and set down the basket she was carrying. "We from over Master Thomas Nash's place, Sara and me, just pas' the orchard there. Keysa from here with Master Robert." She gestured toward the left, then surveyed the cabin and clicked her tongue. "Jupiter sent us over. Said you'd need extra hands t'get this heap presentable."

The other women didn't wait for orders, just set to cleanin' and setting up the assortment of bits they'd brought with them in their many baskets.

"Thank you, Aunt," I said, remembering my manners. Jupiter sent them? I hadn't heard that man say one word much less enough of them to direct these women.

"Don't think of it," Elinor shot back. "Can't imagine what Master Robert was thinkin' . . ." Her words ran out as she dipped both hands into a steaming bucket of water and pulled out a thick cloth dripping with suds. "But it be good t'have a midwife 'round the place." She nodded toward Sara, whose rounded belly I had noticed. Almost six gone, I thought. The girl nodded at me, her cheeks turning red.

"Your first?"

"Yes, ma'am," Sara said, smiling with pride as she patted the roundness.

I nodded my head. *Yes, ma'am.* I wasn't much older than she was. But I was the midwife and she would be in my care. She was young, barely sixteen, looked healthy, well fed at least, and the child was placed where it should be. My thoughts flew to a day not long from then when Sara's child would come.

"And Mistress Thomas breedin' again, too. Her sixth," Elinor added, busy scrubbing the floor on her hands and knees. She stopped to wipe her forehead then attacked the floor again. "Tho' they never come to much."

"How far she along?" I asked, reaching into the water to pull out another cloth and help, taking to mind what Elinor said.

"Just pas' puking stage," Keysa answered. "She ne'er get much pas' that. Two misses ago, she near made four months then . . ." She shrugged her shoulders. I nodded, making a plan in my head and thinking of the herbs and roots that I would need.

"The mistress, she ever carry through?"

"One boy," Elinor answered, "Thomas Jr. She fawn over him like he shit gold." Sara giggled. I couldn't help but smile. "He ten now. No babies since. Seem like she can't."

The woman named Keysa scowled at her.

"You bring bad luck, El'nor, you say that," she warned. She made a gesture with her hand that I recognized as a sign to send away bad spirits.

They scrubbed the rough-hewn floor while I swept out the tiny hearth and scoured the iron cooking pot left behind by the previous occupant. When the floor was dry, the women carried in a thick woven rug and together we unrolled it. What had started out as a dingy and depressing little room now looked warm and settled even though it had little in it.

"That should do you for now. Master Thomas send over his man James to fix up that roof fore it rain" — Elinor and I looked up at the gap between the beams that allowed the daylight in — "And make ye some shelving for your potions and such." She clicked her tongue and frowned. "And you'll need a better table 'n that," she said, gesturing toward a sad-looking contraption no more than three rough-hewn boards barely supported by four unmatched planks. One of them rested on the surface of a small boulder. Elinor glanced around the space again. "And a bed. Mercy! What will you sleep on?"

"I slept on worse, Aunt."

I took a deep breath and smiled. I had slept on much worse than this. The musty smell of damp and emptiness was gone. The little room smelled fresh and clean. And Sara had brought out two quilts from one of the baskets that seemed to have no bottom. Even if the carpenter man did not come today or tomorrow, at least I need not rest my head on the floor.

"Thank ye, Miss Elinor, Miss Keysa, Sara. I am grateful." I placed my palm against my heart. Keysa touched my arm, her touch gentle despite the torn chafed fingers that had worked the fields this morning.

"I fetch you for supper. Iris, Mister Robert's housekeeper, she cook for all us. And she want you to eat with us." Keysa winked at the other women. "She from down near Savannah way. Prob'bly want to talk you to 'bout whether you seen any of her people there."

I felt tears prick the corners of my eyes. It had been . . . a long time since I had had the company of other women. Listening to their voices, gossiping about this person or that, people I did not know yet, Master Robert and Mistress Robert, Mistress Thomas, Patience was her name, and her sorrows, the giggles and laughter, the deep no-nonsense orders issued by Elinor, Keysa's mellower yet strong scolding, and Sara's lilting laugh. It 'minded me how much I missed the sound of my sisters' voices, even when they were tormenting me. How much I missed the orders issued by my mother, my aunts . . . I caught Elinor's eye and quickly wiped mine with the back of my arm. I didn't want to embarrass myself or her.

"Ain't nothin'. You part o' us now," she said, giving me a hug. A small frown disturbed her face as she looked around the small room, glancing up once more at the roof. "But I do hope James get here, soon enough fore it rain."

I don't know how much time I spent unpacking and arranging the bits from my basket and the leather satchel after they left. Funny as it seemed but Master Robert was right. The innards of the old physick's bag had become my friend. And the slow meander from the Low Country to this Virginia had given me opportunity to forage both in the dark pine forests and along the marshes and ponds. As Marie Catherine had taught me, the plants, roots, and herbs that I knew from Caesar's Key and from across the dark waters had cousins here.

"Regard, this leaf is the same plant, just wears a different dress. And what it does for the pain in the gut here, in the cay, it does in the Carolina and the Virginia. The pain is the same no matter who it belongs to." Her voice was in my head, guiding me.

And so I found the sassafras, the sage and lemongrass. Willow bark to soothe the headache and cut fever, mint for stomach pains. I found the herbs I needed to help the labors of a birthing mother, to ease the pain of a woman's monthly bleeding. Inside the old physick's bag I had discovered empty vials and jars, which I scrubbed out and cleaned, finishing with boiling water to remove any contagion. The bottles and jars that I'd kept covered the top of the rough wood table. Some of them had marks on them, writing. But I had not learned that skill yet. So I scraped it off and made markings of my own so that I could tell the one from the other. I looked around the room as if a row of shelves would appear out of the air. They didn't. I had no talent for making, could stitch up a leg but not a hem. I could cut brush and shrubs and boil herbs to make a paste or cut linen and make bandages but I could not cook. I could not conjure a shelf.

"Afternoon, Auntie."

The man's voice was deep and smooth, his tone respectful.

I turned around. He stood in the doorway, haloed by the afternoon light, a hammer in one hand, a large wooden toolbox in the other. Slowly, he stepped into the gloom of the cabin and the silhouette became a person. He seemed as surprised to see me as I was to see him. He was tall, lean, and the look of his face stopped the breath in my chest.

"I — I am old enough to *be* an auntie," I stammered out, thinking of my oldest brother's child, born not long before Jerie and I were taken. "But not old enough to be *your* auntie."

He laughed. It was the most beautiful sound I had heard coming from the most beautiful man I had seen.

"You right about that! My apologies, ma'am," he said, nodding. "When Master Robert said that the midwife had arrived, I . . . well, I 'spected an . . . older woman. Not . . ." He bit his lip and then smiled again. "I am James, carpenter-mason-smithy and all-'round man on Master Thomas's place and here, too, on White Maple Grove, Master Robert's. He sent me over to fix up this cabin, used to be Maisie's place. She was nanny to the Nash family since . . . well, since. Master Thomas Senior's day anyhow. Maisie pass on a while back." He gestured toward the rafters, the east-facing window with a missing pane. "It been empty long time."

This man, this James . . . His voice was . . . His words wrapped 'round me like arms. The smile never left his face. And his eyes never stopped reaching into mine. My breath stopped. I opened my mouth but no words came out. My heart was beating hard in my chest.

Finally, I said, "My name is Maryam. I am the midwife."

16
THE BORDER LAND

It hard to talk about him, say his name out, tell the story of his deeds, of our life. I keep him to myself though the children say I shouldn't. Time. It works out we were with the other twelve years. Twelve. I have had seventy and more without him yet I feel the heat from his hand on my shoulder, I see his face clear, cataracts or no. His . . . James's . . . voice, he speak to me in the rustling of leaves, the quiet singing of river water touching the rocks against the dock, in the song of the first bird that sing before the sun up. I will always hear his voice. It been four lifetimes. I think . . . Was only with him long enough to miss him for the rest of my life.

It will be different, Little Maryam, with a man you love.

Marie Catherine's words, how was it she knew? It *was* different, from the first time I saw him. Would not be the same with any man I would know from that day.

My throat closed when I heard his voice, heart beat so hard that it hurt. Sound of his laughter made my stomach flutter and it didn't settle until he appeared in my sight. Even then. In the mornings, before the sun up, before we went to the fields when the land was quiet or late at night when, back from a delivery, seem like I thought to hear the sound of his hammer, the echo rolling over the fields or the *whack whack whack* of ax against wood, 'specially when the days cooled. When the air lost the moisture that coated sound, I could make out the rhythms, sharp, clear. Was like James standing at my side. I would listen. And wish. It could've been anyone working 'round here. Master McKay's men were clearing trees over that way; might have been Jupiter, too. But I liked to think it was James just so I could think of him, see his face cross my mind, feel his touch, gentle on my shoulder, around my waist, my breast.

James had a pass from Master Thomas that allowed him to come and go much as he wanted. His work took him 'cross the Nash farms, the county, and beyond. When it was tinkering, fixing, and making that needed doing, James did. Thomas Nash hire out James just as Robert Nash hire me. And when he worked on Master Robert's farm, he was often at Elinor's cabin or Iris's, talking and laughing, or on some errand with leave to linger a while.

"Miss Maryam, I would like to visit with you if I may," James said one evening, before mounting the dark bay that would take him back. "If you are . . . amenable."

Wasn't sure what the word meant but from the way that James smiled, I knew it was good.

As my days increased on White Maple Grove farm, there was always James. But there were spaces between us. He call me "Miss Maryam"; I call him "Mister James." In the before time, there would have been talk between our families only. Not us. My father would meet with James's father, many days, weeks of talk and debate. I would lower my eyes whenever I saw James as if he were a stranger to my country. He, too, would not speak, would have nodded, the only acknowledgment of my presence, showing respect for my family, in obedience to my father's words. We would have been apart yet growing together.

Where had he learned these things, these ways that were so like the ways I had known? But this was wasteful thinking. James was a man of near thirty years, had a wife before who had died in childbed, a child who had died also. I was now a woman grown, my first blood many years behind me. I had not had a husband but I knew how to be with a man. The one child I had borne was buried on a bluff on Caesar's Key, her head toward the rising sun and the eastern lands of her mother's birth, beyond the dark waters. No more children since. James and I had traveled many miles alone. Our parents, sisters, and brothers were ancestors now. We were not children. We would come together to make our own agreement. Or so we thought.

Because there was Durfee. And he was always there on Master Robert's place. While James, who had a pass to come and go, lived on the Thomas Nash farm, and was hired out most days. That Durfee knew about James. James knew about Durfee. When they saw each other, they took a long way around, hardly spoke. Did not mess with each other. But, like two snakes coiled on the same rock, there was danger there. Durfee meant much to Master Robert. James meant much to Master Thomas. And I was the border land.

In the king's colony, I was property, a slave, with many eyes watching my comings and goings. This was the first time I ever spent on a farm, a "plantation" they was called, with a master and overseer directing my steps. My body and my labor had been bought and sold a fair bit since the before time, two, three times that I recall on the march across the lands before I crossed the dark waters, once when the *Martinet* dropped anchor in the bay in Jamaica before its sail north toward Savannah. Some of us changed owners but stayed in the hold. On that occasion, our delivery was not to be, thanks to Caesar. But that time was behind me. Durfee saw to it that I ne'er forgot that I was on a farm, that I was owned by Robert Nash. And that he, Durfee, was in control.

"Master may set much by yew bein' a midwife," he crowed at me, "but fair as I see, yew're a field nigger like all the rest. And yew'll werk the fields if I have the say of it."

And he did and I did. I worked from before the sun rose until long after it set, many times from sunrise to sunrise if I had a delivery. Spent the days in the fields, was called out to tend this or that ailment, back to the fields, then supper, then out to a laboring woman, then back to the fields. The small sturdy bed that James had crafted often went unslept in: I spent many a night sleeping in a chair or on a pallet spread on the floor, next to a laboring woman or one ailin'. Didn't mean nothin' to Durfee. I staggered in at sunrise then staggered to the fields directly after. Spent near a day tending to an old Welshman, one of Master Thomas's tenants, who was dying. By the time I made it back to White Maple Grove, I was near dead myself. Durfee sent me to the tobacco fields along the creek to help with the harvesting. In the season, we did nothing but pick tobacco, day and night.

"Ain't right he do that," Yellow Annie commented, passing over a cup of water and a cloth to wipe my face. We were working since daylight. And I felt near dead. "Ya'll out all night with Old Man Llywelyn."

I drank as much of the cool water as I could swallow, its smoothness dripping down my throat and my chin. It felt good. Wiped my forehead and handed the cloth back to Annie. "Ain't nothing."

She frowned and turned her attention back to her work, her cheeks red from the sun. Little spots of brown — they called freckles — sprinkled themselves on her nose like stars 'cross the sky. They called her "Yellow" Annie because there was another Annie on the farm and because she was the lightest-colored person in the quarters, near as white as Master Robert, Master Thomas, Mistress, any of them. With her dark gold-green eyes and sand-colored coiled hair, which she corralled into a tightly wrapped kerchief, Yellow Annie was an interesting-looking person; she 'minded me of someone. Was James who told me who. She was the old Master Nash's child and sister to the man who now owned her.

"Ain't worth no coin to me," she said. "It don't mean I get my papers." She did not waste a breath as she wrestled with the tough leaves. "Robert Nash, Thomas Nash, Old Master Thomas, all of 'em work me as much as they do ya'll. Robert Nash sell me just as quick as he would ya'll. And I the only sister he got."

It was late July and we were picking what tobacco these poor backwoods acres of Master Robert's would yield, and it wasn't much. What leaves we got were small and discolored, there'd been a lot of rain this spring and the fields had flooded; whatever grew there was spoiled. The soil was poor and tired, the rainwater just stood with nowhere to go. The mud wrapped itself 'round my ankles thick and heavy.

"You oughta say somethin'," Annie went on. "To Master Robert. He listen to you. You ease Mistress's ailments and ever'body else's. Bring him money these fields don't. Say something, Maryam. Fore you just fall out yourself."

I patted her on the shoulder and walked into the next row to begin my work.

"Like you say, Annie, not worth coin nor papers to me."

There was no way I would say anything to Master Robert, Mistress, or anyone. I was so tired and hadn't slept in so long, I knew better'n anyone that I might just soon fall down and never get up. Better that than say something and have followings that I wasn't sure yet how to handle.

Durfee showed up one evening, late, not long after I got to the Nash place. Followed me like a shadow from Iris's cabin where I was tending to her boy. Walked through the door of the cabin that ever'one still called "Maisie's Cabin" like it was his door and stood there, watching me as I emptied my basket.

"You a busy neggar," he said, leaning against the door frame, chewing on a piece of straw.

"What you want, Durfee?" I asked, not looking into those dark blue eyes of his, the ones 'minded me of a mean dog's. I called the other white men "Master" this or that. Not him.

"*Master* Durfee," he barked at me in his reedy voice.

"What you want?"

I wasn't 'bout to call him Master anything. I had been in the fields all day, tending to Iris's boy and other children down with the chest soreness near all night. And still had plasters to make, mustard seed to mash up to ease the tightness in their chests, steep sage leaves for the next morning. Was dead on my feet, and my back felt like it wanted to leave my body and move on. No sleep for me yet, too much to do. I was not feelin' any conversation with Durfee, overseer or not.

He grabbed my arm and jerked it the wrong way. I bit my lip to keep from crying. Wouldn't give that man the idea he had a thought over me.

"I'll whip you gal, you don't give me proper respect!"

"Whip me? You can't whip me! Master Robert say so!"

Durfee's grip tightened around my arm. He knew I spoke true and the thought of it ate at him. Master Robert and Master Thomas, too — they owned the farms together — had said that I was not to be disciplined, whipped or otherwise; that I was too valuable to them with my healing skills and deliverin' babies and such. If there was discipline to be given, it would come from them or Mistress Robert and no other. Some of the other people held it against me, too, grumbling-like when I walked past, cutting their eyes. But Durfee hated me for it. I should have been afraid.

But that night, I was too wore out. Wrestled my arm away from him and picked up the iron. It was cold. But it was still an iron. I waved it at him.

"What you want, Durfee?"

He glared at me but backed away, his hands held up, his blue-black eyes boring into mine.

"Make a bargain with yew, Africky gal. An arrangement like."

Tightened my grip on that iron.

"You work yourself into an early grave with all your healin' potions and brews and such, tending births an' buryin's day and night, working in the fields."

I said nothing but thought, *What you tell me I don't know, Irishman?*

"I can make your workload light." He lowered his voice until it sounded like the hiss of a cat. "You be . . . friendly-like to me, I keep you outa the fields at daybreak, give you time to rest up from your labors. The ones with me" — he smirked — "And the tendin' to others." Before I could move, he lunged toward me and grabbed my hand, the one that held the iron. With his other hand, he stroked my cheek. Felt like a nest of ants crawling up my face. "I'll see you come out all right."

"No."

"As I see it, you got no choice. Robert Nash plan to put you with Hewes . . ."

Hewes? A fuzzy memory of a lanky man, funny-colored eyes, toothache. I remembered people by their ailin's.

"For what?"

A grin.

"Breed you. Like any cow."

I could not say anything.

"So. You breed with Hewes or you breed with me."

I felt my stomach move and my hand, too, at the same time. I felt that hand shake off his grasp and push that iron into the Irishman's cheek. Felt a smile brush my lips watching him stagger away yowling. Knew he would whip me for it. Too tired, too angry to care.

Durfee rounded back on me, smacked me wide across the face. That blow sent me staggering. But he was hurt, his cheek bleeding, and he stumbled back, his eyes running with tears, the red stripe across his face widening.

"Bitch! I'll beat you till . . ." he hissed. He staggered at first then set his shoulders, lowered his head, and lunged forward. This cabin wasn't but so big, I jumped aside but I was near within his arm's reach.

"You'll have to kill me fore you do that!" I shouted, wiggling my nose — numb — then feeling my cheek carefully with my hand. I still held the iron, tightening my grip around the handle, my breath coming in bursts as I waited. Waited for him to lunge at me again. Waited for him to raise his hand so I could either brain him with this iron or die trying. Waited for him to grab me, waited . . .

But Durfee stopped, stared at me. His face, he wasn't as pink-faced as some of the others, had lost its color. And he backed away from me, slowly, as if he was studying every step, waiting to see what I would do.

"Cailleach," he growled, his voice rough and low. "Cailleach." He made the sign of his Jesus's cross and stumbled out of the open door, looking over his shoulder at me, his eyes burning with fury and fear.

I stood there, did not move, my mouth open, the iron having more weight now in my hand, felt ready to drop it. I thought Durfee was just gathering his strength to come back in a rage, beat me or worse.

Instead I heard him staggering through the night, cursing. Slowly I set the iron back on the hearth and grabbed the rickety chair, wedging it against the door. Then I sank to the floor, my legs wobbly, strength draining out of my body like water from the pump.

I woke up before dawn, sat straight up in my bed, my heart beating as if to spring from my chest, as if Durfee were still there. He wasn't. But his image was, with eyes wide, mouth open and slack, his pink skin drained of all color. I had cursed at him, warned him away from me. He had called me a "Cailleach" whatever that was, made a sign to protect himself against my evil ways, and left. Why had he . . . I remembered.

When I wake and at night before the dream spirits take over my thoughts, I think in the words of my parents, in the words that I used last with Jerie. And when I am bothered or angry, these are the words that come to me before any others, before English or Akan, before Fon, before the Portuguese. That night I had cursed the Irishman in those words, my first words. It was the first time I had spoken them aloud in a long time. It would not be the last.

226

17

Once in a while they'd give us a li'l piece
of Sat'day evenin' to wash out clothes in
the branch.
— MARY REYNOLDS

For a while, Durfee lurked along the edges
of my world but he didn't come close. I still
put that chair against the door. Treated me
like he did ever'one else much as he could,
barking at me to walk faster, pick more,
hurry back from whatever tending I did.
"You malinger, I'll beat the breath out your
body!" He'd check on my return to White
Maple Grove after the deliveries I made off
the farm; oftentimes he'd get in my way,
telling Master Robert that he was escorting
me, protecting me. He filled up my load as
high as he dared without attracting Master
Robert's notice, without putting himself in
the way of whatever potions and rubbings
Mistress Robert wanted for me to fix.

Mostly I ignores him, don't hear his voice. My load heavy enough without it. I come in late from the field, or from a birthing or just tending someone ailin'. And I'm filthy, with mud and plant leavings and blood. I need a wash. I need to sleep. Most nights I just set in the chair that James mended up for me. I set and rock and think till I fall asleep. Mostly think about James. He near all I think about. And the idea of him soothes me.

But over the past month, when I set and rock late, I been thinking about other things, worries, and . . . I'm not a fore-knower, not like my mother, not like Marie Catherine. But I get . . . feelin's. And I have a sense when something ain't right; I feel like there's something I should know, that I've seen but not seen. Can't figure what that is. But it's bothering me like a shadow over my shoulder and that's not good.

Seen but not seen, mentioned and then forgotten. *Hewes.* I had forgotten about Hewes.

"I've got a secret!" Mistress Robert say to me like she singing. She's grinning, which she should not do. She missing a tooth in front and the rest are near rotted black. She like sweets but they don't like her. "There's going to be a wedding!"

"Drink this up, Mistress," I say, passing over a cup of mint leaf tea. Martha McKay Nash got the worst stomach ever was, it's always sour and giving her trouble. Seem like the tea work but Master Robert had the doctor from Bedford come to give her a swallow of something thick and evil-smelling in a bottle that makes no difference at all 'cause it give her the trots and make her gassy. She tolerate the mint better than most anything else. She drink but don't stop chattering. Her singsong way of talking rubs my nerves and I got too much to do for that. Mess of babies coming real soon, one in the quarters on Master Thomas's place, Mahala on Owen McKay's, plus Mistress Thomas due most any time. I watch her real close because she ain't carried a baby full time in ten years.

"I just love weddings like the one you darkies have. Where you jump over the broom, dance, and sing!" She clap her hands together then belched, turned bright pink, covering her mouth, giggle and talk some more. In my head, I was so far into the preparations I would need for the next week that I did not catch her meaning. Her words washed over me until —

"Mr. Thomas says he'll fetch the colored fiddler over from Fletchers Walk. It will be so much revelry! You and Hewes!" A sigh. "You all will have such precious babies."

Hewes?

I near spilled the tea in her lap. Durfee had said the same that awful night and I had been shocked then, but in the passing weeks, I had been pushed over with running here, running there, had set aside his ugly words, his talk about Hewes, and gone about my work, what with harvests and folks' ailings and the babies coming. But hearing these words made me still.

What it mean to be owned like a cow, like my father's goats. What it mean to have a person to decide that I will be put with a man of his choosing and not mine. Yes, my father would have decided for me had I stayed.

But that was family ways, my peoples' ways. And if a husband was brought forward, my mother would have woven herself into the fabric of his family relations. If there were shadows, if her guides whispered that my intended's family had dark rivers that should not be crossed, there would have been no joining. Father respected Mother's gifts; he listened to her. That is what family does. Even Caesar would have given me leave to choose my own husband.

Robert Nash is not family. He paid king's

money and tobacco for me, pocket the coin I make when he hire me out. He decide my life in the leather-bound book that he keeps, where he counts all the lands waters fields cows horses pigs and people that he own.

Master Robert decide to join me up with his man Hewes just as he join up the bay mare he just got with his mean-temper stallion, the one Jupiter call "Diablo"; it near stomp a man to death. He just marked this up in his book and tell Durfee and tell all the other white people but he don't think to tell me. Or Hewes. Or Yellow Annie, who's been Hewes's woman for two children. *He,* Master Robert, decide.

Mistress Robert belch again.

Giggle.

"You like Hewes, don't you, Maryam?" I am too shocked to speak. "I know that he likes you, I've seen him look at you."

Thirty, forty, more, men work Master Robert's farm, most of them on the back acreage and northwest of the creek. They hardly ever come near the main house. Mistress Robert wouldn't know Hewes from any other black man work this farm. So why she think she seen him look at me?

"Yes, Mistress."

I sweep up my packets and vials quick into my basket and leave the room before my head spin off, hear Iris call after me, say thanks for looking in on Aunt Bella. I wave and fly out of that house, walking so fast I trip over my skirts, waving at this one, that one, Durfee in the distance bark words at me, I wave him off, too. And yes, I know he can beat me for that and yes, I know he think I'm a witch woman. I just want to get someplace quiet, out the way, where no eyes can see, where I can hear my own mind, figure what I can do.

There's a small cove at the edge of White Maple Grove, the waters come in from the ocean mix with waters from Glady Creek just south. It's borderland, not Nash land. Don't know who it belong to. There a grove of trees just across from the landing on a barrier island made up of sand and grass, like Caesar's Key. I go there when I can, look out beyond, wonder how far away is the land I come from, just wonder for wonderin's sake. Sometime, I see fishermen. Other times, I'm alone with the water, the breeze, and my thoughts.

You like Hewes, don't you, Maryam?

Yes, I do, I like Hewes just fine. He's a quiet man, work hard, don't drink, keep himself to himself. He and Yellow Annie and their two little ones.

You all will have such precious babies.

232

"You don't have your pass, do you?"

I knew he was there.

"No, Master James, I do not."

His laughter rolled across me, the humor to match the calm warmth of his hand on my back. I sighed. It been a few weeks since I see him. He was hired out to a farm one day's ride south.

"Good thing Durfee don't know you come here."

"Nobody know I come here. But you . . ."

His lips brushed the top of my head and I could feel them even through my headwrap. He took my hand, turned it upside, and kissed my palm.

"What got you worryin', Maryam? Why you look sad? You quiet, off by yourself . . . in this place."

The words poured out of me, what Mistress Robert said, what Durfee had said before her. I told him what I imagined Robert Nash writing in his thick leather-bound book. James's jaw tightened, his lips formed a straight tight line. I talked around and around what Mistress Robert, Durfee, had said until I started repeating myself, the thought of it all brought me to crying. I choked and stopped. Dried my eyes, blew my nose. And waited for James to speak.

And waited. Listened to the birds 'round

us, heard a splash or two of fish trying to catch a bug floating on the waters. Listened to the water lap against the shore, a lightning-fast bird the size of a thumb darting here and there. Still, James did not speak.

My James listened in a way I have not known often. He ne'er push into my thoughts, cut off my sayings. He wait until I take a breath, two breaths, three. He look at my face when I talk, fix his gaze on my eyes; sometime, he even take my hand and hold it. But he don't speak until I stop. He listen as if my words the most important of his life.

"Hewes. He and Yellow Annie . . ." James's forehead folded itself into a frown. He spoke slow like he think over every word. "Master Thomas tried to match me up with her. Long time ago now, after Arrabeth pass over but . . ." He stopped. I knew that it was hard, would always be hard for him to think about his wife, to say her name out. "But I knew that Annie did not want me. Said so to Master and he say, 'All right then, James, we have to match you up with someone else.' " James took a deep breath. "Next I knew she and Hewes were together, jumped over a broom before Reverend Jeremiah and Katie come, then Little Bari." The furrows in his forehead deepened. "Master Thomas know that Hewes with Yellow Annie. Why he —"

"Why he do what he do is because he can. He know that Hewes got two babies in five years on Annie but no more. Least . . . not yet." It must have seemed to Thomas Nash that Yellow Annie was an indifferent breeding woman and he wanted to try his luck with another. Because Yellow Annie have no babies till Katie and Katie was near five years when Bari come. The boy was just near two now and still sucking and Yellow Annie did not want to have another baby so soon.

James's jaw tightened more when I said this.

A thought came to my head.

"He . . . Thomas Nash try to put you with another woman 'sides Annie?"

James smiled.

"Yes. Maria until Routt sold her off when he went bust. Artemis but she is . . ."

Now it was my turn to smile. Artemis live five miles up the creek on Donovan Kilpatrick's farm. She was the most beautiful woman I ever seen in my life in any place, across the dark waters, in the Caribbean, or here. She was the daughter of a Creek man and Igbo mother, tall, straight-walking, features like a carved ivory mask, and mean as a spider. Artemis, she like men, all kinds, all ways, and they like her. And she was what they call a good breeder, too, a baby every year or so, fathers various. But few know she have the babies she want when *she* want them, that's women's business. Problem was, like some spiders, Artemis got the temper, she near kill every man she lay down with. Didn't seem to bother them none though.

"Evil as a black snake," I said.

James shook his head.

"That true. But her last two babies look more like Master Donovan than any other man on his plantation. And she a good spinning woman, a seamstress, so he won't part with her. That idea went the way of smoke."

"Thomas Nash must be thinkin' to fix you up with someone if Master Robert plannin' to match me with Hewes."

I could see from James's expression that he reckoned this, too.

"I don't want to be with Hewes."

James's grip on my hand tightened.

"I don't want to be with . . . anyone but you, Maryam. And 'specially not Artemis!"

There was no more talk 'round this. I would do what I could do. James, who sometimes had Master Thomas's ear, would do what he could do. It seem there was a barricade going up, made of earth, timber, and stone, to keep me from James and James from me. Master Robert, Master Thomas, Durfee, all building as fast as they could to order our lives according to their plan. And then there was Jeremiah.

18

Break up your fallow ground,
and sow not among thorns.
— JEREMIAH 4:3, KING JAMES VERSION

Being a midwife is hard on a courtin'
couple. What with all the going out at all
hours and in all weather, the standing for
hours, the holding and pulling and tugging
on the mothers, the cleaning up, washing
up, mopping up, the brewing, grinding, and
stewing of herbs and potions, not to mention the time spent away: a delivery can happen in a matter of hours or a matter of days;
you may as well try to get married and be
with each other at a crossroads, one going,
the other coming. There is not time to be
with each other. It wear you out. A midwife
never leave the mother during labor. Never.
That mean you stay for a hour, a day, or a
week, but you don't go nowhere until the
baby come, dead or alive, and the afterbirth,

too. You make sure that it handled right. Some women 'round here bury it. The women of my mother's people burned it and chanted prayers to a god whose name I never learned. It was women's business and in that time, I was not a woman. I don't leave until everything is done, the way I was taught. Which mean that much as James and I wanted to wrap ourselves up together and never leave the little bed that he made for me, for us, we did not get the chance.

"Maryam, there a meeting over at Glady Creek Sunday before supper. I would be pleased if you would come over with me. There will be baptism, Fielding's oldest boy and much celebratin'." James smiled. "I can fetch you if you're agreeable."

There was a gathering on the banks of the creek, and all of the people who worked on these plantations were give leave to go and most did, when the white folks allowed it — the Nash brothers, Clyde McKay, the Wormleys, Baggotts and Routts, Kilpatricks. Except for harvest time, many didn't work on a Sunday, leaving out the house people who were always at work. It was a special day and folks used the time to rest, to visit with family members who lived away, to cuddle babies and consult elders.

We gathered 'long the shore in a clearing

on the Routts' acreage on the west bank of Glady Creek near an ancient oak that had been split by lightning in the times before people ever set foot in these lands, when all gods were children and the world was new. They listened to the words of the preacher shouting heaven, salvation, and sin, sang songs, and performed their rituals in the waters of the creek, cleansing away the bad, greeting the good, washing each other's feet as a form of respect. I went along if I wasn't attending a delivery or resting up after one. The songs were soothing, the rhythms familiar. I had no family there so the food and company were welcome; I never liked eating by myself. I took my big coiled basket with me as I did every time I left the cabin because there was always some ailment or round belly to look to.

While I was agreeable to most anything having to do with James, I was of two minds over the meetings.

Because of Jeremiah.

I sat on a quilt in the shade of the oak, rocking little Deacon back and forth to get him to settle. Jeremiah marched up the bank to greet the people, tipping his hat to the women, shaking hands with the men, patting the little ones on the head, the seductive tones of his voice dancing in my ears.

He was dressed like a gentleman in a coat and trousers, his white shirt bright in the early-afternoon sun as if it were lit by a lamp, a thin tie 'round his neck. In all this heat. His boots was polished to a high shine. His garments were from Master Thomas's wardrobe, discarded for some invisible imperfection and reworked to fit him. He was proud of his suit, said to anyone listening that it gave him standing. His wife, Rhoda, was proud of it, too, but told me privately that the shiny boots were too small and pinched his toe — and would I look to it? She worried about its becoming septic. This I learned a while back when treating her for the change in her monthlies. Marie Catherine had told me that my craft would make me privy to secrets, big and small. Knowing that Jeremiah's big toe pained him with each step gave me a sense of satisfaction.

"Fielding. Afternoon, Miss Leta. How Aunt Pegg getting 'long? Cyrus, how ya'll? That the new baby girl? What her name? Aggy? Miss Fanny, afternoon. Hitt, you comin' 'long? Un-huh, the Lord will provide."

And so he wove himself through all the people like a bright white strand of yarn slipped back and forth through a black rug, though I saw him more as a snake slitherin' through the grass 'round peoples' ankles, whisperin' in their minds and making the world right for his way of thinking. Tipping his hat to this one, bowing to that one. He was a preacher, this Jeremiah, a hostler on Master Thomas's place. The people called him "Reverend Jeremiah," which he pretended was too grand for him and might not please his lord. But he did not stop them saying it. It please him. To my mind he was as false as the false gods he warned about. I had trouble saying out some of the Bible names and Jeremiah's was one of those so I called him "Miah," which did not please him. He said that I needed to set aside my pagan words and pagan names and use the language of the lord, meaning *his* lord. I did not tell him that there were many words that I knew belonging to Christian people and other people. I had the names that my parents had given me that were mine alone and the names passed on to me by Caesar and others. I did not tell him that I had the skill of pronouncing many words and names. I let him think what he wished. I continued to call him "Miah." Away from my hearing, he called me a heathen witch.

Abednego, Iris's oldest, was always into some mischief or other, getting a scrape or a scratch. So it was almost every time I saw Iris that she'd ask if I'd patch up that boy, and so I was doing when Jeremiah slithered his way through the grass leading up the hill to where we were sitting.

"The Lord take a rest on the Sabbath," Jeremiah said.

Iris snorted, swatting at Abednego to be still and giving little Deacon a pat on the bottom while he slept beside her.

"Then the Lord bes' tell Masters Nash, 'cause they's few Sundays that we don't do some kind of work." Iris look at me, I look at Iris. The laughter left us feeling light but brought a sour expression to Jeremiah's face.

"Master Thomas and I in full 'greement . . ." Like he had some authority with a white man. "Best to keep the Sabbath holy."

Iris snorted. I grinned at her.

"Babies come when they ready, people sick or need tendin' when they do," I said, not looking at him. "And my job is to take care of 'em when they come to me, Sabbath or no."

"You in the king's land now, Miss Maryam," Jeremiah said, using the tone I hated, the one he used to scold rowdy children. "Time to set aside the heathen ways and embrace the word of the Lord. To be baptized and born new and clean —"

I cannot say how weary I was of hearing that man call me "heathen."

"I seen babies born time and again," I said before I could stop myself. "They new but they noways clean."

Iris giggled and Jeremiah's jaw snapped shut like a trap 'round a fox's leg, then he said, "Miss Maryam, I 'scuse you because you don't know no better. You come from a dark place with dark . . . ways, heathen ways. I don't 'spect you to know the light the way I do, the way . . ." He looked to the side. James was walking toward us. "The way Brother James does. So I try to be merciful and patient. I know Brother James will lead you into the light and away from . . . Oh! Brother James!"

"Jeremiah."

The men shook hands and Jeremiah stepped back as James greeted Iris and touched me gently on the shoulder, then brushed the top of Abednego's head.

"Sit still, boy, let Miss Maryam take care of your arm."

"Yes sir," the boy mumbled.

I look at Jeremiah, he look back at me but says nothing. I shrugged my shoulders and went back to tendin' the boy. He and James walked away, talking, their voices blending together in a harmony that make me worry. Jeremiah count on my James, he like him. And James think much of Jeremiah. I worry that maybe he talk James away from me.

"Never happen," Iris say, reading my thoughts.

I wonder. It seem that Jeremiah's speaking always pointing at me. He spread his arms wide and ask all the faithful to come to him, the true believers. He tell story about a soft place with light and gold avenues and freedom for us. He shout about idols and evil gods and witches. And how they all going to hell where it hot, and I think, Hotter than here? Hotter than where I from? And when he say these things, he look around, he walk around, but some way, it seem to me, he always bring his eye back to where I am. All his words about that soft place, that heaven, they for James, Iris, the rest. The words Jeremiah say about the hot place, that hell? He mean those words for me.

It had been a day. Worked in Iris's garden and in the kitchen; she'd been ailing with the headache, and, what with the cooking, cleaning, and tending to Mistress that she did, I knew she needed the help. Wasn't my time to work in the fields, so I looked to the cooking and got Iris's children situated to sleep, then took to my cabin to ready myself for the day coming.

Was near dark when he came. I was set about what I always did this time of day if I wasn't out on a delivery, much to do fore the sun set. My days had been full, I had not been to the fields but once, so caught up with one thing or other. Durfee didn't like that but wasn't much he could do. Was Mistress Robert who sent me out on these errands. Phelia's boy took the back part of one morning, Mister Rubin's dyin' the afternoon and only me and his woman Kora to lay him out, I never saw a white man so alone. Then there was Mistress Robert's usual stomach troubles.

Near all my provisions were low, so I foraged 'round as much as I could while it was still light then moved inside to prepare for the next day. Hung up sage to dry, set the sassafras along with mint to steep, ground up cloves. The scents were risin' 'long with the steam from the bowls. I loved the smells, they reminded me of the before time and of Marie Catherine and the smell of the salt in the air 'round the key. As I had a few moments, I fixed to grind a mixture of cinnamon and cloves down fine as I could. Was another birthing coming up: Mahala was near her time, six babies and she never had an easy way of it. The smoke always calmed her and I thought to have the salves, infusions, and candles ready and set aside for when the summons came. I let the memories caress me so they put my mind into my work so deep that I didn't hear footsteps. But I knew he was there. Felt that prickling on the back of my neck. A knock on the door frame.

"Sister Maryam, good evenin to ya."

Sister. I know it mean a greeting of respect but I don't take to it, not with this man. Only people to call me "Sister" are across the dark waters or walking in the land of mists and whispers. This Jeremiah, he speak at me with oil in his words.

"Miah."

He had taken on the name of this prophet who was a hard man, calling out transgressions and passing judgments but pure in spirit, so James said. Maybe the prophet but not *this* Jeremiah.

He had a dark heart.

"Are you ailin', Miah?" I asked without looking at him. Because why else should he be at my door? I knew that his jaw tightened. The others called him "Reverend" out of respect. Not me. He had small ideas about

247

what women should do. And he had smaller ideas about me, said so to everyone who would listen, but never to me, never in my hearing. And never to James.

"Make ye a tea to sooth your innards." A dark heart made for a bitter stomach, which made Jeremiah suffer. Cookie, who worked in Master Thomas's kitchen, told me that the preacher ate food bland enough for a baby.

"Thankee, Sister, but no," he answered as polite-like as he could. I knowed it made his stomach more bitter.

"I come on an errand. For James's sake."

The sassafras was boiling, putting off bursts of white steam, soft enough for me to see the man's eyes and his wide-open mouth, white teeth gleaming. A smile he wore but did not feel.

"Did James send you?"

"The Lord sent me."

I said nothing. Folded up clean rags to guard my hands when I moved the pots from the fire. I settled them on the stones to cool and checked each one. Sassafras is tricky. Too much steepin' time, its strength can unmoor the bowels. Too little and it is of no help at all.

"What your Lord want?"

Jeremiah's eyes flickered and again I felt

that chill on my neck.

He was still smiling.

"Say you and James must stand afore him. Say first I baptize you in the river t'save your soul, wash away your sins. Say . . ." He looked at me, his eyes hard and flat-like, pebbles looking out his face. "He say you stop your heathen ways."

I looked back at him, hoped my gaze was just as stone-like as his.

"My ways like your mother's ways."

I smiled inside.

Jeremiah looked shocked.

Uncle Lemuel's mind and words had wandered when I tended him as he was dying. That man had seen the sun's ups and downs for more'n eighty year since early times there, had come to White Maple Grove with the old Master Nash's father when there was still Indians living in the hills nearby. He come from the Indies, lived some in the Bay colony north and down in New Orleans, worked on a river keel, chopped cane, waded through rice fields. He had seen what they call "snow." He told stories 'bout bringing in the sugarcane then fishing in the Gulf waters south of Louisiana where he'd lived as a child. Some nights when I tended him, his ramblings mixed Creole *français* with the English and Span-

249

ish. Once he spoke to me in words of the Hausa, his words clear and confident, but his eyes did not see. I knew that he could not tell how or why he knew them. He remembered bits and slivers of his life, pieces that never fit smooth next to each other, parts always missing. But they made good stories once you put the threads together.

Uncle Lemuel's parents had come from "the Africa" as he called it. He could not remember his people's name, said the Christian god had taken its memory from him. Jeremiah's mother had come from there, too, on the same boat, sold to the same farm in French Louisiana, then north to the Nash family in North Carolina. Said she'd had marks on her face and teeth filed straight 'cross.

"Prettiest woman I ever seen. Tall, queen-like when she walk." His sightless eyes had a glow to 'em, the kind the dyin' gets when they begins to see beyond the shadows. "She go . . . can't right . . .'member where she go on to . . ."

Lemuel say she worked on one of the Nash farms for a while and then just moved on, sold off or run away or died, he couldn't remember what. Just remembered that she was beautiful. And strange. And wild. If

Lemuel knew who her son's father was, he had forgotten that, too. But one thing he did know was that she never named her boy anything like "Jeremiah"; said he was named for the day he was born, a name from his mother's people. I wished I had met her. I wondered what she would think if she saw her boy now.

"She was a heathen and ig'nant. She never met Jesus. I pray for her soul," Jeremiah said, his words sharp and mean. He gestured toward my cupboards, the shelves groaning under the weight of my medicines, teas, and herbs. "Just as I pray for your soul."

"Don't need your prayers."

He gasped and murmured, "Forgive her, Lord, she don't know. She just a heathen —"

"I'm a midwife, tend to mothers and babies, Christian, heathen, and not. What I know . . . I know. Been passed to me from times before you or I was born."

"You do the devil's work," he hissed. "What you did to Netta . . ."

So that's the way of it.

It never take long for a lie to travel. The truth, with its layers and colors, take its time.

I willed myself not to look at him, not to grab his arm and try to twist it off. Not to throw hot water in his pinched-up face. There had been talk ever since I stumbled back into camp that morning from one of the McKay farms, talk that probably started with Beck, who was too young to know better. I did not blame her. She could not take in what she saw, she could not know that what she thought was one thing was . . . some other thing entirely. And me, I didn't explain. Because there was one lesson Marie Catherine had pressed into my head, telling me that if I only remembered one thing, it should be this: "Never tell them all you know."

The big coiled straw basket was light in my hands that morning because I had used up near everything I had tending to Netta. But she was too far long her path for me to do much.

Seven babies in five years: McKay was using her as a breeder, and when the men he brought in didn't or couldn't make the babies he wanted quick as he want 'em, McKay did it himself. And it was killing her, Netta, slowly taking her life. Four born before my time there, one baby lived, just barely, and he was sickly still. Twins dead born, blue and quiet as if they were only wishes, come too soon, come too close after her last. I helped Netta birth them, then washed and dressed them for burying, a chore that always makes me sad. And the seventh.

The smell of blood is like nothing else. It's like iron. I smelled it before I opened the door to her cabin, smelled it just walking across the quarters. The hounds smelled it, too, they were nervous, baying and howling, pacing. In the distance, I heard McKay's horses snorting and whining in the barn as if they wanted to get out and run away. It was like there was smoke in the air. That dark strong odor told a story I didn't want to hear. But I had no choice. I knew what I would find before I opened the door.

Li'l Becky and Alvine, who'd been tending to Netta, turned and looked at me, their faces blank with horror and dark with fear. Becky opened her mouth but there was no sound. I slid my gaze slowly from her face and looked over at Alvine, whose cheeks were wet with tears, then to Netta, legs open, her belly swollen and contorted. The expression on her face spoke of pain, terror, and —

"She been like this five hour, maybe six." Alvine's voice was hoarse. Her arms were covered with blood, to the elbows.

"Beck, fetch me more water, hot now, and cloths." I moved quickly over to Netta and checked her forehead — no fever — then examined her. I pulled a vial out of my bag and handed it to Becky. "Pour boiling water over these and bring me the cup. Quick-like now. Alvine, let's you and me . . ." Gently, we propped Netta up on a pillow to ease her breathing. I changed out the quilt — it was soaked to both hems with blood — and bathed Netta's face and forehead with cool water.

She groaned. Blood was trickling out of her, slow but steady. My heart pounded in my throat. I leaned close to her ear.

"Netta, what you done?"

Her dark eyes met mine. There was pain there but no regret. Just . . . triumph, satisfaction.

I felt sick.

Netta licked her lips.

"What I . . . should have long time ago."

"Ima . . . try to keep you alive." The words were like ground glass in my throat.

"It fine if you can't . . ."

Netta closed her eyes. Shrug one shoulder, all she had strength for.

Beck brought me the cup and then I sent her away. She was young and had pledged herself to a young man on McKay's northern place. She did not need to see this. None of us did.

McKay poked his head in the door. I was too busy to talk to him, just heard his voice grumbling and raspy, Alvine telling him what was what, answering his questions, all except the one: "How soon can she breed again?"

I will never know what she used. I didn't ask again, she didn't tell. I took that child out piece by piece, a leg here, an arm. Netta bled a lot and then a lot more. I did not think she would live. It was up to the gods now, any of them that was interested. It took me near all the afternoon and into the next morning to finish, to clean her up, to pack her womb. I gave her something — it had a strong tight flavor that I masked with honey and cinnamon — to fend off pain. But there was nothing more that I could do, nothing else I knew for sure, except to tell her, "No more babies now, Netta."

She heard me, sighed.

"Good."

Never tell them all you know. What I knew could get Netta a whipping, could get her sold off. What I knew could get me, Alvine, and Li'l Beck a basket of questions that we would not want to answer. What I knew but what people thought I knew could get me a whipping, too, maybe worse.

"I do women's work," I said to Jeremiah.

Whatever it turn out to be. " 'Less your Jesus plan to deliver the children."

I looked over at him. His smile was gone.

"There was some . . . devilry there. I know it."

So much I wanted to say to this bitter-stomached stone-face man. He waited for a moment, hoping that his words might make tasty bait. I said nothing.

"James wants a marriage blessed by Jesus." This wasn't a lie.

"Not what I want," I said, pouring the cooled tisane into a jar.

Jeremiah's face darkened like the sky before a storm.

"You're a woman, daughter of Eve. And you a heathen witch." His voice rumbled toward me like thunder carrying venom and envy.

"You call me a heathen witch to James?" Jeremiah snorted.

"No," I answered my own self. "No, you didn't."

"You put a spell on him, a hex! He won't listen!" Jeremiah shouted.

"You are many times a fool!" I told him.

"I pray for his soul," the man continued. "I have counseled James against a marriage with you. For you will bring him low."

"Me bring him low! You, with your bitter

words and your sour face, you're bringing my teas low."

"Saint Paul says women should not —"

"Saint Paul don't birth babies, some . . . woman had to do that for him and for every other man I know. 'Less you here for a salve or tea for Rhoda, I have work to do. Got to get ready fore Mahala's baby's starts to move. 'Less you need something for that rumbling stomach of yours."

"Do not mock God, woman!" he bellowed at me, raising his hand to make some sign of power against me.

I pulled myself up as tall as I could and tried hard not to grab the nearest jar to throw at his head.

"Are *you* a god now? Get out."

For one who thought all women were beneath him, Jeremiah couldn't move fast enough. His eyes widened then he snorted and stalked over the threshold. I laughed as I saw the back of him scurrying down the dirt road away from the camp as if the devil, his and mine, were after him.

"You shouldn't have done that," James said to me later when we were alone.

"Done what?" I asked. "Laughed at him?"

James's expression was grim, as if he expected Jeremiah's god and any others passing near to punish him with blindness or plague.

"Yes, you shouldn't have done that. Jeremiah is Master Thomas's man. When he talk, Master Thomas listen. If Jeremiah tell him you a witch —"

"I am not a witch! And you Master Thomas's man, too. You talk, he listen. He just as likely to do what you say as what Jeremiah say." I was trying to hold my temper but these men were testing me. "I am the only midwife for miles. Robert Nash make a coin ev'ry time I go out."

James grabbed my arm and held it and brought his face close to mine.

"But he will sell you in a blink if his brother tell him you put a hex on Jeremiah."

I snorted.

"Not fore Mistress Thomas baby come. If he sell me, he sell after that. Anyhow, I don't know how to make hexes. Why would he say that?"

"Maryam," James said, slowly, his voice low. "Jeremiah say you curse him in the heathen tongue, that you use Africky devil words."

I closed my eyes and felt the breath flow out of my chest. "And you believe him?"

"There's no devil in you, Maryam. But . . ."

I had told Jeremiah Nash to get out in my first words. The words of my parents and my family, the ones I speak only to myself because there is no one else to know them.

"I . . . forget sometimes."

"I know you do," James murmured, his lips brushing my forehead. "I do not blame you. Jeremiah means well but he tries the patience of Job. You must be careful, Maryam."

James folded me into his arms and held me so close that I thought I could feel his heart beating.

"Jeremiah say you going to . . . hell, you stay with me," I told him. "He say I go to hell, too."

James laughed and kissed me.

"Then I go to hell. If you there, no heaven can hold me."

James was right. I needed to be careful. I needed still to learn the ways of these people. To accept their power over my life and his. James and I wanted to be joined. But we needed Master Thomas's and Master Robert's assent, though it galled me to know it. James proposed to build us a cabin in a clearing at the edge of a marsh, in a field called Murray's Corners. Owned by the Nash brothers, it was a near barren strip of land that had belonged to their mother.

James said that Old Master had promised him the acreage though he didn't say why. If that Jeremiah whispered his mean words in Master Thomas's ear, there was no telling what would happen. He might not sell me: a midwife was valuable and these people were all about coin. But Nash could do worse.

He could keep me from my James.

19
PATIENCE

I had four babies coming that month though I knew about only three of them. I filled Mahala's cabin with so much spice smoke we both near choke on it. But the heat and the scent worked and we end up laughin' and coughin'. Her little boy slid into my hands wriggling like a fresh-caught fish, kicking screaming like he mad at us all. He strong. Mahala never stopped grinning and when I put the boy into her arms, her eyes were full of tears. Her man Tom brought their children in to see their brother and I was paid with a quilt and one chicken.

Nel's baby came fore I got there good, right there in the middle of the cabin floor! Another boy, screaming his little head off, a mouth wide open with nothing but pink gums to show. Fat little thing. McKay give me a coin, Nel give me a length of fine cloth to make a dress. I don't ask where it come from.

When Patience Nash's time came, Master Thomas himself came to White Maple Grove in his carriage to carry me over to his place. Said he could not trust anyone else. He never stopped chattering the whole way. Couldn't keep from it, nervous like it his first child.

"S-she seems calm, settled," he said, his voice quivering. "Like she knows what to do, that she knows the baby will . . . be . . . well . . ." Thomas Nash glanced at me, his cheeks pink, then turned his attention to the horse then back to me. "She will be well, won't she?" he asked. "It seems so. But I'm afraid to be too hopeful. It's just that . . . this is the first time since Tommy that she's . . . carried so far . . ."

I murmured, "Yes, sir," and kept my mind on the hours to come.

First day I come there, I was told that Patience Nash ne'er carried past "pukin' stage." This time, she had. Nine full months far as I could tell and it didn't look like no puny child. Her belly was enormous. And because she was so terrified of losing another baby, I was sent for near every week of the last two months.

"Oh, Maryam, thank the Lord, you're here."

Rhoda and Mistress Penn, Patience's

sister on a visit from Richmond town, had prepared the bed, folded up fresh linens, and had water boiling. Rhoda is a wonder. Why she married to Jeremiah . . . well, better things to run through my mind.

"You need anything else?" Rhoda ask me in passing.

"When the last time she eat?" I asked.

Rhoda grinned.

"Not since yesterday," the woman said in satisfaction. "She groaning a bit then and I thought . . . best not feed her much. She don like that!" Together, we chuckled. Few things Mistress Thomas like better than food of any kind. "I thought, she near ready and Maryam don need to be cleanin' that up!"

"Thankee," I told her, pushing up my sleeves. Patience let out a yelp. This baby was coming fast. "Mistress," I said, moving toward the bed, "let's see how you are now."

How she was — well, it was a sight. It been a while since I seen such a mess. Mistress Patience made a nest of that bed like a wild animal, linen bunched up into a ball despite what Rhoda and her sister had done. Pillows on the floor (Rhoda pick 'em up, Mistress Patience throw them down), water split ever'where, and Mistress Patience . . . well, she a mess, too, hair all over, matted, face dripping, hands in a fist.

"Maryam, I'm in so much pain! I hurt all over!" She let out another yelp, rose up and flop over on her knees, grunting like a pig. Her sister look at me as if she never seen such a monster. I guess Mistress Penn never seen a woman have a baby. Rhoda smile a little.

I rub the mistress's back, place the warm towel Rhoda give me across.

"I'm here now, Mistress Thomas. It be all right. This baby just in a hurry to see you is all. Now . . . turn over so I can see . . ."

Was what I thought, the baby was coming back end first. I nodded toward Rhoda to help me. Looked for Mistress Penn but heard the sound of someone vomiting in the next room. Shame. I could have used another pair of hands.

It took Rhoda and me — and Rhoda about the size of a twelve-year-old — to lift up the mistress and turn her 'round. Set her gentle-like on the bed but you would not have known it. She scream like we stuck a knife up her, swing her arms out like she gonna strike us.

Rhoda roll her eyes.

Most times I'm gentle with the mother. She going through a lot. It hurt. The baby move, make her feel sick. And scared, near all laboring women scared. Scared for themselves, scared for their babies. But Mistress Patience screaming like a fool with her head cut off and that mess with me and what I got to do. Then she get to wriggling 'round and I cannot get my way to check her for the baby's situation. It took more time than it should have and with the baby coming fast . . .

"Patience!" I yelled at her. "Shut your mouth!"

Rhoda's eyes got big as plates. The room got all quiet. The vomiting sound coming from the side room stopped and Mistress Penn poked her head 'round the door frame.

Mistress's mouth was open but no sound came out. She just look at me.

"Now if you want your baby sometime this week here, you need to stop that hollerin' and listen to me. Your chile coming out back end first and I need to turn her 'round. It gonna hurt some so bite yo' lip, ball up your hand, hold your breath, whatever you got to do. But you can't holler. Scare the child. You know what I'm saying?"

Patience still look at me. I know what she thinking. But she took a long breath, closed her mouth, and nodded.

That baby girl twirled 'round like she was a little top and slid out near before I was ready. Wriggled, kicked well-formed pink legs at me, and screamed. Screamed like she was ordering a carriage. Screamed like she was leading a regiment. Screamed with her little mouth wide open and her pink tongue poking out. Strong. Healthy. Lots of spirit.

Her mother could not decide whether to cry or laugh. She did both. She barely waited till we got the child or her cleaned up nice before she took her and kissed her all over. Pulled her breast out and started to feed her even though there was no milk yet. Just sang and rocked the child and cried and laughed. Master Thomas near broke the door down coming into the room and sat on the bed, in the middle of the sheets we hadn't taken up yet, in the middle of the blood and water and fluid. He didn't near care. He just cried and laughed like his wife and stroked the cheek of his newborn daughter.

It took some doing for me, Rhoda, and Mistress Penn to get the room and the birthing bed clean and freshened out (because the mother would not put down the child and the father would not leave) but we managed it.

Patience Nash yawned and sighed. Her daughter, who had worn herself out getting born and feeding, was asleep with her little mouth still open. Patience wiped tears away with the back of her hand.

"She . . . she's healthy, isn't she, Maryam?" Her eyes were wide with exhaustion and worry.

I patted her on the arm.

"Mistress Patience, she healthy. You got no worries there."

Patience bit her lip and nodded.

"You knew that . . . she . . . that I would have a daughter."

I was folding up a quilt to put away and turned toward the open chest.

"No," I murmured, remembering clearlike what I had said and when.

"You said . . . you said you had to turn *her* around. That's what you said."

I said nothing, just kept folding.

"Do you have . . . the sight, Maryam?"

I got some kind of sight but even after all this time, I'm not sure what I see, what it mean. Whether it before time or after, things that will or things that might.

"No, mistress, no sight for me. Just figured it was either a son or a daughter."

When I turned around, I realized that Mistress Patience wasn't listening. She and her little girl were sound asleep. I packed up my basket. The birth had been easy on the mistress, the afterbirth slid out whole and right-colored. The baby was already sucking like she would never be satisfied. Rhoda and Mistress Penn was there, no need for me to stay 'round then. Despite the smell of rain in the air and the rumbles of thunder I heard off and on, I wanted to walk back to the Robert Nash farm, stretch my back and legs, breathe the air, and settle my mind amid the birdsongs and the quiet.

"Maryam, Durfee's here to carry you back to White Maple Grove." Thomas Nash stood in the door, still grinning. He'd cleaned himself up some. "Was going to take you back myself but . . . Durfee's here, so I'll send you and the good news about our daughter . . . Elizabeth Rose . . . back to Robert and Martha." He glanced out the window. It was two in the afternoon but getting dark as wintertime. "It looks like rain."

"Yes, sir," I murmured, thinking I'd rather walk through a wall of water and a chorus of thunder's songs before taking two steps much less a wagon ride with Durfee.

"I will be grateful to you forever," Master Thomas said, placing several coins into my palm. He tapped the side of his nose. "This is between us. There is no price high enough for . . . what you have done." His eyes were wet. "I'll settle up with my brother. No need for you to give anything back."

"Yes, Master Thomas."

I got up in that wagon with Master Thomas's hands to lift me. He took my baskets and settled them in the back of the wagon, tucked them in gentle like they were made of gold, then covered them with a wax-coated blanket to keep out the rain. He ordered Durfee to drive careful-like, to make sure that I arrived safe at his brother's home and that he delivered the message about the birth of Elizabeth Rose. Durfee said yes sir and yes sir and yes sir.

And he drove that wagon out of the gates and west toward the old Charles Nash farm, acreage that now belonged to the Nash brothers together, but worked by Master Thomas.

"This the wrong way," I said.

Durfee grunted.

"We s'posed to go east."

"Need you in the quarters," he said. "Master Robert won't mind if I take you by while we're near."

Not unheard of to go look in on someone ailin' while close. But I had checked on the people last time I came to see Mistress Patience. No one was ill and no babies were coming.

"Who you taking me to tend?"

Durfee shrugged his shoulders.

"Jane."

"Sadie's girl?"

I thought back to the last time I saw her some weeks ago now. She work in the kitchen. Pretty little thing, light with dark hair; her mother, Sadie, was brought in from Maryland or the northern neck of the Virginia colony, someplace like that. Jane was eleven, maybe twelve, tall for her age and healthy far as I knew. I said nothing, just watched the land pass by and took notice of the sky and how close the storm seem to be. Wondered if little Jane had come down with some contagion. It about that time of year. Thought about what I had in my basket that might calm a tight chest or ease coughing.

"What's this then?" I said by way of greeting when Sadie opened the door of the cabin. Her face was ravaged with grief, wet with tears. My heart seized up. "Sadie? Sister? What is it? Where's li'l Jane?" I swept past her and stopped.

Janie lay on the bed, her face gray with pain, her belly round and low, her legs open. I swallowed my next question. Told Sadie to bring me more water, hot and cool. Told her to grab me up another quilt and bring me a clean cup. She nodded, she said nothing.

That little girl, Jane, she the bravest laboring mother I ever tended. She whimper some but never scream, never cry, really. Her baby came out whole but near dead. It was too small to live long. Too poorly to breathe much less suck. I comforted Jane best I could but said little. She said nothing. And when the baby took his last breath, she turned her face toward the wall.

I tend to Jane in quiet. Sadie quiet, too. I keep my face tight, my words low and soft. I do this for Jane. For every mother like Jane. Every time a baby die, I die a bit, too. But I can not help a grieving mother if I lose my face.

So I grieve inside. And at night, I cry myself to sleep.

Sadie washed the child and wrapped him tight in a blanket. Together we took him, through the light rain, to the Nash slave cemetery and buried him, head facing east. We made a stack of flat stones to keep the animals away, to mark the place for memory. I chanted the words of my people. Sadie, born also across the dark waters, chanted the words of hers. I gave her the afterbirth to prepare a ceremony as the grandmother.

It took us no time to clean up that cabin,

change over the bed, wash and tend to Jane. I gave her a serum of poppy and left chamomile to help her sleep.

"I am grateful," she said.

"May the gods look after him on his journey," I told her, remembering a few of the proper responses. Sadie nodded, tears filling her eyes.

"The father . . ."

The door swung open and Durfee stood there. He wore the expression of a thundercloud.

"Are yew ready?" he barked at me, ignored Sadie altogether. "We go now, before the storm hits." No asking after the baby or after Jane. Nothin'. The Irishman turned and marched off, his heavy boots made slipping and sloshing sounds in the puddles and mud.

Sadie's dark-eyed gaze locked with mine.

"Thank you, Sister Maryam," she said.

20
CLOUDSPLITTER

The horses race going east over the old Indian Road, as it was called. We were several hours behind the time it should take to reach Master Robert's farm and Durfee knew that. Master Robert would not be pleased. The Irishman did not spare the horses, use his whip to urge up their speed. The storm had turn the sky charcoal and the thunder explode 'round us bringing lightning with it. I was angry as that sky. The faster the horses gallop, the harder Durfee whip them. The harder Durfee whip them, the angrier I got.

Because I remember now.

Remember all of it.

A tobacco-rolling woman from Angola, part of a crew passing through the county, stay on the Chandler place long enough to get a belly and give birth.

The crew move on.

She leave that baby behind.

A girl, Mary, on the Posten farm, a baby boy to put with the other baby boy she'd had the year before. Her womb wore out and she no more than fifteen years.

Thea on the Hayder place, fourteen and she had another belly now, so soon after the last child I helped her birth who died.

Jane. Little Jane. Twelve years old.

Thunder.

Rain falling hard and loud as bullets. The horses strain to get through Durfee's whip.

A little girl, not much past her first bleeding, dressed in boy's clothes, running. Alleyway close and dark. The sound of the devil's breath. Hands. Everywhere, hands, a wound too deep to heal. Terror. Shame. A belly too large for a girl so small. A baby too small, born too soon.

A white baby. They was all white babies.

Weather and storms passes west to east 'cross the land but it different in the sea. Everything different in the sea, 'specially the wind. The salties teach me that. This one blow in from the dark waters, the winds high and loud, screaming. The rain was hard and sharp like blades against my skin. Wind god howled, his voice bend the trees to breaking, fill Glady Creek till it pour over, cross the fields, and into the road near high in places as the horses' knees. I knew land storms of water, thunder, and light, with pebbles hitting the ground, little balls of ice, call hail. No matter how much it rain, or light the sky, they baby storms, violent and loud but just children.

This storm. It different. I knew its name, I had heard its voice before. It was mean, unforgiving, and secretive. It hid in the sun and the soft breezes that played along the tops of the waves. It curl around the clouds and kiss them, then with a sorcerer's breath prodded them to move, to change color, to rain spears on the heads of people. To destroy. I had no name from my parents' words to call this storm that grew out of the dark waters, stirring them until they rose high as the sky. Our home was too far in the land. But I had seen one, been with one. The *Martinet* cabin boy call it *furacão* in his Portugee words, Caesar called the winds, the breath of the gods. Marie Catherine's words came from three of the four directions of the world but after one of the dark-water storms passed over Caesar's Key, she glowered at it and called it in the words of her mother's mother *hotahlee.* And it was. The big wind of the gods.

It roar as it pass over us, sent water down in waves, the horses rear up and scream, Durfee had all he could do to keep them from bolting and us from being thrown out. And I, so angry that I could not see anything but his face, so angry that I did not care whether I drown in this water, so angry that I would fight the big wind's mother to have my way, I . . .

Durfee raised his hand to whip the bay again. It was raining and the leather was soaked through and slippery. I grab that whip from his hand and swing it across his face and chest instead.

Screaming in pain, he called me foul names in his Gaelic tongue, drop the reins and let the horses run, his arms raised as a shield, fighting me and fighting the wind and the rain that was moving side to side 'stead of down from the sky. And I call him foul names back using the words of my mother and my father, using my first words and every word I had learned since the before time and not caring if he thought me a witch.

I shove him, I kick him, I lash him with the whip, I scream at him. He say he will beat me, whip me, he say Master Robert will sell me — or hang me — when he find out. I tell him, "I don't care if you kill me! I-I don't care if he kill me! You a fiend, a devil!"

He fight me back but he stare at me and I

know he think I have sickness in my mind, that I have a demon, his, mine or the two, in my soul. I know he afraid of my words, those he can hear. And the big winds roar around us. I think they as angry as me.

"They were children!" I scream at him using the Anglais words. "Little girls, barely old enough to bleed, too young for . . ."

Durfee's eyes widen. He understand my words now.

"You taint them! What you do destroy them inside, their babies die, too. *Your* babies! They all your babies!"

The wind came from nowhere, pick up the wagon. The horses rear up and one of the linden trees crack open and fall in front of them. I remember Durfee yelling . . . or was that me? His mouth was open and then . . . he wasn't there anymore. I remember the feeling of my feet leaving the floorboard, my arms rising above my head, I was flying, through the walls of water, I was soaring in the air. I know I made a strange bird. Something hit me on the head.

James tell a story about the Christian Jesus. The Jesus wandering through a wasteland where there no food, no water, no living things. He have no home. He see things not there, hear voices that come from the air. The trickster play games with him, taunt him, then leave him there to die. I wander through a wasteland of green and water and birdsong. But the trickster play with me, too, make me think I hear Durfee's voice calling, then James's voice, then Jerie. Make me think I hear a panther's growl, a baby's cry. A choir of babies. I know who they are. They are ghost babies, all of the little ones fathered by that fiend Durfee on Mary, Thea, Jane, the Angolan woman, and who else? And . . . me. My little one was not from Durfee but she could have been.

I think the sun rise and set two times when I wander. I think I sleep. I listened for the panther and for the growl of the walking lizards who live near the water's edge. I cry each time I hear the babies' choir. And I wander until I reach a place familiar but quiet and sit on the edge of the dock, looking out over the cove and the mouth of Glady Creek and the barrier island that blocks my vision from the dark waters beyond. I have not eaten since two days or three. I think I light enough to float across.

"You don't have your pass, do you?"

I afraid to turn 'round, afraid that what I think is James's voice is really the trickster god come to taunt me again. But then I feel a hand on my shoulder and it warm and gentle and I know that it's real and it's James.

"No, sir, Master James," I answer. "I do not."

He carry me to the wagon, say I in no shape to walk, and take me back to White Maple Grove. Iris there, Elinor, too. I remember . . . they smile. Warm water across my body, my face, then I sleep, I think. They make me eat . . . bread? Drink tea? My hands scraped and sore, more from slapping at Durfee than the wandering I think but do not say. My feet got no soles left, it pain me to stand. It take a day or more for me to come back to myself, to remember where I am and what has been. I sit on the edge of the little bed with a bowl of chicken broth in one hand and a ladle in the other. James washing my feet like that Jesus do in one of Jeremiah's stories.

"H-how you all . . . come through the storm? The folks out on the back farm, anyone need tendin'?"

James stop his washing and look at me as if I have two heads.

"We fine, Maryam! It's you we worry about! You lost in the storm. For two near three days. You gone. Durfee stumble into camp out of his head, mumblin' then fall out. The rain move off by then and we all come runnin', Master Robert, Master Thomas yelling for us to hitch up the horses, me, Hewes, Jupiter, we look all over. No sight of you. We find the wagon broke up, good for nothin' but kindlin'. The horses bolt then head into the farm but they cut up so bad, one of 'em, Jeremiah afraid he have to put it down. And you nowhere. Mistress Robert crying herself sick 'cause Iris can't make the tea like she want. Mistress Patience red-faced and wailing like some fury, she lunge at Durfee, say he better find you. Say if he don't, she make Master Thomas send him away, back to a place call Ulster where he come from. Durfee say you a witch. Mistress Patience, and her just have a child, get up from that bed and smack him so hard Master Thomas step in."

I feel cold.

"Durfee —"

"He gone."

James stop his story to pass a cup to me. I stare at him. I cannot believe what he is saying.

"Drink, Maryam."

"But you find me," I say, near choking on the cool water.

James smiles.

"Yes I do. Said I would find you if I had

to walk 'cross this county and back. Look everywhere first then remember your little place where you like to sit and look out."

I feel the warm tears running down my face. My head is full. Of rememberings.

"James . . . the babies . . . Durfee . . . I . . ." I cannot say it. Cannot mention the little mound where she rests. Cannot find the words to tell the way Jane looked at me when her child was born then died. And the rest of those girls.

He closes his eyes and nods. He been on the Nash place long time, I wonder now if he knew what the Irishman was doing. James takes my hand.

"Don't fret Little Maryam," he says, his voice soft. "You here, you safe and not hurt. Eat the food Iris bring you, drink the water. Sleep. You will need your strength. There is going to be a wedding."

I see his face even though my eyes are full of tears. He is smiling.

"Mistress Patience say you can have whatever you want. Say that Murray's Corners acreage is ours to use, to build a cabin. And that we can marry when you heal up."

"You and me?"

James nods.

"Jeremiah . . ."

James touches my lips with his finger.

At the mention of that name, my stomach twitches.

"I will not hop over a broom."

James pulls me toward him and kisses me. "I know."

Later, back at the farm, I learn there was another storm. But it didn't have winds that turned up trees or blew over wagons. It didn't bring rain.

It was a storm named "James." And it rolled all over Jeremiah after he told James — proud like, so the people told me who heard it — that what happened to me was his god's vengeance because I was a devil heathen witch. The people said that James roared at Jeremiah with a voice that sounded like the wrath of many gods. Said he pushed him — hard — and would have struck him if not for the other men who were there. Said James told Jeremiah that he was going to join with me and be with me and give me children and that if Jeremiah's god didn't like that, there were other gods that did.

The reverend pulled himself together enough to beg James's pardon and offer to perform a ceremony. James said that he would ask me.

21
THE WEDDING

About 1781

I marry James Nash at midday on a Sunday on the banks of Glady Creek that was situated on the border between George Routt's lands and those of Thomas Nash. James wore a fine dark suit with a white shirt like the ones Jeremiah like, only his fit. Master Thomas give it to him. I wore a white dress that even the Mistresses Nash said was finer than anything they had seen in these parts. Artemis Kilpatrick (for that what she was calling herself) stitch it up for me special at James's request. I wish I had that dress now. It finer than anything I ever owned. Artemis was a fiend but she could sew.

The ceremony was more like a baptism and a prayer meeting than a wedding. Jeremiah took his time talking about this and that, I did not listen close to his words. I look only at James, think only of James. Jeremiah, he say this prayer, "Amen!" and that prayer, "Amen!" and walk up and down the bank so many times he wore a path through into the soft earth. Finally, he got down to it and said the words that made our joining proper. "Do you, James?" and "Do you, Maryam?"

And we both said, "We do."

There was food and dancing and laughter. That Iris! She must have cooked day and night! The rice and chicken, roast venison, corn bread rich like cake and a rabbit stew she call a "fricassee." Master Robert sent for a colored fiddle player from up Bedford way and he play and play, never seem to tire. There was near as many white people as colored, people from all over the county. It was my wedding day but I am a midwife and my calling never leave me. I checked on a few of the folks who'd been ailin', the little ones and babies new born. Mahala's and Nel's boys were fat and always hungry. Mistress Patience's little girl was thriving, too. And Jane . . .

I took her aside, away from the noise and any ears that might be nearby.

"The bleeding stopped, Miss Maryam," the girl said quietly. She would not raise her eyes. "I don't feel pain no more."

"Good. That the way of it. You feel cramp or tightenin', you send for me, hear?"

Jane nodded. Off to the side, I see her mother, Sadie, looking at us.

"Yes, ma'am." This time, she did look at me. Her expression broke my heart. There was no gods anywhere in this world or any other who could explain to me why a child this age should wear the face of a sad woman who had lived through too much in a world too old. "Thank you for what you done."

I will see little Jane's face for as long as I live and after. I have worn that face myself.

The celebrating went on past sundown. The banks of Glady Creek were glowing with moist air and fireflies. Storms had left the earth damp and the air thick. It was warm and the breeze was not strong enough to push through the trees. It was dusk. I saw the light-colored clothes of the people moving away toward the quarters, heard laughter and their voices, full of good feeling and whiskey. Tomorrow was a work day but for today, for now, there was celebration. James took my hand and we walked together, following the others, but silent. Being with each other was better than words.

Midway, James moved off the old cattle trail and headed toward the mouth of the creek where the fresh waters blended with the salt water of the sea.

"Where we going?"

"You'll see."

It was so dark that I could not see his face clear but I could tell that he was smiling. I knew the path we were on. It led to the little cove. There was a man standing at the water's edge, whose face was lit by the firelight. Jupiter.

He wore a white robe of woven cloth and held a gourd that even I knew was used only on sacred occasions by the elders of my people. The last time I saw such a thing was in the before time. I had not been permitted to stay for the festival's end, had been taken away by one of my sisters and sent to sleep. I had not known that Jupiter was a priest, had not known that he was from the place of my father's father's people. I bowed. James did the same.

"I am told by the gods to bless your union, to seal it by the ways of our people." Jupiter's voice was low and hoarse, rough as if his throat was injured. He spoke slow as if to pray over each word. It was the first time I heard him speak. Durfee had told me, away from Jupiter's hearing, that he had a falling fit, what the whites called "apoplexy," and that he could not speak. But it seemed that away from the white peoples' hearing, he could. It had served him to let them think that he could not. Now, with only me and James in his presence, he spoke in the words of my parents.

"What are you called by your father?"

I told him, noting James's surprise. Jupiter nodded.

"I ask the gods' blessing, Little Bird, for your union with this man, this James, and ask for their guidance as you live together, raise your children, and follow your calling."

To James he spoke using the words of the Anglais. To me, he spoke with the words that I had heard from my first days.

He told James to honor and respect me, to support my calling as a midwife, to guide our children along the paths of our ancestors, his and mine, so far away across the Atlantic waters.

To me, he said, "You are far away from your people, Little Bird, as am I. As are all of us. We . . . you will form a new people in this place . . . with these people whose ancestors came also across the waters long ago but who have forgotten . . . whose memories of that place and of their voices grow dim. You must remember even as many will forget. You must pass on the words, the stories, the names, so that our ancestors will not wander alone. That memory of them will carry them forward. Do you understand?"

"Yes."

He turned to James and said the same in the Anglais that James knew. And James said yes, also.

Jupiter nodded and said that it was good and blessed us and asked the ancestors, those in this place, this Virginia, and those across the dark waters, to watch over us and guide us.

Before we left the cove, in the very late hours of night when the stars had come to light the sky, Jupiter touched me lightly on the arm and asked to speak with me. James nodded and said that he would wait down the cove a way by a blue-bottomed boat beached in the rushes.

"I won't talk much again," Jupiter said, his voice sounding more hoarse than before.

"Uncle, may I help you?" I asked him. "I can brew a tea that will soothe your throat."

He shook his head slowly.

"Thank you, no, Maryam. Soon I leave this place," Jupiter said. "Tomorrow I may be far away. It please me to see you, to hear your words, watch you heal and make our babies strong. You are a treasure, Little Bird . . . The gods will bless you and the ancestors, they will watch."

I could only nod. I took my leave of Jupiter, walked along the water's edge toward the blue boat where James was waiting, turned to look back and wave at the old man but he was gone and the fire was out.

. . . the ancestors, they will watch . . .

22
JAMES'S WIFE

The cabin — I don't call it *our* cabin or *my* cabin, 'cause nothing in this place belong to us. In this English-king land we do not even belong to ourselves. I know this. James know this. But he like to say "our place," "our land," as if this little strip of grass back of the camp writ up on paper and filed at the courthouse in Franklin. It is not. But James like to think it so.

In the days after the big windstorms, the Brothers Nash raised up a crew of men from all their places and Owen McKay's and cleared the trees from the western edge of Murray's Corners, then raised up a two-room cabin on the spot, built it up in not much over a week, sealed up good against rain, and my James laid a roof that could hold against the next *furacão.* They used the hardwood from an old forest in the foothills to make a floor — no dirt floor for James — and he barter with Albert, a free man who hire out from Georg Routt, so there real glass in the windows. Albert scratch his mark in the corner, say the pane a wedding gift.

Iris, Elinor, and Rhoda carried over armloads of quilts, "To make your bed soft" Elinor whispered, giving me a hug. And a feather pillow. She would not say where she got that. And a little stool.

"For you to rest your feet on after a day . . ." She did not have to say a long day. All our days was long.

We walk back to the Robert Nash farm through the camp and west. The cabin stand there at the edge of the clearing, lamplight glow pouring through the windows. The women been here before us. Water in the jug, sweet-smelling grasses spread over the hearth — it too warm for a fire. Bread, cheese set out on the table, covered with a fancy tea towel. Iris "borrow" it from Mistress Robert I know. And the bed made up tidy, white sheet gleaming in the light, Iris quilt, one of her special ones, its colors 'mind me of the birds in the before time, folded and laid across the bed. All to welcome us to rest, to sleep. Or not.

James close the door behind us. When he turn the key, the door give a *tick* sound like one strike of a clock. No slave cabin s'pose

291

to have a lock but James make his own arrangement with Albert to fix up one and he
do. Neither Master Robert nor George
Routt have to know.

He turn around, wipe his palms 'cross his
thighs, and look at me. And my stomach
turning circles. It not like I have not been
with a man before. I have. Not like I do not
know what to do. I have done this . . . we
both have done this before.

But not with each other.

And now we are alone in a place that is
ours to use and no one will meddle with us,
least not until just after sunrise when the
work horn blow.

Still we stand there, together, alone, in the
quiet and look at each other. It as if I see
him for the first time. James tall with skin
the color of my people, the sharp ridge and
flared nostrils of the Igbo and strong hands
— I am fascinated by his hands — that can
hold and lift and pull tremendous weights
yet stroke my cheek with the lightest touch.
When he smile at me, I feel warm, everywhere, and in every way. His gaze does not
study me or pierce me, it do not pull me to
him. Yet I know when he there even if I
don't hear him, even if he don't speak.

It will be different with a man you love.

When Marie Catherine say that to me

292

long ago I did not believe it. I do now forever.

I can tell that I loved James, tell of our cabin, of his hands that could form anything, patch up anything, that he could calm a horse, dig a well, make a barrel as fine as any cooper. I can tell that James, he catch deer and rabbit, that he have only to touch the ground and whatever plants there will grow. That he have the singing voice to soothe the babies. And me. But when it come to talk about James close, about how we are together. How we touch . . . I cannot tell. My throat tight, my mouth dry. My eyes fill with tears. I say nothing. My children think my quiet mean I forget.

But you don't forget tenderness, the softness of his skin, his shoulder so warm against my palm. His back, the muscles strong and firm, his long legs wrapped around mine . . . He tickles my belly with the tip of his tongue. Gentleness. Is it possible to forget a man so strong and yet gentle?

He take my hand in his and raise it to his lips, kiss my palm. Kiss my lips. Kiss the warmest part of my body until I forget to let out my breath. And when he parts my legs, I am not afraid.

I am not a girl, I have walked this path.

James will not hurt me. His breath against my neck will not take me to a dark place of pain, terror, shame, or past understanding. Because it is James, and I love him. And he love and treasure me.

When the mornings come, we unwrap ourselves and go our separate ways. On paper, James's labor own by Thomas Nash, mine owned by Robert Nash. He work under Master Thomas's direction, I go where Master Robert or the new overseer, Wilkins, tell me. Sometime we don't see each other for days. Master Thomas hire out James to Richmond or Norfolk or west to Bedford. I go where the babies are or where people ailin'. But it don't matter. When we see each other, we are with each other.

Gilchrist Wilkins, the new overseer, cut from different cloth than Durfee. Short, stocky, redheaded, and ugly, he was transported to the colonies from Scotland and still owe two years labor to a Master Williams down in Suffolk. In a way, he speak like Durfee but not, he from a place he call Cardeness. He make the Jesus sign, too, as Durfee did, and say, "Jesus, Mary, and Joseph!" when he vexed about something. But he don't mess with none of the women and he work in the fields 'longside us 'stead of on a horse, looking down. It hard to figure his words and what he say sometimes, but he never say them in meanness or loud. He like James and he like me and he try to get along with all the people, say he not more than they are. We know he mean well but he not like us. Two years, he his own man. Two years, twenty years. We do not belong to ourselves.

And this the thing that roll over and over in my mind. This not belonging to myself. I want a baby so bad it hurt. Every time James and I are together, I send a prayer to the mother of the sky god, the only goddess name I can remember my mother calling to when she was giving birth. I want to hold a child of my own in my arms, feel its little head against my breast, kiss and cuddle a little boy with James's nose and my pointy-like chin. It been more than twelve years since the little angel I bore took her first and last breaths. So I wonder now if I can even get a child. And if I do . . . whose child will it be? Mine and James? Or Master Robert's?

But I want a baby. So badly I want a baby. That I do not chew the weed that stops bleeding. I do not drink the tea that I make for others. I think about everything bad that can happen to a child born into this slavery and then I joyfully open my legs for my husband and sigh in delight when he enters me and think how wonderful it will be to have a child at my breast.

And it is wonderful.

Eli is born nine months to the day after I lay with his father. He sends me into a labor that lasts two days — time enough for me to deliver Artemis's child, too (her third for Donovan Kilpatrick) — and then walk home, lie down on my own bed, and push him out. He eats as if he is hollow. His father is so proud of him that he cannot stop grinning. And two years after that, my little Shadrach come, so quick-like that I barely have the moment to squat. No babies after. But I am content. My boys grow strong, tall, and smart like their father. They learn quick. Eli calm the horses and the dogs like a magician and James send him to Jeremiah to train up as a hostler. Shadrach like his father, he can take anything and turn it into a tool, a machine, a beautiful carving. He good with his hands. And both my boys are learning to read and to write. It against the law of this Virginia, it against the law of the Brothers Nash, but still we send them to a secret place where a free colored woman teach at night. That where Artemis take her children to learn.

Time go by most fast when it seem like it go slow, creep like an old turtle. It pass so slow when you hardly notice the days passing, the seasons, a storm so bad you think you will remember it all your life then a dry spell come, one of the worst the farmers say, and you forget. A contagion push through one rainy spring, make everybody sick, even me, and kill all the babies in the womb before I can stop it. Old Man Routt pass on and so does Master George. One of Iris's little ones. Sadie. Bad summer. Then time, it move on and I forget 'cause life, it move on, too. Mistress Janet McKay get a swelling in her belly that she think is a baby even at her age though her monthlies finished. I think she wish for a baby so hard that her belly pretend to give her one. It can happen but not this time. Something growing but not a baby. McKay he call the old doctor from Franklin way, don't like what he say so then he call a new young doctor down from Norfolk. He say the same thing I say and Mistress die. They bury her in the family crypt and Master Owen, who never seem to care much for his wife, grieve like one of them stone monuments in the yard. Then he shut himself up in his house and drink.

Iris's Abednego grow up and get a woman

and a baby but they sold away to Pittsylvania County. Master Robert sell him there, too. Elizabeth Rose Nash grow like a dandelion weed and become the most spoiled child ever lived because she the last child but at least she not mean. And my boys, my Eli and Shadrach grow up tall and strong, my James, we all live quiet-like in our little cabin on the sliver of land that Masters Robert and Thomas own and we work hard, and save whatever coin we can get and think about ways to belong to ourselves.

A war came and went and there was much talk about independence and no taxes without having a say. The English white men marched in red coats. The other men marched in any coat they could find. And they all, when their numbers were low, talked about putting sticks, pitchforks, and muskets in the hands of black men to help them with their causes. James went to a gathering in the middle of the night where some of the king's men spoke to sign up colored men to fight. They promise food and wages. They promise land and bounty. And they promise freedom; at least the king's men do. The Virginia militia want help from black men but that all they want. James say he think about it. I say leave it alone, it's white man's mess.

And it was. Black men who help the king's men, some got to go to his country, others got sent to a place north where it cold. And the rest stay like they are and belong to others not themselves. So much for freedom.

I think about Abraham's cow. Abraham a free man, got him a two-room cabin and a wife, and a boy. He got him a hound and a space of green to plant crops. The Virginia soldiers they talk with him about the good things come when they defeat the king's men. So Abraham sign over his cow. The soldiers come, the battle go. Abraham get no coin. And no cow.

23
FOREKNOWER

I loved the little cove off Glady Creek at Newton's Mill but I hated it. I loved that the trees were green and fragrant, the grasses in the marsh swayed in the breezes, and the sun was warm and comforting. The birdcalls woke me in the morning and there was a little yellow bird that I liked to watch, the people call it a "goldfinch." When they was small, I'd take Eli and Shadrach with me when I was foraging. We'd watch them, the goldfinch birds, flit from branch to branch, tree to tree, as like children playing. Eli was learning to count and I was teaching him in his father's English words and my words. "One yellow bird, two yellow bird . . ."

The morning mists covered the water lands then disappeared like magic as the sun rose. At night, if it was cool, the crickets chirped and hummed. If it was summer, the cicadas buzzed in the choking heat, and the toads croaked and belched. Flying beetles with yellow bellies lit up the land like clusters of flowers that bloom in the night.

But I hated Newton's Mill, too, more than any place I had lived since Caesar's Key, because it *was* close to the water, because I could see the little island and beyond. It 'minded me of the places where the white-sailed ships docked in Ouidah, in Savannah. The salt-thick air clogged my lungs, brought back the counting of days I had been away and thoughts of my parents, my sisters, Jerie, of all that I had lost to the dark waters. The low country near the mill was beautiful, green, and restful. I listen to the waterbirds call to each other, sing love songs as they fly past. But their songs also make me cry.

I got up in a crying mood that morning, carrying the mist and the water-heavy air with me as I walked toward the main house. I'd risen with the sun, helped Albert, Hewes, Yellow Annie, and the others with the corn, gathered eggs, and helped the other Annie catch a chicken for Iris's dinner pot, then got Mistress Martha's leave to forage for herbs and greens I would need for my medicines. That woman was always worryin' about this or that, heart flutterin's, headache or the vapors, her sour stomach. Martha

Nash was nothing but a basket of nerves, always sure she was dying of something. Her mind wouldn't rest just kept spinnin' 'round. I told her, "We all of us dyin' just a matter of when." Nothing I did would soothe for long so her digestion was in a confusion and her bowels were even worse. She claimed that the sassafras and mint teas I made eased her suffering and that the berry compote helped her bowels to move. So I spent the afternoon picking berries, pulling up watercress greens, and digging oysters. I prowled along the water's edge, using some of the shells I found as tools, rinsing them careful and returning them to the waters when I had finished. My back gave me a twist and I stood up, rubbing it until it eased, thinking how much I missed my "helpers," my boys, who were better at crouching down than I was most days. My back was getting to be a misery but I didn't wonder at that. Was getting on forty years now by my reckoning. I was old.

It was just me today. Nash had sent James, Eli, and Shadrach and some of the other men to a farm just over the county line, to help bring in the corn from a section of acreage he owned there. They had been gone a whole day and night and I missed them, the boys' laughter and games, James's warm hand on my back. Yet I admit it was pleasant to be on my own, listen to my thoughts against the birdsong and the snapping of the dying fire at night.

"You like a spider, Maryam," Annie teased me. "Settin' up in your web just happy to be there."

I grinned at her and wiggled my fingers like a spider's legs, bringing them close to her face.

"Until I catch me a fly!" I teased her back.

So it was I had a quiet day and would have a quiet night, too, with Master Nash and most of the men gone, Mistress in her room tending to her nerves. I'd give her tea to soothe her, now it was up to Iris to look after her.

Iris held the little packet I'd prepared up to the light and shook it gently.

"If she ask for more?"

I shook my head slowly.

"That what she should have. More'n that, her bowels do nothing but move. That another misery. She get restless, brew the chamomile, that help her sleep." Half of what Mistress thought was worryin' her was a gnat's sneeze.

Iris nodded. She placed the packet on the shelf next to the jars of tomatoes and pickles she'd put up. She pushed back the curtain with her hand and peeked out the window.

"You bes' git on, Maryam, it getting dark. Mosquitoes bad after that las' rain, you don't go now, they'll eat you up. You need another light?" She gestured toward a low-burning lantern on the table.

"No, I know my way, even with my eyes closed. I see you in the morning."

And I did know the way. Sometimes it amazed me that I had been here long enough to call every plant and animal, to know the people on all Nash's farms and the ones around us, black, white, and other. I had tended to folks or delivered babies on near every farm and plantation between here and Lynchburg. I had been joined with James here, given birth to my sons in this place. There were some days that I forgot I was "country born" and not from here. Other days, that notion worried at me. Since two, three years, I had met few who had taken the journey across the dark waters as I had. Seem like every colored person I met was born here, in this America, and some of them had the markings and colors of the white people, like Yellow Annie with her freckles and sand-colored hair. On nights like this one, as I walked, alone, down the dirt path between the main house and the quarters to Murray's Corner, I wondered what had happened to the rest of us, and to the few faces 'sides James and my sons who had meant anything to me in this place. Where was Caesar? What happened to Marie Catherine; did she get to New Orleans to live with her children? James didn't like it when I started turning my mind over like this, said it didn't do to live in the past. That I had to . . . let go of the sadness because it worried the boys. Mostly, it worried him.

"Momma, what you cryin' for?" Eli asked, wiping the tears from my cheeks.

James and I locked eyes and he smiled then pulled a hair in Eli's head. Eli yelped.

"Ow! Papa! Stop!"

And then that rumble of laughter that came from deep in James's chest, the sound that I loved.

"Oh, your momma, she's a mysterious one. With her notions and potions and her African ways." I shake my head at him. And his eyes soften. He knew. "She just thinking of her home, boy, that's all."

Eli's face would twist up with the question.

"But this our home."

My before-here home, I said to myself, thinking that my sons could not think of a place, a home besides this cabin on the Nash farm. Their mother could have a home

305

before here.

I could never be near the waters off Newton's Mill without a catch in my throat, wondering . . . how far away was it? How many risings of the sun? I had tried to count them when I was on the boat but despair and the darkness confused my counting. Where was it that Jerie was thrown over the side? Did her body float home? And her spirit . . . The sadness came over me, and for days I would say nothing or close to nothing. James tried to understand but it was hard for him. He was born in Georgia, his mother and father in Virginia. And the boys as they grew tried to understand but they, too, were from here, had been born here. I taught them my words, the words of the Edo, but their first words were the English, the words of their father and of the other people here. My words were strange to them, the sounds funny to their ears and hard to form in their mouths. And as time went on and they grew older, it became harder for me to explain what it meant . . . to be from somewhere else. A place so far away that it had no one name. Days like this felt like a heavy blanket fall on my head, covering me and leaving me in darkness. Days like this I felt like I was alone. People all 'round me. But I by myself.

I walked back to the cabin that evening, tired, feeling a little sad, rolling these thoughts over in my head. It was getting dark but still light enough to see my way and light enough to see that the door to the cabin was ajar.

At first, when Nash give me and James the cabin in Murray's Corners, I was not certain that I liked it. It was a little ways from everyone else. And when the babies came 'long, I wondered why my boys had to walk so far. But as the days and years went by, I came to think it a good thing to be more out of sight. It made me feel more free to be myself and do what I had to do.

Behind my back and out of James's hearing, I knew that Nash call me an African witch. He wasn't foolish enough to believe that I rode a broomstick or some other nonsense like the white witches that folks talked about, but he thought it best I live as far away from the main house and from him as possible. Guess he thought distance made it hard to cast a hex. And so when I came toward the end of the row, there was no one but me to see that open door.

I set my basket to the side, pulled my knife from my apron pocket, and pushed the door open slow in case the hinge squeak. Sometimes there were vagrants in the fields, trekking from here to there, and they might set for a bit under the oak tree nearby, catch their rest. They harmless. Other times, it was a child from another farm, sometimes colored, sometimes not, lost its way or run away, and these I would send or take along home. This time was different. The air was shimmering-like around me, moving, and there was a cool breeze. My shoulders rose without my knowing why.

"Who are you, what you want?" I held the lamp up toward the corner of the cabin. The flame flickered wildly but the light didn't reach the farthest wall. A long dark form, frozen into stillness, had pressed itself to the wall next to the hearth and two eyes glowed in the reflection of the lamp. For a breath's time, I was afraid, reminded of stories my brothers told to frighten me, stories about demons that could catch me in the forest and eat me. But I no longer believed in that kind of demon. Whatever this was, it lived and breathed and walked on two legs.

"I mean no harm, Sister. I ask for water and food only." The voice was rough and low, a growling whisper of a sound.

"Where you from?" I asked him in the few words I knew of his language.

"You speak my words."

"I ask."

"I escape . . . from ship grounded in the marshes south of here, place call Owl Creek."

I stopped. Even I had heard the story of Owl Creek. It had spread north up the coast to Virginia and west through Georgia like a contagion, it spread through the quarters faster than that, scairt Nash and the other planters 'round here more than any nonsense about the king's armies returning or raids by the Tuscaroara. I looked over my shoulder but the road was empty, only the flicker of candle lights twinkling through the curtains in some of the other cabins 'round the bend beyond. I walked quickly inside and closed the door. Then I held the lamp high and turned it toward the corner where the man stood trembling in the cool evening air. What little bit of clothes he had on were near shreds and filthy, his arms and legs was striped with scratches and sores. One of his legs was dripping blood. His face was long, gaunt, his eyes sunken, and he was marked on both cheeks. I recognized the markings. Igbo.

"You speak my words," he repeated. Slowly, painfully, he unfolded himself and stood up full. He was tall and strongly built despite his injury.

"Some." I set my basket and the lamp on the table and stared at him. "The slaver ran aground months ago," I said slowly, my mind struggling to find the right words. *Long way from here.* "Where you been?" I poured water into a cup and passed it to him. He took it with both hands and gulped it down, nearly choking. He nodded his thanks. I refilled the cup.

"Lost, wandering. In the marsh."

The hissing growl-like rumble of his voice made my skin crawl.

"That a long time to wander. Are there others who . . . others . . . like you?" The marsh was way south of the Dismal Swamp. It was beautiful and lush when the waters from the sound came in. But treacherous in the cold times when the waters rose and dangerous even in the best of weather. There were snakes in those waters, large cats that prowled at night, and, in some places, *el lagarto,* the huge walking lizards that the white people called "alligators," roamed the shores.

"There were," he said, draining the cup again. "But I do not see them now. I do not know where they have gone." There was despair in his voice. He picked up the bread that I had cut for him and held it in his hands, an expression of wonder on his face.

I chuckled and sat down.

"You ne'er seen bread b'fore?"

He look at me then look back at the bread, his fingers wrapping around the crust as if he expect it to float away.

"It . . . been awhile."

I nod. I know what it is to go without food for a long time then eat. On the slaver, we went without food for so long that when we finally were given something real to eat, our stomachs could not hold it. It was as if our bodies had learned to live without nourishment even though the starvation was killing us.

"What they call you?"

"Kalu."

I took clean linens from my pack and poured out water into a bowl.

"My name Maryam. You need tending." I set the lamp on the floor next to him and knelt down to study the gash on his leg. In the light, it was red swollen and looked as if it had already turned rotten. He groaned when I touched it. Warm.

"Tell me . . . about what happen," I said, as I dipped the cloths in the water and began to clean his leg. I knew that it pained him but hoped that by getting him to talk, I could move his thoughts away from his suffering. And move mine toward what to do

311

with him. I could not hide a runaway in the cabin, even if I wanted to. It was dangerous. If I was caught, it could get me and him strung up. There was much to do. James and the boys were due back in the morning. Children cannot keep secrets. And Nash's hounds had good noses and the run of the place. Wouldn't take them no time to come to my door, sniffing out a new scent, braying at the top of their throats to announce their catch.

At the same time, Kalu was starving and poorly. How he had survived the marshes up to then was a mystery. But with this leg, he wouldn't survive them again. I set water over the fire and banked it up, then grabbed some willow bark. If I could cut his fever down, might be a chance. It was total dark now. Good. Whatever needed doing, I would do. Just had to do it before the sun come again.

The tall boat was from a place called "El Elmina" which I had heard of from others country-born. Its name was the *Citadel* and its captain was a man named Farr. The slaver left the country with over one hundred people in its hold, bound for a place near Savannah. The people had already been paid for by a trader there. Most slavers have a cargo of people from different nations, of different languages, like the *Martinet*. The people in the *Citadel*'s hold were of the Igbo and among then was a chief. In this America, the Igbo have a reputation for revolt.

"You are not of this place," Kalu said to me, wincing when the cloth touched his skin as I tried, gently as I could, to clean away the mud and filth from his leg. I kept my expression calm; the cleaner his wound became, the more I saw that it was beyond my skill to help him.

I shook my head.

"I am of the Edo."

"Ah," he said. He smiled slightly. "Our people were sometime enemies."

"It mean nothing now," I said.

As the ship got close to shore, some of the Igbo men mistook the Low Country coastline for their homeland coast and, elated that they were near, convened and decided to take the ship. Despite their chains and leg irons, they overtook the crew. The boat went aground on a small barrier island, the Igbo waded ashore, celebrating and singing, believing that they had returned home. But as the local citizens, hearing of the ship's distress, came out of the forests to help, the Igbo realized that they were not home.

"I was in water up to my middle," he said touching his waist with his hand, his strange whispery voice hoarse from his travails and from the fever. "But I did not care. I knew that I was home and that Chukwu would protect me. But I was wrong. We were in . . . this place. And the white people were at the shore to buy us, not to help us.

"Chief called out to us, 'It is time! We will walk home across the waters!' "

I held my breath when he spoke those words. I had heard them before from others who whispered the story across the miles. The Igbo, chained together and singing, walked into the waters and drowned.

"My people called out to Chukwu to protect us." Kalu closed his eyes and sank into the back of the chair. He was exhausted. " 'The waters brought us, the waters will take us away. The waters brought us, the waters will take us away . . .' "

"You . . . walk into the water . . ." The words froze on my lips.

He nodded. The air around us shimmered.

"I thought to wake up away from this place. But I am still here." He opened his eyes, and even in the dim light, I saw his pain and confusion. He had wanted to go home or to die. But he was not home.

I made him drink more of the tea that I

had brewed to cool him and cut the pain. He fell asleep sitting up against the wall, though I tried to persuade him to rest on Shadrach's cot. I covered him with a quilt, banked the fire again, and settled myself in the chair. I would wake before the sun. A midwife learns the art of sleeping in whatever position or place she finds herself, standing up, lying on the floor, or sitting in a hard-backed chair. I closed my eyes and dreamed of waterbirds calling to each other, of toads bellowing in the darkness, and of Igbo people singing as they walked across the shimmering waters.

The waters brought us, the waters will take us away.

"Momma! Momma!" Eli's and Shadrach's voices hit my ears like the screeches of a hawk. I hadn't meant to sleep so soundly. I had not meant to sleep at all, just nap like a cat in the sun. Dazed, I felt my heart thump in my chest and I stood up so fast that the room spun around.

What was I going to do about the Igbo man?

My sons gave me no time to figure it out.

"Momma! We did —" Eli slammed into me, chattering so fast, wrapping his skinny arms around my waist. "Papa says —"

"Shadrach fell in the —"

"No, I didn't!" This from Shadrach, who grabbed me, too, burying his head into my chest. That boy was getting tall.

"Maryam, I missed you." James's voice bubbled through his laughter. "And so did my very naughty sons."

I was in a panic. Kalu lying in the corner, a strange man in the cabin, my sons there, what would they think? Worse, what would they say? And then James . . .

Before I could explain the man wearing the bundle of rags sleeping in the corner, James swept me into his arms and gave me a kiss on the forehead.

"My beautiful wife, we are returned and find you sleeping in like Mistress Nash!" he teased me, turning his head to look around the room. "The fire is out, no water drawn . . . What have you been doing?"

The words and breath caught in my throat. How to explain . . . I turned toward the hearth on the back wall and the breath left my mouth in a rush. There was no one there. I jerked my glance toward the opposite corner. Nothing. No person, no rags, no . . . The blanket I had covered him with was folded neatly on the chair. The cup that he had used for water sat on the table, dry inside, next to the slice of bread that he had held in his hands and not eaten.

"Maryam? What is it?" My husband's brow furrowed with concern. "Are you sick?"

"No, I . . ." My mind traveled across the past few hours, when I had bathed the man's leg, poured two cups of water for him, and cut a thick slice from the loaf of bread that now sat, covered with a towel, in the middle of the table. He had left without waking me. I was a light sleeper, my craft demanded that. I would have heard him get to his feet. And the door . . . Gently pushing James aside, I ran to the door and opened it slowly. It squeaked.

James chuckled.

"Ah, yes, my wife. You remind me. I must oil that door. Maryam? Maryam, what is the matter?"

There was talk. Some of the Igbo survived the walk on the water, were dragged to shore and sold. Others ran away but were caught and hanged, their heads displayed on stakes as a warning. There was also talk that some of the Igbo who drowned still walk there, the sound of chains scare the fish; their song terrify anyone who walk that way late. But Owl Creek a long way from here. Yet I had entertained a lost Igbo who was looking for a way home, across the fields, across the marsh, across the dark waters.

The same chill that covered me when I approached the cabin last night came over me again. I took in a long breath but an unease prevented me from releasing it. Had I given shelter to an angel unawares, as James's Bible story said? Or was I visited by a ghost? Did the seeing make me blessed? Or cursed?

On the fifteenth day of September, the year of their lord 'round 1794, Robert Murray Nash's tobacco crop burned and his creditors called in his loans. Mistress Nash sold her silver plate and the small acreage left her by her older brother to save the family home but it wasn't enough. To make up the difference, Robert Nash sold the equivalent of five thousand dollars in people: two women, four men, and three boys, including my husband, James, and my sons, Eli and Shadrach. They were carried over to Nash's acreage in Pittsylvania County to work one morning and from there were loaded into wagons for the trip to the slave auction in Danville. I knew it in my bones when I saw Nash returning that evening with an empty wagon.

Just after dawn the next day, singing the song of the Igbo, I walk into the waters of Glady Creek off Newton's Mill.

■ ■ ■ ■

PART III
WISE WOMAN

■ ■ ■ ■

24
TOMORROW

Was Iris who found me. She come looking when I did not bring the ground leaves for Mistress's morning tea, thought I might be foraging along the banks of Glady Creek. Said that seeing me laid out near beneath the waters gave her three kinds of fright. I'm not a large woman but it took all her effort, Hewes and Wilkins, both good-size men, to pull me from the marsh waters. Iris say that was some work for them, my clothes tried to pull me back under; they were heavy with water. I think but do not say that it wasn't my wet clothes that held me, that it was the Igbo walkers reaching up to grab my hands, wanting me to join them on their journey home.

I coughed up the water and the weeds and mud, slept for days, came to myself after a time or so Iris told me. I don't remember the green stalks of weeds wrapping around my arms and legs, the egrets picking at the insects floating along the top of the water. I don't remember Wilkins's strong arms grabbing my waist so hard that there were marks below my ribs. I remember only standing on the shore, looking out past the sound, past the barrier island toward the Atlantic, the Igbo song filling my ears, my feet wet, my shoes floating away. Wondering what else I got to lose to this place.

"Maryam, you must eat."

How long had she been standing there? I shook my head.

Iris took a breath, her lips pressed together.

"You have not taken bread for three days and no water enough to make any," she said, her voice stern. Her lips curled upward slightly. "And Mistress is 'bout to whine 'cause she out of her tea, the one that keeps her insides runnin'. She say I don' make it right. Maryam."

I looked at her.

"You got to come back to us now. Got to."

I knew what she thought, what everyone thought. I had died and now I was not dead. But I was not the same Maryam. I would never be the same Maryam. I stared at Iris and her face transformed, growing thinner and browner with large dark eyes and a beautiful mouth. The Fulani woman who had brought me water to drink on the slaver after my sister died, after the Portuguese sailors threw her bones into the sea and I died, too.

We thought you were gone away.

I had become another someone else after Jerie died. And now I was becoming someone else again. Iris knew it, too. I could see it in her eyes.

Fear.

From that day, everyone on the Nash farm and everywhere else treated me like the witch they'd always whispered I was. I was a walking ghost. Mistress Nash's ailments came back full force. It took me a while to know that she had poured out my teas and medicines because she was afraid. There was a baby coming on the Kilpatrick farm, two in the quarters on one of the big cotton plantations to the south. The overseers called other midwives to help with the birthings. No one wanted a ghost or a witch to deliver their children.

How could I have been the same woman? My husband was gone. My children, two boys, gone. I did not know where — "South of here" was all that Wilkins could tell me; even he did not know. South of here were Alabama, Louisiana, and Mississippi. South of here were miles of cotton fields in middle

Georgia, shimmering white in the late-summer sun, and ugly tough fields of sugarcane, tearing and ripping into dark flesh as it was cut. No, I was not the same. And would not be again.

In time, I recovered, came back to myself as Iris said. In time, Mistress Martha stop pouring out her teas, the people sent for me again to tend their laboring women, to their ailments, and sit with the dying. But there were still whispers about me being not right in the head. And about the other thing.

Near dusk one evening, I was hailed by another Igbo hiding in the trees near my cabin, a woman. She was cold and she was hungry and she had scrapes that needed tending. She run away from a master in North Carolina, one who had beat her and threatened her for years, and she figured she might as well be killed free as killed slave. She'd heard of a pathway, some kind of road that would take colored people north into Canada, a cold place where there was no slavery.

I listened to her speak, remembering the Igbo words that Kalu . . . the ghost had spoken. I watched her careful to drink the water, and she ate two slices of bread. I told her that she had to be gone by sunup and she agreed.

"Come with me, Sister," she said, her eyes brimming with intelligence, boring into mine. "We go free together. What you got here to stay?"

I had no answer. All I had now was my name that no one knew and my life, just what I had when I stepped on the *Martinet*. I did not even need a cotton sack to carry those with me.

What else could they do to me? I had been beaten, sold twice before I was twenty, lost one baby to death and two to slavery down cotton way. My man was gone, too. All was left was to kill me.

She left before sunrise, slipping out of the cabin like a cat. I slept on. The door did not squeak, because James had oiled it months before.

A few weeks later, a man and boy stopped through; one month after that, it was a woman and son — the woman was of the Mende, whose words I did not know. So many people strolling away that the land-owners formed a band of deputies to find them.

Owen McKay and the others sent their hounds loose 'cross Newton's Mill whenever there was a runaway. Those dogs tore through the fields and gardens, stood on their hind legs and tried to take doors down;

a pair of 'em ran through Lula's cabin, knocking over the chairs and table, breaking dishes, chewing up the bedding and clothes. Scairt Lula's Sallie near to death. The child was only four. They plowed through the quarters, galloping like wild horses, didn't care whose ownings they destroyed. Mistress Nash's roses and her what-she-called it, "English" garden fell under their paws' destruction. Martha Nash was put out by it all. "Chase down the niggers," she shout at McKay, "but don't tear up my rose garden!"

But the hounds didn't come near my cabin. Walked a wide circle 'round but didn't come close, dropped their big heads, whined, then moved on. Their handlers couldn't drag them through the door. Nash told whoever would listen that it was because I was a witch and had cast a spell on my place. With James and my boys gone, I didn't care if he thought I was a witch or not. I knew that it was not a hex or evil spirit turned those hounds away.

Marie Catherine's kitchen was a wonder to me but I learn after my first visit, real quick-like that you did not assume what she was cooking was to eat.

"*Non! N'est pas mangez!* Don't touch that!" How many times did I hear that warning in Creole French, English, and Portuguese?

"So what is it?" A question I must have asked her as many times as stars in the sky.

Her lessons still serve me.

"*Attencion.* Do not ask what it is, *ma petite* Marie, ask what it does." And Marie would tell me the purpose of whatever tea, potion, or balm she prepared, how to make it, warning me to measure correctly and what dosage to use for man, woman, child, or animal. "There is a purpose for almost everything, each plant, dirt, what you call *le weeds,*" she taught me. Even to turn back a hound from tracking a scent.

But I could not figure how she knew this or why she needed to. Marie Catherine had been born free in Haiti, her father and her grandfather were French and white. She looked near white herself with her straight, light brown hair, visible only when she unwrapped the white turban from her head, sharp features, and ebony-dark eyes. When I spoke that observation, the warmth pouring from her dark eyes toward me cooled, making the pupils of her eyes black like obsidian.

"Maman taught me a good lesson about *les blanches,*" she said, her voice low with strong emotion. "As far as *les blanches* think, as far as they see, I am a colored woman. I am black enough. To be . . .

327

handled. To be . . . bought and sold. *Et maintenant . . .*"

Marie explained that she had been taught her art by her mother, who had been taught by her mother, a wise woman of the Dahomians, a worshiper of the loa Legba, who was captured in a Portuguese raid. When she reached Haiti and then Jamaica, she and others ran away to the mountains and formed their own community, without the white men, living in their own world. I had a short visit near the Jamaica but even I had heard of the fierce Maroons living beyond the mists of the mountains.

"The plantation owners planned raids on us," Marie Catherine said, "when I was *très jeune,* very small. They assaulted us with guns and with dogs." She chuckled, her eyes glazed over slightly as they reviewed the memory. "When they could find us, and that was not often, *les chiens,* they seem uninclined to track us!"

Dried red pepper, rotting meat, and the thick sappy mucous squeezed from the glands of a land rodent, a groundhog, possum, or skunk, worked the best. Mix all these together and heat. Caesar removed himself from Marie's presence when she cooked up a batch. The stench could turn the stomach of an elephant.

"Best to make this in the open away from the cabins," she told me, a mischievous smile on her lips. "Or in a cave where no one see you."

"Or smell you!" I managed to gasp out before dashing out of the room, my stomach whirling. Marie laughed — a musical sound like the tinkling of bells.

"*C'est ça*! It will make the dogs cry," she said, calling after me. "Don't use much. Just a drop every foot or so around your cabin or the opening that you want to protect. And if you are running yourself, my Maryam? *Eh bien*. A few drops smeared" — she demonstrated, placing her hand across her heart. "*Comme ça*. That enough to turn around hound and horse."

And so, when they came looking for the Igbo woman, and the man and his son, and the Mende woman, the hounds fled from my place, whining. And after very little thought, Robert Nash made what he figured was a smart business decision. He sold me away.

I been kidnapped, bought and sold five times in my life, so the auction at Wigfall Turning was not much doing to me. The trader poked and prodded us — I swatted his filthy rough hand away from my privates and growled when he tried to pull my dress open. He moved to smack me but I put my heel on the toe of his boot and he thought better of it. Best not to mark the merchandise in front of possible buyers. So he marched back and forth like a cock at dawn, kicking at the dirt with his boots, his arms waving 'round as he talked up the value of his "goods." His audience, a group of men as filthy and crude as he was, hooted and prodded him on, raising their flasks in the air and spitting out tobacco on the ground, trying to wait him out as part of their wagering, hoping to get the prices down. Could they get this negro for five hundred instead of eight? Would this gal breed? What about this boy? Not very big now but in time . . .

"And what will you give me for this comely wench? Bids in gentle'men, looks may be deceivin'. She's nary a spring chicken nor an old hen, but she has a strong back for farm labor or" — and here he must have winked, because they laughed and nudged each other in the ribs — "any other activities you might like her to perform. Sold to settle debts, temperament good, so her owner tells me. She has healing skill and is a vouchsafed midwife for your breeding wenches. I've heerd told that she's tended white women, too. Good investment, sirs. Hire her out and make a profit."

He did not mention that I was a witch or that I was feeble in the head or that I had walked into Glady Creek, because Nash did not tell him.

"Opening bid, gentlemen, eight hundred. Can I get eight hundred?"

The ruckus went on from there and I didn't much pay attention until the filthy man raised his hand and pointed, saying, "Fourteen five, do I hear, fifteen?"

He must have heard fifteen because his next words were, "Sold! To A. W. Mc-Culloch."

25
THE SCOTSMAN

It was three day's ride to McCulloch's farm, a long, quiet stretch of sunrises and -sets, marked only by the sound of the horses, birds calling, and a boy named "Jemmy," the only other person McCulloch had bought at the auction, sneezing and coughing. The man spoke more to the horses than he did to us and when he did speak, I couldn't figure none of his words.

"He's a Highland man, Scot," Jemmy whispered.

Didn't mean nothing to me, just another kind of white man. The English, the Spanish and Portuguese and the French. And now . . . This A-Dubya, for Abraham and William. The third name I could not say at all.

"He speak English but . . . ," Jemmy said. "You have to listen careful so you can take his meaning."

He explained that he'd had a master who

was a Scot.

I frowned. "How many masters you had?" I asked, curious. Jemmy could not have had more than fourteen, fifteen years.

"Four, but I born here, not country-born like you," he said then sneezed again, a sound that set one of the horses snorting.

I patted Jemmy on the back, rummaged in my pack, and pulled out a small piece of clean linen. "Wipe your nose. I can mix up a powder to help that," I said, handing it to him. "Once we get where we goin'."

"Thank you, Miss Maryam," Jemmy coughed out, sneezing at the same time.

The Scotsman spoke and near spooked me out of my seat.

"We'll stop now." He hadn't said one word to us since midday and it was getting on to dusk. He reined in the horses and turned to look at us. "You," he barked at Jemmy, the word sounding like *ye-uw,* "tend the horses, I'll make a fire."

"Yessir Master McCulloch," Jemmy answered, jumping down from the wagon faster than a squirrel.

What sounded like a growl emerged from the man's lips. Jemmy and I froze.

"Ye-uw no call me master, just McCulloch," he said gruffly. Jemmy nodded, murmured, "Yessir, Master" anyhows, and disappeared to the other side of the wagon, where he sneezed again loudly. One of the horses whinnied and stamped a hoof.

"Ye-uw!" This time the Scotsman was speaking to me.

"Yes . . . ," I almost said "master," too. I pressed my lips together before another sound slipped out. Habit. Near every white man I had met demanded to be called that. But trying to say McCulloch's name stretched my skills. I could not get my mouth to form the sounds.

He fixed me with a hard stare. "Get yer pack o' the back and mix that lad up a po-tion or powder or some-un to stop him dewin' that! Christ almighty, he'll fright me horses!"

I bit my lip to keep from smiling and nod-ded. I would have to get used to this rough man and his rough words. I would have to not laugh, because he struck me as funny. White men did not want colored people to think they were funny.

I been a journeying woman since I was ten years old, crossed the dark waters of the Atlantic, ran my palm across the smooth blue waters of the western Caribbean, wad-ing through the marshes of Georgia colony and the Carolinas, and now, journeyin' once again in the back of a wagon that rolled across a road steady climbin' into dark near-black green hills toward rocky peaks — they called mountains — of the Appalachian. First time I could remember traveling west, toward the setting sun. Farther and farther away from the dark water and the tall white-sailed ships. Farther away from any boat that could take me . . . I pushed the thought out of my head, crushed it and blinked the tears back. The only thing I could do was take another breath and then another breath and then another. But I would not cross those dark waters again. That I knew was true.

The farther we get from the coast, the cooler it get, 'specially after the sun set. It never got cool in Virginia like it do here — the Scotsman passed over a plaid-like blanket for me to wrap up in but I couldn't stop shiverin'. My bones ain't made for this weather.

I watch the trees and study the grasses and shrubs when we stop. Some look like hardier versions of plants I knew in Virginia and on the key, some even 'mind me like a tea my mother made in the before time. The Scot give me leave to forage and so I do. I pull the leaves, rub them between my fingers and sniff their scent, rememberin'

Marie Catherine's lessons to me.

"Know where you are, pay attention to the smell of the place, the feel of the soil, and the size and color of animals. Remember, in most places you will find a sister or brother to a plant that you know. *Attendez*. Always know your place, *ma petite.* The land will not deceive you if you know it. And it will give you what you need."

I look up at the stark gray crags that bring me in the mind of the Blue Mountains in Jamaica and wonder if there are bands of runaways in those hills, especially the ones beyond the clouds. The Scotsman says that south and east of here they're called the "Great Smokies." He speaks abruptly and sharp-like, and gives only a few words at a time as if he's 'fraid he'll run out. And always he fixes me with a stare, like he's studyin' me. But it ain't like the studyin' Old Man McKay did or the way that Durfee would look at me — at all of the women — in a manner that made you want to wash yourself and hide. He look at me like I'm some kind of strange creature, one he ain't seen before and can't make up his mind about. But he seen colored people before, he seen African-born before, so I ain't nothing new. Still.

McCulloch's plantation was not what I

thought. He say don't call it a "plantation," call it a "farm." Jemmy, who understand the man's words, say he got hundreds of acres, fields, timber land, two barns, one for his horses only, and chicken coops and a mill. His "big" house don't look nothing like the ones in Virginia or saw on the journey through the Carolinas. No columns or fancy porticos. No elaborate workings at all. It's big, two floors and whitewashed but plain, tidy and sparse as a Quaker meetinghouse. Row of rough-hewn whitewashed cabins to the rear beyond the kitchen and smoke-house, and it is to one of these that he leads me.

"This is yours," he say, opening the door. "Put your things there and go to the kitchen. Dolly will tell you what to do, give you anything you need." Jemmy, he takes with him.

The door closed slowly behind him and fit snugly into the jamb. No squeaking, no rubbing. I stepped back a few steps to see how good it fit. No daylight coming in from under that door, which mean no cold air neither. I turned 'round, looking, from one wall to the next, each of the four made from rough-hewn logs, fitted tightly, and the windows — there were three of them — had glass in them, the sun shining through clear.

I leaned close to see where the glazier had scratched his mark into the surface. There was a rug on the floor and a hearth in the back. Clean, not a speck of dust or dirt. Way different from what old Maisie's place was like at Master Robert's when I got there. I'd seen many slave cabins but none better built than this one 'cept the one my James made for us. Fact was I'd delivered white babies in places that were meanly built and decrepit.

"You could do worse than have the Scotsman as a master."

Dolly, she say her last name "Reyes" after her father, who was from Cuba, is the housekeeper and cook, did the washing and the sewing and weaving, tended garden and fixed the meals for everyone on the McCulloch farm, white and colored, did cooking for other white folks, too, at their gatherin's, weddings, and such. She was paid money for it. I thought it strange that McCulloch was the only white person on the farm and said so.

"Widower," she commented, placing bowls and plates of food on the table in the kitchen for me and Jemmy. "Typhoid came through long time back, his people wiped out, his wife, all his children. Buried out there" — she gestured toward the left. "He likes women and he take . . . well, care of hisself you know what I'm sayin'. But he ain't bring one *here,* none good enough to marry, tho' there's plenty wouldn't mind him. I think he jes like being by hisself." She studied on me then chuckled. "No, it ain't like that neither, if that what you think-in'."

Dolly glanced at Jemmy and frowned. "Boy, you gonna choke if you don't take a breath! You slow down now! That food ain't gonna march off your plate!" She smacked the top of his fuzzy head but I know it didn't hurt none. And Jemmy didn't stop chewing either. Just mumbled, "Yes Miss Dolly," with his mouth full. Dolly looked at me and we both grinned.

"The McCulloch a gruff sort," Dolly added, returning her attention to a large pot on the back of her huge stove. Whatever it was she was fixing smelled good. My stomach grumbled even though I was eating and near full. "But not a mean one. You and I lived long enough to know what that like." She fixed me with a knowing stare that went over Jemmy's head. His face was buried in a bowl of beans and meat. The boy's stomach had no bottom. "He fair, to colored and white both. No overseer here.

The other white folk don't like it, say he too loose like, but" — she smiled — "They ain't bold 'nuff to say it to his face. Mind" — she held up one finger — "The McCulloch got a temper, white or colored, you wrong him, you got troubles. That man 'rupt like a cloudsplitter you cross him. But no negro ever been whipped on McCulloch's place nor sold downriver neither less they ask. And I been here ten year."

Dolly explain that the Scotsman allowed his colored people to hire out and keep a portion of any trade or coin they got. Now that was news. Nash kept every penny I ever brought for tending the sick or a lying-in; I got to take only what was given secret-like from a grateful husband or master. Now I began to wonder if I could build me a purse heavy enough to buy me a freedom paper and take myself out of Virginia.

"You a midwife he tell me, that good. There plenty breedin' 'round these parts, colored and white," she said, wiping her hands on her apron and sitting down at the table next to Jemmy. "My husband Hercules say he'd like another little one 'round the place. I told him he got a better chance digging one up from the potato patch than he would with me!" Her eyes took every detail of my face. "Look like you and I near 'bout the same years, so no babies from you neither." She shrugged and smiled slightly. "Least, not for much longer."

Much as I hated to hear it, I knew she was right. I was still bleedin' but it didn't come regular-like. Marie Catherine had told me that if I lived long enough, would happen like this. But then she had also told me I'd have four sons in my life and two daughters. Considering Eli, Shadrach, and the baby girl that had died right after she was born, I had only three children. Marie was wrong.

I hadn't seen any children on the place — no one younger than Jemmy anyways — and wondered if Dolly had any children. But I didn't want to ask. Like me, like most colored women I knew, children were a blessing and a curse. If you had them, you worried yourself to death about if you could keep them. And if you had lost them . . . to disease or . . . that was another well of sadness and worry, one that could not be filled. But she sensed my question.

"Had me six. Two died as babies, my sons Antony and Francisco hired out — not with McCulloch but with another master — they bought their freedom papers." Her voice was filled with pride. "They live in Washington. Blacksmiths. Got their own shop. My daughter Delores live on the Burnes plantation north over the ridge. She the cook and housekeeper. Burnes promise to give her papers and I say a prayer that he do. Juana, she the one I couldn't hold on to . . ." At this Dolly bit her lip. "My last owner, before McCulloch, sold her off to the fancy girl market in Lexington. I don' know where she gone. But I still keep her" — she placed her palm across her heart, where a gold cross on a chain lay flat against the calico material of her dress — "Here."

I thought about James, Eli, and Shadrach, sold to only the gods knew where, and the gods, they don't talk. I placed my palm across my heart, too.

26
NED

Seem like not too long ago I was near young. Now I'm near old. Too old for a man to look at. Too old for a baby. Just. Too. Old. The years they marching down fast, seem like. I been in this middle Virginia more than five years, said almost that many words to the Scotsman in that time, he being a man of few words but not a hard man, just like Dolly say. He hasn't sent any troubles my way. But I've worked myself sunup to sundown. Babies, tending to ailin' folks, seeds in, crops out, help Dolly in and 'round the house. And I saved me up a fair amount of coin, too, now that's somethin' I never done afore. Nash b'lieved in hiring out and taking the fee. But the Scotsman take only a jot of what I get. I keep the rest. Not close to the $1,500 he pay for me. But more than I ever had b'fore. There are bargains I could make, to buy my freedom. Many here do.

But when I think clear about it, early

before dawn break or late when the fire's dyin' . . . I wonder if it matter at all. Not free. Free. There's free colored over the ridge north of here in White Sulphur Springs. Or free somewhere else. That Ohio just west of here, the Pennsylvania colony just north. But it still be me. Just me. I wonder what good it be to be free but alone.

I miss my family, the times that were and won't be again. It been so long ago that there are parts that I forget. But not the feel of my boys, in my arms, like when they was babies, the soft brush of James's lips on the back of my neck. That I won't forget. But that's gone now. It's in the before time like everything else worth anything in my life.

Then there was Ned and everything changed.

I saw him for the first time when I was in a place where I wasn't supposed to be, at a time when I should not have been anyways near. Had finished doing something that I wasn't supposed to do. Had I been caught, pass or no — the Scotsman's pass was sparsely worded and sharp like the point of a needle ("Let Maryam Grace pass and repass. McCulloch") — I could have been whipped or worse. Nash had sold me because he needed the money and because he said people thought I was a witch and touched in the head. But he also sold me because he thought, but could not prove, that I was helping runaways. Which I was. And which I still was, thanks to Dolly Reyes.

I had lived on the McCulloch place a good while before the opening presented itself, before Dolly reasoned she could trust me. Called out to deliver a baby in the quarters of a farm a few miles away, I passed by McCulloch's neat white house as I walked toward the road. It was still light, would be for a while, so I heeded the summons now, figuring that I could get Mister Joseph's man to carry me back in a wagon.

"Maryam!"

I turned to look at the open kitchen door where Dolly was waving at me. "Stop here will you? Eva asked me to send her mistress some of my honey and you just as good a carrier as anyone."

I nodded and changed course. Even if I spent a quarter hour chatting with Dolly, because she liked to talk, I could still reach the Joseph place before dark.

She'd set the honey and a half-dozen eggs out on the table and started to wrapping them in brown paper and talking.

". . . and her hens ain't layin' good . . . ," Dolly murmured, talking more to herself than to me. Her small hands moved quickly, arranging the items in the basket. "You goin' for Susie's child?"

I nodded. "Uh-huh, she started this mornin'. Her first, it take some time."

"Miz Burdett still ailin'?" Dolly asked. "She gonna carry that baby through or not?"

I shook my head and tried to think good thoughts about the woman; she was puny and always sick. Six pregnancies, six years, only two lived and one that was stunted-like and always coughing. Now the woman was breeding again and I wished I could cast a good-luck spell on her to give her least one more healthy baby because I didn't think little Amos would see his second birthday. As for this next child, she was four moons along. But the way she was vomiting and losing weight, I didn't think it would happen and I told Dolly that.

She sighed.

"Shame. Roger Burdett's a devil of the first water but she all right. Just married to the wrong man. You go past the ridge near Falling Spring right? 'Long the Rappahonnick?"

I shook my head no, gathering up the honey and eggs and placing them in my basket. "I will if I take the long way 'round."

"Take the long way 'round. I need you to

346

drop off this basket." She pointed to another basket that I hadn't seen before.

I shrugged. The ridge near Falling Spring wasn't too far out of my way.

"McCulloch got a crew working up on that ridge?" The Scot owned acreage there on the north side, and the back parcels of his farm ran up to it. From time to time he'd send a logging crew up there to cut timber.

Dolly smiled.

"No. Got me a couple fugitives hiding out in Indian's Cave."

I set a jar into the basket, carefully, because my hand was shaking. I stared at her. Dolly's dark eyes didn't waver and her chin was tilted up, challenging me like.

"Fugitives," I said, looking over my shoulder. I lowered my voice. "You mean runaways."

Dolly's smile widened.

"If you like. Don't worry, he ain't here. Gone to Roanoke on business."

I looked at the woman, my eyes asking the question before my lips could form the words. "Why you think I'd do something like that? Something could get me killed?"

Dolly's dark eyes had a look in them that reminded me so much of Marie Catherine's. There was a kind of knowing in them that gave you to think she knew what you would say before you said it. She smiled again but when she spoke, her tone was somber.

"I trust you. And you got a pass. Folks used to seeing you goin' here, goin' there. And you, more'n anyone on this place, know what it like to be free." Neither of us spoke for a moment after she said that. I guess she figured, like McCulloch, she'd used enough words and the right ones, too. And that I understood everything she was saying between those words.

"How you get . . . how you start . . . doing this?" I asked her. Before . . . when I lived on Nash's farm, the people came to me on their own like, out of the blue. I never had a sign they was coming or where they'd come from, unless they said, which I discouraged them from doing. They were just there. And I would feed them or tend a scrape or cut and then they were gone. Like a puff of smoke from a dyin' fire. But I was never part of nothing, least not that I knew, and there was no plan. The people were at my cabin and then they weren't.

Dolly shook her head slowly as she wrapped up a half loaf of bread and placed it in the bottom of the second basket.

"Maryam. You don't get to know that."

"Be easy for me to tell the Scotsman."

Which I would never do.

Dolly snorted.

"You won't tell him squat," she barked out. "Only person say fewer words than him is you. 'Sides . . . you African. I know what they like. My pappy was one. You just like him." Her dark eyes twinkled again. "Born free, you all never take to bein' owned, never." Her expression grew solemn again. "Even after all these years, something 'bout you still free. You still you own woman."

Never met Dolly's father, never would, if he was still alive; he lived in Cuba, where she was born. But I knew what she meant. And I knew that she was right, that I could do what she asked without much notice — babies came when they got ready, not when you wanted them to. And a midwife moved at all times of day and night, and as long as I had the Scotsman's pass, I was let alone — and no. I wouldn't talk either. To anyone, colored or white.

And so I took the basket to Indian's Cave, where three people ate its contents like they were starving and thanked me with such gratitude that I was embarrassed. And from that day on, I took many baskets along to Indian's Cave and other places deep in the woods of Falling Spring Ridge, anytime Dolly had "friends" passing through — and how she came to such a position I never knew or asked about again. I delivered food, water, and medicine, treating wounds and sickness and delivering a child or two for the next five years. Who these people were, I did not know. Where they were going, I would not let them tell me. Some days, I wanted to go with them. Other days, I did not. But on one of my visits to Dolly's friends, I met a logging crew in the forest, consisting of colored and white men and Sullivan, an overseer from the next county. That was the first time I saw Ned.

I had taken the long way home from the Washington place. Washington, his wife, and two of the children were down with the influenza as were four of the workers. It was a bad contagion this year, harder on grown folks than children, but I had shivered through it twice in my life, the first time on Caesar's Key, so I wasn't scared. And none of the other midwives would come near the farm, nor would the white doctor in town. So they sent for me. And since Washington's little farm was on the north side of the Rappahonnick River and not far from Falling Spring, I choose to walk through the forest instead of 'round it, and brought food and medicine to a group of fugitives hiding out in the cave. On the way down the ridge, I walked straight into the logging crew.

"Auntie, what you dewing here?" Sullivan's nasally twang hit my ears like the screech of a red eagle. I near dropped my baskets. "Yew hear me Auntie?"

Just how are we related? I wanted to ask him. Sullivan was one of many white men whom I did not like.

"Over at the Washington place," I told him, gathering my skirts 'round me to keep them from blowing. It was late October but November was coming fast. I felt the change in the air, could smell it. It was still mild out but I knew that the cold and rains were on the way.

Sullivan spat out a wad of tobacco that landed a few inches from my feet. It looked like a piece of dog shit. And I forgot myself and looked the man straight in his red-tinged eyes. He grinned at me, proudly displaying dark-pink gums and near-mud-colored teeth stained dark with tobacco juice.

"You a long way around, Auntie," Sullivan barked out.

"Yes, sir, I am," I barked back.

It was then that I noticed that the crew had stopped work and was standing in a semicircle watching us. There were eight, no ten of them, most colored but a few whites, too, probably in debt and working off the sum by clearing forest land and logging.

Sullivan spat again and half-walked, half-staggered closer to where I stood. Even in the cool air of early fall, the stench of unwashed skin, dry piss, and liquor saturated the air. My stomach lurched and I swallowed. The man held out one large filthy paw.

"Pass."

I unfolded the coarse gray-ivory colored paper that the Scotsman had scribbled on. I could not decipher the symbols but I knew what they said. Sullivan pretended to read them without comment (everybody knew that he could not read), refolded the paper, and passed it back to me. I had already known that I would not have any more trouble. The man would strut and swagger a bit for the benefit of his audience but he wasn't stupid. Sullivan and everyone else in the county knew that I worked on Mc-Culloch's place. McCulloch's ways were strange to the other white people, they whispered behind his back, rolled their eyes at his thick, gravelly voice, and made comments about the way he "let his niggers run loose." But it was all talk. They were too afraid of him, too intimidated by his landholdings and his presence to do more. And he did not hold with anyone meddling with any of his people. Sullivan would show off in front of his crew but he wouldn't do more than that.

"So you been at the Washington place. Somebody breedin' there?"

"No, they got the contagion."

Sullivan couldn't step out of my path fast enough. The smirks and chuckles from the other men provoked a rebuke from him but the damage had been done. The drunkard had been undone by a colored woman and his fear of catching a chest ague. As I moved to leave the tree-stump-filled clearing, I nodded and spoke to the men, most of whom I knew, if not by name then by face. Except for one. A tall, muscular man whose smile lit up his face and whose eyes grabbed mine. He'd taken off his shirt and though he was covered with dirt, sawdust, and sweat, his shoulders were strong and well formed, his waist slim, belly flat. He nodded slightly and my breath near stopped in my throat.

"Good mornin'," he said, polite-like, his voice smooth. My ear picked up the roundness of tone that I associated with parts of the Virginia colony and Georgia. He was not country-born, too young for that.

"Good morning," I said.

"My name's Ned," he added in a lower voice.

The quivering in the pit of my stomach was so pronounced that at first I thought I might throw up. It was the same sensation I'd had when James held me in his arms and murmured his love into my ear. A sensation that had been so long absent from my life that I near didn't recognize it.

Desire.

I thought about no one and nothing else for the next few days. So much so —

"Maryam!"

McCulloch standing in the doorway of the chicken coop, where I been gatherin' eggs for Dolly. Or thought I was. How long he been there I do not know. How long I been there I do not know.

"Sir?"

He clears his throat although it sounds more like he growling at me.

"Get your wits about you, gal, and see to the barn. Abner's men, the logging crew, waiting there along with Wash and Clayton. One of the men is hurt." He frowns.

"Yes, sir," I say quickly, wiping my hands across the front of my apron and moving toward the well to draw a bucket of fresh water. In my mind, I mark off the things I'll need: cloths, aloe, willow bark tea, vinegar, something to cut the pain, to clean it . . .

"You ailin', Maryam?" the Scotsman asks, his voice rough as always but not unkind.

"No, sir," I say as I brush past him, walking quick-like, chiding myself. Seem like I lose myself more and more in my dreams lately, thinking about what was then and what is now. Somewhere, I remember my mother's grandmother . . . or was it my father's? A small, dried-up-like woman who sat in the corner of my mother's house, chewing . . . what was she chewing? Wearing a toothless smile and a blank look. My mother said that she was looking backward, that she had to focus her eyes in a way that we children could not. I wondered if I was becoming like that old woman, eyes focused backward on what was and could not be again. Looking forward to something that also could not be.

Dolly's husband, Hercules, was sitting with the men in the open doorway of the barn; they'd just come in from the forest. Will, and Clayton, and Wash and Godfrey from Master Russell's plantation, along with Abner's men. McCulloch had hired in more men to help with clearing a creek bank to open up a dam. Hercules stood up and gestured for me to come over where he was.

"Maryam, need you o'er here. This man here . . . seem like it a bad cut."

He stepped aside so that I could see the man sitting on the hay, his filthy shirt torn, an ugly red gash across his shoulder. He had his head down and seemed to be breathing hard and I knew from what I saw that this wound pained him. I knelt down and pressed my hand gently on his chest.

"Let me see."

He lifted his head and looked at me. The breath caught in my throat and my heart stopped midbeat.

Ned.

"Yes, Mistress Maryam," he said, his voice melodic and strong.

I felt the tingling start at the top of my head and travel down, stopping midway, low in my belly. If I'd been standing up, my legs would have give way.

He was working on Master Russell's place, brought from Russell's brother-in-law's farm some miles away across the Blue Ridge. He was dark mahogany brown in color with a strong arrogant nose like those of the Igbo, full lips that curved slightly upward, and a form that showed he was a strong man, a hard worker. And handsome. 'Minded me someways of James and someways not. The look in his eyes told me that he was not a preacher, his look was too bold for that; and he wasn't a prophet either, there was nothing distant or thoughtful there. Ned was a man of the earth, a man of the practical, of things he could touch and hold.

I cleaned and bandaged up his wound as quickly as I dared and left while I still could keep my face still and my thoughts to myself. Ned's gaze had near pierced my skin. I planted myself against the side of the barn and closed my eyes, willing my heart to slow its racing, my breath to slow its pant. It was foolishness, pure. I was past forty years old; this man, this Ned, was in his twenties, thirty at most. My daughter, the baby born on Caesar's Key, the child whose face I never saw, would be about his age.

Not that it mattered. He came to my cabin a few nights on, his wound still raw. His touch was light as he unbuttoned my dress, gentle. I tore the shirt from his body. And neither of us slept that night or the others that followed. The wound on his shoulder I dressed and redressed because our couplings broke it open again and again. I was sore and glad of it. My lungs filled with the scent of him, my ears strained to hear the sound of the men working in the woods adjacent to the farm, my heart leapt whenever I heard his voice, whenever he touched me. There were weeks when I did not see him at all — the crew finished McCulloch's work and moved on. Russell's crews went everywhere in this part of Virginia — but I had only to hear his name to feel my heartbeat race and the space between my legs grow damp.

We met in my cabin. We met in the barn and in the woods. Through that autumn and winter and early spring. There were times when he walked away from Russell's farm, met me near Falling Springs, and pushed himself into my body against a tree. I could not get enough of him, the feel of him, the smell of him, the sound of his breathing . . . Ned was a sickness that I had but did not want a remedy for. Filling my body, filling the empty spaces in my soul.

27
BABY EDWARD

First, I thought the trickster god was play-ing a game with me. I wanted a child, had wanted a child for so long but knew that I was near beyond that time. Had to reckon with myself that I gettin' old, fat, and that my courses had stopped as Marie Catherine said they would. But I'd been a midwife too long not to know the phases. Not to know that it was possible. And not to know that this was Ned's child I was carrying.

For the first time in more years than I could remember, I was smilin' all the time, hummin' to myself. Herc looked at me sideways, I could tell he wondering what was wrong with me. Jemmy and Clayton just nodded, said, "Hello Miss Maryam," and gave each other a quick glance. Even McCulloch . . .

Dolly watched me give up my breakfast several mornings but said nothing until one day, near five months in, when I stopped by the kitchen to get some whiskey to mix up a medicine to treat the cough that was going 'round. The children had it bad especially.

"Got it here, Maryam," she said, passing over the small flask. "McCulloch say you can have what you need for your medicines. Should be 'nough there to hold them a week or so. You need more, you ask. And here some mint too, hold you until this rain leaves off and you can forage again."

"Thank you, Dolly," I said, meaning it. Her little supply was helping me to do my work until the fields and land dried off enough for me to find more. It had been a rainy spring, leaving most of the land still too wet to plant, and the herbs and greens that I used just couldn't get rooted in the soil, rotting out before they could take. The damp had also brought more than the usual coughs and contagions, which used up near every dried remedy I had put by.

Dolly turned back to the stove — she was making a soup she call "gumbo" and it near always took all day and most of her attention.

"You feeling better now?"

My hand went to my belly, now swelling and getting firm with the growing child. I couldn't help it. I smiled as I looked up at her. I had told no one about the baby. It

360

was a treasure that I had been keeping for myself. And for Ned. But soon I wouldn't have my secret anymore.

"Yes. Nothing serious. Little indigestion." I bit my lip to keep from smiling and busied myself with organizing vials, bottles, and packets in my baskets.

"Maryam, Ned . . . I know you and he . . ."

This time, there was no reason for me to smile. "Yes. We are. I am. And it ain't none of yours." I spat out those words, feeling the venom rise in my chest.

"You're . . . like a sister," Dolly said slowly, her Spanish inflections creeping into her words, which meant that she was either nervous or worried, or both. "But you got to know . . ."

"Know what?"

"Maryam, he a young man. You . . . I . . . none of us wants you to be hurt . . ."

"Dolly, I know he young. I know how old I am. Every turn I got one of y'all reminding me."

"Maryam . . ."

I felt the anger rising in my chest. Swept the rest of the packets into the large coiled basket and turned to go. "What."

"How far you 'long, Maryam?" A question and not gently asked. Dolly's words had been spat out like she'd held something bitter in her mouth. I looked over at her. The spoon was still in her hand but now held over the pot so that the juices could drip back in. She was not smiling.

"Five months." Saying those words made me feel as if I'd found Caesar's chest of gold, hidden somewhere on the key. I was grinning again, a huge face-splitting grin and I knew that I looked like a fool. But I didn't care. This baby was the best thing to happen to me in a long time. To me and Ned.

"Where is he these days?"

I felt my shoulders stiffen. Dolly never asked a question without a reason or a message behind it. Fact is, she never asked a question that she didn't know the answer to.

"Master Russell hire him out. North somewhere, Greenbrier County" — I tried to remember what Ned had told me — " 'long with the twins. Just till the tobacco takes hold, then he comes back." I inhaled and patted the soft roundness. "By then, the baby ready to be born."

"You been to the Russell place lately?"

Another question.

"Dolly, you asking me something? Or tryin' to tell me something? Goin' over today. Taking the medicine for the children's coughing spells and seeing to Mistress Sourpuss for her monthlies." I frowned, trying to remember the last time I'd actually been on the Russell place.

This time, it was Dolly's turn to take a breath. Her black eyes, so prominent in her dark honey-colored face, bored into mine with a sharpness that now unsettled me.

"Dolly . . . what?" The only words I could get out.

"Did . . . you see Nini the last time you were there?"

Nini?

The silliest woman I'd ever met, and I'd met a lot of women in my days. Nini was more a girl than anything, a housemaid on Russell's place although no one thought his house was grand enough to need one. But Nini was pretty and easygoing and smiled a lot. And the word was that her workload had been lightened because she now slept in Russell's bed since his wife died. So she wasn't stupid. Dumb like a fox, a phrase I'd picked up from Petal. Ever'time I saw her — I didn't have cause to go to the Russell place more'n once e'ery few months — she was pleasant-like, nodding to me, calling me "Auntie Maryam" like I was old enough to be her grannie, which I wasn't. Least, not yet.

"Was there four, six weeks ago, tended to Uncle Augustus. Spent all my time with him, hardly saw no one."

Dolly nodded, remembering. She made the sign of the cross. Augustus was the oldest person either of us knew, ninety years by his own reckoning, could have been older. Over the years, I'd tended to his swollen crooked joints, rubbed his aching back, and treated him through the influenza and a bout with the flux. But with the winter we had that just held on and the cold, rainy spring, Gustus got a chill in his lungs that he couldn't shake and nothing I could brew up would rid him of it. He said he'd been born in a place called Angola, still remembered some of those words. I did not know them, those words. He talked in his final days about places far away and people long gone to their gods. We all loved Gustus and missed him.

I turned to go.

"Saw Nini from a distance, she was on the portico near the grape arbors. Just waved at her. Why you asking?"

"Maryam, you need to know something."

"It getting late, Dolly . . ."

"Maryam . . . when you see Nini . . ."

I was out the door. "No reason for me to see Nini unless she ailin' or breedin'," I

364

snapped, angry about Dolly's words, wondering why it was anyone's business but mine and Ned's.

Being Master Russell's bed warmer had turned out well for Nini. She wore a pretty satin-like gown and as she walked the snow-white petticoat showed itself with her steps. Her head wasn't covered so she had the chance now to show off her hair, which was a dark brown and thick but long. She'd plaited it tight and wrapped it up. Little ear-bobs danced on thin hoops dangling from her pierced ears. And as she walked toward me, I saw that her belly was round and high. Russell had moved fast, that was sure. But his widowed sister had taken over the running of his household after his wife left and I wondered how this situation was going to work out. For Nini.

"Auntie Maryam." Nini's voice was high and light. She didn't carry a thick slow drawl like some of the people did, especially those from farther south. And her voice did not carry the cadence of those like me who'd come 'cross the dark waters. But then it wouldn't. Nini was pecan colored and had the slim nose of the English or other of the white people. And she made it her business to make her way of speaking flow with her looks.

I stopped and smiled, lowering my eyes to her belly.

"I see you got a little one comin'."

The girl flushed and patted her stomach.

"Yes, ma'am," she said proudly. "Esha say in July." She sighed. "It be hot then."

"Yes, it will," I agreed. "How you feel?" I reached out and placed my hands on her stomach. The child was fairly large for six months, and her belly was hard. Good-size child. Maybe twins?

Nini signed again. "No vomiting in the morning but sometimes ache in the belly. Can you give me something for it?"

I was digging in my basket for a packet of mint leaves. Was probably just indigestion. I had it myself. "Master Russell . . ."

The girl glanced quickly over her shoulder, then grabbed me by the elbow and moved me toward the door and out on the portico. Her eyes were dancing with laughter.

"Yes, Master Russell. He all happy about this. Miss Bella not so much but she can't say nothing." She giggled.

"Well, it been a bit of time since he had a baby 'round here," I commented, holding the mint. "This should help. Brew it up in a tea, steep but not too long, the water still be light color."

Nini nodded and grinned. But her smile

did not reach her eyes.

"Master Russell think this his baby," she said in a low whisper, in a voice that I near didn't recognize.

She leaned close to me.

Well, this was news.

What Dolly would give to know it.

I still had the mint between my fingers. Nini's light brown eyes flickered and she smiled slightly as she pried the packet away.

"No?"

"This is Ned's baby," she said.

Her eyes locked with mine then slid down my face to where my breasts, large and drooping, rested above the raised and now loosened waistband of my apron, then lower to my belly. She snorted and I felt the indigestion that had been brewing in my stomach turn hot with rage.

"You look like you breedin' yoself, *Aunt,*" Nini said, turning to leave. "But I know you too . . . old for that." The sound of her heels clicked across the polished wooden floor. She waved the packet in the air. "Thank you for this, Auntie Maryam."

I wanted to grab her, throw her down on that floor, and kick her until she bled. I wanted to snatch the packet from her fingers and give her something to make her bleed away the baby she carried. My mind filled with ugly evil things so dark so mean that they made me sick. But not her. Because I walked away.

I made my other rounds, checked on this woman, that man or child, passed out more medicine, dressed a wound, moved like a dead woman, hardly said any words to anyone. I don't remember seeing the trees. Someone waved and greeted me, I don't remember who. Made my way back to the farm feeling as if I had been kicked in the stomach. Near walked into McCulloch. I did not see him, did not see anyone.

"Maryam? What . . . are you ill? Do you need tending?" McCulloch waved toward the house where Dolly was standing.

I shook my head, tried to walk away. The Scot held my arm and would not let me go.

"Did you . . . Dolly said that you went on your errands. Did you . . . visit the Russell place?"

I looked up at him, looked him full in the face, and knew in that moment that he, like everyone else, knew about Nini, about Ned, about their child.

And about me.

He cleared his throat.

"Russell sent that crew . . . the one that Ned is on, out to Green Pines. He owns a spread there. They'll be there for some time.

I thought that you would want to know."

"Why you think I want to know? Why? Why it any of yo' business? Huh?" The backs that had been turned away now turned in my direction. My next words were in Edo. McCulloch's eyes widened slightly. "I with Ned, Ned with me! Least . . . for a while! Why you care? Because now you got another worker with this child! That your concern? That why you ask? How much will he be worth to you?"

The growl came out of his throat. I took a deep breath. And woke up. The shouting I had heard was my own voice. The words . . . . my parents' words . . . were spoken by me to the man who owned my labor. I had forgotten myself, forgotten what I was. Forgot who I was talking to.

"Yew are not well. Dolly will look after you . . . and the child."

I jerked my arm away. *No.* He let me go. I stalked down the dust road toward the cabin, Dolly at my heels. The moment she shut the door, I collapsed to the floor.

Edward was born on June 7 in the morning, his first cries blending in with the sound of light rain on the roof. He was small but strong and well formed, all his fingers, all his toes. He had Ned's round nose and my forehead. His little body was the color of dark sugar. I cuddled him, kissed him, fed him until he was near to busting. Mc-Culloch had Dolly tend to me and told her that I was not to work until she say I was ready. If anyone needed healing or a midwife, they would have to call Esha or Mrs. Ames. So I stayed in the little cabin or in a chair next to Dolly's big hearth, nursed my baby, and watched over him. And watched over him as he caught the contagion that was still spreading through the countryside, watched as he stopped feeding, stopped crying, just stopped. He lit up my life for a month. And then the light went out.

McCulloch had him buried in the family cemetery and had Clayton fashion a little marker for the grave: EDWARD SON OF MARYAM JUNE 7–JUNE 30 1804.

I did not sit in a corner and pray to die. I did not walk into the river and call for the gods to carry me away. I did not turn away food or water. I did not cry. I was in a sorrow beyond tears. After Hercules poured the last shovel of earth on the tiny box that held my son, I turned and walked back to the little cabin and pulled a length of white muslin from the chest that sat in the corner and bound my breasts as tight as I could. Then I put a straw hat on my head and went to the fields. I was the only one there. The rest of the people were still in the graveyard singing a song to guide my Edward's soul to the clouds.

28
BUT THEY WILL NOT
ALL BE YOURS

He was born on a summer day. A day that started out fine and stayed so with each ray of the sun, each chirp from a bird, the breezes caressed my face, the air was sweet and soft and comforting. It was one of the most terrible days of my life.

I was hunched over the tobacco plants and my back felt as if it were cracking into pieces. The ground beneath my feet was damp, my shoes were covered with mud, but the cool thickness felt good, as if it were nourishing my feet. And my hands were cramping — a condition that I noticed in myself more as the days and years passed, a condition I used to treat others for and now I had to look to myself. The salves I made I used on myself as often as I did on Herc for his gnarled arthritic fingers or Dolly for her back. Time was passing.

When I looked across the acres of green, the feathered tops of the corn plants bend-ing in the breeze, the notion came to my head that I had now more fields and ridges and rivers . . . and big waters behind me than I did ahead. I sighed. The day, the time of my birth, was so long ago that even I had forgotten how many years I had seen, but I knew one thing: I was an old woman. In my mother's circle, I would be a wise woman, with a brain and body better suited to tending laboring mothers (which I did), spoiling children, and giving unwanted advice than for hard labor or quivering with desire under the touch of a man's hand, though I longed for it. I pushed Ned's image from my head. My breasts tingled. I would have to change the bindings soon.

"Is the way of t'ings," Marie Catherine often said.

She was right.

The blue cloudless sky distracted me again and again but I could not stop, my work would not get done. I focused myself on the plants, listened to the cardinals signal each other and the goldfinches tweet. A blue jay cawed a warning. The cicadas buzzed in the trees, their last song before dying and turning the chorus over to nocturnal crickets. The cycles, the circles, the seasons, turning over and over . . .

I heard him before I saw him.

"Maree-yum! Mareee! Where you at? Maree-yum!"

I stood up like a deer checking for the sight of a gun barrel. It was Wash from the Russell place. He waded through the rows of corn until he got close enough then stopped and collapsed over his knees, head down, gasping for breath. I chuckled.

"Uh-huh, Wash, Tousy been feedin' you too much cake and buttered corn bread." He looked up. The expression on his face stopped me from making more light comments about his girth. "What is it? What the trouble?"

"It's Nini. The baby's coming." He spat the words out like breaths he needed but couldn't take.

I shrugged and look down at my sack near half full of corncobs.

"Didn't have to come all this way to tell me that. Esha take care of her." Esha and I had had our moments, useless tensions arising mainly out of the conflicts between our two peoples, but even the gods knew, her gods and mine, that was a long time ago in a place that neither of us had seen for more than thirty years and would not see again. In this place, we were the same. Nini had asked Esha to attend her; that was no surprise. She would have cut off a finger before asking for my help.

"Was Esha that sent me." Wash's voice grabbed me with its urgency. "She say you come quick. Nini in trouble." His light brown eyes caught mine. He was frightened. I dropped my sack and ran toward the cabins. If Esha was asking for my help, Nini was in more trouble than Wash could know.

I had attended hundreds of laboring women, maybe more. The faces of the mothers blurred in my mind, their moans and screams became one moan, one shriek, the cries of their children blended into one long wail. Even when there was a sadness, the lines between births faded into the softness of my brain and all mothers became one, all babies became one. All except for Alexander. I will remember Alexander's birthing every day for the rest of my life.

Because it was so quiet.

By the time Wash came to fetch me, it was already too late. The silence met me at the door of her cabin, a presence that near stopped my steps. Nini's throat had given out from all the screaming, leaving her with barely enough strength to moan. The cabin floor was flooded with blood. No battlefield had ever seen so much. Esha was standing in the corner, her face ashen, her dark eyes rimmed in red. I heard her voice, low and hoarse, the unfamiliar words coming quickly as she chanted prayers. Tousy and Nedra stood in the opposite corner, wrapped in each other's arms, sobbing silently, doing nothing. I remember thinking, *Why don't they help her? What is wrong with them?* and being angry, then realizing: What could they do? What could I do?

And then there was the blood. So much blood.

The baby was still inside her.

"Maryam? Mary, is that you?"

The strength in Nini's voice startled me. She did not sound like a lighthearted girl now.

"Nini, it's me. You just be still, I'll . . ." What? What was I going to do? "We gonna get this baby out now."

My hands were moving but I had no idea what they were doing. Esha and I cleaned her up as good as we could and I tried to examine her without causing more pain. She moaned a little but said nothing. I think Nini was beyond pain.

"I need . . . you . . . tell you . . ."

"Hush, Daughter," I barked out gently. *Now where did that come from?* Esha's eyes caught mine but she said nothing. I had used an Edo word, a word of endearment from my childhood. It was not Esha's language but she knew it. "Be still now, we talk after."

"No. I . . . tell you now . . . Maryam . . ." Nini's voice was fading but she barked out my name, using precious energy to get my attention. My throat tightened. *"Please."*

Esha nudged me gently, her hands replaced mine performing a massage of Nini's belly. I wrung out a cloth and dabbed her forehead. Nini no longer looked like the girl I knew. She was pale, almost gray, her dark eyes sunk into her face, her lips drawn and chapped. Her long dark hair spread across the pillow like the legs of a large spider. My heart filled.

A kind of . . . knowing washed over me, taking with it the jealousy, bitterness, and fury that had marked my dealings with Nini. Love can be a sickness. We had almost come to blows: I had near slapped her across the face when she told me that her rounded belly was from Ned, had wanted to stomp her to death. I had wept for days until my eyes were dry and my head hurt, imagining them together, his lips brushing hers and worshiping her body in ways that I knew. I was sick near every day after that day, while Nini, with her youth and health, seemed to float through the weeks, her breasts becoming full, her belly rounded but soft and sensual. And Ned . . . gone. And my baby . . . his baby, born and also gone. I had wished all manner of darkness on this woman.

And now? I was her midwife, sent by the gods who watched over laboring women, to serve her, to conduct her child through the portals of life. Nini had been beautiful once, amber skin, dark thick hair that she kept braided and pinned up. Luminous dark eyes and a body that any man would want. Young. Had I been more clear-eyed, I would have known why Ned wanted her. But as I gazed back across the landscape of my life over the past few months, I realized that none of that mattered at all. An ocean of hot tears filled the wells behind my eyes. I tipped my head back, willed the tears to return to their source. I had work to do.

No matter that they are dying before your eyes, that the child is dead or ill formed, you wear the face of the goddess. She is powerful and wise. The goddess does not weep, she does not show despair. She is making and unmaking itself. Marie Catherine's voice filled my head as if she were as close to me as Esha. I took a deep breath and said a prayer to this unnamed goddess. Then I spoke.

"Nini, what this all about?" I asked her

with a no-care tone in my voice that I did not feel. "I got me a baby to deliver."

Nini's eyes were closed but she smiled.

"You hate me."

"Come now, girl . . . we got to . . ."

"No. You listen. I know that I . . . that Ned . . ." She sighed and the sounds that came from deep inside her throat sent cold down my spine. No death rattle could have been louder. Esha's eyes met mine again; this time hers were full of tears.

"Ned . . . he . . . didn't love you . . . didn't love me either. S'over now. And he gone. Sent away. But Maryam . . ." Nini grabbed my hand with a ferocity that I wouldn't have thought she'd be capable of. "Take my boy, Mary. Take him, feed him, you still got milk. Raise him up. I got no people here. Please . . . please don't let him be alone." The sob hit me like a wave, like the ones I'd seen years ago when I crossed the big water — the Atlantic — a "rogue wave" the salties called it. They could come out of no place, formed by only the gods knew what, and for what purpose, only the gods knew. Sometimes they brought sea monsters with them. Sometimes they knocked over the tall-sailed ships like they were toys. Sometimes they drowned everyone and everything. And always they sent rivers of dread.

Fear washed over me like a bath of needles but I could not let it consume Nini.

"Nini, don't worry." The Scotsman would have said, "Dinna fash." *Don't fuss.* "I'll take your boy till you better. I'll take him."

Nini opened her eyes and smiled at me.

"Won't get better, you know that."

Yes, I know that. Shame on me trying to fool the dead. Or almost dead. They can see through the mist.

"Tell the child about me. Tell him about . . . Ned."

"Yes."

"Will you love him, Maryam? Please?"

This time, I couldn't speak. I had no words. I pressed my lips together and nodded.

Nini's boy — and she had known that — was born almost the moment she let go of life. I didn't have to pull him out. Esha and I didn't have to cut him out. He slid into the world, stretched, kicked, then wriggled. Took a breath so deep that I thought it was gonna tire him out then screamed. We all smiled with joy then cried. His mother never heard his voice.

Esha, Tousy, Nedra, and I cleaned Nini's body, with water and tears, and wrapped her in a sheet. The men carried her to Wash's cabin for the wake; it was going to take some doing to scrub all of the blood up from the floor. Brother Willard, the preacher from the McCormick farm, was sent for to say a few words. Nini's body would rest in the Russell slave cemetery in the woods behind the quarters before the sun go down.

"What you all going to do with that baby?"

Mistress Bella's voice, twangy and sharp, cut through the grief-filled silence like a cleaver.

"He's my property," she cackled. "Or least ways . . . my brother's." Mistress Isabella Russell Ellis was living at Mr. Russell's on his charity and at his pleasure because her husband run off with some other woman and taken their money with him.

Esha shrugged and said nothing. She was from the McCormick place, Mr. Russell didn't own her. It was Tousy who answered.

"Mistress . . . we . . ." She looked 'round, over her shoulder at Nedra. "This baby gonna need a titty and I'm too old. Nedra all dried up." Tousy looked me square in the eye. "Maybe . . . Maryam take him for a while."

Bella Ellis snorted.

"As if that's going to happen," she snapped, tossing her head slightly so that her fat lacquered sausage curls could swing.

"That nigger baby is my brother's property. He stays here."

Now it was Esha's turn to snort.

"Maybe you can nurse him, Mistress . . ." She bit her lip. The rest of us did, too. And, as if to seal the point, the baby started crying.

Bella Ellis turned four shades of red.

"Me! Why that's . . ." She stopped herself before saying that she was too old, had never even had any milk in those droopy bags she called breasts, and no white woman in these parts was ever, had ever, put her breast in a black baby's mouth.

She composed herself. And looked at me.

"Maryam. I know that you all . . . . McCulloch told Mr. Russell that your baby died a few weeks while back. Do you . . . can you still . . ."

"Yes, ma'am," I said as if my body hadn't already betrayed me. That baby cried, my breasts leaked and leaked and the milk soaked through the bindings I had wrapped myself with, soaked through my dress, too. I stood before her looking as if someone had thrown a bucket of water on me. The baby buried his face into my chest.

"My brother is away," Bella Ellis said, choosing her words carefully as she thought it through. "I'll send Washington over in a while with a note for Mr. McCulloch. Perhaps, if . . . he . . . you could foster the child for a few weeks. Just until he's weaned."

"Yes, ma'am," I repeated, feeling a hundred years old and as if I'd gone a hundred years without sleep. My pack was already on my back, along with some swaddling that Esha and Tousy had found in Nini's cabin. I couldn't talk anymore, I was just that tired. I turned and walked back toward the farm. Back to my little cabin. The one where Ned had made love to me so many times. And where I now would foster his son.

"Maryam! Hold up now, I take you in the wagon!" Was two days or more before I remembered that Wash, Tousy, and the others had yelled after me to wait for the horse to be hitched up. I didn't hear nothing but the sound of that little boy — Nini's boy — snuffling and whimperin'.

It was only a mile and a half. Should have taken me a half hour, three quarters. But I was wearing down, and the baby was waking up. And my breasts were so tight and full that I thought they would explode. I could see the smoke rising from McCulloch's chimney but I had to stop. My legs were giving out. And the baby was hungry.

There was a small ridge that overlook the

fields, now full with everything that growed in late summer. No one came there much but me and folks passing through who didn't stay long. McCulloch was so fierce-some that few of them dared to step a toe onto his lands. I sank onto the fallen log I'd fashioned into a bench for myself and set down my pack. The baby looked up at me with dark eyes and his father's nose. I bit my lip. This was my penance for being such a fool.

My dress was so tight, damp, and sticky, I could hardly get it open but I did, pulled it off my arms. And that baby latched on and drank like he was hollow inside. I sang him a song that my mother used to sing although I had forgotten the meaning of the words.

His little head was covered with dark hair, his eyelashes inky and fine like feathers. Oh, god, his little nose! So much like Ned's. And his tiny hand wrapped around my little finger.

I looked up. Thought I heard something. Held my breath. The baby suckled on, oblivious. A poacher? The patrollers? I looked slowly around me, hoping I wouldn't see a pair of eyes — human eyes — staring back at me. But there was nothing. Not a deer, not a squirrel or rabbit. The baby nursed himself to sleep. I did up my dress,

and walked down from Falling Spring Ridge
with Ned's son in my arms.

29
MARYAM'S BOY

I didn't see or speak to McCulloch for near two, three weeks. He was in and out of the house, on and off the farm. Hercules mentioned something about him going over to the McCormicks' and the Russells' and to town on business. It didn't matter, his place near ran itself, we all knew what we were supposed to do and in this season we were busy doing it. The corn wasn't going to pick itself. The chickens didn't gather their own eggs. And Dolly cooked whether the man was home or not. I had one laboring mother to tend to; Mistress Smith from over at the south right sent for me to deliver her daughter Peg's child, so I was gone for two overnights. The baby came after sundown and I didn't like being on the roads at night so I slept on a pallet next to Miss Peg. I came back early in the morning, when the sun was just coming up. No one was on the roads at that hour to challenge me and anyway, I had the pass McCulloch had written me. And wherever I went, Nini's baby went with me.

I dragged myself in at about six in the morning, lay the sleeping boy in the little cradle that Clayton had crafted for my baby, for Edward. It had hardly been used. I hadn't even shut the door good yet when there was a knock. I answered. McCulloch's form filled the doorway.

"So we got a bairn on the place now," he said.

"Yes," I managed. The tiredness poured out of me. I hoped that he wasn't going to give me any grief over this. Hoped that Mistress Bella's note had reached him to explain.

"Mistress Isabella wrote of the circumstances." He walked over to the cradle. For a few moments, he said nothing. Then, "Are yew well enough to . . . look after the boy?"

I nodded, was too tired to speak.

"How long before he's weaned?"

"Six . . . eight months. Maybe more but . . ."

"Dew whatever it takes, we want the bairn to be healthy." McCulloch leaned over the cradle and stroked the baby's cheek with one large work-worn finger. "Such a wee lad . . . does he have a name?"

Tears slid down my cheeks.

"No. Nini died . . ." I shook my head. The rest of the words stuck in my throat like a fish bone.

McCulloch nodded slowly as he stood up.

"Aye. Afore she could name him. Awful thing. Ah, well . . ." He looked down at the sleeping child again and smiled. "We'll call him Alexander for now till Russell tells me otherwise."

As if he were answering to his new name, the baby stirred, stretched, and opened his mouth. At first, nothing came out but a yawn but then a cry so loud that McCulloch gave a start. I pressed my lips together to keep from smiling.

"He just a baby, sir," I said. "He won't bite. Least, not yet he won't."

The Scotsman looked at me and I, in one of the few times since I'd been on his place for years, looked back. I had never looked him straight on in the face. From the time I stepped onto these shores, into this place, one of the first lessons I learned was not to look long into the face of a white man.

He was a tall man, broad across the chest, fit-looking despite his age — he was a good ten or more years older than me, way past being young. His beard, black white and gray in places, he kept cut short and close;

he was picky about that according to Hercules, who barbered him. He had high cheekbones and his skin was more tan than pink for all that he was from the Scotland, where was said that it was cold and hilly and rained a lot. His eyes were the color of dark honey, and they moved over me like a rain shower in the fall, leaving my skin chilled. I let my breath out slowly. Alexander whimpered.

The Scotsman's eyes flickered and then he turned and walked toward the door, saying gruffly before closing it, "Look to the bairn, woman."

The bairn — Alexander — cried loudly with hunger.

The front of my dress was soaked through.

"He's a fool about that boy, that's for sure," Dolly said, looking down at the large bowl of beans in her lap. We had just picked them and they snapped loudly with moisture. "Who would have thought . . ."

"Uh-huh, who woulda." I echoed her words, keeping one eye on the beans and one eye on Alexander. Made me nervous what McCulloch was doing. He had gathered Alexander up into his arms and was marching around the corral with the boy and his huge horse, Ben, setting him in the

saddle at times. Alexander giggled and Mc-
Culloch giggled and it would have been a
satisfying sight if not for the fact that Ben
was a gigantic animal and Alexander was
still just a baby though he was good size.
And then there was the fact that McCulloch
was a white slave owner and Zander was,
well, property. Not McCulloch's but still.
Not that you woulda knowed excepting that
they weren't the same color. McCulloch
looked on Alexander as if he were his own
son. He'd been a fool like that since I
brought him to the farm. I couldn't explain
it to myself or anyone else so I just let it be.
But it worried me. Alexander was ten
months now, near weaned and ready to
walk. He was bright and tried to speak
although it came out as babble except for
one word, "Da" which McCulloch took to
mean him. I expected any day that Master
Russell would send Wash over to carry the
boy back to his farm. Every day I had him
ready to go despite the fact that it would
tear my heart out. But he was property. Mc-
Culloch knew that, so what was he going to
do when Mr. Russell showed up?

"Probably 'cause his wife and chil'ren
gone and he lonely," Dolly murmured.
She'd been talking, I hadn't been listening.
"And in all these years, he's never brought

a woman here. He coulda taken another wife, had more babies. Shame. He too old now."

I looked over at the man holding my boy . . . I could think of Alexander only as my boy even though I knew that soon I'd have to give him up. McCulloch was old, yes. But not dead. He glanced my way and I returned my attention to snapping the beans in my lap.

The story of McCulloch's family was a familiar one. His wife, whose name I had never known and Dolly had forgotten, came over with him from Scotland, twenty years ago, maybe more. They'd bought and worked their lands and she'd given birth to five children, all healthy, all thriving. Until the typhoid came through and killed them all. In one day. His wife and the baby fell ill and the Scot went to town to fetch the doctor. When he returned, his wife and all but one of the children were dead. That child struggled for another day then let go. It was said that McCulloch tried to kill himself.

After what white folks say was a "respectable time," his neighbors commenced to invite the Scot to this or that gathering, introducing him to unmarried young and not-so-young ladies. He was a fine prospect with land, frugal if gruff ways, and a hard-working John Calvin ethic, although there was talk that he was a Catholic. No one knew for sure, because he never showed his face in any church. Spent a part of every Sunday paying respects to the row of head-stones in the northwest corner of his back acreage: MCCULLOCH, BELOVED WIFE, JOHN, BRIDGET, JAMES, JOAN, ANGUS.

"A lot of man there gone to waste," Dolly said in her usual judgmental way. She frowned as another thought entered her mind. "I do 'member some talk 'bout him seeing Miz Henriette Perkins some time back. And I mean a long some time back!" Dolly grinned then adjusted her expression. She lowered her voice. "But, it didn't take. Next thing I heard was that Miz Perkins visited her aunt up in Baltimore City and married a widower there. Merchant I think she said. 'Course she was a silly woman and McCulloch's not one for foolishness. Was also talk 'bout him and Isabella Russell . . ."

We looked at each other and started gig-gling like children. Isabella Russell? I could not imagine.

"That wouldna work," I murmured, mim-icking McCulloch's way of speaking. We giggled some more, then Dolly nudged me.

"What?"

"He's looking at you now."

"He can look on. I'm too old. And so is he."

Dolly snorted.

"You weren't too old to open your legs for that Ned, nonsense that he was. And you weren't too old to get a baby either."

I did my best to give her the evil eye.

"Dolly . . ."

"Well."

"It's over. I gots my work and my . . ." I almost said "my boy." But Alexander was not my boy. And soon, sooner than my heart would be able to stand it, Mr. Russell or someone in his employ would come and take Alexander from me. And I would be alone again.

" 'Sides . . ."

" 'Sides what?" I snapped back.

"He's . . ." Dolly's grin near split her face open. She ran the tip of her finger down the side of her face. Her light honey-colored cheek was sprinkled with freckles. "And I just popped up in the melon patch."

I nudged her this time, hard.

Dolly sucked the inside of her cheek. "Maryam, you lived too long to say that and think it's true. Wouldn't nobody blame you. Wouldn't nobody blame him. He a good man in his way. And —" She clapped her mouth shut and returned her attention to her work.

McCulloch bounded over to where we sat, the hound Ginger at his heels. He handed the squirming bundle that was Alexander to me and stepped back, the largest silliest grin on his face that I had ever seen on a grown man.

"That lad's a born horseman, ever I saw one. He'll ride that roan afore he walks!" McCulloch tapped Alexander on the nose and was rewarded with a huge grin and a giggle. To Dolly he said, "I'll be late for dinner, set it on the back of the hearth."

"Yes, sir."

To me he said, "Graham Brown says that you'll be tending to his lady soon."

"Yes, sir," I answered, looking down at the near overflowing bowl of green beans in my lap. "She won't be long." This was Mrs. Brown's sixth lying-in.

"Mind, if you're called away after dark, come get me first. Word in town is there are patrollers out."

"Yes, sir," I answered without looking up. Alexander was damp on the bottom and I got up to change his britches and hide my startled expression.

Patrollers.

McCulloch walked away and Dolly and I looked at each other again. We had been expecting a visitor for several days but he or she hadn't arrived. And now, with slave catchers out, especially if it was the one I'd had a run-in with, the one they called "the Kaintuckian," our visitor, wherever he was, could be in danger. And there was no way to get word. I hoped that Mrs. Brown's delivery would give me the cover I needed to persuade him out of hiding, tend any wounds or sickness, give food. But despite the number of babies Amy Brown had, I figured she was at least four weeks away.

I was wrong.

30
THE INDIAN'S CAVE

The Browns' oldest rode over to fetch me to their farm.

"Ma says the baby's comin'," the freckled-faced boy said breathlessly, his straw-colored hair stuck out wildly about his head. "She says for me to carry you back quick as I can!"

Babies didn't keep time and couldn't, as far as I could tell, know when they were or were not s'posed to arrive. So outside of a few notions that needed to be gathered or picked right before, I always kept everything in one place, ready to go. I sent the Brown boy to the kitchen to get a cold drink, then gathered up Alexander and his blankets and went there myself.

Dolly was doing ten things at once as she always did: cooking supper, setting pies out to cool, scrubbing the tables and handing off a cup of water to the ginger-haired Brown boy. McCulloch passed through on his way to the stables, exchanging a gruff greeting with the boy as he went.

"Boy, you ain't had no water today?" Dolly chided the yearling.

"No'm," the boy mumbled, between gulps.

"Uh-huh," Dolly said, taking the empty cup from him and turning it upside down. "You want another?"

He gulped, belched, and nodded, much to Dolly's and my amusement.

"You all take the north road," Dolly instructed, and directions not being part of her usual conversation, I fastened my attention to her words. "It be cooler that way, going through the Shawnee woods."

"Yes'm," the boy said, nodding. "Mam always tells us t'go thata way."

"Good," Dolly said. "It be cooler there."

The Brown boy belched out his gratitude then headed for the door.

"You'll watch over Alexander?" I asked her, knowing that she would.

"Yes," she said, taking the chubby bundle from my arms and kissing him on the cheek. She leaned over to look through the connecting door that the Scotsman had passed through just a moment before. "The cave," she whispered.

How she knew that I had no idea. It was not my business to know. Just to mind her words. To my pack, we added bread, jerky, apples, and a jug of water. A blanket.

"How soon he be there?" I whispered.

Dolly's gaze flitted toward the open door. McCulloch's footsteps were heavy and close but not that close.

"Today, may be there now if he come early." She stuffed the blanket deep into my pack. "Mind yourself, patrollers still out." She sighed. "They chased after . . . well. That over now." I had heard the whispers. The man had been caught but more than that no one knew.

I nodded. I had my pass but that wouldn't save me from a beating or worse if they caught me. Alexander hiccupped then frowned as if he ready to cry. He did that when he sensed that I was leaving him.

"Baby boy, Momma be back soon." I nuzzled his neck and he giggled, a sound that made the breath catch in my throat. Dolly shot me a look of pity. I knew what she was thinking: *She loves that boy too much.* And she was right. But until the Russells took him away, he was *my* boy and I was *his* momma.

"He be all right," Dolly said.

"I know."

"*Vaya con Dios, Maryam,*" she called after me. *Go with God.*

Had I been one to gamble, I would have put silver on Mrs. Brown's baby coming so fast I would forfeit a fee. But I would have lost that bet. Five babies in twelve years; I'd delivered the last two, easiest birthings I had. All Amy Brown ever did was fart twice, grunt, and the baby tumbled out. But not this one. I guess six wasn't her lucky number.

I got there and she was pacing the room, grunting like a pig one moment, screaming like a terror the next. Every time she opened her mouth, her husband flinched. He had the look of a caged animal desperate to run yet knowing that he had to stay, and 'sides, where would he go? I handed him my basket, put my hand on Amy Brown's shoulder, and guided her back to the bed, talking to Mr. Graham over my shoulder as we walked.

"Kettle on? Blankets?"

He nodded.

"How long since the pains start?"

"Since before supper. She say it's never been like this. Says she feels like the baby's splitting her apart." His face was so white I could see through it to his bones.

"Having a baby kinda feels like that —"

I was interrupted by a bloodcurdling scream. Amy grabbed my hand so hard I thought that she was going to tear it off.

"Maryam! Help me! This is killing me! I can't do this!"

"Miz Brown, let me see now," I said with a calmness that I did not feel. She'd been laboring for eight hours by my count. No way a woman who'd had five children should have been in this much pain for so long with nothing to show for it. I spread her legs wide and examined the birth canal. Amy screamed again and I held my breath. "Pant slow, Miz Brown, slow . . . slow . . ." I closed my eyes and gently massaged her huge belly, hard in some places, more giving in others, then I reached inside the birth canal and found what I expected to find. I looked over at Brown. He swallowed slowly.

"Miz Brown . . . Now, you need to take a breath when I tell you. Ima turn this li'l one 'round then. It's gonna hurt. But —"

"Do it!" she growled.

"Yes, ma'am," I murmured. The little one settled himself into my palm as if he knew what I was doing and why. Amy held her breath and said nothing, didn't scream or even moan. The room was still. Even Master Graham, who looked as if he was either going to vomit or faint, just stood there and held his breath. Don't know how much time passed exactly, but the next sounds I heard were those of a small but healthy baby boy and a wiggling angry baby girl who wasn't happy about making an entrance into a bright but cool room. Her face turned red from squawking and she kicked me on the nose when I tried to situate her and cut the cord. That done, I wrapped her up in a shawl and handed her over to her mother. Brown held the little boy and was grinning like a fool. He did not vomit or faint.

"Maryam, you don't want to stay over?" he asked later after he recovered himself. He watched me as I packed up my baskets. "You can stay here with Amy and the little ones until it gets lighter." He held back the curtain a little and peered outside. It was five thirty, six o'clock, still dark with a ring of light along the edges of the horizon, the prophecy of morning to come. "It's foggy out, won't be easy walking in the hills till it lifts. I can send my boy with you."

"No, sir, I be fine. I know these roads as good as my hand, fog or not. Thank you, sir." I needed to move on, had a job to do. Miz Amy was fine, was already feeding both babies. And her mother and her oldest, Maureen, were there to help. 'Less Brown sent word, I would look in on his family in a few days. Told him not to let Miz Amy get up for least two sunrises.

Took the road that hugged the eastern edge of the Brown farm. Brown's corn was planted here. Like everywhere else in the valley this year, it was growing well. The stalks were tall as a man in some places. The fog had settled over the silk tops like a cloud that had lost its way. I wasn't surprised that there was no one around, it was hard to see, so hard to work. But my feet had taken this way so many times that they moved without my having to think. The road branched off at the boundary of Brown's farm and John Eastman's. Here the fields bumped against a bastion of white maple trees, venerable hardwood giants marking the opening to the uncultivated higher ground. McCulloch said the trees there were older than God's coat, that they were old even when Cherokee hunters moved in and out of the country following bison and hunting elk. This had been a logging road once and there'd been a mill on the creek until it ran dry. I took the northern way and followed the old Indian hunting trail into the woods.

This part of Virginia was different from the lowland area where I had lived before, different from the Georgia marshes and the heat of Caesar's Key, and oh, so different from the place Edo where I was born. The forests were dense, so tight packed with trees it was like dusk, and here and there were outcrops of rock — and caves. Some of them lead a soul deep into the earth, all of them places of mystery, the source of ghost stories and the lair of fairies, trolls, or monsters, depending on who was telling the tale. Even I had spun a story about a blond spider the size of a cat who ate rabbits and squirrels for supper and used the cave as a nest. Because I had a reputation, was called an "African witch" by some and a "geechie woman" by others, the story held and kept the curious away. And it wasn't entirely a lie: I had seen a light-colored spider but it was more the size of a fingertip, and so it couldn't eat squirrels on any account.

You could stand within ten feet of Indian's Cave and not see it. A copse of small trees framed the entrance; flowering shrubs, sunflowers, and ivy-covered rock so that the niche appeared more like small mound than an opening into a hill. No people lived in this part of the woods. The cave was isolated and situated midway to the top of a ridge and out of sight from the creek, where deer and coyotes came to drink in waves at dawn and dusk. And that made it near perfect for hiding runaways. It was off the path; the nearest work that could be considered a road was at least half a mile away. Even men on horseback who might have been following the old bison trails through the hills, who might need to stop and give their horses a drink, would have no reason to climb out of the ravine and up the ridge.

The cave was secret but not undiscovered: it had been a trysting place for lovers, a shelter from rain for trappers, a camp for Cherokee hunting parties and anyone who needed a place warm and dry but invisible. Over the years, I'd found animal bones, pipe stems, campfire remnants, and a broken teacup. "A" and "J" had carved their initials into soft limestone near the opening. At the back of the cave where it narrowed to a near-solid wall of limestone rock, leaving an opening large enough for only a small animal to crawl through, an earlier visitor had drawn a hunting party across the side wall, men on foot with bows, arrows, and spears, elk and bear, traces of red ocher and charcoal outlines still clear in the dim light even to my tired eyes.

It was so quiet that you could hear a butterfly breathe. I whistled. The trill of a goldfinch that used the huge sunflowers for games and nests. Another goldfinch answered. I pushed the lilacs aside and stepped in.

He was waiting for me.

"Thank you, missus," he said after devouring the food I'd brought and drinking near a half gallon of water before taking a breath. He belched loudly. His cheeks colored. "Excuse me."

I smiled, rummaged in my basket, and held up a roll of linen and a small tin. "Let me see your arm."

He'd cut himself. The wound wasn't festering but it needed to be cleaned and treated so that it wouldn't. He winced while I tended to him but said nothing, only smiled with gratitude.

"What's your name?"

"Har . . . Henry, Missus."

I smiled again. The young man had manners that showed.

"Have you chosen a second name for yourself? What was your owner's name?"

"I've chose my own name," Henry said quickly. There was a story behind his sharp tone. "Johnson. It be . . . will be Johnson. John was my father's name."

"All right, Mr. Johnson." I patted his arm. "Done." I handed over a folded length of linen and the salve. "Fore you sleep this night, you take that off" — I pointed — "Rinse it with clear water, then pat it dry. Let the air see it for a while then wrap it up careful before you set out."

I wanted to ask him where he was from and where he was going but I wouldn't. I was to know only enough to feed him, treat any wounds he had, and prepare him for the next stop on his journey. What the next stop was . . . that was not my business nor was his destination, although Mr. Johnson felt no qualms telling me.

"Going to Canada, Missus," he said. "This may be the land of freedom for some but it ain't for me. My cousin found work on a farm up in Ontario near a town called Amherstburg and that's where I'm bound."

"Goodbye Mr. Johnson," I said before I left him. There was a tightness in my throat, something about this young man made me weepy. Dolly's words came into my head and I said, "Go with God." *Vaya con Dios. Go with any gods you can find.*

As I walked home, I couldn't get him out of my mind. He was so young, so determined. The glint of fury in his eye when he said that he would not take his former owner's name. The glimmer that took its place when he spoke about Canada and a farm where he would have work. And a life.

How old was Henry Johnson? Eighteen? Twenty? Somewhere in the world, my Eli, Shadrach, near his age. Alexander would be eighteen or twenty someday, if the gods went with him. If backbreaking work didn't kill him, if he wasn't sold downriver to cut cane in Louisiana, if he didn't take up an infection or a lung-wasting sickness, if he didn't back talk a white man and get killed, standing up for himself, having his say, and acting his measure. In my head, I saw my boy's face as he grew — whether the Russells took him back or not, he would always be my boy. Alexander at five, at twelve, his legs long and skinny, his voice cracking between high and low, Alexander at . . . fifteen, at sixteen . . . too soon a grown man. Wanting to be his own man.

I had helped more folks than I could remember cross this backcountry moving north or west or anywhere out of this Virginia. I had seen the lash marks, treated ankles and wrists gone bloody and raw from chains, heard the stories about rape and separation and death. So much death. Their lives were mine, and my life was theirs. I had ministered to the hurt, the weary, and prepared the dead for their last journey. And I had sent them on their way with the best that was in my heart. But this was the first time in a long time that I had allowed myself to wonder if any of these journeys could be mine. Now I was. Because of Alexander.

What kind of life would he have here? Percy Russell wasn't a hard man but he knew hard times. When he took Alexander back — how long fore he decided to make a profit on a "likely negroe lad"? And Mc-Culloch . . . Alexander was near a year old and cute. What happened when he was grown up and not cute anymore?

Could I run? Take freedom for myself and for Alexander along the ways that Dolly and the others had constructed? Was it time? If I went now I'd have to carry him but soon, very soon, it could be me and my boy in that cave, me and that boy making a way to Pennsylvania or Ohio or maybe the Canada that Henry Johnson spoke of.

These thoughts turned over and over in my head as I made my way down the ridge from the cave. I kept moving, followed the trail down toward the creek. From there, all I had to do was walk along the creek bed then across the ridge and down to the back acreage of McCulloch's lands. Was halfway to the creek when I heard men's voices, a dog barking, and woke up from the walking sleep that had covered me. Ahead of me was Lacey's Creek and four men, two standing, two mounted. A large hound rummaged in the undergrowth. One of the men was Mc-Culloch.

I stopped short, lost my footing, near slid the rest of the way down the slope. But I caught myself and crouched low and held my breath, pulling my shawl tight around my shoulders. The hound turned its head in my direction and lifted its snout towards the sky, sniffing. One of the men reached down and patted the animal on the head and glanced upward, trying to follow the direction of the dog's attention. But I was wearing gray and brown and blended into the foliage like a jackrabbit. The hound stood up then swung its large head in the opposite direction and its handler was diverted. I took that moment to exhale the fear slowly then grab another breath. Nothing I could do except wait.

And listen.

". . . no right . . ." McCulloch's voice.

". . . the law and Ima uphold it . . ." The high jarring cackle of the slave catcher they called "the Kaintuckian."

"Yew think yourra one to tell me the law? I know the laws well enough. And on my land, I am the law."

The hound scratched the ground with its hind legs then swung its head back toward its master. The Kaintuckian's weird high-pitched laughter carried up the ridge and sent a chill down my spine.

"Well," he said, stretching the one word into two, "you right there, sir. And Ima one to mind the laws as I am sure you can appreciate. I have to respect them too and I have a job to do. Now any runaway niggers I find, on your land or anyone else's, b'long t'me. And there's talk, sir. There's a lot of talk 'bout them finding refuge hair in these woods and —"

"You'll na do your job on my lands, sir, I'll take you out m'eself." It had been years since McCulloch left Scotland and the time had softened his accent except when he was agitated. And the Kaintuckian had him good and agitated. "Any negroes — that aren't mine — that I find on my lands, I'll deal with. D'ye ken? D'ye understand my meaning, sir? I am the hand of justice on my property, not you."

The Kaintuckian laughed again. There was a hardness to his voice but I pushed away the urge to shudder. The hound's attention had shifted again in my direction.

"Singular idear o' justice you have there, Mac," the man said, and even with the distance, I could see the Scot's jaw tighten. "But the federal law goes afore yours." McCulloch's body twitched, the motion sent the Kaintuckian back a step. He wiped his forehead with the back of his arm and

410

giggled. "However . . . I'm not one to trample on the rights of law-abiding citizens." He bowed low in a mock concession. "I'll take ye word for it. A word o' warning . . . if your niggers are out on . . . your business, they carry a pass. I would hate to pick one of 'em up. By mistake like, y'understand." The man grinned.

This time there was no twitch. McCulloch took a full step toward the man. I was sure that he was going to strike him. The Kaintuckian's grin disappeared. The hound lowered its head and growled. McCulloch growled back. The hound went silent.

"Should that happen, mistake or no," McCulloch said, "I'll bring ye 'afore the sheriff if I don't hang ye up meself."

The Kaintuckian flinched then giggled again, from nerves. He mounted his horse, tipped his hat, and whistled for the hound, which took one last look up the ridge then followed his master and the other men away from the creek. McCulloch stood at the creek side for a long time, long after the sounds of the Kaintuckian, his men, and the horses melted into the breath of the forest, and the only noise that came to human ears was the water running lightly down the creek bed and the goldfinches laughing as they played their games. Finally, he swung himself up into his saddle, used the reins to turn the huge mare's head, and rode off south toward his farm.

I waited until I no longer heard the sound of men and horses moving through the forest then picked up my pack and basket and made my way down the ridge and across the creek.

31
ALEXANDER EDWARD McCULLOCH GRACE

"He wants you," Dolly said, greeting me at the kitchen door, Alexander squirming in her arms. Dolly's nose twitched and she took a step back. "*Dios mío . . .* what is that smell? Oh!" Comprehension flooded her features as she batted the baby's hand away from me. She frowned. "Trouble?" Our eyes met and she nodded with understanding. *Later.*

"Hello baby boy," I cooed at Alexander, who was reaching toward me with both chubby hands. "No, no, baby. Momma's got to wash up first . . ."

"I wish you could," Dolly said, turning her nose up again. "*He* say to send you soon as you come." She nodded her head slightly toward the stable and sighed. Her expression folded into a frown of worry and she lowered her voice to a loud whisper. "Was he . . ."

I nodded. Mr. Henry Johnson was on his

way to someplace north.

"A few cuts, not festerin'. Can't you give me something to wipe my face?"

Dolly grinned. "Wait there." She wagged her finger at me. "Don't you even think about coming into my kitchen smelling like that!" She disappeared into the kitchen and returned with a wet cloth.

McCulloch was waiting for me in the stable. Jemmy took care of the horses except for Ben; McCulloch was the only one to lay a hand on the mare. He was brushing the animal's flank when I entered. Ben swung her huge head toward me. She snorted, whinnied, then stamped the ground as if trying to get away. Then she reared up, almost knocking the Scot off his feet.

"Woman! What the . . ." McCulloch grabbed the reins and tried to get the animal calm. "Coo, coo, dinna fash girl." He glanced at me over his shoulder, a dark expression on his face. "Shhhh . . ." A low growl sent me backing out of the door. Ginger barked, then let out a mournful howl.

"Dolly said . . . ," I shouted so that he could hear me over the ruckus.

"What . . . in the name of Jesus, Mary, and Joseph is that godawful smell? You fall into a den of skunks? Shhh . . . there,

there . . ." McCulloch glared at me as much as he dared since he was still struggling to get the horse settled. He looked like the wrath of God that Brother Willard shouted about in his sermons. It was Willard's favorite subject, a bitter hot sharp rain burning itself through the skin of unsuspecting sinners who thought they'd gotten away with some transgression or other.

I'd wiped my face with the damp cloth as I walked to the stables, my stomach in knots, knowing that I would get dressed down, or worse, by the angry Scotsman, terrified that he would send his own patrollers after Henry Johnson and others like him although I had to admit I'd never heard of the man doing such a thing. But if Ben's and Ginger's reactions were anything to go by, I hadn't washed up enough. The hound wouldn't stop howling. I was satisfied. The repellent would do its work. No dog could or would follow young Henry's scent. I couldn't help but smile even when I met McCulloch's fierce gaze.

"Get out! Go wash y'self, woman! Yew smell like a raccoon's arse!"

I was pleased to hear that. He used near the same words as Henry when I'd saturated him with the salve.

Henry had coughed, sneezed, then

coughed again. His eyes were watering.

"Excuse me . . . Missus . . . but what *is* that? It smell like . . . beg your pardon . . . the wrong end of a possum."

I'd grinned and continued with my work, spreading the mixture across his back in a layer as thick as butter. The residue went on my neck and arms and across my chest and the front of my skirt. I didn't want no slave catcher's hound to follow my tracks back to McCulloch's farm.

"It's for the dogs. T'make sure they don't follow your scent. Take this." I handed him a vial.

Henry blinked a few times then raised his hand, which I grabbed before he could wipe away the water from his eyes.

"No!" I shouted. "You don't want it in your eyes! Let me . . ."

I wiped his eyes out gently then dabbed his face dry.

"What's in it?" he asked, coughing as if he'd like to choke.

I smiled.

"Well, it a secret. Just a li'l bit of this and the other, a drop of that and a pinch of red peppers to give it flavor."

He chuckled.

"Any hound who comes up against it will regret it for the rest of its days."

I was proud of the repellent, part my own concoction and part borrowed from Marie Catherine. Nothing on four legs or two, no matter how large and fearsome, wanted anything to do with it. The stench sent horses into a frenzy. Now the Scotsman had two things to be angry at me about.

Dolly roared with laughter when I returned to her kitchen to take Alexander and told her what had happened. She sniffed me around my neck to make sure I'd washed properly before she released my boy to my arms.

"That better," she said, smiling. Alexander yawned and nestled his head against my shoulder. "He all wore out. I tell you, Maryam, he walk soon. I spent the day chasing him 'round the house, him crawlin', me walkin'!" I kissed my boy and buried my nose in his black curly hair. Dolly had bathed him (she loved giving him a bath) and used a soap that she made herself, scented with herbs, lavender, and dried flowers. It smelled like fresh grass and lilacs.

"Get you some rest," she added, passing me a basket of food. I'd forgotten about supper. "Heard from Lewis over on the Burleigh place. His Norma's been suffering and Master Burleigh give him leave to get you to have a look in."

I sighed. It'd been a long night with Amy Brown and now it might be another one with Norma.

"When I'm supposed to go?"

Dolly rubbed Alexander's back.

"Note from Master Burleigh say he'll send Lewis with the wagon to fetch you tomorrow. They busy with picking today." I remember hoping that Norma didn't drop dead in the orchard.

So I was to get one night's rest, anyway. I walked slowly back to my cabin feeling ever' one of my forty-some years and every pound of Alexander. The boy would have to walk soon. He was getting too heavy for me to carry. I nursed him then settled him into bed and collapsed into the chair, too tired to eat, too tired to get into bed. Just wanted to sit and think.

I stared at the hearth. It wasn't cold enough for a fire but I saw one in my mind. Blazing, the flames yellow, red, and orange, leaping and dancing, warming a room that was mine in a cabin that was mine, cooking food that was mine, nourishing my life and my son's life in heat, plenty, and safety. In a place that was not here, not in this western Virginia but somewhere north, across a dark fast river. A place that would be colder than I was used to but a place where I could . . .

and Alexander could . . . just be. Sent my mind back.

What it like to be free, Miz Maryam?

Columbia's voice was as clear as if he were sitting there. He had twisted his ankle badly trying to escape from a patroller's hounds. How he managed to make his way to the quarters at the edge of the Nash farm I did not know. Only that he did. Back when my husband . . . after James, Shadrach, and Eli were sold, before I was brought here to this western Virginia valley.

Seemed like to me there were more of us then, those born in "Africky" as some called it. They did not realize that we "country-born niggers" were from many places, with many names, that we spoke many words. All of us dropped onto a farm mixed with people who looked like us but were not the same. Born here and been no other place but here and in chains, the iron kind and the kind that wrapped themselves around your thoughts. It was as strange as a thought of taking wings to the moon. Many of the "native born" had parents who were from across the water, too, but they had been separated from them and there was no one to guide them or answer their questions. Except someone like me.

What it like . . . to be free?

I answered with few words. My job was to heal, to clean a wound, to serve as midwife. Conversation was a distraction I had no time for. So many times I was asked this question, so many times I answered and sent the soon-to-be-forgotten one on his way. Columbia was different.

He was an older man, in his fifties and dying from an untreated gash on his leg delivered by an overzealous overseer. The wound gone days without cleaning so when I was sent for to tend him, fever and rot had set in. He was dying and would never see free here on this earth. All I could do was ease his way to his gods. Maybe that's why I remember him. Because I knew my answer was the last one he would get.

"You one of those Africkys, Miz Maryam," the man said slowly, his words slurred by the high fever and worn as the sole on a shoe. "My mammy was from Africky. Had a . . ." He brought one large scarred hand to his cheek, his fingers were gnarled like a broken branch fallen from an old tree. "Marks . . . right here. On her cheeks."

"Um-hm . . ." I murmured, taking his hand down and laying it as gently as I could at his side. "That sound like the people who live south across the great river . . . their women are warriors. It is said . . ." He did, he had the true look of them. Tall, somewhat stout, with wide flaring nostrils and a noble forehead. I remembered . . . how strange that his words sent me back to my mother. "My mother say their people work gold."

He closed his eyes and nodded. Then he smiled.

"My . . . . mammy say it beautiful there. Say . . . the trees they . . ."

The trees. I closed my eyes and saw them, the trees near my parents' home. Smelled their fragrance. In the before time.

"She never could . . . settle here."

"Columbia, rest. Don't talk."

He was past hearing me.

". . . told me she'd jump . . ." He lifted his hand again, his veins swollen and dark, gestured toward some place that only he could see. "She'd jump in the river if . . . not for me." He sighed and his hand dropped like a stone onto the bed. But he open his eyes and look at me.

"What it like to be free, Miz Maryam?"

I lied to him. I told him what I thought his mother would have wanted him to hear before he died. And when he passed over to the place of shadows and spirits, I imagined her, standing on the shore of that river, holding out her hand and smiling. How could I tell him my truth?

I'd lived more years in this place than in my mother and father's land. As far as I could figure, I was a child when the white-sailed boat left the port of Ouidah, I hadn't even had my first blood yet. Before the traders grabbed me, before they sold me to the Portuguese, who traded me off to the English, I was a little girl, playing games with her friends, being teased by her sisters and her brothers. I helped my mother with her babies, fetched water, and walked the paths with my father, who called me his . . . little red hawk. I was a girl, a middle child, neither the treasured first son nor the most beautiful of daughters, a child whose mind was fixed on the next game and doing her chores and what she would eat. I had not even known that I was such a thing as "free." And with each passing year, the images had begun to drop away, one by one, and the ones remaining started to retreat to a place in my mind that got harder to reach, the memories more pale in color as they disappeared behind the curtain that led to the mists of time. I could not bring myself to tell Columbia or anyone what it was like to be free, because I had not realized then that I *was.*

That is not what I wanted for Alexander.

A knock on my door and the memories

shattered like broken glass. How long had I been sitting there, staring into the past? Another knock. I stood up feeling dazed, smoothed my dress around my aching thighs and knees. My back was stiff and my head ached; there was a storm coming, I had seen its clouds forming over the west ridge, dark gray and angry. It was late. But I am used to knocks on my door when it is late. Babies come when they ready. Folks sick when they sick. Figured it was Lewis from the Burleigh place, come to tell me that Norma needed my help. Thunder rumbled, faint but not faint for long. I glanced over at my pack setting in the corner. I'd have to move fast if I was to make it to the Burleigh place before the rain. Take Alexander to Dolly and Herc.

It wasn't Lewis at the door, it was McCulloch.

"Sir." I wasn't glad to see him but least he knocked. Durfee never knocked, just opened the door and walked through like he owned the place and me.

"I'm a sorry to come so late, Maryam but . . . there are wards to say." He threw a look at the cradle, lowered his voice. "Is the bairn asleep?"

I was too tired to say anything, one word or two, so I just nodded.

"You did a fool thing this morning," he started, his voice low and tense. He moved to the other side of the room. I did not hear his footsteps. For a large man, he moved like a cat. "I told yew to send word from Brown's place so that Jemmy or Hercules could fetch you or ask Brown to let their boy to walk with yew to the northern edge of the farm. I told yew not to walk in the dark. The slave catchers are prowling 'round the county, tramping across my lands. And that Kaintuckian . . ." McCulloch's voice filled with contempt. "He's a godless fiend. He has no qualms about snatching you up and carrying you away." The Scotsman's eyes gleamed in the dim light of the lamp. "Pass or no."

I nodded again. He was right and I knew it but I was far away, lost in my thoughts. His voice sounded like someone calling to me from a distance. McCulloch grabbed me by the shoulders and shook me.

"Woman do ye hear me? Do ye mind me?"

"Yes!" I shouted back at him then looked over at Alexander, sleeping through the storm of words as if we'd said nothing. "Yes," I repeated in a loud whisper.

"How many this morning?" the Scotsman asked. My blood froze. He released his grip on my arms and brought his face closer to mine. "How many?"

How did he know? A moment's clear thought. *How did he . . . how could he not know?* The pieces fell into place. Workers coming, going. Never a talk about an auction or selling someone on. Dolly's contentment. Hercules's absence for days at a time. And the Indian's Cave. The conjunctions . . . so organized. So secret.

"One."

He nodded.

"I want ye to stop."

I shook my head.

"Think, woman," he growled. "That Kaintucky boy has got a holy mission in his head. He thinks he's clever and he smells gold. I willna be able to protect ye if they catch ye at the cave or in the forest. What happens to your boy if they snatch you up?"

I shook my head again but this time tears fell. I hadn't thought of that.

"Don't mean nothin'. He's not m-my . . . boy. B'longs to Mr. Russell." Wiped the tears away with the back of my arm.

"Belongs to me. I bought him off Russell six month ago."

I broke my rule about not looking white men in the eye. And McCulloch was looking back.

"You? B-bought him?"

"Aye."

"So he yours then."

"No." McCulloch paused for a moment, then said, "He's yours. Ye brought him in the world and took care of his mother's last breaths even with the bad blood between you. Yew fed the child at your breast and yew . . . are the only mother he knows. But you're a headstrong woman, Maryam Grace, and reckless. And ye have a will just as fierce. I know —" He stopped. "I ask of yew one thing. And think well before ye answer."

The boy fretted and both of us, startled, turned our attention to him. He had kicked off his blanket, as he always did, and was lying on his back, his round belly moving softly up and down, his little mouth open. He was snoring. I couldn't help it, I giggled and patted him on the stomach to settle him. He inhaled and his tiny eyelids fluttered. He smacked his lips. Alexander didn't even know that I was there.

"He's a fine lad," McCulloch said. He was so close that I could feel his breath on the back of my neck.

He would be, I thought, with his beautiful young strong parents: Nini and her exquisite face and body, now gone. Ned, whose love and body I had shared with her, his

426

broad chest and back, his strong yet expressive hands with their long fingers, his deep-textured voice . . . gone. My little Edward, that little boy, he might have been lovely, too, had he been stronger, had the contagion not taken hold.

"I know yew want to run. Ye canna help all these pur souls without wantin' a taste of the freedom for yourself. You're strong and you're wise. Yew have a craft to make your way. If I give yew papers of emancipation, for yourself and Alexander, will ye take him north with yew, along the . . . paths that the others know, and raise him up, see him schooled and trained? I'll pay your passage. And no hounds or patrollers will track yew." He sighed and his shoulders drooped. He was tired.

McCulloch placed the back of his hand against Alexander's cheek. "I'm old. I'm wantin' to see Cardoness again. I'm no slave master, never was. Owned people to get the work done and . . . but was near owned me-self in Scotland. My folk had nothing. So . . . I'll send ye and the boy; Dolly, Herc, Jemmy, and the rest can go on later when they wish. Then I'll sell up and sail off. Go home." He chuckled as if remembering another time and place . . . as I had been remembering before he walked in that night. "And live me days out in a thatched-roof cottage next to a hollow hill somewhere near the loch with a few sheep, horses, a pipe, and a bottle of whiskey."

A sob stuck in my throat.

McCulloch frowned then spoke under his breath using the words of his faraway home.

"Home. You want to go . . . to your home." I imagined his Scotland, a place I'd heard talk about; I saw it as a cold, wet, green place with mountains and plains and wind. The deep lakes he called "lochs" so different from the place I called home and could not remember and could not return to. I felt hot tears streaming down my face. I also felt the palm of his hand on my cheek, cool and soft.

"I'd send ye there if I knew how . . ." He spoke as though he had read my thoughts.

But his touch had stopped my words.

"W-what are those words? What did you call me?"

He pulled his hand away and took a step back as if he had just realized that he had touched me. He shook his head as if to clear it then looked down. But before he lowered his gaze I saw the shadow of embarrassment and a sadness of the heart, longing . . . the loneliness of a man whose true home was far away, whose wife and children had been dead for decades, who had nothing but his work to warm his heart, no woman to warm his bed and had not loved anyone in a long, long time until a small chubby little boy showed up one day before the corn harvest. I saw the face of man who wanted tenderness.

I knew what he was feeling. I knew, perhaps more than anyone on his place, the pain . . . the unfillable hole of loss, loss of husband and children, a scar that was unseen but would always be with me. I would be buried with it. And I also knew the longing that had sometimes driven me out of my head, the loneliness and the longing . . . for an endearing word, a gentle touch.

"I — I'm . . . I said . . ." When he looked up at me again, I didn't look away. "I called you 'my heart.' "

When babies sleep, it's the sleep of the righteous. They haven't lived long enough to have regrets. Alexander slept beyond that. Dolly said that he slept like a stone, and it was true. I worried whenever thunder rolled across the valley, bringing with it waves of water like the storms at sea that I remembered, the lightning flashes in the dark as if they were fugitive bursts of sun. I'd run to the cradle and grab Alexander, tuck him in next to me, and lay there in the bed, trembling because it sounded as if the gods were angry and had sent giants to destroy us with thunderbolts and light rays and winds strong enough to drop trees. I couldn't sleep until the storm passed but Alexander could, he slept through it all. So when the storm that had made my head ache finally arrived from across the ridge and into the valley and when the storm that was McCulloch and me erupted, Alexander slept through them both.

He took my hand in his and, bringing it to his lips, kissed my palm.

"I . . . havena done this in a long time," he said, his low, softly growling voice barely audible over the sound of the rain on the roof. I clasped his hand in mine and pulled him close until I felt his body against mine. I hadn't done this in a long time either.

I stop here. Close my mouth. Blink my eyes in the sun. I won't say more words about this. About . . . him. McCulloch.

Have I forgot? Who ask me this? Forgot what it was like with him? With McCulloch? Have I forgot how gentle he was, how he look at me as if I . . . how he touch my shoulder as if he had not touch a woman before? When I reach for him . . .

No. I have not forgot. Ne'er will forget.

The mists may cover my eyes sometime, send fog o'er my rememberings, but not all the way. And not these rememberings.

These are the things that I hold close, keep for myself. They are mine alone now. Treasures of my heart hid from sight like Caesar's gold wher'er it is. And these things I cannot say to the young ones, to my children, my grandchildren. They are not for them. They are not theirs.

What I will say. That being with him, with McCulloch, was just as she'd said it would be, Marie Catherine, all those years ago. She had told me near word for word what I would think, how I would feel inside, how his body would feel, warm and soft, against mine. The child I was had listened but not understood. Had heard but held out her hand against Marie's words. At twelve you think you know all but you know nothing.

"Never," I'd spat out. *"Jamais!"* I'd used her own language, my pronunciation coarse. The memory was as clear as if it were before me, in my cabin. And in some ways, it was.

She'd smiled, Marie Catherine had, and placed her palm against my cheek, then brushed away the tears that it found there.

"Cherie, what happened to you was . . . not how it will be with a man you love. It was not the way it should be."

431

"I don't want a . . . m-man to touch me! Ever!" I'd shouted back, my throat closing from emotion. All I knew of a man's touch was that of the man who had grabbed me, used me in a cruel way, then smacked me, hard, across the back of my head, shoved me down on the cobblestones, busting my lip. I wonder that Caesar didn't notice the black and purple bruises, the swelling on my forehead. He was good at seeing everything, a pocket too full, eyes shifting one way to another, a rival's expression that spoke of agreement or deception. But he didn't see. And I never said until Marie saw through me.

"Listen, *la petite* Marie," she said. "Know that what I tell you is true. I do not call it 'love' but . . . if you have a man who treats you well, who listens, accepts your words and your wisdom, touches you with restraint and tenderness, take him. Do not bother about his language, or his wealth or poverty. Do not concern yourself with his status. Take tenderness where you find it. And know that sometimes, it comes in a form that you may find hard to accept. But . . ." She passed her hand gracefully across her body. "These bodies are of no importance. It is what is in the heart that matters."

She spoke true, Marie Catherine did. I

saw a flash of uncertainty in the Scotsman's eyes, as if something had given him pause. I place my palm against his cheek. The coarse hairs of his beard rubbed against my hand.

Take tenderness where you find it.

In the County of Pittsylvania,
Commonwealth of Virginia
Comes this day 6 May 1806, Abraham William McCulloch, who hereby emancipates Maryam Prescilla Grace and her son, Alexander Edward McCulloch Grace for consideration as agreed upon. Said emancipation to be honored from this day forward.

Signed — "X" his mark — Abraham William McCulloch

I STILL HAVE the paper.

PART IV
MOMMA GRACE

32
THE RIVER

Was some time passing before I left the Virginia. There was much to do with plans to make and conjunctions to see to, messages to send. Would be plenty of sunrises and -sets until Alexander's legs strong enough so that his old mother would not have to carry him all the way to Ohio.

Even with papers — and the Scotsman would not be satisfied until I had a satchel full — there was no promise that patrollers wouldn't trouble us. To their way of thinking, we were walking money. My salve could put off the hounds but men had sharp eyes. There was always folks watching. Coins talk. A coin in a palm could shake aloose any worry 'bout the right or wrong of owning people or seeing them gone. Tricksters take the coin and the papers. McCulloch took his time because he didn't want nothing to happen to Alexander. Or to me. So my journey to this chair on a porch in a clap-

437

board house on a ridge in Highland County began long afore I took one step.

McCulloch hired Jasper Schilling and Isaac Cupp to carry us up. They were too young, I thought, nephews of McCulloch's cousin who knew the land and the ways to get through it. I won't tell the way we took. The children say I should, say it history and good for people to know. They say, "Momma Grace, the war's over, slavery's finished. Nobody comin' to take you back." I laugh and tell them, "Who pay a bounty for a old woman who don't see good and walk even less than that?"

But it ground into me, this no telling. It ground in from the days I spent alone in the cabin on Nash's farm tending to runaways, ghosts, and others. It ground in from my knowing Dolly and what she did to help folks all those years. No one person knew all the ways and safe places, the calls and signals. I look back through the mists and wonder if even Dolly knew the whole way. And though I will see the roads and the trees, the hills and the sky along the path we took, I cannot . . . will not say how I came to Ohio. The roads we took were only for us and changed for the ones who came after. And changed again for the ones who next came. And changed. Known once and then forgot.

We left the Virginia, I hugged Dolly and Herc and Jemmy, his wife, Sinde, and his baby, Li'l Sinde, and the others. For the last time, I cast my eyes over the green vastness that was the valley of McCulloch's farm, the land I'd worked, rich and green, the fields generous with their gifts, the woodlands thick with the trees that the Scotsman said were older than God's coat, that stood so close they were like grass. The mountains, Jasper called them "Alleghenies," I decided they were gods who were old, older than I am now, and had got tired from their wanderin's, settled their big feet into the earth, and now were stuck, thunder their grumblin's like old men do, smoking their god-size pipes until the smoke mixed with clouds and covered the tops of their heads.

It was August, some crops in, some not, but the weather was turning, slow-like, from the choking hot of summer to the cool dry of autumn, and the plants and the crawling things did not know how to manage. At night under a full moon, we fought off the mosquitoes and the biting ants that flew and listened until our heads hurt to the grinding buzz of cicadas. But as we moved into the foothills south of the river valley, the air cooled and the days not so long as afore.

The hopping bugs call "crickets" began a song at sunset, and the cicadas' songs got shorter and quieter as if they were listening. Not long 'fore we came out of Mason County — where we changed wagons at McCulloch's cousin's farm — the cicadas stopped singing and left the darkness to the hopping bugs.

Alexander rode in the wagon, Alexander rode on my back, Alexander walked on his little feet, wearing out one of the two pairs of boots that McCulloch had the cobbler make for him. He was three and fussy. He had his father's long legs and his mother's temper. Every word Jasper and Isaac put down, Alexander pick up. Sides "no," his favorite word was "goddamn." His next-favorite word was "why?" He marched so close around the horses I was feared that he'd get trampled but he was never afraid. McCulloch had trained him. I saw Ned's strength in the set of his little jaw. Nini's beauty in his perfect nose. He was their boy in my keeping. And he would grow up a free man.

"Ma'am? Missus Grace? We're here."

At the end of the dock, a tall man wrestled the ropes then stood up. Jasper and Isaac wave at him, he wave back. Wipe his hands on his britches and take long steps over to the wagon, holding the horses as the boys jumped down.

Jasper and Isaac greeted him, pat him on the back.

"Mister Ellis run the ferry, Miss Maryam," they say.

The tall man take me down from the wagon like I weigh nothing, Alexander, too. He tip his hat.

"Nathan Ellis, ma'am." He look down at Alexander, who looking at him like he a giant, which he is.

"Fine boy, ma'am."

It take me a while to get used to white men calling me "ma'am."

"Sir. Mister Ellis, you got people over Bedford, Pittsylvania County way? A Mistress Isabella Russell Ellis?"

Ellis's face, long and raw-boned, give away nothing.

"Yes, ma'am," he say. "Unfortunately, I do."

Ellis manage that ferry boat so it glide along, hardly make a sound in the water. Maybe he know. This only a river but I don't like water. Not since the before time.

A clear way, marked on both sides by shrubs, small trees, the side of a dilapidated whitewashed house. A landing like the one near Newton's Mill and a small ferry dock.

Beyond the trees and the little house and the landing, a town followed the shore, barges, a riverboat with a wheel turning, buildings, a smokestack in the distance and a hill covered with trees and houses. And in between a river, wide, largest I seen since coming to this land, its waters sparkled in the sun, the sound of splashes as it touched the shore.

Everyone who see it give it a name. The people who once live here, gone now, call it "Spaylaywesipe"; those who went north call it the principal stream. The *français, "la belle riviere."* It is wide in places, so deep that the whiskered fish that swim the bottom grow as long as a man. It bring people, trade, and contagions. When it flood, the water turn brown. It run fast and it kills. They call it the "Ohio." I call it the river.

Jasper grinned, his skinny face bright. Isaac nodded, wipe his face with a red-print handkerchief. He was grinning.

"It's a beauty, ain't it?"

I nodded, all I could do.

"Momma! See! Big water! *Big* water!" I picked up Alexander, getting heavier each time. I kissed him.

"Yes. Big water."

"This is your house, Mrs. Grace."

442

The woman named Mrs. Gordan look around like she nervous.

"I hope it will suit."

My house.

I looked around the front room of the clapboard house, felt a swelling in my chest. The room was small like the cabins on the Nash farm, but that wasn't all there was. A door led to another room. And there were windows and a wooden floor. The little hilltop house had been swept and scrubbed down, probably by this Mrs. Gordon herself, and my throat was so tight with gratitude that I could not speak to tell her. The house was rented for what Mrs. Gordon say was "an indefinite period" and the fee had been paid. When I left the Scot handed me a pouch of coin that he said was mine and only mine, "to be used for you and the bairn." I call it "Alexander's treasure" and hid it in a small space beneath a floorboard. The house had what they call "furnishings," so there was nothing for me to do but put away the few belongings I had and get a feel for the earth of this Ohio under my feet. Jasper and Isaac had taken their leave, bidding goodbye with their hats in their hands. Alexander cried because they had become his friends and I, despite the warmth of the welcome from Becca Gordon, her husband, the Reverend Gordon, and the members of the free colored community whom I met, was again in a strange land with strange people. I grabbed up my boy and hugged him close. At least on this journey, I was not alone. We settled in, my boy and me. And every night, I said a prayer of thanks to whatever god was listening.

Yes, it suit fine.

Some weeks later Becca Gordon was visiting, unpacking a basket of goodies that made my mouth water. The woman could cook and live close, which was a good thing! Two babies come right when I did so I had not time to cook, hardly time to eat.

"You a godsend, Maryam. What Lulah would have done I don't know. And Uncle Edwin. We need a midwife here, so many babies comin'. O' course" — she chuckled — "Soon, it'll be your turn." She wave her hand toward me. "Don't you worry, we'll all pitch in when the time comes. And you can tell us what to do."

My turn?

My cheeks were warm.

I was getting old *and* stout. The journey north was backbreaking what with the walking up and down and over fallen trees and rocks, climbing in and out of the wagon, crossing the little creeks on foot. It had made my body hard but not lean. I had filled out, plump now like the old woman I was. So much so that in the past few months, my dresses push at the seams. And my belly . . . well . . . from eating too much bread and too many slices of Becca's pies and cakes since we been here. I had been greedy. Eating too much of everything.

"No, I'm too old for *that.*" I chuckled and patted my rounded stomach. "Just fat. No, I'm . . ." As I searched my mind for the right word, something inside me thumped the palm of my hand.

Can't be.

I looked up at Becca, who looked back at me, an expression of amusement on her face.

Dios mío! as Dolly would say. What kind of midwife didn't know that *she* was going to have a baby?

Becca cleared her throat then said, "When do you think your baby will come?"

33
Partus Sequitur Ventrem

Partus sequitur ventrem. Latin. "That which is brought forth follows the womb."

The pains came at midnight. My child would be in my arms by dawn. *Let her be strong,* I prayed to the goddess of rainbows and laboring women, *Let her be well.* I was too old to lose this child. My heart would not survive it and I was too old to have another.

There are stories that midwives can deliver their own babies, can tend to the labor of their own bodies and childbed as easily as they do for others. That is not so. I called on Becca Gordon to attend me. Becca was not a midwife but she had given birth ten times and knew what needed knowing.

My daughter *was* born just before dawn. She kicked and threw her arms around, screamed at the top of her lungs. Nursed as if she were hollow inside. Becca grinned from ear to ear as she tidied up.

"You got you a beautiful child, Maryam," she said, stroking the baby's head and then kissing it. "Prettiest baby I seen in a while. 'Cept for Blessing o'course," referring to her youngest child and only daughter. She patted the baby on her back and was awarded with a belch for her trouble. We laughed. "What you gonna call her?" As she passed the squirming bundle back to me, her smile faded some. "Got to ask you, Maryam. You . . . you said that this child would be a girl. How . . . did you know?"

It was a question that I did not have an answer for, least not one that I could speak. *Blessed is she who remembers . . . How many years gone now?*

The back room of a small cabin on Caesar's Key and a woman pressing on my stomach and making me drink spiced water. Marie Catherine. The woman who had healed me, calmed my mind, and taught me what she knew about birth and death, about healing, the things that can be taught and the things that a woman has to learn for herself. I had not forgotten that she also had the eyes to see beyond the veils of time, past the mists of what was and see that which would.

That little room, evening, quiet except for croaking frogs and tiring cicadas, giving up

447

their song as the sun set. The room lit by candles. I was sitting on the pallet that she made for me, wincing as she wrapped white strips of linen around my breasts, which had filled with milk to feed the child who was no more.

"I am sorry, little one," she said, pulling the bandages taut with a practiced hand. "But I must do this . . . to dry up the milk." She shook her head sadly. "Unfortunately for you, none of Caesar's women have given birth lately, so there is no need for the wet nurse. *Eh bien . . .*"

My head hurt with the thinking, the confusion, the pain. I was a child. No. I was a woman. I had *had* a child. But my child had died. My mother had said that her children were like flowers, a pleasure and a gift. A door to the future. If I had no children . . . if the death of this baby was bad luck, would I have more bad luck? Would the gods take the rest of my children and leave me without a future?

Marie Catherine's expression was soft as I told her of my fears and she patted me on the hand.

"It is not *le mal chance.*" She parted her lips as if to speak again, then left the room. When she returned, she was carrying a tall wide candle, red in color, its flame steady despite the breezes coming through the open window that faced the sea.

I opened my mouth to speak, then thought better of it. It was time for silence.

She look at me, up and down, then into my eyes. I squirm.

"Be still," she whispered.

I nodded, swallowing in fear.

"You are . . . so young and yet . . ." She looked at me, a strange expression on her face. I thought she look sad. Now I think she was wondering just how much to tell. I had lived by her words: *Never tell all that you know.*

"You will live many years, Little Maryam. And you will have much love and one husband."

I smiled. I was a little girl then, despite what I had just suffered. The thought of "much love" and a husband held appeal to me. I knew nothing of the world.

Marie Catherine looked into the flame again. When she spoke this time, her voice was low and strange and did not seem to belong to her. The candle flame flickered and I felt cold.

"You have traveled far and will travel still farther." Again she looked at me. *"Sans compagnie."* Her voice had dropped to a whisper.

"Com . . . pa . . . knee?"

Marie frowned.

"Alone. And yet . . ." She waved her hand slowly in front of the flame. It did not waver. Marie sat back, her hands limp in her lap. My questions came one after another. The answers came when it was their time.

I will have a man?

Ned. McCulloch.

A husband?

Yes, she said. And I had James.

Will I have children?

"Yes, but they will not all be yours." Then I could not figure what she meant. Later, I knew. She had told me four sons, two daughters. And over the years and the losses I had forgotten. But now?

Four sons. Eli, Shadrach, Edward, and Alexander.

But they will not all be yours.

Two daughters. The angel whose grave looked out over the dunes toward the sea and this girl child of no name in my arms.

Marie Catherine took my hand into hers, the palms warm, her fingers firm.

"Listen and remember, Maryam. There are places in the world where the mists are thin, where what is and what will be may cross each other's paths, where an unsuspecting traveler may step through a door and find herself in a strange land, both once and forever. Do not be afraid."

My daughter had put me on the path to a strange land, the future. I had no choice but to go.

She was pale compared with my skin. Her hair was near black. I noticed highlights of red and gold, so brilliant that I thought they might be dreams of sunlight, but no, they were really there. She had her father's eyes, the color of dark honey and the whiskey he liked to drink. They were warm and true. Her forehead reminded me of my own, and her nose, long and slim, sent me back to my mother's face with its dark copper hue and sculptured cheekbones and . . . my heart stopped like a blow to my chest. The memory of my mother's face was fading into a fog of shadows and mist.

This forgetting. It came to me like an escaping wave, like the gusts of wind that serve as heralds of a storm. McCulloch's farm, Nini's taunts, the red-coated soldiers, James . . . my beloved James and the sweet softness of baby Eli's neck, Caesar my savior, the white sails so beautiful and deadly and the door of no return, my father's voice, my mother's face . . . All of the faces and stories, the places, were fading away, disappearing behind a wall of forgetting to a place that I could not go.

When I first came here, to this Ohio, it crept up on me, taking one small memory from me each day or so, leaving me with a new one, but never enough to match what was taken away. My mind twirled around, searching for faces and voices and streams and smells of my other lives and those who had lived there. The longer I stayed in this place, this America, the more I fought to remember what I come through and where I had come from. At first, it was my way of staying alive, of keeping my mother and father and sisters and brothers near me, to keep them, and especially Jerie, alive. But as the days and weeks and years traveled on, so did I. And in the darkness of evenings when I was alone, my mind wandered back and met a wall of nothing. Did this town still exist? Had the dark waters swallowed up the world I'd come from? Were my sisters now old women with grandchildren, my brothers head men of the village?

Blessed is she who remembers when all have forgotten.

And now I was forgetting. Every memory, smell, sight, or sound had become a blur, and I was terrified. If I forgot, who would tell the stories?

Becca's voice shattered my mind's wan-derin's.

"This little gal remind me of a calico cat," Becca said as she washed the baby. "All brown and gold eyes, red in her black hair and cream color." She hummed a tune that I recognized as a hymn.

McCulloch had named Alexander but I had given my boy a second name, Edward, after his father. I would do the same for this child. I named her "Ediya" after my mother and "Maeve" after McCulloch's mother. But no one ever used those names.

Everyone called her "Calico."

34
BLACKJACK

My cabin set on a hill among hills. Built tight with the hardwood from trees Mc-Culloch said were old when his god was young. It hug the land like a child its mother, set up tall against the cold winds that blow through, shake that wind off like it was a sneeze. My house stay dry as a desert even when it rain. It beautiful here on my hill, the land green, it go on and on, the forests unbroken. Fields give up whatever seed you plant, pigs, sheep, cow, people, all eat good. I make my way as I always have, tend to ailments, help babies into the world, ease the way for those leaving it, raising up my Alexander, he getting so big! And Calico, who talk as good as the Reverend Gordon. She got up to walk the day she turnt nine months and she *fast.* I can't get old. Got to chase my girl!

The people, the colored people anyway, they welcome me, good to me and the children. Becca is near the best friend I got in this place and so is Benjamin, the reverend, her husband. I like him but I don't go to his church. Becca knows that and it make her wonder. Benjamin though he a preacher, he don't wonder. Just greet me, set and talk a bit, listen when I tell him what to do for his joints that ache. He say his grandmother was from "the Africa" and he say that I hear the voice of other gods and that fine with him. Says those gods were old when Jehovah was young. Makes me smile when I think of it. Jeremiah Nash woulda never said that!

This Ohio a beautiful place. In the mornings, I look out across the hills, the valley, try to see through the morning fog. East of here there small hills that the first people in this land made with their hands. I want to see them but it a long walk from here. So I just look east. And dream.

The white people here like everyplace else, some fine, some not. They came north once they wore out their lands in Carolina and that Virginia. So they brought their animals and their ways of thinking. I live near the settlement, name is Eaton's Stop after the Englishman who put up a trading post. All the colored people live here. The white people live over the ridge and in town. Eatonville, Becca say it the "county seat" where business is done, is ten mile away, take half day by wagon. They got no slavery here in this Ohio. But they do got laws to keep people like me from doing, from being, from having the same as them.

Some across the ridge and in Eatonville town ease the way of the slave catchers come over the river from Virginia and Kentucky. They watch and whisper. They put out the word. Then they send for me when their children cough and their women need help. They smile and say "Thank you, Miss Maryam." And they pay me with coin, maybe the coins that the slave catchers give them as they drag away people, some who ran and some who did not. Some who have papers — like me — and some who do not.

The people in Eaton's Stop help those who run when they can. They feed them and hide them away. They point them to the next stop. They are the north star. I tend to their ailings and wounds. We know that more are coming, runaways and those who chase them. After Nat's risin', the chains tighten up. Some of the free people here — the Browns, Jamie Smith and his family, young Elijah Highwarden and his bride, Becky Taylor — have decided that this beautiful land, this Eaton's Stop, is not safe. And so they have moved on, north, way north, slipped along the great Erie sea to Detroit and into Canada. There are times when I wonder if I should not go myself, take my babies and move again where no slave catcher will follow. But this land, my land, is so green and soft and I am weary of journeying. I have lived this life just like the waves on the dark waters that brought me to this place . . . and I have taken, without being asked, this journey that was not always mine to steer, but when it was, I had to steer it alone. But now I have my Alexander and my Calico. I have my home and my work. I will not journey again 'less the gods call me.

Sunday the day of rest — that what Benjamin, the Reverend Gordon, say. It only a day of rest for me if I have no ailin' folk to tend, no baby to deliver. And if that so, then I work in my field, milk my cows (Becca's middle boy Abednego does it when I'm away), and watch over my babies. Alexander, he four now, he say, "Momma! I'm no baby!" He isn't. He big for his age and look just like Ned. As for Calico, mercy. That child never was a baby. Went from nursing to walking to talking to telling ever'one what to do. Even her brother. And when she don't get her way, her face cloud up into a look that only her father could wear. It a look that make rain, lightning, and thunder.

Today a Sunday. It quiet on my hill and in the valley, all the people in church, Benjamin's little church, Pastor Mitchell's AME church, and all the white peoples' churches. Leaves me by myself, the heathen as Jeremiah would call me, a sour look on his face. But I got too much work to do to think 'bout him. I'm tired with my old self sittin' up here on my porch with my two children playing 'round. And me old enough to be their grandmother. I worry though what I've left undone: mendin' (and Becca better with a needle than me), cook up that old hen, sweep out that shed, mix up some herbs for the next lyin'-in, prob'bly Amelia Allen down the way, and then —

Gideon barking his head off 'round back. Start me outa my musin's. Never had no dog in my house till I came here. No gun neither. The people said I had to, being up here out of the way. Said it would protect me, guard me and the children. Once that hound made himself comfortable, all he did was try to eat up everything that was cooked and sleep in the sun. The shotgun never hungry.

The dog barking then stop. I hear somethin' make my stomach turn over. And then nothing.

He standing there looking like a corpse walking, his face gray, his eyes moist and red with yellow 'round the iris. Sick. Drunk. He grinning, too. Not as many teeth as before. What hair he got is a muddy gray, stringy. His clothes too big for what's left of him. But his hands, still large, still muscle, wrapped like bird's claw 'round the neck of my son.

"I knew it was you." His voice the same. "When they told me was a Africky witch woman up on the hill, I knew. Heard you run away. Or did Mac send you north after you fucked him?" He laughed. I never could take the sound of the Kaintuckian's laugh. "See you gots littl'uns now. Good. This boy will fetch —"

"That boy is free. So am I." *Where is Calico?*

"Witch, even if you got papers, I'll tear 'em up. Don't mean nothin' t'me. This boy worth a king's ransom and you ain't so old I couldn't get a few dollars." He looked 'round and so did I. "Heard you had a little half-breed nigger here too. The Scotsman's? She'll bring five hundred dollar or more. I can sell her as a fancy girl in Lexington."

"You ain't sellin' nobody nowhere."

I aimed the shotgun at his head, willing

Alexander to keep still. The Kaintuckian laughed.

"I got your boy." He pulled my son closer and giggled. Pulled his pistol from a pocket and cocked it. "Put that down, witch. I'll strangle or shoot this boy if I have to. Then go find that little half-breed you got and take her."

"I'll kill you," I said. "And I'll kill him, too . . ." I wished I hadn't had to say that, with Alexander standing there looking so afraid. But for that moment, seeing that creature with his hands on my boy, threatening my little girl, I woulda killed to keep them from the clutches of this demon. Took a breath. Tightened my grip 'round the barrel and narrowed one eye.

"Momma!"

Calico.

The Kaintuckian turnt around. Alexander kicked at him and wriggled aloose and away. Calico tripped on something as she ran toward me. Then she stumble and fall.

I cocked that shotgun and fired.

The rest of that Sunday comes to me as a dream, in pieces, blurred, sounds like water rushin' past my ears. There was shoutin', men's voices, angry voices, horses, smoke. Church bells ringing across the valley and into the hills. Not calling the believers to pray. Calling out a warning.

There were four of them, the Kaintuckian made five, come 'cross the river to pick up bounties on runaways and if none could be picked off, then to grab any colored person to be found, papers or no. The residents of Eaton's Stop faced down the four and chased them off. The community settled itself for a siege. We figured they would come back. If not to finish their job than to rescue the Kaintuckian.

He was beyond rescue.

The men of Eaton's Stop dug a grave deeper than six foot up on the little ridge where the berries grew. Out of respect — for his god but not for Amos Cockerill, for that was the Kaintuckian's name — the Reverend Benjamin said a prayer. I watched as the shovels of dirt fell across the face of the man who seemed to have followed me through several lives, through that Virginia, 'cross the river, and into Ohio.

"What you want me to do with his horse?" one of the Highwarden boys asked, holding the animal tight. Was an older animal, a bay gelding, made for riding and not for work.

"You take him," one of the others said, stroking the animal gently on the nose. A long thick stick bounced against his side.

"What's that?" I asked.

461

The boy snorted and untied it, handed it to me.

"They call it a blackjack. Here. You take it, Mrs. Maryam. Case you need to fend off any more slave patrollers."

The wood of the stick was smooth, hard, shiny in the sunlight. But I knew the Kaintuckian. This stick had done much pain, had fed on suffering. I went to the foot of the grave and threw it in.

Blueberries blackberries strawberries grow on this hill. 'Specially around the grave. The next spring, I take the children there to pick berries, give most of the sweetness to Becca. She make better pies than me. The months go by and I wait. Wait for that demon to rise up outa the deep grave that was dug for him. Wait for his comrades to return. Jump every time my second dog, also name Gideon, bark. Wait. Some ways I'm still waiting. But they did not come. And as time went on, as the war came and went, the little hill that had no name came to be call Slavecatcher Hill.

35

Eaton's Stop, Highland County, Ohio
Summer, 1870

I yawn. Blink open my eyes. The memories just . . . float away. I been thinkin' all this story, my life. No. Been dreamin' it. Waking up. Now it come to me, after my nap, that Calico had not come home. It would be time for supper soon. I could smell the aromas floating out of Fannie's kitchen.

"Where your momma?" I asked my grandson as he carried two buckets between the barn and the house.

Nicholas chuckled.

"You know how she is, Momma Grace," he said. "She's at the women's group they starting down at the church. She and Mrs. Gordan and Mrs. Powell."

I nodded. My daughter was always away organizing this, guiding that, putting her thumbprint on any and every little thing that went on in Eaton's Stop. Calico was not one to let a cause go if there was work to be done; she did it, put her shoulder into the plow and moved forward. I chuckled, thinking 'bout that. Her father had kept himself to himself but quietly did what had to be done when needs must, as he said. McCulloch was a doer, not a talker 'bout doin'. Me, I kept to the edges, the shadows, deliverin' babies, mending broken arms and legs, steeping teas to soothe folks' innards. Somehow, between the two of us, the Scotsman and me, we had bred a daughter who had no fear of anything or anyone, who spoke her mind. All ways. It was a wonder that she and Rodam had stayed married as long as they did. Calico had six babies in between women's group meetings, church activities, teaching, and the gods know what all. Can't say I know how and when she managed to get those babies! But here I was living with her youngest and his family.

"Here she comes!" Fannie's voice heralded my daughter's arrival.

"Who's that with her?" Nicholas asked.

I looked up and squinted, turned my head slightly to the left to favor my good eye. The wagon chugged up the hill, I heard it and saw my daughter, her reddish brown hair blazing in the afternoon sun — I could not get that gal to wear a bonnet — and a man sitting next to her, brown-skinned, a bright white collar framing his neck, wearing a suit.

Humph, I thought. *Another preacher.* Eaton's Stop was a highway road for preachers. Nicky walked alongside as his mother slowed the horses and Fannie came out of the kitchen, wiping her hands on her apron, her hand to her forehead as she squinted in the afternoon sun.

Some murmurs between my daughter, her son, and daughter-in-law and then I saw the man jump down from the wagon and reach up to help Calico. She smoothed her dress and took down a basket. The man whose face was dark but seemed pleasant gestured for her to walk first, and she nodded and said something to him. *Ah, so my daughter has a suitor.* Calico had been a widow for several years now, how she grieved when Rodam passed. But time it goes. She wasn't young anymore but she was still a beautiful woman and I didn't like it that she was alone. Alexander didn't either. Far away as he was — that Washington, DC, where my son, the teamster, had the charge of all the horses that pulled the city's fire brigades — worried about her, too. Sending letter after letter. I know 'cause she read them to me and her answer was always, "No, Mother. No, Zander. When

465

would I have the time for a husband?" And with her causes and projects, she had a point. But as I watched her coming toward me, the man at her elbow, I wondered if she had changed her mind. She laughed. In response, the man laughed, too. And the breath caught in my throat.

His laughter was warm and rich, deep. It emerged from between his lips in a sound calming and familiar. It made my heart ache. I squinted my eyes as they approached. Wished I had done what Alexander had said and gotten me a pair of those spectacle whatnots. The man stopped at the bottom of the hill and Calico continued toward me.

"Momma," she said, her beautiful face glowing in the warm sunlight. "I want you to meet someone. He has come a long way, from Texas, to see us. To see you." She looked over her shoulder. "Momma, this is Reverend Holland. Ah . . . Reverend, this is my mother, Maryam Priscilla Grace. We call her Momma Grace."

The man came forward and stopped, turning his hat around in a circle in his hands. Then he bowed deeply and smiled.

"Mrs. Grace, it is an honor to meet you, ma'am." His voice was deep and smooth and sent vibrations through the soft late-summer air. I felt the hair on the back of my neck stand up. I had heard this voice before a long time ago. The vibrations surrounded me in swirls and the air felt heavy, as if lightning were on its way.

"Reverend," I said slowly. "My daughter say you've come from a long way. You mus' be tired. Sit down and tell us about it. Calico, fetch Reverend . . . Holland a cold drink."

My daughter chuckled and walked away, her skirts swishing around her. "Don't let her intimidate you, Reverend Holland. Momma likes to do that now that she's reached the age of Methuselah's wife."

I wasn't much on the white man's Bible but I did know some of the stories including the one about that Methuselah.

"Methuselah's wife died young!" I called after my daughter. "No woman could put up with a man for nine hundred years and not want to die!"

Calico's and Nicky's laughter filled the summer air.

"Where are you from now?" I turned my good eye on to the young man who sat across from me, with his familiar face and his familiar voice and his familiar laugh.

"Adams, Texas, ma'am," the reverend answered. "It's a small town, a spot in the road if you want the truth. Not far from the border with Louisiana. Do you know it?"

"No, sir, I do not," I said and asked him another question. Truth was I asked him question after question just to hear the sound of his voice when he answered. It was like I had a burn on my hand and his voice was the balm that soothed it.

"Tell me about your people," I said.

"Here you are, Reverend Holland." Calico's voice cut through the conversation. Nicky was carrying a small table from the porch and settled it on the ground next to me. Calico set down a tray on its top with an arrangement of glasses, cookies (the vanilla ones I liked), and a pitcher of tea, so cold that its sides dripped with moisture. She poured me a glass. "Momma, this one is yours." Then she handed one to the Reverend Holland and smiled. "I hope my mother isn't pounding you with questions. She likes folks t'think she's all quiet-like." I felt my daughter's warm hand on my arm. "But she's not. She's fierce."

"I am not!" I said. "Don't call me names!"

Calico's laughter filled the air.

"It's a good word. It means that you are intense. And strong. Very strong, Momma, with what you've been through in your life." Her voice trailed off. I looked up at her surprised to see that her eyes — warm maple syrup golden brown like her father's — were damp with tears. Why?

"Your daughter tells me that you have had quite a life, Mrs. Grace. I would enjoy hearing some of your stories if you would care to share them."

I thought about that for a moment but let it go because, well, because I felt those vibrations again when he spoke, a swirling that I needed to mind. It meant that my life was 'bout to take a turn, either good or bad.

"I don't mean t'be a rude old lady, Reverend, but I want to hear 'bout you. Who your people are, how y'all got to be in . . . what was the name of that place you from?

"Adams, Texas, ma'am," the young man said once more in his pleasant tone. Now, the Reverend Holland wasn't exactly young; he was more near Calico's age. But when you as old as me? Ever'body is young!

"Momma Grace!" This time it was Nicky who was scolding me.

"No, it's all right," the reverend said. He set his glass down and rubbed his palms together as if to warm them even though it was a pleasant day. And I wondered why he was nervous.

"I . . . well, ma'am, my people . . . that is, my mother's people are from Texas, least they are for two generations. Her folks came along with their master back in the early 1850s, their place went bust in Alabama, the land just plain wore out and there wasn't anything for them there. My parents met in church, in Adams, and got married there."

"Do they still live there? In Texas?" Calico asked.

"No, ma'am, Miss Calico. My father died in a . . . what they call a typhoon in the Gulf. He was a merchant seaman. Momma carried on best she could but she was never strong and when I was five, she caught the consumption and died."

"God rest their souls," Calico murmured. "Did you have any sisters or brothers?"

"One sister, but she gone now too. Was my grandfather that raised me."

He stopped then, as if he was at the end of the story, answering the question that Nicky was about to ask and then saying nothing. Only I knew — and maybe Calico, too — that he was not finished. My mouth went dry and my heart pounded in my chest. I felt my breath coming in spurts.

"Your mother's father?" Calico asked.

"My father's." Again, he stopped. Then he did something I wasn't expecting. He reached over and picked up my hand. And I knew.

"Tell me," I said.

"My name is Eli Holland, Mrs. Grace. My father was Shadrach Holland and his father's name was Eli. I was named for him. Papa . . . that's what I called him, Papa . . . well, Papa Eli and his brother came with their father, James, to the Texas territory, they'd been sold away from their home in Virginia. Papa said that the master, Nash was his name, needed to raise capital, to pay his debts, so he sold some of his people to do it. My great-grandfather James, my grandfather Papa Eli and my great-uncle Shadrach were some of what was sold. Papa's mother . . . was left behind."

I heard Calico take a deep breath. She and Nicky looked over at me, I could see them out of the corner of my eye but I couldn't look at them. Not yet. The only thing I could see with my one good eye was the face of Eli Holland.

"I was five when I came to live with Papa and from the day I went there, he told me . . . stories of when he was growing up in Virginia, about his brother, Shadrach, his daddy James, who died before I was ever born, and his mother . . ." He squeezed my hand.

"Papa said that she was an African woman, brought across the sea and that she was beautiful and smart and fearless. He said that she was a midwife, wise, skilled. The plantation masters asked for her when their wives and daughters gave birth. Papa said that . . . he would never forget her . . . He made me promise . . . that when I could, I would find his mother or any of her people. He made me promise to tell her people how he and his father and brother fought, that they tried to find her. That they never forgot her." There were tears in his voice now, and for a moment, the mists of time parted and I heard James's voice, warm, strong, and deep, telling me of his love, little Shadrach all grown up and my Eli . . . whispering to me, *Momma, this is my boy. Listen to him. I sent him to you.*

"I . . . I have been looking for you since the war ended. Papa told me the name of the man in Virginia that sold you but there was nothing there, nothing left after the war. Then I learned, from a colored preacher man, that you were sold to a Scotsman who lived in the Shenandoah Valley in central Virginia. I went there, too. I found his grave but . . ."

His grave. McCulloch's face swam into view.

I felt my heart in my throat. McCulloch wanted to be buried in the soil of his Scotland but he had died before he could go back. Before he ever saw his daughter's face.

"And then I met some people who remembered stories about a geechie woman, they called her, an African medicine woman who had helped people run away, who had been a midwife. And then I knew. I knew where to go. But I never thought —"

"You never thought I would still be alive," I said, sounding out the words carefully because my throat was so tight. I saw James's forehead and eyes on this boy, I saw my nose and my mother's lips. My father's eyes, too. He had his father's build and his father's voice. And he had my son Eli's name. Maybe I was still alive for a reason.

"Papa told me . . . to say . . . that he never forgot you. That your face was always the first that he saw when he woke and . . ." Eli's voice cracked. "And would be the last face he saw when he died."

We had a celebration, that week, on the farm. Every person who lived in Eaton's Stop and beyond was there. Eli preached the message that Sunday at Benjamin's Baptist church and *I* went and sat in the front pew. I knowed some folk thought the church might fall down on us! And that Sunday evening as the sun was setting, and the festivities continued, I hobbled up to the back porch and sat down in the rocking chair away from the noise and the music. My great-grandson Eli walked with me, holding my elbow, arranging the chair so that I could sit down, asking me questions along the way.

"What happened to Aunt Calico's father? You didn't say."

No, I didn't. It hard. Ever'time I see my girl, I see him. I remember what he did. And how he never saw his child or his Scotland ever again.

"I'm sorry, Momma Grace," he said, sounding out the two words as if they were precious stones. "I've tired you out with my pestering. You rest now."

I shook my head.

"No, boy, I'm not tired. I'll tell you anything you want to know."

He smiled and again my heart skipped a beat. *James.*

"Is it true?" he asked. "All those stories about you . . . about Africa and pirates and . . . all of it. Is it true?"

"May be. May be not, I don't know what those stories are. My story, that's all I know. My life."

The sun set on my great-grandson and me sitting on that porch on that hill and it rose on the other side of the world, in the place where I was born, in the place of the "before," the place where it all, where I began, where I walked through a door of no return with only two things, my life and my name.

ACKNOWLEDGMENTS

The seeds for *Things Past Telling* were planted in my childhood with stories told primarily (but not exclusively) by grandmothers about *their* grandmothers and grandfathers and the times they lived in. These were wondrous tales of adventure that spanned vast landscapes and featured brave women and men and exciting times, equal in narrative power to the best bedtime stories and fairy tales. Only later did I realize that these stories were about real people.

I am a genealogy/family history geek. But once the paper, microfiche, digitized ledgers and books are scrutinized, one must return to the "once upon a time." I owe much to the storytellers on both sides of my family, but specifically to my great-grandmother Jesse Highwarden Gardner on my dad's side and my great-aunt, the indomitable Emmie Montgomery Reid, on my mother's. Without their words — spoken and written — I would not have dared to create the stories within these covers. Gratitude also to "The Thursday Gang" of volunteers who, with great skill, assist family history seekers in the Family Search Center of the John Parker Library located within the walls of The National Underground Railroad Freedom Center in Cincinnati, Ohio. My colleagues Sue Mehne, Dr. John Bryant, and Dan Daily offered advice, patience, and enthusiasm. I didn't always follow the paths they recommended but I hope to be forgiven for the diversions.

I consulted many independent sources, narratives, and books to provide the context and background for Maryam's story. Sources that recounted the lives of midwives, including African American midwives, and their patients over the decades and centuries were also consulted. The WPA Narratives of formerly enslaved African American citizens were a rich resource. The accounts of these brave individuals often left me overwhelmed. There were many loose threads but, as my colleague and friend, writer Lynn Hightower, would say, "Nothing is ever wasted."

It occurred to me often during the research and writing that I needed to be precise concerning names, dates, places, and events of historical significance. But as the story evolved, I realized that this approach was implausible. The events that meant much to my heroine personally were not recorded officially on a historical record. And the conversations I had with revered elders forced me to rethink the use of a rigid date/time/minute structure. It is the storyteller's prerogative to adjust time and geographic location on occasion. "Black Caesar" was an intriguing historical figure who roamed the Caribbean during the golden age of pirates earlier than the story I tell. The mysterious Igbo who wanders to Maryam's cabin from Owl Creek is homage to an incident that allegedly took place around 1803 at Dunbar Creek on St. Simon's Island, Georgia.

The appearance of Nathan Ellis (1749–1819) is a thank-you to writer and colleague Ron Ellis, the first reader of this book. Nathan did indeed operate a ferry between Kentucky and Ohio. He was Ron's four-times great grandfather.

My character may or may not have been born in 1758. There will never be a way to verify her exact year or place of birth. As a result, some chapter headings include a date with the word "About" as a prefix. Character names may not appear to fit and and dates will be imperfect. My research yielded a richness of detail as well as nuance. There were so many stories that I could tell. And there were many for which I had to read between the lines to extract what was too painful, brutal, private, or treasured to relate directly. These were the things past telling.

Multiple thanks to my editor Patrik Henry Bass and to the publicity and marketing team at Amistad/HarperCollins as well as to my agent Matt Bialer. My family is a source of delight, inspiration, and support; I give them my heartfelt thanks. And especially to my husband, Bruce, who is always there.

SJW

ABOUT THE AUTHOR

Sheila Williams is the author of six novels including *Dancing on the Edge of the Roof,* which was adapted for film by Netflix under the title of *Juanita,* and *The Secret Women.* In addition to her published works, she is the librettist for *Fierce,* an opera commissioned by the Cincinnati Opera. Sheila lives in northern Kentucky.